If I
Could Sing
You Home

Drifters, Book Eight

SUSAN RODGERS

Cover design by Alanna Munro. All rights reserved.
Edited by Kathy Gillis and Stephen Reaman.
Book design and formatting by Valerie Bellamy, Dog-ear Book Design.

ISBN: 978-1-987966-06-0

For Josh,
who inspired the Drifters story
in the first place

Contents

Chapter One

*C*reamy sunlight streaming sideways through the master bedroom window of the Upper East Side condo nudged Jessie awake. She lay there blinking. It took her a few moments to come to her senses; too many changes in sleeping arrangements lately were leaving her confused and uncertain. The place felt strange, sterile. The sunlight was welcome, a beacon of hope in an ambiguous setting.

She slipped out from under the rich gold duvet her decorator had purchased during the busy first two weeks of the small family's occupancy in the five bedroom, 4600 square foot space, and sat on the edge of the bed. Stretching catlike, yawning deeply, Jessie scanned the room. Her eyes landed on an exotic birch dresser on the interior wall. She knew some of her clothes had been carefully folded and placed in the slim drawers—she did that part of the moving in herself. Yet the furniture was foreign. It didn't feel real. Its presence felt forced.

As she eased herself upright and padded towards the large ensuite bath, itself fitted out with an exotic light wood vanity along with a luxurious white marble mosaic floor, Jessie pondered the many elegant hotels where she'd laid her head over a fifteen-year career. They always felt unfamiliar and strange, but all were temporary. This new place was hers; she bought it last month after pretty much fleeing Vancouver.

Intentionally butting out a past where she'd laid her head in smaller, homey residences never filled with excess, as was this fancy-shmancy condo on Madison Avenue just steps from Central Park, Jessie had 'purchased up.' Hell, she could afford it. She needed a change. She wanted comfort.

She needed guest room space for Charles and Dee, and Carlotta, and even Steve and Sophie or Charlie and Jane, if they ever came to visit. Plus there were the two Sawyer children to consider. Emily-Grace was three-and-a-half, almost four now, and David was a rambunctious seventeen months. The kids needed as much stability as their mother could provide, given their new routine of cross-country travel to spend time with each of their parents, and Jessie figured part of that would come from setting the children up in their own rooms, where they could decorate at will with their favorite toys.

What she didn't count on was the sick lonely feeling overtaking her in the large, bare space. It wasn't home. The hotels over the years? They were always fleeting. She could always go home. But now there was no going back, not to Vancouver to stay, at least. Visits, sure. The downtown condo was still Jessie's, its glistening baby grand piano often beckoning her in late night dreams to caress its ivory keys once more. The starry view of distant mountains and the homey distinctive buzz of seaplanes over the hum of the west coast city's busy traffic flow had been taken for granted—now, those sights and sounds were deeply missed. La Casa was there, too, just over the Lion's Gate Bridge, buttery yellow and pretty—always welcoming—surrounded by Deirdre's Olde English roses and an assortment of colorful, gaily flitting hummingbirds.

The UBC house Jessie shared with Josh? With its comfy rooms, warm beckoning pool, and dashing view of jaunty sailboats harnessing the Pacific's wild winds? Was it welcoming? Not so much. Not anymore. Its comforting presence in Jessie's life had been ruthlessly sucked out the shattered window of her old SUV.

Even now, remembering, the pain was enough to clench Jessie's gut, causing her to bend over and grab the doorframe of the ensuite bath for support. The loss of her and Josh's home clung to her soul like a never-ending grey canker sore, red-rimmed and raw.

One thing was certain. This $ 6 million dollar luxury condo may as well be a 200 square foot hole in the wall when the children were in Vancouver with their dad. At least, it sure as hell felt that way—empty and dark and foreboding. There was nothing soothing and comfortable about the rich window coverings or the expansive kitchen with its expensive appliances, or even the new white Italian leather couch in the living room. Not without Emily-Grace's sweet voice echoing through the rooms in little-girl song, or David's happy babble as he foot-pumped a wooden toy pony around and around the family room, which Jessie mostly utilized as a playroom since its close proximity to the kitchen allowed her to keep an eye on the two kids while she was cooking.

There was one 'plus' that sometimes alleviated the pain of Josh's refusal to accept Jessie back into his life. Not always, no, it didn't eradicate the big hurts that left her crushed, but it did manage to at least mitigate them on some level. Now, after her morning pee and a quick duck of her head under the bathroom tap for a drink, Jessie padded out to the living room to find that 'plus.'

She found it—him—on the new leather couch, an iPad in his hands. He was checking the number of YouTube video-plays for his and Jessie's new ballad, which Charles had just released. All they were able to offer fans was a live version of the song, filmed during the recent domestic violence fundraising concert. Plans were underway to shoot a more dramatized music video sometime in the next month or so.

Jacob.

Adorable in unbuttoned faded jeans and a navy blue T-shirt, bare feet crossed at the ankles and resting on the brand new Danish coffee table sourced from a boutique down Madison Avenue, Jacob was, at first, unaware of Jessie's presence in the wide hall.

Taking advantage of her covert position, she silently watched him for a moment, her stance against the wall carefree and easy, her smile wide. An endearing, naïve innocence surrounded Jacob like a halo. He was a comfy presence in Jessie's home. As he tapped his fingers and sang softly along with the ballad on YouTube, she couldn't help but think he was blending as nicely into the new couch as the two quilt-patterned pink rose cushions she'd picked up at a home décor shop last week.

Quietly, Jessie stole into the high-ceilinged room and slipped onto her new-old man's lap, facing him.

It only took Jacob a second to size up his options—the iPad versus Jessie. Dropping the portable computer at his side, he opened his arms. Jessie snuggled in.

"Did you have a good sleep, baby girl?" he asked her, eyes closing and a small contented *mmmmm* following the query as he engulfed her tightly, rubbing one warm hand up under the back of her tank top.

"Yeah," she sighed, still sleepy, leaning her head against his shoulder and burrowing both hands under his arms and around his back. "The sun woke me." As if in protest, she yawned.

Wiping loose hair back from her forehead, Jacob grinned wholeheartedly. "It's nine-thirty. We actually have to meet Maggie at ten."

"Oh, shit! Is it that late? She's not going to be impressed."

Jessie made no move to jump up and get ready. Their coffee date with her *Drifters* friend was at a café just around the corner, so she wasn't too concerned about being late, although she was glad she'd remembered to charge her cell phone, since a few apologetic texts would likely be in order.

"It's that late," Jacob ascertained. "But you, beautiful girl," he kissed her pink lips delicately, "need your beauty sleep these days. So I let you sleep in."

"First of all," came a muffled murmur from the general vicinity of Jacob's neck, "I don't need sleep for beauty. I am what I am, and it's all good. And second of all, you didn't *let* me sleep in. I chose to do that all on my own."

"Yes, but had I decided to blast this tune in the bedroom, you might have been jarred roughly awake. So indeed, I did let you sleep in. By choice."

In response, a happy girlish giggle vibrated against Jacob's skin. Jessie stayed snuggled into the strong, hospitable shoulder while her left hand reached for the iPad. "What are we at now, oh sexy singing partner?" In a lazy, drowsy way she rubbed one eye before squinting at the screen saver.

Jacob took the computer from her, tapped lightly on it, and found the video again. He scanned the number displayed at the bottom left of the ballad. "We hit 11 million this morning." Dropping the iPad again, he nuzzled Jessie's cheek, moving loose curls out of the way and planting gentle kisses on her eyes, forehead, and lips as he did so. "We're magical, you and me."

"I'm glad," was her whispered response. "I love you, Jacob. Thank you for flying back in from Toronto last night. I don't do well here when the kids are gone." A whole body sigh accompanied the honest statement.

"No worries," he said, slipping a hand down the back of her panties to give her a gentle rub. "Being with you is my favorite place to be, ever. I'm a mess when I'm away from you—I'm all lost and alone. When baristas see me coming into their coffee shops, they duck behind the counters." He mimicked a woman's high-pitched voice. "'It's that guy again, the one Jessie Wheeler lets sing with her, the one who is so sad when he's not with her that a dark cloud hangs over his head.' I rain all over them. I get their fancy espresso machines all wet. They're not fans."

A smile lit his face then. Jessie could feel it through his kisses, which she gratefully leaned into. "Babe, you just got 11 million views in three days. Practically everyone out there in the big 'ole world is your fan."

His kisses stopped then, his lips freezing before Jacob sighed and hung his head. "I can think of one person who isn't. Actually, I take that back. Your entire circle of friends are not my fans."

"They'll deal."

"Or not."

"Maggie is. She's a fan. You'll see." Raising her head up off his shoulder, Jessie added, "And I don't care what they think. I only care what I think, when it comes to sexy Jacob Ryan." For emphasis, she pulled up his T-shirt and planted a loud raspberry somewhere in the middle of his stomach.

"So that's how you want to play this, is it Jess?" It only took Jacob a second to force her head away and flip Jessie onto her back. Despite her protestations and squeals of *we'll be late,* he managed to cajole her into a little loving before they had to duck into the shower to clean up for their visit with Maggie.

At the café, Maggie was visibly annoyed. She raised her eyebrows at Jessie's flushed cheeks and buoyant stride as the couple pulled out wooden chairs and plopped down beside and across from her. "Only thirty-five minutes late. That gives us twenty-five minutes to get caught up before I have to run to my appointment."

"What is it today?" Jessie asked coyly, winking at Jacob. "Bikini or Brazilian?"

"None of your beeswax." Frowning, Maggie rotated the paper newspaper she was reading towards Jessie. "Read this while I get a refill." She sent a glowering look in Jacob's direction before rising, taking her empty coffee mug with her.

Jessie eyed Jacob carefully before glancing down at the article. "Can you get me a flat white this morning, Jacob?"

She heard the screech of his chair as he stood, and felt a reassuring touch caress her shoulder as Jacob obligingly passed behind her to make his way to the cash. Going by the thinly veiled 'look' Maggie fired in Jacob's direction as she gave Jessie the paper to read, Jessie figured there was a good chance this article would not be in her new boyfriend's best interest. Despite Maggie's kindness towards him when he bailed out a very despondent singer a few months back, now that he and Jessie were a couple, Maggie's attitude had undergone an adjustment that even she did not completely understand.

Scanning the article, which featured a small black and white photograph at the bottom right of an entertainment news page in the New York Times, Jessie quickly gleaned it was about Nadia, the exotic coffee-skinned woman Josh started seeing when Jessie was missing. Emitting a slow *hiss* between her teeth, Jessie's blood pressure escalated quickly as she realized Maggie's intention in showing the article to her was, no doubt, meant as a reference to Josh.

"Humph," was Jessie's displeased reaction after scanning the short piece. She studied the picture. Decorated from top to toe in some slinky, stylish, haute couture gown, accented with glittering accessories, Nadia was front and center, with a tuxedo clad tennis star on her arm. The Gucci bracelet gifted by Josh noticeably dangled around one wrist.

Maggie slid back into her chair across from Jessie, and sat on the edge leaning forward, her toes, in red ballet flats, tucked over the bottom rung. "He's not seeing her anymore."

"I knew he was lying."

"Hmmm?" Biting into a butter croissant, Maggie looked inquisitively at her old co-star. Tossing her ponytail, she grabbed a napkin and wiped her greasy fingers.

"The day he told me he was going back to her. At the lawyer's office. I had a feeling he wasn't telling the truth. To my knowledge Josh hasn't left Vancouver, according to Steve, anyway. Apparently Nadia hasn't been around, either."

Before continuing, Jessie peeked across the café and eyed Jacob to be sure he wasn't within earshot. He wasn't—he was still patiently waiting for their handcrafted beverages at the far end of the counter.

Leaning towards Maggie, rotating her gaze back around to study the curious disapproval fleeting across the woman's face, Jessie added, "I guess Josh just wanted to be sure I got the message that he's done with me. Well I got it, Maggie. Loud and clear." Sitting back, Jessie's lips trembled slightly. Talking about her estranged husband brought the angst back a hundred-fold, as if releasing his name out loud somehow gave the pain more power. Grabbing one of Maggie's napkins, she squished it between suddenly damp fingers.

"Honey," Maggie started, taking her friend's hand. "He's not done with you. Josh will *never* be done with you. Steve says he's got this weird idea in his head that Jacob's a better partner for you. He saw you on stage at the fund-raiser and then after, when you were, uh, 'slow dancing' shall we say, with Jacob, and he just gave up."

"He's always been nervous about Jacob." Raising her chin defiantly, a bitter edge suffused Jessie's words. "I guess he had reason to be."

"Honey…" Maggie, too, looked over her shoulder. She met Jacob's hush puppy baby blues, and frowned before turning back to her friend, whose heart was melting at the sight of her musical soul mate slouched over at the end of the espresso bar with both hands shoved deep in his jeans pockets. "I am so, so glad Jacob came to your rescue when you needed him. He's a sweet, soft place to fall. A gentle loving island to float on. But he is not your husband. And you are not divorced. Might I also add there is an entire contingent of your friends counting on you not to give up on Josh. He needs you."

Jessie pulled her fingers out from under Maggie's. Sitting back, she placed both hands in her lap and eyeballed her old co-star from underneath long lashes tired of streaming tears over a love that seemed dead. "He needs me about as much as I need Deuce McCall back in my life, Maggie. Josh made it crystal clear."

"Only because you let Jacob climb into your bed, Jessie. Period." Annoyed because she was quickly running out of time to say her piece, Maggie's voice rose in pitch. "Let him go. Now, before your kids get too attached to him. Before Jacob gets too attached to you. For the sake of his heart as well as your own."

"He knows the deal, Maggie," Jessie cut in quickly. "We're taking it slow—he's away half the time anyway. His schedule's nuts this year, between touring and guest appearances here and there. And FYI, my kids were attached to Jacob the moment they were born. Or maybe when they were conceived, I don't know. With *Mystic Nights* and music, by the time they were born they knew Jacob's voice better than their father's!"

"As your friend, Jessie, I'm begging you. Let Jacob go. Josh doesn't deserve this."

"The hell he doesn't!" Jessie's icy eyes flashed. "Maggie, I know it was bad for him. I know that."

"It wasn't bad, Jessie, it was hell! There's a difference!"

"Yeah, okay, whatever, still…he is the one who has all the power here. He's making all the choices. So I don't get why all of you are coming down on me!"

"Because Nadia meant nothing to him, Jessie, that's why! She was a warm body. But everyone knows what Jacob means to you, and the thing is, unfortunately, what it means to Josh and to your children is that you are putting up one giant stop sign. A stop sign that has the power to hurt a lot of people—not just Josh, but your kids, and last but not least, Jacob! I know you're lonely, I know it hurts, but you're using him and he doesn't deserve that, your kids don't deserve it, and your husband doesn't deserve it!"

Glancing over at Jacob, who was watching her inquisitively as he wrapped his fingers around their coffees, Jessie shot back, "For six and a half months I had no choices, Maggie. None, practically, besides when to do Yoga or play guitar. I came home and Josh decided we were through. Not me. I simply acted on the decision he, at first, voiced, but didn't really have the courage to make. Then, in Vancouver the day we sorted out custody, I tried to convince him to try again. He quite clearly said no. So… Jacob. He is my best friend, he's my musical soul mate, and now he's also my lover."

Pointing a finger across the table at her, Maggie threw in, "You told me Josh was in the stratosphere. At the fundraiser. In terms of love, you said he is out of this world. Seems to me that kind of love is worth fighting for."

Skidding back her chair, Maggie rose. She felt a presence behind her—it was Jacob, who had just landed back at their table. Realizing he'd likely heard her, she inhaled sharply and slowly blinked her eyes shut. Turning, she met Jacob's downturned lips and misty gaze as he stood immobile, holding out his and Jessie's takeout coffees as if they were peace offerings, or perhaps targets, if one chose to swing an arm and send them across the room to accent the heated feelings flying around.

"I'm sorry, Jacob," she stated sincerely, drawing up both shoulders as she reached over the back of her abandoned chair for a multi-colored bohemian bag. Maggie hoisted it over her head so it angled across her chest and rested against a hip. "But despite the wishes of Charles Keating, Jessie's friends are hoping against hope for an HEA. That, my friend, would mean happily-ever-after. For our friend, Josh. Since she won't listen," she glared pointedly at Jessie, who stood slowly, fingers gripping the edge of the table as her face went white, "I'm appealing to you. Walk away. You're breaking up the sweetest little family, and you're hurting someone very close to me. To us *Drifters* friends."

Without looking at Jessie, Jacob reached past Maggie to set the two hot coffees on the small round table. Wiping his hands on his hips, he swallowed nervously.

"Maggie," he entreated numbly, his voice hoarse, "I get what you're saying. I wasn't on *Drifters*. I wasn't around at all in your old glory days. I'm not one of you, and I never will be. I know what I represent to all of you is someone who has the power to take your girl away from you. But I'm not stupid."

Raising her eyebrows, Maggie waited. "Would you care to elaborate, Young Padawan?"

"Meaning I don't know how long I get to keep her. So if you and your righteous clan don't mind, for now I'm just going to soak her up."

She blinked. "Intuition?"

"Reality. It's too perfect with her right now. But perfection is not a thing. It's not possible."

Jessie moaned. She knew which bullet Maggie was going to aim at him before the gun was even loaded.

Maggie fired it right between Jacob's puppy dog eyes. "Sure it is, honey. Ask Jessie. She'll tell you."

The ensuing silence was Jacob's pain, melting him into the narrow wood slats lining the café's floor.

Maggie flew out the door with a one-armed hug and a light brush of her lips on Jessie's cheek, although neither was reciprocated. Sickened, thinking *well, New York's really going to be lonely now,* Jessie actually turned her head away during the brief goodbye. She resolved to give her 'friend' some space for the next while.

When she finally found the courage, Jessie let her eyes drift back over to Jacob. Watching her, studying her, he stood with his feet a hip's width apart, aching already for what he felt he could very well lose.

Sinking deeper into her chair with a heavy sigh, Jessie patted the seat next to her. "Come, babe," she murmured quietly. "Sit."

Obliging, Jacob exhaled slowly as he dropped his burden down. Staring at his coffee, he left his hands on his thighs, where they moved with a fretful unease as he considered this woman next to him. Jessie was wearing a short ruffled denim skirt and her favorite aged brown western boots. A cropped denim jacket over a floral halter completed her rebel look for the day. The simple clothing choices were soaked with intoxicating memories—the stink of reckless weed and the taste of heady Guinness, accompanied by a liberal dose of love and laughter in a dank old Scottish pub.

Closing his eyes, he wished like hell he could give up all of his fame and money for the chance to go back in time to be with his 'Annie Hayden' in Scotland again, playing music for a small crowd in that cozy Scottish pub. He was startled when a hand, and then a body, landed in his lap in this public Upper East Side café.

"Jessie?" he asked, as she snuggled into him and buried her face in the hollow of his neck and shoulder. Wrapping his arms around her, he sighed deeply enough for the two of them.

A small voice escaped from the general direction of Jacob's unruly layers. "If I have to choose between my friends and you, Jacob—I choose you."

Kissing the top of her head, he pondered Maggie's words as the shock of them sank in, leaving him dazed and unsure. "I'm breaking up a family," Jacob whispered into her loose curls.

"No. Some asshole who smashed my SUV's window did that a long time ago."

"I love you, Jessie. I'm here for you. You know that, right?"

She stilled, before turning her face directly into Jacob's shoulder so nobody could see her cry. She was sitting sideways on his lap, one boot touching the floor, and the other floating just above it. As Jessie had done earlier, though, she tucked her arms up underneath his. "You are more than just a soft place to land, Jacob. Sometimes I think you are all that's holding me together these days. Everyone else just refuses to see the big picture. All they want to do is judge and offer opinions on lives they can't even begin to understand."

There didn't seem to be an answer to that, so Jacob just swallowed and blinked the thoughts away as he buried his lips in her hair so he could offer love the best way he knew how. But he realized, as he did so, that Jessie was the one not seeing the big picture.

Jacob knew Josh's hell. He understood it. Damn it, he lived it too while Jessie was gone, and while the children were missing, when no one had a clue what hideous secrets the shattered SUV window really held. The big picture? What Jacob saw framed in his mind was a man with a history of addictions suffering from a loss he was incapable of managing on his own. And what cowered in a musty dark corner in Jacob's eyes was the realization that the person needed to help that man was the woman who, just now, crawled into Jacob's lap in a very public venue…the same woman who just hit 11 million views in three days on YouTube singing an aching ballad she co-wrote with Jacob a few days after losing that man.

"Jess," he murmured against her neck now, as she trembled in his arms. "We need to go. People are not-so-discreetly taking pictures of us. Come on." Gently, Jacob eased her body away from him. With the sleeve of his jean jacket, he wiped teary streaks off her cheeks.

Jessie climbed off his lap then and, without looking up, wrapped a set of fingers around the coffee he pushed towards her. Entwining his fingers in her other hand, Jacob led his girlfriend out of the small café. Outside, he let go and draped that arm around her shoulders so Jessie could bury her face in him again, and he granted the cell phone photo hounds one last gift— a delicate brush of his lips on Jessie's cheek.

But the iPhone photographers didn't hear what he said to her when he did that. If they had, their knees would have given way altogether. "I love you, Jess. Regardless of everything…no matter what happens. Even if we end up a million miles away from each other in the end. You're everything to me, and you always will be. Okay?"

At her silent nod, he relaxed, just a little. For Jessie was right about one thing. Jacob knew where he stood. It didn't mean he liked it, or thought it always had to be that way. But just the same, it seemed like a good idea to let Jessie know exactly how he felt about her.

Not that Jacob's feelings were ever in question, to himself or to her.

And not that he really understood why she didn't feel *exactly* the same way back.

Chapter Two

With a mixture of curiosity and helplessness, Josh eyed the iPhone image of Jessie sitting on Jacob's lap with her face buried in his neck. Handing the phone back to Steve, he shrugged, feigning disinterest, although his heart felt ready to disintegrate into a thousand tiny pieces at the thought of Jessie lost—body and soul—in Jacob these days.

"Whatever," he muttered, looking away from his good friend as they sat by Josh's pool nursing Starbucks coffees. "If you're going for the shock factor, it's long past. And, in a way, I'm glad she's not alone."

"What, is that affection I hear coming from you, Josh? Finally? Your icy heart's finally melting?"

Steve chuckled as, before him, Sophie and Kayla frolicked with Emily-Grace and David in the pool. The girls each had a child on a paddle board, and were racing them from one side of the pool to the other. Giggles and squeaks reigned loudly in the stifling summer heat. He glanced to his left. His infant son Caleb was sleeping soundly in his buggy in the shade, dreaming of frogs and butterflies, Steve hoped, sheltered from the harsh world and its torturous life lessons.

More like dying, Josh caught himself thinking, in answer to his friend's light barb about his heart melting. Out loud he said, "It's not a surprise that she's with Jacob, Steve. Or were you too drunk to notice last month when she practically inhaled him during that slow dance in New York?"

Leaning forward, Steve pivoted his head so he could stare directly at Josh, who was sitting beside him in a striped deck chair. He used his coffee as a pointer. "Did you even see the photo I just showed you, Josh? Or the

13

one I showed you before that? With him wiping tears away from her face? What does that tell you?"

Shrugging, Josh glanced down at his coffee cup. "I don't know, Steve. What is it supposed to tell me?"

"Duh. You need to go get her. That's what."

"Not highly likely."

"Look buddy, you're doing great. You've had the kids almost two weeks now, and I dare you to show me a beer bottle. Nadia's not in the picture anymore—"

Josh groaned loudly, remembering the decadence of his and Nadia's two week Toronto bender, and her sensuous curves along with the erotic gift she gave him in Vancouver after his and Jessie's unsuccessful joint attempt at therapy.

Steve continued, waving his coffee for emphasis. "You're seeing Trudy, right? Regularly? And Frank too, I hear."

"Just because it's a condition for custody. So they can likely run back to Charles with their slick little reports. Otherwise—" The fear of what might otherwise happen clenched Josh's gut in two.

Filling in the rest of the sentence for him, Steve lowered his voice, one eye towards the pool. "Otherwise your time with the kids goes to Charles and Dee." Exhaling, he straightened. "Look, Josh, I know the two of you needed some time apart. I encouraged her to go to New York. Hell, I set it up and put her on the jet myself. But no more dicking around. You're doing awesome. Go get her back."

"I can't," were the small words that met Steve's ears then.

"Why the hell not?" Aghast, Steve watched Josh struggle with what to say.

"Did you see her with Jacob, Steve?" Finally, Josh met his friend's eyes. "I did. And not just at the fundraiser, and not just in his lap, when, a few days ago? She loves the guy. She's always loved him. They're amazing together."

"She loves you, you big doofus."

Josh's voice remained quiet. "I don't deserve her, Steve. Jacob does. Period. I've been stupid."

"Yeah. You have been. But you're trying, Josh." Steve twisted fully in his chair so as to face his buddy square on. "Look. The longer you wait, the harder it's going to be to get her back."

Josh's silence was unnerving.

Staring at him, Steve hesitated before speaking. "Tell me you want her back, Josh. Please."

His friend's eyes were dark as he answered. "I want what we *had* back. But I don't think that's possible, Steve. Jessie and I have accepted that. We know the truth. I think maybe it's time the rest of you believed it as well."

Draining the last few sips of his Starbucks dark roast, Josh set the cup on a nearby deck table and stood, pulling off his white T-shirt at the same time. Calling out to the kids, he stepped towards the pool. "Who wants a dolphin ride?"

Watching him, Steve found it hard to reconcile the man before him now with the drunk guy whose hair he held back while Josh vomited the night away at an Upper East Side New York hotel last month. Nor could he see the tortured guy he flew across the country to accost in Toronto, in an effort to bring him home, to straighten him out, and whom he had to tell, at the time, that his wife had left him. No, this guy here today wasn't as tormented. Instead, he just seemed sorrowful. Was that a permanent thing? Would the sorrow lift? Would the pain lessen as the days went on? Could Josh maybe start to see the light as the stink of Nadia's breath on his body faded? As the fatal attraction to liquor and beer dissipated?

Well, one thing was for sure. His kids were sure opening up to him again. Even sensitive little Emily-Grace was all laughter and bubbles now as she clung to her daddy's back for dolphin rides around the pool. Her blonde ringlets were soaked now, clinging to her face, and she was giggling with wild abandon, even screeching sometimes when Josh dove a little deeper under the water.

When Josh stopped swimming and brought his daughter around his body so he could hold her, Steve saw the truth in his eyes, a truth Josh was apparently afraid to voice, likely even to himself. It was clear in the way he studied the little girl that he saw her mother in her—in the way Emily-Grace brushed his own wet layered hair off his cheek for him, and in the way the miniature pale Jessie-eyes searched Josh's from a depth founded on thinly disguised lingering sadness. For a moment Josh was silent, watchful, non-responsive to his little girl's request for another dolphin ride. Steve didn't have to wonder where his mind took him—he knew.

To an image of Jessie on her new lover's lap, Jacob's sleeve fringing one cheek as his fingers wiped the water away.

Chapter Three

*N*adia was pissed at the image of her and the tennis star making the gossip rounds on social media. She was so angry she ignored Morgan's requests for caution. Did she give a shit if her hoity-toity neighbors heard her yelling? Nah. Besides, the condo Josh bought for her was so large she doubted a truck would be detected even if it rolled through the master bedroom. *Which it used to sometimes,* she managed to console herself, thoughts of Josh Sawyer's tongue on her body igniting her senses.

She was back in the condo full time now. Josh didn't seem to give a sweet shit if his ex-lover used it or not. Nadia hadn't heard from him since the morning he pulled out of TO, nor did she hear from any lawyers as she half-expected to, in terms of rousting her out, so she started staying there again.

When he was in the city, Morgan stayed overnight there too. They weren't worried about being seen, or being policed. He always wore a hoodie and, as an experienced member of the Keating security team, Morgan damn well knew where the cameras in the building were. He avoided them. The condo was large as far as Nadia's standards went. But Josh had some scruples when he bought it. There was no concierge or uniformed security in the place, not like Jessie's capacious new Madison Avenue condo. So Morgan slipped in and out easily, with no real cause for worry about being discovered.

Now, Nadia whipped around on one of her new Jimmy Choos. "Morgan, why don't you think he'll come back to me? I would have thought me seeing other men would have him writhing at my door." She purred as she spoke, and drew a finger up the front of Morgan's shirt as she did so, like a child wanting candy. "You were with him and the kids last week—he's not seeing anyone else, right? And Jessie's not around. Believe me, the man needs sex on a regular basis. There's no way he's not getting it from somewhere."

"First of all," responded Morgan nervously, wishing she would just forget about Josh already. Shit, she had the condo! The Gucci bracelet, the diamond ring, the fancy new wardrobe…the high profile dates she had met through Josh. How much more did the woman need? "I was only with Josh and the kids off and on, when they went out somewhere. I wasn't with them at home."

Nadia fired a menacing *you asshole, why weren't you parked outside watching them* look, but she had the wherewithal to at least remain silent. She did, however, cross her arms and balance most of her weight saucily on one foot as she regarded him.

"Secondly," Morgan added, avoiding her eyes and lightly running a long finger over an expensive white marble sculpture modeled after Rodin's amatory *The Kiss*, "I haven't seen any evidence of further interest in Jessie. So just get her off your radar, Nadia. Leave her be."

"The hell I will. You and I both know, Morgan, she has to go. Eventually she'll put two and two together, or Josh will go after her again. The stats say 90% of couples that split up have sex again, you know. And many of those reconcile. Josh and Jessie have kids together, they're going to be seeing each other."

"Mmmphh."

"What the hell's that supposed to mean?"

"It means, Nadia," Morgan faced her straight on, leaving the Rodin look-alike alone, "there's not much chance of that. They're not speaking. Usually one of us, or Charles and Dee, shuttle the kids back and forth between New York and Vancouver. So you can rest your overwrought little pea brain. They're done."

In his mind, Morgan wrestled with the truth. Were Josh and Jessie done? It sure seemed that way. Still…the sadness each carried with them was tangible, like unseen ghosts neither could shed, which clung to them mercilessly.

Once, when Morgan was at Jessie's new condo in New York, using one of the five bathrooms in the place, he overheard her crying. It was one a.m., and he had just escorted her back from some charity function at the Metropolitan Museum she attended with her friend Maggie. The plan was for him to stay overnight in one of the guest rooms, just for company, he thought, because he knew she was still wary—or at least Matt and Ulysses and Charles and Dee were still wary—of some sick predator out to get her. Jacob was away on a gig and the kids were with their father. Being alone in that big place was clearly sometimes too much for Jessie.

So when he went to the main washroom on his way back from the kitchen, heading to his room for the night, he stopped outside the door of the master bedroom. Even now, remembering the deep, hurting sobs, Morgan felt a gloom waylay him, traveling up and down his legs and spine like pricks of stinging desert sand, sharp and bitter and biting. He couldn't stand to see her sad. There had been enough of that in the now-burnt Langley house, which he witnessed through the one-way mirror. Her cries then were wretched, lonely, scared, as they were that recent night in New York.

Always, her pain buried Morgan under its power to condemn him for being its cause. It seemed his appalling impact on Jessie's life was far-reaching. Even now, she suffered. Why? For Josh. Morgan knew her well enough to know her husband was the cause. The impending total dissolution of a marriage she did not want to end…was the cause.

Jacob helped matters. But as much as Jessie loved the guy, Morgan knew he would never be enough. Yet, Morgan hoped the singer would soon ease the ache, totally and without mercy, as far as Josh was concerned. And…if Jessie stayed with Jacob, maybe Nadia would take the girl off her diabolical radar.

But…now…it seemed Nadia still had a single-minded focus when it came to Jessie. Perhaps because Nadia, too, sensed the lingering pain in both Josh and Jessie's haunted eyes, when she scanned the gossip sites and searched Twitter for their names and photos.

Nadia was smart enough to know her wicked game was still afoot. And she knew which card to play. Which made Morgan listen while Nadia stood before him in heels and a slinky dress that barely covered her breasts. Which made Morgan want what he was used to, but which he couldn't have unless he did the woman's bidding. Which made him yearn for the sensuous body in front of him now, and which made him the willing accomplice he'd agreed to be.

Smiling wickedly, Nadia took his fingers and cupped them over her breast. "Jessie is playing with Jacob at a few music festivals soon, isn't she? One in Scotland, and one in Montreal? Are you booked for those, Morgan?"

He didn't answer. His eyes were on the tattoo on Nadia's left breast. With a finger, he traced it. *DarinS.*

Morgan bent forward, and let his lips linger on his son's name.

Suddenly, he was reminded that most things didn't matter anymore. Nothing had mattered since the day his and Nadia's five-year-old child died in their arms a number of years ago.

He slipped a hand up under his wife's dress and willed himself to disappear.

Chapter Four

*M*inus security by choice, Josh brought the kids back to New York after their two weeks with him, with explicit instructions from Deirdre that they were to be dropped off to her, not to Jessie.

In her haughty words, "Jessie is not interested in seeing you right now, Josh. And she doesn't want you anywhere near her new place. Bring the children to me before Jessie and Jacob's show at the Beacon Theater, Broadway and 74th. They're booked in there both nights this weekend. I'll arrange to meet you outside."

They set up a time and she gave him directions, but he didn't need them. Josh and Jessie had attended Hozier's show at the Beacon the last time they were in New York. He clearly remembered her saying she would love to play there—its lush red and gold 1929 Art Deco stylings reminded her of the cozy Orpheum in Vancouver.

"It's like a big 'ole hug playing in a place this beautiful, with so much history," she had enthused, holding his hand and breathing in the gorgeous aura of the opulent, yet cozy, space.

Those damn good old days, Josh had thought as he disconnected from Deirdre. *They're going to haunt me forever.*

He arrived in New York with the children as planned, but for some reason Dee was not answering his texts. Josh tried calling, to no avail. Getting around the city was comfortable for him, an actor who once filmed a movie there, and who had visited many times, so he was in a rented vehicle cruising for a place to park—still without news from Dee—when David let out a mighty howl.

The child hadn't been in good shape on the commercial flight down, either. The mode of travel wasn't Josh's first choice, but he was quickly learning Charles and Dee weren't interested in accommodating him anymore if it wasn't easy for them. Today, they had the jet, since they were coming to New York from Montreal, where they were fine-tuning plans for an outdoor festival in which Jessie and Jacob were scheduled to appear. In all seriousness, Josh knew they would have preferred the children, at least, travel in privacy on the jet, but commercial travel was a viable back-up.

But geez-louise, traveling with a seventeen-month-old and an almost four-year-old was an exercise in patience.

I take that back, thought Josh as he scanned for parking outside the Beacon Theater. *Emily-Grace is easy. Her brother's a monster.*

Glancing into the rearview mirror, he grimaced as his son stretched wildly, trying to escape his car seat harness. Accustomed to her brother's antics, the toddler's sister was watching quietly, clutching both her singer-dowwy and bawwet-dowwy to her chest with her left hand, while sucking on her right thumb.

"Just a few more minutes, buddy," Josh apologized, the timbre of his voice elevated as he talked himself through options, should he not reach Dee. Wandering into the theater asking for Jessie didn't seem like a good choice with his son in this kind of hoary mood. Already, Josh was exhausted from dealing with the child's refusal to sleep or sit still on the airplane, or at the baggage carousel, or at the car rental counter.

Thank God for that nice flight attendant, he thought now, wistfully recalling the young Asian woman's motherly knack with his son. Once again an unbidden ache formed in his heart. *Fuucckkk, Jessie. I miss you.* But he shoved the pinpricks at the corners of his eyes away with a squeeze of a thumb and forefinger, and eased into a parking space, finally.

A new panic took hold. Within minutes, he would be dropping his children off for two weeks. Two long, lonely weeks…

Josh was flying back to Vancouver the next morning. Now, terror seized his heart and his breathing changed. Beads of sweat broke out on both palms. Steve would be away—he was shooting a film in New Mexico for the next three weeks. Charlie would be around. Maybe Josh could convince Carter and

Ashley to leave their sunshiny state and drop up for a visit. He felt his pulse returning to normal until the thought of Nadia crossed his mind.

No, he admonished himself, running a hand through his hair. *I am not even considering going there again. Never.*

Another peek in the rearview mirror had him frowning. David was now screeching bloody murder.

"All right, little guy," Josh said by way of hoping to calm his busy toddler, "let's you and me go for a walk." He eyed Emily-Grace. "What do you think, sweetheart? Can you and Daddy keep David from running into traffic?"

He was parked across and down the road from the grand historic theater. A small voice came from the back seat of the rental.

"Okay, Daddy. I hewp. We go see Momma now?"

"Yeah, Emily-Grace. You and David are going to stay with Momma for a bit. Is that okay with you? I bet she'll take you to Central Park. She lives real close to it now."

"Jacob too?"

Groaning, Josh looked back at his daughter. "Yeah," he managed, shoulders sinking and the last of his sanity fleeing as his heart dissipated into a thousand pieces for the forty-ninth time that day. "Jacob too."

Sighing, he reached for his cell. Still no message from Deirdre. Josh had tried Charles too, to no avail. *Maybe I got the day wrong? Maybe she meant tomorrow's show?*

In case of emergency, Josh had Jessie's contact info, and Jacob's too. He stared at Jessie's name on the small screen of his iPhone. It looked weird, distorted. He felt sick, but he bypassed it, letting his finger slide up to hover over *Jacob Ryan.*

"Here goes nothing," he whistled inwardly, pausing to text Jacob.

After a moment, without typing a single letter, he removed his thumb from the screen. Eyeing the backstage door that some burly security guy was guarding, Josh admonished himself. *I'm not fucking texting Jacob.*

Inside the theater, backstage, snacking on a carrot stick pilfered from a veggie tray, Jacob was regarding Jessie who, in casual jeans and boots for tonight's show, was having a last word with the female stage manager. Jessie must have sensed him watching, for she smiled a thank-you at the woman

23

responsible for running the show through smoothly, and wandered over to Jacob. He popped a carrot stick into her mouth and grinned.

"I like that look on you," he said, eyebrows narrowing in fun.

"Ha! You men are all the same, Jacob Ryan." Wrapping her arms around his waist, she made his favorite contented *mmmmm* sound. "Sex, sex, and more sex. You must have been some horny old bastard when you were sixteen, huh?"

"Twelve," he answered, laughing outright as he hugged her back.

An attractive mocha-skinned woman ducked her head out of a nearby dressing room. "Jessie? Can we do your hair now? We're getting close."

"Oops, what time is it, Miranda? I've done this so many times that sometimes I tend to forget. Sorry." She leaned into Jacob and draped both arms tightly around his shoulders. Kissing him tenderly, Jessie sighed when she let him go. "Come see me in ten for vocal warm-up, sexy man." Their fingers slipped out of each other's grasps as she wandered away.

Jacob went to reach for another carrot stick then, a broad grin creasing his face, but froze when he saw Josh and the two kids across from him, silently watching. Thankfully, Jessie hadn't spotted them. She'd be mush for the show if she had to stare into eyes that sorrowful before taking the stage.

Pulse suddenly racing, he started over.

David made a beeline for Jessie's guitar, which was leaning on a padded stand waiting to be moved onto the stage. At the last second, Jacob lunged for the child. Laughing, he scooped him up and planted kisses on the small face. David resisted, going taut in his arms and whining to get down, but Jacob backed up and grabbed a slice of apple off the craft table, which settled the toddler for the time being.

He approached Josh, who was standing still, resigned to the day's incessant challenges, one hand buried in a pocket and the other clenching his daughter's small fingers.

"Hey," Jacob started, trying to be amicable. "Thought you weren't coming until tomorrow's show."

Ppfffttt was Josh's response. "Damn it," he muttered quietly. "Dee told me today. I'm sure of it." He moved to check the calendar on his phone, but Jacob's words stopped him.

"Nah, don't worry about it, Josh. You're here now, it's all good." Jacob looked down at Emily-Grace, who appeared uncertain of what to do. Somehow she seemed to sense her father's sadness at seeing her mother and him, Jacob, together. "Hey, beautiful girl," he said by way of greeting as David munched away on the apple.

"Hewwo," she said softly, raising an arm to wave but not moving towards him.

"Do you want something to eat, too?" Jacob asked her.

At her nod, he moved ahead and selected a couple of carrot sticks, which he dipped in hummus. Handing them to Emily-Grace, Jacob looked up to see that Josh had followed him to the table. A few crew walked by and stared, but they glanced away when Jacob's warning look caught their eyes.

"I'll take the kids to Jessie's dressing room," he determined. "We'll find someone to keep an eye on the two of them while we're on stage."

"Charles and Dee aren't here?"

"No, they're in Europe somewhere. Who knows. Or Montreal. I forget. Can't keep track of those two jet-setters." The nervous fuzz edging Jacob's mumble emerged unnoticed by Josh.

"I guess that explains why I couldn't reach them." Thoughtfully, Josh rubbed the stubble on his chin. "Look, I'll stay with the kids. Or I'll take them to my hotel, I guess, that might be the best option. Since it was obviously me who screwed up."

But Emily-Grace had already seen her mother. Ominous tears welled up in her eyes. She vaulted across to Jacob's side, faced her father, and grabbed a handful of the singer's jeans. "Daddy," she pleaded, unknowingly pouring another layer of cement over Josh's heart, "I wanna stay with Momma and Jacob."

Oh geez, thought Jacob, unable to look at Josh as the little girl's request floated on some stale air current towards the high ceiling. *That's gotta hurt.*

Josh swallowed the bitter pain seizing his chest. *Fuucck. I'm such a goddamned loser.*

Rallying for her sake, and for the sake of his pride, Josh bent before his daughter and kissed her lightly on the cheek. "Daddy loves you," he managed. Then, standing, he leaned towards his son in Jacob's arms and repeated the good-bye. Eyeballing Jessie's new partner afterwards, he asked, "You okay? Are you sure?" He gestured towards the now happily munching David. "This one's been a hyper pain in the you-know-what today."

"Nah, it's fine," Jacob answered, trying to be upbeat for Josh's sake after Emily-Grace's anxious request. "There are people around. Assistants, PAs. We'll manage. Thanks for bringing them to the theater, Josh."

Josh nodded, afraid to let his kids out of his sight. Turning to go, but stopping part way around, he looked back over his shoulder and studied Jacob. Licking some moisture over his dry lips, he hesitated before uttering his next simple words. "She okay, Jacob?"

Silently, Jacob regarded Jessie's estranged husband. Then he shrugged. For some weird reason, he still couldn't help but like the guy. Honesty and decency prevailed. "Sometimes," he swallowed. "Not always."

Dipping his chin to study the toes of his boots, Josh accepted that. "Okay," he managed. Barely. "Thanks, man. And, uh, thanks Jacob. For picking up the pieces of this whole damn mess, I mean."

"No worries, Josh. I'll take good care of your kids, man." Thinking the words probably came out sounding a little pretentious, Jacob added, with a shrug he hoped looked casual, "Making sure they're safe and stuff. Fed. You know." He didn't add *oh yeah, and I'll take good care of your wife too,* but it crossed his mind. Somehow he didn't think that statement would go over so well.

Josh just watched him, unsure, before he swiped a hand under his nose, rotated his head back around, and started to move forward. It was either go ahead or go running back for his kids, which at this point was starting to feel like a viable option.

He made it about five steps before Jacob called out to him. "How'd you get in, Josh? Backstage, I mean?"

Over his shoulder again, Josh said, "The security guy recognized us. He let us in." *Everybody knows us. Our lives are not our own.*

In the SUV on the way to his hotel, he considered the reason why Jacob might have asked him. Was the guy trying to keep distance between him and Jessie? That brought up another thought. Josh saw her, backstage with Jacob. Kissing him. In love with him. And Jacob was right there with her, in his glory, loving the woman he longed for over so many years. It was a bitter pill to swallow, watching the two of them together again.

Josh knew he could have approached her. What might Jessie have said, how might she have reacted? She would likely not have been too hostile, he figured, since he was there with their children, and she wouldn't want to frighten them, especially reflective, watchful Emily-Grace. But would she have been receptive to a chat? Josh wasn't sure. The last time he saw Jessie he'd left her screaming on the floor of a Downtown Vancouver law firm.

But she was so close…

Flicking on the blinker, Josh pulled a hard right, which pissed off a New York cabbie. Ducking his head, embarrassed, he stammered, "Next time, I'm hiring a driver." Soon, he was at his hotel, lost and alone. Within an hour, he was drunk.

Back at the Beacon, Jessie was floored when the door to her dressing room opened and Emily-Grace popped in, followed by Jacob, with David in his arms.

"Momma!" The little girl bounded towards her.

Jessie reached down, grabbed her under the arms, and drew her daughter up onto her lap.

"You little monkey! What are you…?" Laughing happily, she sent the unasked part of the question on raised eyebrows to Jacob, who deposited another wriggling monkey on his mother's lap. Wisely, the hairstylist, Miranda, backed away, hot curling iron in tow.

"Josh got the day wrong. Or Dee gave it to him wrong." He shrugged.

Emily-Grace placed both palms on Jessie's cheeks and tried to get her mother's attention. The ballet doll fell to the ground. Jacob swooped over to get it, but when his eyes left hers, Jessie caught something in his gaze that bothered her.

"Momma, Stewwa has the same bawwet-dowwy as me."

David was wiggly, so Jessie helped him slip down. With Miranda's help, he toddled off to explore the small dressing room.

"She does? Wow, you and Stella will soon have to start your own ballet lessons, sweetheart." Absently, Jessie caught herself thinking with a pang that wasn't likely, since the kids would be spending two weeks in

Vancouver and two in New York—amongst elsewhere—over the upcoming fall and winter.

Letting her gaze drift back to Jacob, Jessie's pulse quickened as she clued in to his weird vibe. She sat taller. "Is Josh…is he here?" She blinked, trying not to let Jacob see her angst at the notion that her estranged hubby might be outside the door waiting to say…hello?

Jacob gave her a look she wasn't sure how to interpret. It was somewhere between sadness and victory.

"He was. He's gone." Twisting the ballet doll between his fingers, Jacob waited to see how Jessie handled that bit of news.

"Oh. Uhhhh…" She tried to look away before he could detect the old sorrow. It was etched in every wrinkle and pore, in every knuckle, underneath every fingernail, and within every beauty mark. It owned her, body and soul. *Josh* still owned her, body and soul.

And Jacob knew it.

He floundered too. Glancing at Emily-Grace, who was sitting on her mother's lap facing her, watching her, wondering at the grief fluttering over her mother's features, he took a pause to bite his lip and lean forward to hand the child the ballet doll.

Settling back on his heels, Jacob let his eyes inch back up to meet Jessie's, but she was still avoiding his gaze. Inhaling slowly, he gestured towards her anyway, unsure what to say or do. "I didn't think you'd want to see him before the show."

"Oh. Okay." Unable to help herself, after Jacob's remark Jessie glanced back at him. Her next question was a whisper, but it was cautious. Maggie's voice echoed in Jessie's head. *Don't hurt Jacob.* "He, uh, he asked to see me?"

Her good intentions landed on the floor with Jacob's dignity. She could see him struggling for something reasonable to say, for a way to say it without appearing desperate.

From Jacob's perspective, he felt like she threw the knife first. So he tossed it back. "No, actually, uh no, Jessie. He didn't."

Immediately Jacob felt like shit for admitting it, the truth, but he wiped a hand across his jaw and stood with his hands on his hips, watching David grab a pile of make-up remover pads from a wheeled make-up kit Miranda had set by the couch earlier. She was patiently trying to keep him from tearing it apart, but he was a curious little guy.

Planting his feet more solidly next to Jessie, Jacob remained silent while Jessie shrank down in the high dressing room chair. She was trying to smile for her daughter's sake, but Jacob knew her well enough to interpret the sudden pale cast to Jessie's pretty face, and the way she now slouched against the chair's back.

Touching her daughter's cheek, she smiled softly before running manicured fingers through the little girl's ringlets. "So pretty," she said in a subdued murmur. "Daddy did good with your hair today, sweetheart."

"Daddy wearned from the computer, Momma." Emily-Grace touched a small yellow duck bauble on the top of her head. "He got me ducky ones." At that, she looked towards the door, and her small shoulders collapsed. Jacob caught the look. The Sawyer women were without their man again. Suddenly all, including the man trying to take his place, profoundly felt Josh's absence from the room. The impact of that knowledge was so strong Jacob almost keeled over.

When he took the stage that night, Jacob felt like an impostor. Jessie could hardly look at him. The bubble was not in place. The magic was 'off.'

After their show, they found Emily-Grace asleep in a little nest Jessie had made her on the couch in the small dressing room. David was nestled in Miranda's arms. As Jessie took her sleeping son from the make-up and hair gal's embrace, she smiled wanly.

"I'm so sorry, Miranda. This is totally not in your job description."

"Oh, I didn't do a thing," the lovely mocha-skinned woman replied. She pointed to the small round speaker in the ceiling. "Your ballad rocked the two of them to sleep."

It put me to sleep tonight too, Jacob thought unhappily as Jessie responded with nothing more than a smile. He reached for Emily-Grace, who snuggled easily into his arms. Miranda helped wrangle the kids' coats on, before she handed Jessie her leather aviator coat and bag.

"I'll see if Ulysses is ready for you," she said, before easing out of the door.

"I'll bet you will," retorted Jacob, grinning finally, as Jessie lightly swatted his arm.

"Yeah, Ulysses is into her," she acknowledged. "I agree. They'll be married within the year."

"Or shacked up." He knew his response was on the haughty side, but Jacob couldn't help himself. Avoiding her stare, he adjusted David's coat so it was a little tighter around the neck. There was a cool August breeze in the New York air tonight.

"What are you getting at, Jacob?" Jessie's cool tone was a warning. "You opposed to shacking up?"

Jacob skipped the warning tone. He decided to play 'cool' right back at her. "No. But I'm not averse to marriage, either." A quick inhale accompanied the remark as his nerves and blatant annoyance at the not-so-magical show caught up with him.

"And whose marriage would that be, pray tell?" She was whispering so as not to wake up her peacefully slumbering daughter, who really needed to be in her own bed about now, or…in one of her own beds.

Studying her, Jacob's eyes were darker than usual in the semi-dimmed room. "I'm just saying maybe it's an option, Jessie. Something we should consider."

"I'm not divorced."

"Ah. I see." He raised his chin, and nodded at his singing partner. "We better get your little ones home before midnight, or we'll have your ex to deal with, Jess, if some paparazzo outside tweets a pic. Provided Josh's still sober."

Tears were suddenly pricking Jessie's eyelids now. "Why wouldn't he be?"

"Duh," Jacob said rudely, throwing his hip against the door to swing it open, "he just left his kids with his ex and her lover. In New York City. Against all odds, we think he may have been sober for the last two weeks. At least we hope so," he added, catching her stricken look. "But by the look on his face when he dropped off Emily-Grace and David, I'd say Josh was on the hunt for booze before he got out the backstage door. We might want to give Ulysses a heads up in case he shows up on Madison Avenue."

Jessie didn't follow him right away. Holding the door for her, Jacob felt like a damnable shmuck. All it took that night to piss him off was that one angst-soaked look on Jessie's face, that one stupid query—*he asked to see me?* And any confidence Jacob had in his budding rekindled romance with Jessie was toast. Yeah, he felt like shit. But it hurt to see that anxious hope in her eyes, not just for him, Jacob, but on behalf of Jessie too. And for these beautiful children, who were suffering horribly because of their parents' inability to get their shit together after a horrendous trauma.

At the condo, Jacob tucked Emily-Grace in, and Jessie tucked in her son. Afterwards, Jessie took Jacob's hand and led him towards her bedroom. Inside, she didn't speak. She started undressing him, from the top button down as she always did. Jessie understood Jacob's hurts, tonight. She could see them in his eyes, plain as day, little flecks of light moving here and there, playing across the surface like they wanted to settle but had no hope of doing so. Lowered eyebrows, misty longish girl-lashes, and Jacob's nervous habit of biting his bottom lip accented them.

He stopped her on the third button down, by placing both of his warm hands over hers. "I'm sorry," he murmured. "I was an ass."

"I'm sorry, too," she replied, peering into her lover's soul. "I'm sorry for a lot of things. But Jacob…don't be asking me about a divorce. Ever. I will never divorce that man." Swallowing, she removed her hands from his shirt. "I understand if you want to go."

"I don't want to go, Jessie."

"Why not?"

"Because I will never give up hope that you might change your mind some day. That's why." Mimicking Emily-Grace's earlier movement, Jacob took Jessie's cheeks between his palms. He bent and kissed her lovingly on the forehead, and then let his tongue tickle her all the way to her lips.

"I won't," she responded stubbornly. "I love you. But I will never let him go. You know that."

"Eighteen," he said softly, still holding her face between his palms, eyes closed.

"Hmmmm?" she asked, legs melting under his gentle kisses.

"That's how many nights I've spent with you now. Each one is precious to me. Each one is a miracle. Each one is one more step to holding you in my arms forever. Someday you'll see, Jessie. It will get easier every day, and then one day you will say to me, 'Jacob Ryan, I want to marry you.' And until that day comes, I'll count us in like I count us in on stage. One beat at a time. One night at a time."

Speechless, Jessie let her knees buckle under his touch.

When she regained her equilibrium, she almost let herself believe in his happily-ever-after hope for the two of them.

Almost.

Chapter Five

osh didn't show up at Jessie's place, but the concierge at his hotel did have to arrange for hotel security to escort him to his room. He collapsed on the bed, alone, in a heap of sodden misery.

The next day, he considered texting Jacob to see if he could get in to see the kids before flying back to Vancouver, but he was hung over and wisely unwilling to let his babies—or Jessie, if he should happen to cross paths with her—see him in this lonesome, loathsome way.

He flew back home with barely a word to anyone. By the time Josh landed in Vancouver, he was so drunk again he had to call a cab to drive him home. More than one cellphone caught him stumbling through the airport. When Jessie got wind of his state upon arriving home, she sat on the floor of her son's room after she put him down for a nap, and sobbed into his crocheted blanket so Jacob wouldn't see her and wonder what was up.

Josh's entire two weeks without the kids were a hazy blur. To his credit, he did his drinking at home. Not to his credit, he skipped his mandated appointments with Trudy.

Charles arrived at his house the day before Ulysses was supposed to fly the children back to Vancouver. He found his grandchildren's father asleep in his media room. The place was a mess of pizza boxes and beer bottles. Josh took a lot of prodding before he finally half-woke to see Charles staring at him.

He eased up to a sitting position, wrapping one arm around his sick stomach and using the other hand to brace himself on the black leather couch. Uneasy, he glanced down at the wrinkles on his white T-shirt and wondered when he'd last changed his clothes.

33

Charles started. "Your children will be here at four o'clock tomorrow, Josh."

"H-how'd you get in?"

Charles held up a key, which Josh half-swiped at. He missed, and groaned with the effort as the room swam before him.

"You haven't been to see Trudy."

"Nope."

"Have you been drunk since you got back?"

"Nope. Since before." Josh wanted to add *you fucking lunatic,* but he knew Charles held the cards when it came to his children's visit, so he bit his tongue.

"Jessie called me." Charles was softening.

Why? Josh wondered, on both counts.

He tilted his head to listen, although he now kept both hands firmly anchored on the edge of the couch to keep the room from spinning.

"She asked me to check on you, Josh. She was worried."

"Fuucckk." He didn't know which hurt worse, the hangover or the fact that Jessie cared enough to ask Charles to check on him. Josh shoved his thumb and forefinger into his bottom lip, squeezed hard, and sucked in a breath, which he held for a moment in this esteemed producer's company. "Tell her I'm fine. Okay? Charles?"

"The thing is…you're not fine, Josh. You're far from fine."

"I'm okay, I'm just…" Josh tried to stand, but fell back down. "I'm just tired. I haven't been sleeping."

"This is how this visit is going to go down, Josh. The kids are coming to La Casa. Give yourself a few days to sober up, and then come see them. But by the Lord Jesus, you better be sober."

Grimacing, Charles stared hard at his estranged son-in-law. "Josh, I will happily drive you to rehab. I want the best for those kids. And they need their father. They need their father alive and sober. And," he added, "for the life of me I don't understand why, but apparently Jessie needs their father alive and sober too. Despite what she said to Steve outside the law office the day we negotiated custody."

Josh tried to look up, but the overhead light Charles all of a sudden snapped on was too bright. He blinked, and shielded his eyes with one quaking hand. "Wh-what? What'd she say?"

"No comment. Suffice it to say it was out of heartache." Sighing, wiping a hand under his chin, Charles sat down next to Josh. He rearranged his blue silk tie as he did so. "Son," he started, "I know this has been a tough year for you. It's been tough for all of us. And it can't help that Jessie is with Jacob now."

Cringing, Josh couldn't fight the small moan that escaped his lips. He turned his head away from Jessie's pseudo father.

Charles continued. "But you need to get on with your life. You need to get some real help, help you want, not help that's mandated to you. You have to want to help yourself, Josh."

"Why do I feel like there's a 'there is always hope' couched in there somewhere?" Josh bit off sarcastically in a husky voice he'd recently only been using to order pizza.

"What?"

"Never mind."

"What happened? What set you off? You were doing so well with the kids before New York."

"I'll do fine this time too, Charles. I'll be fine by tomorrow. I won't drink. I'll clean the place up." Looking down at the pizza box at his feet, Josh couldn't remember the last time he ate.

"No," Charles said. "Take a few days and then come see them at La Casa."

"They need their own rooms."

"They need their father back, is what they need." Charles clamped a hand on Josh's shoulder and stood again. "Please, Josh. I don't know why or how Jessie is still capable of caring for you, after all you've done to her, but she does. Immensely."

At that, Josh managed to stand. He teetered in front of the powerful man. "Can you give her a message for me, Charles?"

The older man nodded warily. "As long as it's not some X-rated curse."

"It's not. I just..." Josh swiped at his eyes. "I just want her to know I did it for her, you know? The whole 'Jacob is better for you' thing? She needs to know I did it for her."

Charles pondered him, this man who once made the girl he considered his daughter so happy. "I would say I agree, Josh, about Jacob being better for her, except that I've never seen her so miserable."

Blinking, teetering, Josh took that in. "She loves that guy. I saw them. In New York, when I dropped the kids off."

"Well, that explains this little bender then, doesn't it, son?" Charles' tone was, surprisingly, kind. He softened even further. "I think she knows the truth, Josh. Or at least she suspects it. And you're right, she does love Jacob. Desperately. But I have a feeling it's you she still cries herself to sleep over when she's alone."

As he moved to leave the room, Charles called over his shoulder, "I wish to hell you'd let me take you to rehab, son. Because I'll tell you one thing. The longer Jacob is with her, the harder it's going to be to peel him off the pavement when you come riding in on your white horse. And the harder it's going to be for me to put him and Jessie back in the studio together."

He barely heard Josh's voice behind him. Charles had to ask him to repeat himself. Then he bent to listen.

Josh was saying, "You have hope. You think there's still a chance for me. For us."

"Yes," he heard the man say before Charles turned to look at him. "Against my better judgment, may I in all honesty add."

"Look at me, Charles. I'm a fucking mess." Josh held his arms open wide to show Charles the 'real' him, stinky and unshaven and still blatantly drunk.

"You beat addictions once before, Josh. I know you can do it again."

"Why? Why all of a sudden do you give a sweet goddamn? You hate my guts. You and Dee both hate my fucking guts!"

"Because Jessie called me today from New York, Josh. She cried the entire time. One, because she is putting those beautiful children on the jet again tomorrow, and flying them miles away from her. And two, because for some godforsaken reason, she is, she was, and she always will be, hopelessly in love with you." He let that digest before slapping the doorframe and walking up the steps towards daylight. "Get yourself cleaned up, Josh. Come see your children. And get your ass to rehab."

After the outside door somewhere above him closed, Josh dropped slowly back down to the couch. He thought about the strange meeting with Charles and wondered why the hell the man was suddenly no longer asking him to divorce Jessie. He decided that Charles, like him, had very little capacity to see Jessie in pain.

And somewhere, deep inside, a tiny light blinked on. It was the old lighthouse, back again, the one from before the New York fundraiser when Jessie first responded to Jacob because Josh showed up drunk.

The lighthouse beacon was weak, but it was something. And its fuel was the words from Charles Keating's own lips—*she is, she was, and she always will be, in love with you.* Not…Jacob? Really? On some level, sure, yes, but…

Sitting back against the couch, Josh closed his eyes. For once, he allowed himself to think of Jessie in a good way, without being accosted by the usual pain. He sent her a telepathic note. He whispered it aloud in the hopes that saying it that way might make it travel quicker, and easier, to her ears. "I love you, Jessie. I love you." And then, in a tiny voice, "I want you back. I want my family back."

At the time, he blanched at his own audacity. *Me, a drunk? A loser? What chance do I stand of getting my family back?*

But then Josh realized that although he hoped the telepathic message would make it to Jessie, he knew the truth of it—the words were really meant for him.

He eased his trembling body upright, pulled himself upstairs by virtue of the steady handrail, stripped off his dirty clothes, and stepped into the shower.

Chapter Six

Matt showed up unexpectedly when Morgan was on shift in New York. He nodded a quick hello to Morgan before knocking on Jessie's trailer door. Surprised to see him, she flew into his arms. Matt represented good times and good memories. Matt was hope.

"Hey, what's all this?" he asked, hugging back, unable to hide his joy at the warm reception.

"What, the hug or the shoot?" She laughed.

"I know what the shoot is. The hug. I'd almost think you missed me."

She shot him a sideways look that clearly said *you know I do*. Glancing at Morgan, who was seated in a lawn chair outside her trailer, Jessie gestured to Matt. "Come inside. Let's talk."

When they were comfortably seated across from each other at the trailer's small beige table, with Jessie casually perched on one folded knee, she shoved a script she was reading aside. "Dee and her never-ending pile of offers," she grimaced.

"Nothing worth pursuing there?" Matt half-smiled and casually leafed through the pile on the table before him.

"No, that's the problem, they're all good. I want to do every one of them!" She grabbed one she'd set aside and held it up to him. "So far this one's the winner, though."

Taking it, he knifed through the pages before reading the synopsis on the title page. "Hmmm."

"What?" Jessie sat back and crossed her arms. "I can tell you don't approve."

"It's a love story."

"Yup."

Scratching his ear, Matt paused. "It's a love story between two musicians."

"It is. Yes."

He let a small curve light up one corner of his lip. "Jacob?"

"Yup."

"He has no shortage of offers, Jessie."

"I know. I just thought it might be nice to do a feature film with him. Big screen stuff. Larger than life." She lifted both hands and wiggled her fingers to accent the 'larger than life' part.

Setting down the script, Matt wordlessly fingered it.

Crossed arms telegraphed Jessie's curious disapproval of his lack of enthusiasm for the project. "So why aren't you jumping up and down, Matt?"

Sighing, he sat back. "Charles was in to see Josh yesterday."

Startled, Jessie hesitated. She recovered quickly. "I know. I called him and asked him to check on Josh. I was worried, Steve and Charlie hadn't heard from him. Charles called back, he said he was fine—look, Matt, is Josh okay? Did something happen?"

Looking around, Matt raised an eyebrow. "Is Jacob…"

"No, he's not here," she cut in, heart rate accelerating. "He's on set, shooting some single shots for the music video." She dug the nails of one hand into the back of the other and sucked in a breath.

Catching the fear playing across her face, Matt reached across the table and took Jessie's hand. "He's fine, Jessie. I think he had a rough go the last two weeks, as I'm sure Charles told you, but Charles felt optimistic that Josh might finally try rehab. I'm not here to hassle you about him. I'm actually in the city on business with Kelly and Michael," he smiled half-heartedly at her small frown, "and thought I'd drop by to see how you and Jacob are getting along with Morgan these days."

"Meaning?"

"Meaning I can swing a few more shifts with you if you like, but I know Morgan's back around after his holiday so I'm guessing you don't need me."

"You're missing me." She winked. "I knew you would, eventually."

"It's not that at all." Chuckling, he sat back, absently adjusting his button-down shirt at the waist. "It's Julie. She wants a bigger house. She sent me out to look for more work."

Jessie laughed, eyes sparkling. "Liar. I know Julie. She doesn't care about bigger houses. You're missing me. Unless…" Her eyes darkened, just a little. She cocked her head. "Is everything okay? I mean…in terms of finding out who wanted me dead last April, that's all. No biggie."

"There hasn't been any movement, Jessie. So no, that's not why I want to hang out with you. I really do have some time coming up when I'm available, and to be honest, I…well, Jacob's going to kill me for telling you this, but he sent me an email. He's got more concerns about Morgan. I talked to Ulysses. He's thinking about letting him go."

"Oh. Hmmm." She looked down at the script in front of her and traced the title with a fingernail. Speaking quietly in case Morgan should hear through the open window, she said, "He's definitely been a little off lately. Since I was rescued, in fact."

"He's the quiet sort anyway, Jessie, as you know, and he doesn't express his feelings much—"

"You security types aren't known for being touchy-feely, Matt."

Swatting her across the table, Matt frowned. "Ulysses thinks Morgan took it pretty hard. The whole…thing. And as much as he and Charles hate to let him go, Jacob has some real concerns." He leaned his elbows on the table and searched her eyes. "Call it intuition, Jessie."

"What, you think I need to be afraid of him?"

"I don't know what to think, Jessie. There's no reason to be afraid of him, is there?"

"No, I mean, I don't know. I don't think so. Yeah, he's quiet, but he's a rock, you know? Matt, I'd hate to let him go. He has a wife in Toronto."

"No kids though, right? He'll be okay until he finds something else. Ulysses will give him a reference. Jessie, I think we need to listen to Jacob on this one. He's uncomfortable around Morgan, and he thinks you can't see the forest for the trees. I'll fill in again as long as you promise to take me to Serendipity for ice cream."

"Okay. I guess. Fine. When and how do you propose to tell him, Matt?"

"What time do you and pretty boy expect to wrap today?"

"We're supposed to be done by five but you know how these shoots go. It will likely be closer to seven. We're already running half an hour behind."

"Fair enough, then. I'll come by. I don't know why, but for some reason I'm doing Ulysses' dirty work."

"That's because he's with my kids, Matt. Duh."

Laughing, he stood and leaned over the table, and gently kissed Jessie's forehead. "Thanks for agreeing to let me come around again, Jessie. I'm feeling a little more like my old self these days."

"You missed your friend." Her voice was low, calm, and her eyes were twinkling.

"What do you want me to do, get down on my knees and kiss your feet?" Matt moved sideways to slide out of the bench seat. Jessie rose halfway to meet him, her weight on one knee.

"I'm not talking about me," she smiled. "Charles will be around when he and Dee fly the kids back in two weeks. You guys can, I dunno, go to some documentary film festival or something. Or—I got it—wander through MoMA together, sipping on Pinot Grigio while you discuss the spiritual transcendence of contemporary art."

"You're killing me."

"C'mere."

He stepped closer and Jessie wrapped both arms around Matt's waist. "I'm glad you're going to be around a bit more, Matt. I miss you like crazy. I miss my old life."

"You like New York though, right?"

Letting go of him, she leaned back. "Is that a loaded question?"

"Maybe." He shrugged loosely.

"There are some things I like about New York."

"Can I ask how things are with Jacob?"

"Things are fine with Jacob. He knows what's up."

"And what's up, Jessie?"

Melting in the steady gaze of Matt's kind eyes, Jessie sat back on her heel, resting one arm on the small table. "Is there something Charles didn't tell me?" She swallowed. "About Josh, I mean?"

"Charles wants you to be happy."

She digested that by glancing down and running a finger over the edge of the script again. When she looked back up at Matt, her eyes were questioning but her voice was a whisper. "Charles knows what would make me happy, Matt."

"Yes," Matt smiled sadly. "He does. He knows. For a long time he couldn't admit it, not really, but…he knows."

"Do you think he was okay with Josh? Not…nasty, I mean? I asked him to be nice. I begged him."

"I think he was fine. He's had some time to process everything. Josh agreed to let him and Dee keep the kids for a few days until Josh cleans up. I think they left on some kind of amicable terms."

"Matt…what aren't you telling me?"

Thinking quietly, Matt wondered how much he could tell Jessie, how much she could take. He thought about Jacob, about how worried the guy seemed to be about Morgan, and about how worried he was about his relationship with Jessie in general. Matt's heart ached for the kid. It must suck to love someone you know loves someone else more. He studied Jessie. "I think Charles left something out when he spoke to you over the phone last night."

Her stomach lurched. "Oh? What?" *Please let Josh be okay.*

A tiny grin lit up the corners of Matt's lips. "He didn't want to tell you because he thought it might upset you. But I disagree. I think this is something you need to hear. Even though…" He glanced behind him. Jacob's distant laughter was pealing through the small trailer window. The guy was on his way back from the set. Matt picked up his tempo. "Apparently Josh wanted you to know he thought Jacob was a better partner for you. Than him."

She swallowed past the hoards of cotton stuffing her throat closed. "That's not a surprise, Matt. Josh told me that himself."

"Did you read between the lines, Jessie?" Serious now, Matt's countenance was slightly tense.

"'Course I did. Or I guess you could say I *hoped* between the lines."

"Well, last night he came out and said it, to Charles of all people. He is very typical of a man dealing with addictions and post-traumatic stress, Jessie. He doesn't feel worthy of you. He wants you to know the reason he spoke so harshly to you regarding Jacob at the lawyer's office that day was about you. *For* you. He thought he was doing the right thing for you, backing away like that. Letting you go, despite how much he loves you. *Because* he loves you. He thought it was best for the kids too, of course."

Taking Matt's hand, Jessie held his gaze. He watched as her eyes turned diaphanous again, pale and misty in the morning light. "He *does* still love me. It wasn't all just about Jacob being the better man."

"And he still needs you, Jessie. More than ever."

"Do you think he's ready? To give me a try again?"

"I think he's finally considering rehab."

"So I suppose when he gets there someone should once again send him a sunny yellow card with the word hope on it."

"Hmmm?"

Jessie colored slightly and absently traced a finger again across the script nearest her on the table. Ignoring the curious query, she shrugged and turned back to the general conversation. "You're not helping Jacob's case any, Matt." Her words were barely audible, just a slight hum, almost, in the small space.

He touched her cheek with his thumb and forefinger. "In the long run, maybe I am," he admitted. "And Jessie, I didn't tell you this so you would immediately go running back to Josh. You need to be strong enough too. But what the two of you had…it's rare. And you've got the two children to consider now. Is it fair to them to be shipped across the country every two weeks like FedEx packages? What kind of a life is that for them? Emily-Grace is getting old enough for classes and pre-school. She needs stability."

"Ah, good old Matt. Welcome back." A wide grin spread across Jessie's face, then. It lasted a moment before it faded. Outside, Jacob's voice was drawing nearer. "The ball's still in Josh's court anyway, Matt. Us getting back together is his call."

"So if that becomes an option, Jessie, how fair is it to Jacob to keep him hanging on?"

"Ohhh, fuucckkk." Putting her hands over her face, Jessie collapsed lower onto the bench seat so she ended up sitting on her butt and dropping both feet onto the floor. "This is killer. Really."

Matt brushed a hand over the top of her head, like one would do to a child. "So I assume you would take Josh back if he asked." It wasn't a question.

"Oh, Matt. Jesus, yes. In a fucking heartbeat. But not with him running out the door to Nadia."

"I think that ship has sailed, kiddo."

"I hope so."

"I also wouldn't want to see you and the kids back there until he's been sober for a while, Jess. He needs to do this rehab thing and prove to you he can beat it."

"He did it before. He can do it again."

"Apparently," Matt moved to go, "that's what Charles told him."

She looked up. "Really? Seriously, Matt?"

He smiled, a 'cat that ate the canary' grin. "I wasn't just talking to Charles this morning, Jessie. I actually had a chat with Josh, too."

She sank back against the seat, hands folded in her lap. "Remind me to give Charles a hug next time I see him. I can't tell you what his trust would mean to Josh, Matt."

"I know." Eyeing the script on the table, Matt nodded towards it. "When would that film about the two musicians go to camera?"

She held it up. "This one? Next month, actually. Soon. The cast they had booked dropped out. We're the backups. And I know what you're thinking, Matt."

"Some backups." He smiled before adding, "Well, we all need our memories, Jessie. Maybe you should give Jacob his."

"Aw geez, Matt. Ouch."

"I'll see you tonight at your place." He held up his phone. "Text me if the time changes."

"Okay. And Matt?"

"Yeah?"

"Thank you."

He pulled down the handle on the trailer door and exited, tossing a knowing smile in her direction first, his hard-soled shoes familiar music to Jessie's ears as her trusted friend dropped down the three metal steps to the asphalt underneath. Jessie heard him greet Jacob and have a brief chat, which she was glad of so she could have a few moments to process what he just told her and why.

In the end, she pushed away any thoughts of reconciliation with Josh. One, because it still hurt too much to wish and wonder without real hope from Josh himself, two because Jacob would be bounding into the trailer in an instant, and he could read her like a book, and three, because all of a sudden she felt like shit about having to fire her longtime bodyguard tonight.

And she still had to finish this music video first, for the ballad she and Jacob wrote together, and for which the live onstage video version now had 345 million views on YouTube.

It was going to be a long day.

Chapter Seven

*B*y the time Matt arrived at the Madison Avenue condo, Jessie was feeling a little more open to the idea of firing Morgan. Partly it was because, with Matt's admission of Jacob's real concerns, she took the time to study Morgan. Lately Jessie was so caught up in her own personal angst she just accepted him as he always was—steady, dependable, strong. But now she saw what Jacob saw. The guy had lost a lot of weight, and he was distant, as if something was troubling him.

Part way through the long day, at the end of the lunch hour, Jessie had dropped into a lawn chair next to him.

"How's your day going, Morgan?" She picked at a strawberry in her dessert crepe, forked it between her lips, and regarded his short blonde hair and broad, chiseled features.

He rustled a little in his seat, obviously uncomfortable with his boss' close proximity to him. Clearing his throat, he said, "Fine. Quiet."

"Thankfully," she smiled warmly. "How's your wife these days?" Immediately, Jessie colored. "I don't mean to pry, Morgan. I'd like to meet her some day, that's all. It seems kind of weird that we've worked together all this time and I've never met her." Instantly, she regretted saying that. Jessie knew she was just spouting words in empty air—she was firing the guy tonight. She felt like a traitor.

"Na—My wife's good," he said, as an interesting shade of crimson bloomed across his cheeks.

"What kind of work does she do?"

Uhhh, besides kidnapping and plans to murder, you mean? Oh, and playing games that involve destroying people and their families? "She was working for an accounting firm, as a receptionist, but she's on a bit of a break right now."

"Oh. Is she well? I hope she's not sick." Jessie had paused with a spoonful of crepe halfway to her mouth. She felt guilty for thinking *well, maybe it would be best if he left the Keating employ.*

Meanwhile, Morgan was thinking *she hasn't been well since our son got sick. At all.* He muttered something without looking at Jessie. When she glanced over at him, he was staring at the pavement, his lips curved downwards, and was absently poking underneath a fingernail.

"Are you okay, Morgan? Again, I don't mean to pry, but…I can see you're not feeling a hundred per cent."

"Hmmpph." Shuffling in his seat, Morgan pursed his lips. Other than the guttural grunt, he said nothing.

Jessie knew she was making him uncomfortable, but she felt immobilized by what she saw in front of her now, and she wondered how she could have missed it all along. Morgan was definitely unwell. His pallor was pale, almost a sickly green, despite the red flush that spread across his cheeks from the discomfort engendered by this particular chat. He was thinner, which in a way didn't surprise Jessie, since she was spending a lot of time working out in her small home gym these days, and not accompanying him to a commercial gym like in the old days. She wondered if he still worked out…?

"Maybe some more time off would be okay?" she asked him, despite the warning bells in her brain. *Might as well test the waters,* she was thinking.

"Uhhh, no, Jessie, that's okay. I need to be here. My wife's fine. She just needs to get her shit together, that's all."

Harsh, thought Jessie. *But okay.*

Jacob eased up to Jessie's chair then, and placed a hand on each of the two armrests. He bent down for a kiss. Scooping the last of the crepe into her mouth, Jessie dropped the paper plate on the asphalt and placed both palms on his cheeks. A view of a lingering kiss was what Morgan got treated to as he sat by them wondering uncomfortably whether he should get up and leave.

"Ahh, Jessie, you taste like strawberries," Jacob was saying as he licked the edges of her lips. "Mmmm. Nice. Maybe we should grab some on the way home."

"You taste like peanut butter." Giggling like a schoolgirl, she leaned back in the lawn chair, taking him with her so that he almost lost his balance. Still, Jacob hovered over her, kissing her lightly, playing around her lips and wanting more.

Morgan couldn't take his eyes off them. Jessie had two lovers, basically. He had half a one, if you broke his and Nadia's relationship down. It didn't seem fair. Life didn't seem fair.

Jessie could feel Morgan's eyes on them. Jacob seemed to be ignoring him, but then Jacob had other things on his mind suddenly, and he started murmuring them to Jessie as he brushed one hand down the side of her neck and slipped a few fingers inside her sleeveless top.

"Nooner?" She could feel his smile tickle her throat as his lips slid lower. "We've got a few minutes."

"Mmmmm, Jacob. I'm not going to be able to go back to work if you keep this up."

"Let's do the nooner," he pleaded, somewhat insistently, kneeling on one knee now and grabbing her hips to pull them forward. Burying his face in her chest, Jacob wrapped loving arms around the woman he considered his. He undid her top button and then the one below it, brushing his lips along the top of her bust line as he did so.

"Babe," Jessie laughed, slightly ill at ease by Morgan's eyes staring where Jacob's lips were landing, "not now, okay? Later." She placed her hand over the third button so Jacob couldn't undo her any further.

Disconcerted, he sighed and stood, then reached a hand out to help her up. "Fine," he replied, grinning, "but I at least want a rain check. What do you say, Mizz Wheeler?" He wrapped both arms tightly around her waist and leaned in for another lingering kiss.

"I say yes," she murmured adoringly. "But not 'til we're home, sexy man."

Later, in the condo, they had to settle the unpleasant business of firing Morgan before they could sink into the sweet oblivion of each other's bodies. Matt started them off. He stepped into the outer foyer and called Morgan in. The kitchen was off the main hallway, secluded from the entryway. Waiting at the kitchen island, Jessie strummed her fingers on her thighs nervously as Morgan's runners tapped out their path around the corner before landing inside the kitchen itself.

She couldn't meet his eye, and she was trying not to wring her anxious hands. He noticed, and glanced up at Matt, who gestured to the seat next to him, across from Jessie.

"We have to talk," Matt began, as he slid into the seat next to Morgan, with Jacob opposite. "There are a few things we need to discuss."

Understandably tense, wondering if Jessie had remembered or said something about the Langley house that tied him into the kidnapping, Morgan's steely gaze shifted across to her before landing on Jacob.

It was unusual for Morgan to hold anyone's gaze, ever, for any period of time. Jacob withered a little from the piercing stare, but he didn't look away.

Matt continued. "We're going to let you go, Morgan," he said outright. "There have been a few concerns raised."

"What?" It was a shock, albeit there was a certain relief in Morgan's eyes as well, which Jacob, watching him closely, found interesting. "Why?"

Matt gestured to Jacob, who cleared his throat and said, "Look man, it's nothing personal. It's just…that night, a while ago. I haven't been able to get over the fact that you must have heard us. Jessie and me. In, uh," he looked sideways at Jessie, who was sliding deeper into her chair, before glancing nervously across to Matt, "in bed. Since then I just haven't been completely comfortable around you, Morgan. I'm sorry."

Adrenalin fueled Morgan's quick rebuttal. "Yeah, that's uh…that's quite the tat you have there, Jacob."

"Wh-what?" *Did he see us in bed?*

"I saw your back."

Jacob gulped. Beside him, Jessie inadvertently shot out a hand and grabbed his thigh. She couldn't breathe.

"On the way back down the hall. After you got Jessie the chocolate chip cookie she asked for." The darkness in Morgan's eyes shifted and bored deeply into Jacob's shocked baby blues.

"You…heard me ask him for a cookie that night, Morgan?" Jessie was almost pleading for the answer to be no. But it wasn't.

"Yeah," was Morgan's answer, "I did." He angled his gaze on her—to the woman his wife was planning to have him kill. To the woman he adored as a boss, and who he once gave what he still thought of as an incredible gift.

"How close were you?" Jacob was quietly insistent, as Matt lowered his chin and poked at a shirtsleeve cuff.

Morgan was silent, but his lips turned up just the tiniest bit. He made a small victory sound in the back of his throat and locked his eyes back into Jacob's.

"Were you watching us, Morgan?" Jessie asked the question because she could see Jacob's lips working in confusion, and she figured rightly that the shock value of Morgan's probable proximity to them was overwhelming for him. She had different levels of experience with sex than Jacob, starting at the age of twelve, and including a short time making erotic films in a Downtown Vancouver black box studio. The shock hit her less in the gut than it did her lover, but still, Morgan's treachery sure as heck was unbelievable.

"You left the door open," the bodyguard said blankly. He grinned wholeheartedly at Jacob. "You're a player, man. I learned a few things."

The clock's ticking and the incessant cranks and groans of the fridge were a strange cacophony in a room where three people were suddenly breathless. The fourth person was shifting in his high chair, which creaked too, in counterpoint to the clock and fridge.

"Jesus Christ," was Jacob's final stunned statement. "What kind of sick pervert are you?"

"Easy, Jacob," Matt said, sliding off his chair. He rested a hand on Morgan's shoulder, but Morgan shrugged him off. "Let's go, Morgan. You're done here."

Before he moved to leave, Morgan flicked his eyes over to Jessie. She blanched, but didn't look away. Lips pressed in a tight line, he said, "I'm sorry, Jessie." In his opinion, she didn't have to know what for. He just had to say it. And mean it.

She shivered. Those drifty eyes…suddenly, something hit her. The eyes… she sucked in a breath and straightened. Morgan didn't notice, as he was getting off the chair, finally. But Jessie's suddenly shocked stare moved sideways and landed hard on Matt, who caught it, and stopped moving. He narrowed his eyes at her.

No way, she was thinking. *No fucking way.* She looked back at Morgan as he rounded the opposite end of the kitchen island and walked out, Matt behind him, with one eye backwards on Jessie until he was out of sight.

Jessie sank deeply into her chair and hung her head in her hands. A throbbing had started in her head; her hands were suddenly clammy and damp.

"Jess?" Jacob laid a hand over her forehead. "You okay?" He answered his own question. "Of course you're not okay. That guy's a fucking freak." He, too, sat lower. He traced a line on the white marble countertop.

She didn't answer. She couldn't.

When Matt returned with a quiet, "He's gone," she met his gentle questioning eyes with a shrug. *It's nothing.*

But Jessie wondered. Was she just freaked out because Morgan admitted to watching her and Jacob have sex on that unreal night when they first got together? Or was she freaked out because…well, because she saw those eyes somewhere before, in some hazy murky dream…

…just before the hands attached to the same body dumped gasoline all over a house she was tied up in, and lit a match.

Chapter Eight

Not surprisingly, Nadia was incensed when Morgan gave her the news that he got ditched by the Keating camp. For his part, though, he was relieved. He wanted to quit anyway—the charade was too hard to maintain, his anxiety over his double-life too difficult to bear. Best of all, he wouldn't have to go through with killing Jessie now, because he would never get near her. He knew the security drill. She would be well covered at all times. However… he did know the holes. And there were, indeed, holes. Lots of them, in fact. But would he tell Nadia that?

In the end, he had to. Because she had other plans.

"You'll get another job, with another artist. One who will also be playing at that outdoor festival in Montreal next week."

"I have no references, Nadia. Matt said Ulysses was planning to give me one but I…I haven't got it yet." That last bit was partly true, but Morgan left out the part where Matt also said *I'll be talking him out of a reference now, Morgan* in his 'my-shit-don't-stink-I-own-Jessie-Wheeler' voice.

"That won't matter. You worked for Jessie, you're experienced doing security at that level. Work will be chasing you down."

It didn't, chase him down, that is, but Morgan did some poking around on Facebook and got hired as temporary security for a band scheduled to play at the Montreal Festival. 'Running In Squares' was a new indie band on the Canadian scene. Because they were also Canadian musicians, they were quartered near Jessie and Jacob, whose superstar status engendered them a large, private tent to use as a green room on the festival grounds.

While Morgan was packing to head to the festival, however, Jessie was preparing to fly across the country to Vancouver. She would miss the first night—Jacob would take the stage alone.

As life would have it, she was on an emergency trip to pick up her children. She, like her ex-bodyguard, was just getting started on the packing for Montreal when a panicked, angry call came in from Charlie.

"I swear to God, Jessie, I could kill the guy. You should have stayed with me."

"What? Charlie, what the hell's going on?" Clutching a pair of white cotton socks, Jessie froze at the urgency in his voice, and anxiously floated the sock hand in mid-air while she used the other to adjust the phone for better listening.

"Josh was keeping Stella while I ran out to Abbotsford to shoot a commercial. Something unwired him, shall we say. I'm pissed, Jessie." Charlie settled momentarily, well aware that prolonged silence on Jessie's end meant she was processing a spate of questions, not to mention likely hiding a desperate angst at this latest fall from grace in her husband's world.

"Jess, look, before you hit the panic button, the kids are fine. I'm at your house with them now. But Josh is not capable of keeping them, and I'm shooting again tomorrow afternoon. I can take Stella with me, but three little ones are definitely too much to handle. Jane's in South Africa, doing her usual 'good for the world' bit, Charles and Dee are away—are they ever home? I know Carlotta's visiting family in the Philippines this week. And Steve and Sophie are still off on his shoot. What are the chances you can get here by morning? Where's the jet?"

"It's, uh, it's—they're—in Detroit, I think, at some music biz convention Charles is attending. That's likely why you're not getting a response from Charles or Dee, Charlie, I'm guessing they're in some kind of meeting or music showcase."

"Look, Jess, I never tried them, okay? I know they're at some conference. And I don't think Charles needs to know about this. But Jesus, Jessie, should I grab this guy by his toenails and drag him off to rehab? He had my daughter here today!" Charlie was close to tears, which was Jessie's barometer for how bad the situation was, because Charlie rarely got choked up about anything.

"Charlie? How bad was—is—it?"

53

A heavy sigh prefaced her old fiancé's unguarded response. "He was fine when I dropped her off. In fact, we've spent a bit of time together lately with the kids and Josh has been really, really great. But something set him off today. When I got here, he was passed out cold on the floor of your media room. The outside doors were locked, thank God, so no pool access, and the kids were fine, but still. Jesus. Emily-Grace just kept saying 'Daddy won't wake up' in that scared little voice of hers, and Stella was crying. David, well he's David, so he was off in a corner puttering with his cars. Everything slides off that kid's back, huh?"

He heard a nervous, stifled laugh. "Thank God for that small mercy." Jessie's hollow footsteps also echoed through the phone. She was pacing the large condo, the forgotten socks still clenched in a hand.

"What kind of place do you have there, Jessie, a fucking mansion? It sounds empty."

"F-off, Charlie. It's big enough to hide in, put it that way. Look, I'm just grabbing Matt, okay? We'll get the jet flown here and be in Vancouver by, when, oh I don't know, maybe by eight in the morning or earlier. Can you…Charlie, can you stay until I get there?"

"Negative. I'm taking all three kids back to Burnaby with me. Josh is fine. He'll spend the night sleeping it off, is my guess."

"What did he drink?"

"Your old favorite, as far as I can tell. Jim Beam. So I'm guessing whatever set him off—"

"Had to do with me. Lovely."

"It'd have to do with you, Jessie, or he wouldn't have gone over the edge like this, not with the kids here."

"I have a feeling I know what it was. Our new video—Jacob and me, for the ballad—was released this morning. The live onstage version's been out for a while, but this one…well, you know how music videos are, they tell a story."

"Ah. You and Jacob, all lovey-dovey, is that it?"

"It's special, Charlie. It was a lot of fun to make."

"I can just imagine."

"Can you take your sarcasm and park it, Deacon? If there's any chance in hell Josh is mooning over me at all, then it'd be nice if he'd share his thoughts in this general direction instead of taking them out on a bottle of Jim Beam."

"Honey, I know someone else who did that once."

"Yeah, and I suffered alone. In silence. Jesus, Charlie." Hanging her head in one arm, Jessie blinked back tears. "Back then I would have given anything to see him one more time, to tell him what was really going on, how I was really feeling. And what have I done, huh? I've left him alone through all this bullshit. So much for 'For Better or For Worse.'"

"The way I hear it, he didn't give you much choice, Jessie."

"Well, that may be true, but people suffering from addictions generally don't. Maybe that's what's really supposed to test us, huh? We love them anyway?"

"To a point, kiddo. Not when it becomes dangerous for the wife or kids. Or kids' friends." He tousled his daughter's hair. Stella was putting on her coat and tugging at his sleeve. "Look, just get on a plane, any plane, and get out here, okay? I'm taking the kids with me. I'll leave loverboy a note so he knows exactly how thrilled I am at this latest escapade of his."

"Not too harsh, okay Charlie? I'll say that in person."

Charlie was quiet. "I don't think that's a good idea, Jess. I'll come back here tomorrow with Matt. We'll talk to him."

"I need to see him. I need to talk to him."

"Ahhh, kid. You're breaking my heart."

"I'll see you, Charlie. Give the kids a hug from Momma. Tell them I'll be there in the morning, okay?"

"All right. Hey, aren't you supposed to be in some big festival this weekend?"

"Montreal. We're on twice, but Jacob can do the first bit on his own. I'll bring the kids back with me and between Jacob, Matt and I, plus Miranda, my new make-up and hair gal—also Ulysses' current girlfriend, by the way—we'll manage. Dee's sticking by Charles at the conference this weekend, something about some kind of reunion. I think Martinique's in Detroit too. Party time for the music moguls, I guess."

When they disconnected, Jessie was hunched over at the kitchen island, still clinging to the socks as if they were a heavy stone weighting her to the ground. She had stopped her pacing to digest this latest turnover in plans, as a niggling worry escalated in her belly. She didn't like the idea of leaving Josh alone all night in a bad state, but Charlie was likely right. He couldn't do much if he was immobile. Silently, she sent a prayer to the universe in the hopes some guardian angel would look down on him and not let him choke on his own vomit or something equally inane.

A long, slow exhalation accompanied her move to the right as she propelled herself to action. Her heart lurched when she saw Jacob standing there watching her, his usual blue-eyed puppy dog appeal already tearing at her insides.

"Uuuhhhh." Groaning, she leaned over and momentarily rested her head on one elbow. "C'mere, babe."

"I'm coming with you," he insisted, moving forward and folding his body into her arms as she raised her head and opened herself up to him. "Please."

"Why, Jacob? Do you think your physical presence is going to change how I feel about him? Or what I tell him?"

"What are you going to tell him, Jessie? That he's a fucking asshole who threw away the best thing he ever had? Eh?" He was speaking into her neck so the words came out muffled.

Then Jacob stood back and grabbed Jessie's chin, a little roughly so that she yelped, and he spoke directly to her, demanding she listen once and for all. "Jess, he is always going to be *that* guy. You know the one, the one with addictions nipping at his heels his whole life. He is always going to be one step away from the edge. You'll be watching over your shoulder always, for Josh to fuck up, whether it's through coke, or booze, or goddamned heroin. Or women! Fuck!"

Spinning around, Jacob dropped his hands on top of his head. He grabbed fistfuls of hair and pleaded with everything he had in him for her to hear, to listen. "What the hell do I have to do to prove to you that I can take care of you better than he can? That I can be a father, a good father, to Emily-Grace and David, one who will come home to take their kid to hockey practice on time, or to ballet or whatever!"

"You don't know what it's like for him, Jacob. You don't know!"

"Thank God for that! I don't ever want to be that guy! I will never be—THAT guy!"

As his words forced themselves inside her roiling brain, Jessie pulled the end of her sweater sleeve over a fist that she shoved against her mouth. The ice blue eyes threatened to leak profusely as she took in the truths Jacob presented before her.

"I can't not try to help him, Jacob. Don't you see? He's like a part of me. He *is* me. We are one. He is hurting, and that makes me hurt. Seeing him hurt our children makes me hurt. And now Charlie's daughter…" She shook her head. "I'm not even saying there's anything I can do. But I'm going there anyway, to Vancouver, to get the kids. So I will go to the house, I will go see him, and I will try to talk some goddamned sense into him. Okay?"

Jacob swiped a hand across his eyes. "So he *is* you, eh? You are one? What the hell does that make me? Your fucking sex slave, that's all? Your island, I heard Maggie say one time. More like your whore, I think, if a guy can be such a thing."

He wheeled around to head back into the bedroom to finish his own packing.

Jessie's angry voice floated past him. "I don't need this from you, Jacob! You've always known how I feel about him! I have enough to deal with tonight without your fucking closed minded judgment hanging over my head!"

"You know, you got lucky this time!" Jacob cried, spinning back around. "Charlie got lucky. All kinds of bad shit could have happened to your kids today. Josh should be arrested. Even if he cleans up, he is always gonna be a bullet in a gun, waiting to get fired, waiting for the right combination of spark and flame to set him off. And who knows what damage he will do next time. He's always gonna be the guy you have to watch to see when he breaks!"

"He's me, Jacob, don't you see? We're two fucked up people. That's what connects us. We're the same *soul.*"

The ache in Jacob's eyes tore at her. But his response was quick. "You don't hurt people."

"Don't I? Jacob," her voice broke, "that's *all* I do. Wouldn't you agree?"

He let the air go still between them, and sucked on his bottom lip before spitting back at her, "Because of him! You should not be going to him. He'll go off the rails again. Josh does things to hurt you, over and over, and you just go crawling back to him! I do whatever I can to help you, and you spit in my face! Is that what you want to hear?"

"It's the truth, isn't it?!"

"Why? Why, Jessie? Why is it the truth?! Why does it have to be the truth?"

Slipping off the high chair, she squared off to face him across the large room. Jacob was steadying his hand on the doorframe at the entrance to the hall, and Jessie was still in the kitchen, half facing the family room.

"I'll tell you why, Jacob," she bit off. "Because Josh is my husband, that's why. Still. And forever. I will never let him go. Ever. I love him."

A salty trail traced its way down Jacob's bristly cheek then. Sucking in a breath, he fisted his chest. "You love me. You say it every goddamned day."

He was choking now, on the effort to get this straight in his head—where did he fit in? Did he still fit in? Where was this night going to land? Suddenly Jacob wanted a bottle of Jim Beam. Suddenly Jacob understood the need for heavy insulation from the hurts of the big bad world.

He didn't wait to hear her answer. Jessie's hesitation was enough. Jacob turned again, and stomped down the long echoey space. The slamming of the bedroom door almost startled Jessie off the edge of the stool, where she had plunked her butt after Jacob stormed out.

Matt was staying in the guest room at the far end of the condo, on the south side behind the cavernous formal living room. He heard the fight, not by choice, but it was hard to avoid.

He found Jessie still on the stool in the kitchen, immobilized. "Do I hear there is a change in plans?"

She looked up, sick to her stomach at the harsh reality of loving two men at one time. "Vancouver," she whispered, a picture of doom and gloom. "We're going on a rescue mission. Can you reach Charles, Matt? We need the jet."

Chapter Nine

Vancouver was rainy and grey when the jet taxied to a stop on the slick tarmac of YVR. The dismal atmosphere did nothing to alleviate the tired, hungry, desolate feeling assaulting Jessie who, from a lack of sleep, an attack of nerves, and an almost desperate wish to have Jacob by her side, was less than pleasing company on the trip north.

Charles' Audi was at the airport. Matt dug out the key he knew Charles always hid over the wheel well of one tire, and once he and his subdued company were settled, he pointed them towards Charlie's large new home in Burnaby. The sleepless night had one consolation—at the end of it, like a big old rainbow, were Jessie's children.

"Ohhh," she almost moaned, holding the two of them close to her chest at once. "Momma missed you both sooo much!"

Emily-Grace pushed her mother away a bit, just so she could see her face. "Daddy's sick, Momma."

"Oh my darling, I know. Momma's going out right now to make sure he's okay, sweetheart. You don't need to worry, honey."

The little girl was twisting her singer-dowwy around and around. "I bwing him watteh, Momma."

Jessie tweaked her cheek as David toddled off with Stella to play blocks. "You are such a big girl. Daddy was lucky to have you with him yesterday when he wasn't feeling well." Inside, her heart was breaking. This child should not have such weighty responsibilities. Her whole life was a mess, it seemed, at least the last ten months were, and they were likely enough to weigh the child down for life. "Baby girl," Jessie said, trying to remain composed, "you go with Stella now, and David, and play blocks. Build Momma a castle, okay? I need to talk to Charlie and Matt for a minute."

Emily-Grace did as she was told, her step a little lighter now that her beloved momma was in her space.

Jessie straightened, crossed her arms, and regarded Charlie, who studied her right back.

"You look like shit," he said, not unkindly.

"Have you heard from him?"

"No. Not a thing, Jess."

"All right. Can you keep the kids another two hours? By the time I get up to the house and back to Burnaby…"

"You stay here. Matt and I will go." He waited.

Her response was immediate. "No. I need to do this, Charlie. The kids, can you—"

"Of course," he said, pulling her close for a hug and inhaling deeply. "Just bring me a coffee on the way back, okay?"

"Don't you and Jane have some fancy espresso machine? Make your own damn coffee!"

"I haven't learned to use the thing yet. My espresso always tastes burnt."

"Then go to ROAM and take some lessons from Chris, you lazy butt. He'll school you."

Saluting her, Charlie smiled sadly. "Will do, Jessie, sir. I'll see you in a bit. Don't worry about the kids, Uncle Charlie's making teddy bear pancakes for breakfast. Matt taught me. Speaking of Matt…" He eyed Matt carefully.

"I'm going with her, Charlie." Matt didn't need to add *just in case*, but it was a given.

"Good," Charlie agreed, visibly relieved. "Call me. I'll see you in a bit."

The drive to the UBC neighborhood house took forever. Friday morning rush hour traffic kept the trip on a slow roll all the way up East 12th and down West 16th. Forty grievous minutes later, Matt finally pulled into the driveway behind Josh's King Ranch. Jessie clutched the seat of the Audi and gulped at the sight of the familiar large metallic grey Ford pickup.

"I can't move, Matt," she lamented, breathless. "The house…so many memories…"

He swung open the driver's side door. "I'll go first, Jessie. Stay put for now."

She touched his arm before he managed to exit the sleek sedan. "No, Matt. It's okay, I can handle this." A quick inhale while looking into the steady strength evident in his eyes provided much needed courage. "Look, if I'm not back in twenty minutes, come down, okay? In the meantime…wish me luck."

Her fingers slipped away from his arm.

Slowly, Jessie made the trek past the King Ranch, which she couldn't help but give a lingering, trailing touch as she passed, as if its energy could somehow fortify her for the next twenty or so minutes. At this time, she had not seen Josh since the day he left her in a puddle on the floor of the fancy law office in Downtown Vancouver.

Pausing at the iron gate as thoughts of Jacob rolled through her mind, Jessie swiped a hand through her hair. Jacob who, when she left the condo, had given her a cursory hug because he couldn't stand to see her go without a final soft caress, despite their angry words and the jealousy Jessie knew rightly consumed him where Josh was concerned.

"I'm sorry, babe," she murmured to him now as if, thousands of miles away, he had any chance at all of hearing her.

Fingering the gate, Jessie finally found the courage to open it. She sucked in a breath and stepped lightly and slowly down the remainder of the flagstone steps.

Josh was standing as she came around the corner. He had been reclining on a deck chair, by the look of the half-consumed water glass beside him. His hair was wet but he was wearing jeans and one of his ubiquitous v-neck white T-shirts. Shaven, but pale and a little bent over, he actually seemed sober, or was working his way towards being sober, at least.

Their eyes met and locked themselves inside each other.

"I knew it would be you," he whispered, a hand half-reaching for her while his mind screamed *she's not yours to reach for.*

It took Jessie a moment to gather her wits from the various corners of the large outdoor pool deck to where they'd flown when she met his solemn gaze. She couldn't help herself—she let her eyes flit over the faded jeans, the bare feet, the strong biceps peeking out from under the T-shirt…her baby blues flitted, too, over that desperately loved bit of rogue hair falling over one cheek.

When her eyes finally drifted back up to his face, she saw that Josh was doing the same thing—looking her over, *maybe just to be sure I'm real*, she thought. At least, she knew that was her intent, the other way around.

Drawing up her shoulders, she dove in. "What happened, Josh?"

Already Jessie had both arms wrapped around her belly, partly from sheer relief that he was here in front of her, okay, alive, breathing…and partly to hold herself together.

He floated a hand in the air before answering. "I was stupid."

In truth, he seemed apologetic, sincere. Near tears, in fact. Jessie was a little afraid he would break down, but then she considered maybe that was what he needed, a good old-fashioned Jessie Wheeler style meltdown—a good old cathartic cry, to let loose some of the unforgiving demons haunting him.

"No kidding," she said, with only a hint of judgment.

"Did you come here to lecture me?"

Her voice was soft, tender. Shaking her head slowly, she stepped towards him. "I came here to make sure you are still on this planet with me."

"Why?"

"Because I couldn't bear it if you weren't."

Stopping five feet away, Jessie recognized the man before her now. The sorrowful eyes were the ones she loved; they gave his face a weighty sadness that here, today, consumed him. They were not the angry, hard eyes that greeted her at the hospital the day she was rescued, and that she saw for so many days after that.

"I've been so cruel to you."

"Pretty much. Yeah." Sniffling, Jessie hoisted her hands away from her belly and shoved them in her back jeans pockets. "Asshole." But a tiny smile snuck through before her countenance turned serious again. "Tell me what happened, Josh."

He shrugged. "Does it matter?"

"Yeah, babe. It does."

Her singsong voice today calmed him. She wasn't here to fight, it seemed.

"I saw your video. With Jacob."

"Mmmm. Thought so."

He guffawed, just slightly. "You know me too well, Mizz Wheeler."

"I'm glad, actually…that I still do. I was worried there for a while, Sawyer." She resisted the urge to add *Wheeler-Sawyer* to his comment.

"It killed me, Jess. To see the two of you together that way." She barely heard him, but Jessie detected a glowing mist in her estranged husband's chocolate eyes. "You…and him…always, he was one step behind me. Always."

"I let him go, Josh. To try to bring you back to me, that day…the last day I saw you. You threw me away. You told me you didn't want me."

A dark flicker crossed Josh's face at the hard memory. "I was scared. I didn't…I don't…deserve you, Jessie."

"The hell you don't. Look where I come from, Josh. You know everything about me, all my dirty little secrets. You know my soul better than anyone."

"Not better than Jacob. You two are something together, Jess. Really something. In that ballad? It's crazy, the way you light up the screen with him. *Mystic Nights* was nothing compared to this one song and the video behind it. Even the fucking live video is magical." He swallowed. "So was the night it was recorded. I couldn't stand it. I can't…stand it."

"So you poured a drink."

"It was just one. I thought I could handle it. I thought I could stop."

"But you didn't. You poured a few more."

His silence was her answer.

"Not just your own kids, Josh. Stella was here."

"I don't know who I am anymore, Jessie. I'm this monster…I'm back there, in the black death again. Only this time I feel like it's winning. Without you…"

"You are the father of two beautiful children, Josh."

Josh's blood pressure spiked at what she wasn't saying. "Is that it? You have Jacob now, so –"

"This isn't about Jacob. This is about you, and what you did. To us."

"You don't know what it was like—again. You were gone—again."

"Wasn't my choice, Josh. Not this time."

"I thought I was gonna lose my mind, Jess…I thought that was it."

"Then you got the kids back and you found it again—your mind—with Nadia."

"She was a warm body. Something to hang on to."

"Did you love her? Or…do you? Was she your Jacob?"

He shook his head slowly from side to side. "No. Not even close. What I felt for Nadia—it wasn't the same. It hurt at the time…when…" He swallowed, and blinked back the hurtful thought he almost unleashed. "But it was never—like you and me…"

"It hurt at the time?" She was whispering now. "At the time, Josh? You mean…when I came home. That's what you mean."

"No, Jess. No." He reached out to her. But they both knew that was exactly what he meant. "I needed some time. To let her go, to find myself again. Please, try to understand."

"It's funny, because…well, all I really understand, Josh, is that somehow my presence seems to hurt everyone I love. You all do better when I'm away."

He threw his arms out to the sides. "Look at me, Jessie. Is this me doing better? I'm a fucking drunk."

"You remember that time? When we met? You remember the garbage outside Charlie's club? You remember when Deuce caught up to me and I knew I had to leave you for a while? You remember in P.E.I. when you were so angry with me for not trying to get help when I needed it? What about our vows? Do you remember those? In sickness and in health, Josh. Do you remember how you felt when our babies were born?"

A glimmer of light appeared in his eyes. "Yeah. 'Course I do, Jessie. 'Course I do."

'Then you should know by now, Sawyer, that there is someone in your corner who loves you. Who will always love you. Even if—" She bit hard on her bottom lip.

"Even if what, Jessie?"

"Even if it's not working for us right now. As a couple. To be together. Even if we've used up all our hope."

He took that in, pondering her as he did so. Jessie was wearing a light pink cardigan over a sleeveless white lace-trimmed top. Her hair was tossed back in a loose ponytail. Even so, the grey Vancouver humidity was frizzing it so the ends looked a little frazzled. Josh thought she looked adorable. He sighed deeply as the memories of their time together came rushing back.

"I don't want it to be over for us, Jessie. I want—I want my family back. All of you. I don't want you standing back and loving me from a distance. I want your self-righteous bullshit about hope, and your 'always and forevers.' And I want to believe in our fucking vows, Jess. But I can't hope for those things while…" He let the thought drift off.

She waited a moment before cutting the silence with, "While what? What aren't you saying, Josh?"

"While you fuck Jacob."

"Hmmm. You called the shots this time, Sawyer."

"I needed her. And I thought you were better off with Jacob. I guess in my heart I still do. But that doesn't mean I have to like it."

"You didn't wait for me…." Jessie's attempt at self-control was crumbling. Suddenly she was a sandcastle on a windy beach while the tides rushed in.

"How long was I supposed to wait, Jessie?"

"Josh, I'm not talking about while I was away. I'm talking about when I came back." She spit the words out at him, punctuating them with shifts of her weight and swipes of the back of a hand across her eyes.

Josh was incredulous, shocked, quiet, but the emotions crisscrossing his face were troubled; they were multiple masks and layers that changed like the aforementioned relentless tides. The final layer was the most truthful. He answered almost silently. "So am I."

This was a brand spanking new awareness. "I was not the problem, Josh. I caught you masturbating in the goddamned guest room bathroom, with Nadia on the phone, for Christ's sake!"

"You were only half there, Jessie. You were still in that basement hole in Langley, in your mind."

"I was here. *You* were in that goddamned basement hole in Langley. You still are."

She turned to leave, but he grabbed her arm. Sobbing now, Jessie tried in vain to pull away, but Josh wouldn't let her go.

"No," he demanded. "You don't fly all the way out here to see me and leave mad. No, you don't get to do that, Jessie. We have to talk this through."

"This is too big for us to talk through, Josh. It's bigger than either of us is strong enough to handle. You need to get help, and I need to get back to the man you think is better suited to be my partner and to raise your kids!"

Flailing at him, Jessie managed to break loose from his grip. Josh stood poised, afraid she would run, but she didn't. To her credit—and because of her everlasting need—Jessie took a few steps in a small circle, the way Emily-Grace liked to do with a doll dangling incessantly from one hand—then she turned back to him, hands on her hips and eyes pained.

It only took her a few steps to finally collapse in her husband's arms. She beat lightly on his chest a few times as he held her, as he breathed her in, placing a big hand behind her head so he could bring her as close to him as possible.

"You fucking dork, I so want to hate you these days, but I can't...I fucking can't..."

"Jessie," he whispered into the lavender scented hair he loved and missed, "I'll get help, I swear. I swear I'll get help."

"Oh, God," was her answer. "Please, God. Please." She didn't need to voice what she was actually praying for. Josh knew. And Jessie was well aware that God knew too.

Josh's dusky voice stilled her sobs. "I can't do this alone, Jessie. I can't do it alone, knowing you and my kids are with Jacob. Knowing how you feel about him."

Leaning back so she could see his face, Jessie managed, "Jacob, Josh? Seriously? *Thank God* for Jacob. That's all I can say about him. And you should, too. He's been a rock for our kids. You and me fucked up pretty good. So thank fucking God for Jacob."

She paused to let this sink in. It did. Josh's face went white again, and he nodded. "Okay. I get that. That's fair, Jess." He pulled her down onto the end of the long deck chair, so Jessie ended up sitting in his lap leaning against his chest, his right arm around her shoulders, and her fingers wound around his left.

"And yes, you can," she said. "Do this alone, I mean. And you will, Josh. Look at me. Look at me. Not for me. For our babies, okay? For Emily-Grace and David. Do it for them."

"I need you." He buried his face in her hair.

"I'm a phone call away, Josh. Or a plane ride. Okay?"

"Jessie…don't go. Please. Stay with me."

"I can't…Josh, I…"

"It's Jacob. Isn't it? I fucked up big time."

"I don't know about Jacob. I just don't know, we…we had a fight. A big one. About you. About me coming here to see you."

"I get it. He loves you. He's scared."

That stilled the air between them again. Jessie twisted her body around so she could face her husband. Carefully, fingers trembling, she tucked the favorite loose strand of hair behind his ear. "Yeah," she said. "He is, babe."

A long inhale to the count of seven prefaced Josh's next murmured question. The same one was on Jessie's mind. It took Josh a moment to ask it. "Should he be scared, Jessie? Should Jacob be scared?"

His eyes searched hers as he brushed her hair back off her cheek.

"Y-yeah," she said, a last lonely tear falling slowly home. "Hell, yeah."

The tiniest smile lit the corners of his lips then. Josh moved his left hand up to Jessie's other cheek, and he used his thumb to wipe away the last tear. When he pressed his lips to hers, finally, she thought she would melt away. The kiss was long and beautiful, sensual and wanted, but it had no desperate quality about it. The time for desperation was passed, at least for today. Now was all about finding the way back home.

There were two issues at play—one, Josh needed time in rehab. And two, Jessie needed time with Jacob, to sort out the higher truths, to step away from the man who caused her so much pain, to gain some perspective. Only time could do that for her. Only time had the power to choose her future.

Jessie lingered in Josh's arms, letting him kiss her, on the cheeks, behind her ear, over her eyes, on her neck. When he reached up underneath her top and sweater, though, she placed a hand over his and stopped him. He hesitated, rubbed her back a little, and removed his hand.

"Jacob," he determined softly, with remorse but not unkindly.

"I need to be fair to him, Josh. If you and I…well, if we have a chance, I need to be fair to him first."

"Do you think we have a chance, Jessie?"

"I fucking hope so. Because the pain I feel in my gut 24/7 is killing me, Josh. I want it to go away. You need to make it go away."

"What if—"

She placed a finger over his lips. "No, babe. Not now. No more ifs. Just possibles, okay?"

"I can't live my life with Jacob one step behind me. Not anymore."

"No worries there, Josh. He agrees with you on that lovely point."

"I'm sorry."

"Me too."

She sighed and, one more time, wrapped her arms around the broad shoulders she adored. "God, I miss this. I fucking miss you." The tears started anew.

He held her another few minutes before Matt's sharp footsteps could be heard on the flagstone steps. Jessie wiped away her tears and brushed a few off her husband's cheeks as well.

"Get help, Josh. Please? I'll call you tomorrow, okay?"

"You will?"

She smiled. "Yeah. I'll call. Get help, and come get the kids again when you're feeling better, okay? After rehab?"

Behind her, Matt's voice rang out, a little nervous. "Everything okay down here, kids?"

Their laughter buoyed him.

"Come say hi, Matt." Jessie still couldn't take her eyes off her husband, who seemed to have a new light about him now. "Come say hi to Josh."

Later, at Charlie's house, as Jessie carried David to the Audi, she spoke to Charlie. Emily-Grace and Matt were behind her, saying goodbye to Stella. An undercurrent of strength marked her words.

"'I know you're angry with him, Charlie."

Covering David's ears, Charlie replied, "He fucked up pretty good, little girl."

"I'm afraid to leave him alone. At least until he cleans up and gets some help."

"What, you think I'll abandon the guy? No, he's my friend too, Jess. Yeah, I'm pissed at him right now, but no. Jane will be back early this evening. When I'm done shooting, she can hang with Stella. I'll get Josh to an AA meeting and then I'll take him downtown to see Trudy, or maybe the other way around. I've already called Trudy to give her the heads up, in case Josh is open to seeing her. We'll go from there."

"Meaning checking him into rehab? Tonight, maybe?"

"Meaning even if I have to drag him there by the balls, yes. Even if it's midnight. He'll be okay, Jessie. Trudy and I'll make sure of it." Leaning forward, he brushed his lips against her forehead. "Now go do that show in Montreal. Bring the house down."

"Charlie…" She placed the baby in his car seat and strapped him in.

When she stood, trying to find more words than just his name to cover the impossible emotions of the last many hours, Charlie shook his head and swooped his old girl up in a big hug. "There's nothing more to say. Love you, girl."

Grinning, Jessie's pale eyes lit up with relief. "Love you back, Charlie. So much. Tell Jane I'll call, okay? She'll be pissed."

"Nah. She's a helluva gal."

Jessie paused, her eyes misting over again.

"None of that. I know what you're thinking. Yes, she's amazing, but so are you. And I've still got all your drama in my life anyway. Just not the sex."

Laughing, Jessie punched him lightly in the belly as Matt wandered by and muttered, "Too much information."

Once Emily-Grace was settled, Jessie stood holding Charlie's hands for one last goodbye. Stella, who was hanging onto her father's leg, got a hug and a kiss too.

"You promise, Charlie?"

"I promise." He held up his cell phone. "Calling him now. And every hour on the hour. Okay?"

"K. Luv you. Bye."

An hour later, as the jet disappeared into the clouds above Vancouver, Jessie couldn't help but notice the sun was out. She fell asleep with a wide, hopeful smile on her face, thinking about her kids and for once not feeling sorry for them.

Montreal was a different story—it was a turbulent landing as the warm inland air met the cooler Atlantic air, and it was dripping rain.

But Jessie had a festival to do, with an angry hurt Jacob nonetheless, and so she and Matt packed up the kids, got them to their hotel, and faced the music.

Chapter Ten

While Josh settled in to rehab at a private treatment center on Bowen Island, a quiet, 20-square-mile forested sanctuary just northwest of Vancouver, an exhausted Jessie prepared to face Jacob. She had a little free time between putting the kids to bed and dealing with what she knew would be confusion and uncertainty on his part, since he was on stage when Jessie and Matt checked in. Still, having time to think wasn't necessarily a good thing. Jessie's mind was in overdrive. Her heart was leaping—*hope*.

Deirdre had an assistant who occasionally hosted Jacob and Jessie at festivals and engagements if she couldn't be present. Pam was in her forties—a grey-streaked, bobbed hair fitness addict whose only son was now teaching in Korea, she was a high energy devoted Deirdre Keating apostle. It was Pam who called Jessie to tell her Jacob would be signing autographs at a booth on the main festival grounds before heading home.

"That gives me about an hour," Jessie muttered to herself as she tucked her toothbrush and toothpaste into one corner of the vanity, and a floral make-up bag into another.

By the time she heard the card key at the door, she had their suite in some semblance of order. David had woken once, upset at either the new environment or a painful molar trying to break through his tender gums, so she had crawled into bed with him and softly sang 'You Are My Sunshine' over and over, brushing back his hair and cuddling him until he settled.

"You're not the rock everyone thinks you are, are you, little guy?" she whispered to him. "All this moving around, and Momma and Daddy in different places all the time...it's gotta be tough for a little fella, huh?"

He rolled onto his side and drifted back off into sleep with one small set of fingers wrapped tightly around his mother's thumb. Calling to mind the months without her children was something Jessie tried not to do. But sometimes that nightmare came unbidden. Tonight, watching her son's healthy chest rise up and down, studying the features that so closely resembled the child's father, she was overcome with love and devotion. She was a wealthy woman, but that was nothing compared to the simple blessed joy of lying here with her son's fingers wrapped around her thumb, Emily-Grace sleeping peacefully in the bed opposite him, and the hope these children might one day find their mother and father reunited.

Jacob...what to say? What could Jessie share with him that wasn't already spoken in hope and fear and faith that the future would turn out the way it was meant to? What simple words could possibly ease the hurt she intuitively felt was coming his way?

Worse...all Jessie had for hope herself was a few minutes on her husband's lap, his tears mingling with hers, her arms in a desperate hold around his neck. His words were encouraging, yes, but they were just words, thrown loosely out into the air of a grey Vancouver day. Josh had a lot to prove. He had a long uphill climb ahead of him.

His treatment center was encouraging...Jessie had scoured the website earlier. The counselors were mostly addictions survivors, so Jessie knew Josh would have people to talk to with whom he could relate. A holistic method of healing was their focus. A mind, body and spirit approach along with good nutrition and private sessions would bring Josh a long way. Instinctively, Jessie knew that.

She planned to call Trudy the next morning, to check in—Charlie had left a message on her phone saying he and their trusted therapist planned to ferry over to Bowen Island a week from Sunday, after Josh's first 'no visitors allowed' week, to see how he was getting along. To let him know he was loved. Rumor had it bubbly Kayla was planning to jump in with them.

"No one's giving up on you," Jessie murmured aloud now as she watched her baby boy sleep. "You are one special guy, Josh Sawyer. You can fight all this bullshit that's got you cowering in a corner. You can come back to us."

As the card key slid in the lock and the door opened, though, she tensed. Jessie kissed David on one baby pink cheek, and slid off the bed carefully so as not to wake the little fellow. Sleepy, yawning, she tiptoed through the door, closing it behind her so the children wouldn't wake if words between her and Jacob got heated.

She needn't have worried. Jacob was too brow-beaten for a knock'em down fight.

"How'd the show go, babe?" she started, hands in her jeans pockets, facing him.

He stopped in the middle of the suite and took her in, his lips working as he tried to sort out what to say or, even, how to feel.

"Crazy, as usual. Your husband's stupidity pissed off a lot of Jessie Wheeler fans."

"I'm sure sexy Jacob Ryan placated most of them."

"Jacob Ryan wasn't feeling too sexy without his girl beside him on stage."

"Good, then Jacob Ryan probably didn't have thousands of women asking him to sign their boobs."

"Only two."

"Two women, or two boobs?"

"One boob each. So that'd make two women."

"Fine."

"Fine."

She shrugged, tipping one ankle over on its side as she tried to read beyond the exhaustion lining his face.

"Jessie…I'm tired," he started, unwilling to wait for her to unload the day's trials. "Skip the small talk and tell me what I need to know, okay? I am making the assumption Josh is okay, or you wouldn't be here. And you're not a mess of snot on the floor so I'm guessing your chat with him went okay. What I don't know is where I stand."

She raised her chin. "You know where you stand, Jacob."

Slowly, he shook his head from side to side. "I have days when I say to myself, God, I am a good person. I am taking care of another man's children, because he is incapable of caring for them himself half the time. I don't always get to church, but sometimes I do, and when I'm not there I subscribe to the

72

whole 'love one another, be nice to people' thing. So on those days I find myself thinking God will reward me. I just need to be patient."

She started to speak but he air-palmed her. "Don't bring up the material things. The career and all that. I'm grateful for it, but I'd throw it all away just to have you by my side for always, Jessie. Loving me, not some jacked-up boozehound."

"Ouch," she flinched.

"On the bad days, like today, I wonder what I've done to piss God off. Because I can see it in your eyes, Jess. That little glimmer of hope. You can't hide it from me any more than you can hide the rain pouring down outside right now, soaking all those people who paid a shit-ton of money to come see me play tonight. So I ask God, what do you want from me? But you know something, Jess? He doesn't answer. I don't know how to get Him to answer."

"Maybe you're just not listening, Jacob."

An angry flash in his tired blue eyes telegraphed Jacob's thoughts about that particular statement, which he thought was mighty mean and uncalled for. "And what, pray tell, would I hear if I was listening, Jessie?"

"You'd hear God telling you to move on, Jacob. You'd hear Him shouting 'save yourself' from that crazy Jessie Wheeler! Stop counting the nights. Stop hoping for something that's never going to change."

"Let me ask you this—would you rather be alone than take number two?"

"It's not about me, babe. You know I love you. This is about trying to save a family. This is about those two babies in there," she gestured behind her, "who need their father back."

Lowering in pitch, his voice took on an angrier edge. "I asked you if you would rather be alone, Jessie, than be with me."

Her answer was a whisper. "No. No, Jacob. I don't want to be alone."

"Did he ask you back?"

She swallowed. "He agreed to go to rehab. He was checking in tonight."

"That's not what I asked you. Did he ask you to get back together with him?"

"He wants his family back, Jacob. But there's a long road between here and there, you know? What he wants and what he gets might be two different things."

"So we're back to square one. Good 'ole Jacob picks up the pieces while Josh and Jessie try to get their shit together. Jesus, Jessie."

"Babe, please." Reaching for him, Jessie met only dead air. He backed away.

"I need a little space tonight, okay? I just—" Jacob shoved the heels of his palms into his eyes. "I can't even think right now. And I sure as hell wish I couldn't feel."

Wheeling around on one booted heel, Jacob headed to the opposite side of the suite where his bag lay open on a wooden fold-up suitcase stand. Rummaging through it, he dug out his toothbrush and toothpaste, and he headed to the washroom.

Watching him, Jessie ached to go wrap her arms around his waist, but she doubted he was much in the mood for comfort from her tonight.

Yawning, she slipped out of the room and ducked downstairs to the hotel bar.

A familiar figure sat at the rich mahogany bar, handsome eyes glued to a Toronto Blue Jays game.

"Ahhh," Jessie sighed, sinking into the high chair next to him. "You couldn't sleep either."

Matt turned his head and grimaced at Jessie. "Did you even try?"

"I laid down with David for a bit." She covered her mouth as yet another wide yawn threatened to crack her jaw in two.

"You have two kids on your hands, no nanny, and a big show tomorrow, Jessie. You should be in bed."

"Yes, massa." She saluted him, then frowned. "Maybe I should hire back their old nanny."

Groaning, Matt plucked a pretzel from a small dish on the bar and tossed it at her. "Nadia was never popular with the kids in the first place, from what Charles told me. They just tolerated her."

"Whatever. Fucking Nadia." A gloomy shadow crossed her pale eyes as Jessie forced the salty pretzel between her lips.

"Did Jacob get back?"

"Yep. Festival security escorted him home. Mister Sunshine is hopefully tucking into bed at this very moment. I hope he is snoring heavily by the time I slide in next to him."

"You two need to be shut away in a closed room for a day so you can sort out what your relationship really means."

"There's no sorting. We know what it means. Agony, that's what it means. Pure, sweet, fucking agony."

Laying her head on the bar on top of folded elbows, Jessie studied Matt as he chewed on the end of a green plastic swizzle stick. "I need to cut him loose, don't I, Matt? To be fair to him."

Even Matt's stomach clenched at that comment. "And if Josh doesn't get his shit together?"

"Jessie Wheeler becomes a lonely old lady with fifteen cats."

"What does Jacob think?"

Sighing, she sat up straighter and leaned back in her bar chair. "You heard what he thinks. I think he was pretty clear the other night in New York."

"He keeps hoping you'll see the light."

"I do see the light, Matt. And today it got a little brighter."

"In Vancouver."

"I want my family back. I want my husband back."

"Then yes, Jessie. You need to let Jacob go."

"I don't want to. Not yet." The words emerged thick and hurty.

"He's been your rock, Jessie. I know that. But I think you're doing great these days. You are a wonderful mother to those two children, and somehow you're managing them with very little help from anyone else, which surprises me, given your means to hire help."

"I was averse to having a nanny long before the beautiful Nadia wormed her way into my husband's bed. I want my kids to know I'm their mom, you know? I don't want them to get attached to someone else."

"They'll always know you're their mother, Jessie. And I've got news for you. Kids have big hearts with lots of room in them for more than one person."

"Apparently so do their mothers."

"Ah. And reuniting with Josh could be a ways off. But what I saw this morning sure looked promising. Was it?"

"He's on Bowen Island. Charlie texted that Josh is all checked in."

"Do you think he'll stick it out?"

"Yeah. I do. It's in the woods, apparently, so not too many distractions.

I hope he does. He signed on for a 28 day program. The first seven days are a total immersion. He's not allowed to have visitors or leave the center."

"Is that the same place he went to before?"

"No, the other one was in the States. Near Seattle, where Zach and Hilary could keep an eye on him. It was a much higher profile kind of place. This one's intimate and set in nature. Maybe he'll even get some kayaking or mountain climbing in. It's got a spiritual component. I think once he taps back into the big guy in the sky he'll start doing a lot better, Matt."

"Did you get that yellow card yet?"

She smiled at his remembrance of her comment about the card that day in her trailer, forced her eyes downwards, and traced a deep crack in the otherwise pristine bar while her cheeks flushed pink. "Nope. Tomorrow morning I need to do that, before we hit the festival grounds, okay?"

"You got it. I'll mail it for you."

Another yawn stole Jessie's next words. She laid her head back down on her elbows and looked through sleepy eyes up at Matt, raising a hand in a 'no thank you' gesture to the approaching bartender. "Maybe I need to tap into God more to see if He can help me sort out Jacob. Otherwise, I'm at a loss. Although Jacob says he's tried and he's not getting a clear answer."

"Sure he is, Jessie."

"Mmhmm?"

"Josh checked into rehab, didn't he? Maybe God just doesn't answer all at once."

"Or maybe Jacob just doesn't like the answer."

"I can't imagine that he would, kiddo. Now get your butt back up to your room. Get some sleep. I'll see you at breakfast."

Moaning, Jessie raised her head and blinked sleepily at the ball game. "I'm surprised they have the guts to play a Toronto game in a Montreal bar."

"The Jays are losing. They'll likely change the channel if things turn around."

"Sounds like me." She frowned. "I could just switch the channel. If only it were that easy, Matt." Slipping off the high chair, Jessie pondered his amber beverage. "Why do you suppose some people can't just sit and have a drink, Matt? Why do some people go under?"

"I think some folks just need more insulation than others, Jessie. Until they develop the tools to get insulated in another way. Or maybe they just chip away at what they're hiding from until they no longer need to hide. But that's just me."

"I guess I should know that, huh? Since I did it myself for a while?" Frowning, she pondered him as she started to back away. "Booze really is a good place to hide, you know. Until you wake up the next day and realize you're still alone. And life still hurts."

His small smile wasn't quite enough. Matt stood and took Jessie's arm and pulled her close. "I'm glad you're here," he said quietly, his voice a little crackly. "I'm glad you clawed your way back out of…well, everything, Jessie."

A little surprised at his gruff emotion, Jessie smiled into the comfort of her good friend's neck. "Well, I'm glad *you're* here, Matt. Thank you for helping me claw my way back." She leaned back. "That Julie really is some lucky gal, you know."

"I tell her that every day." He laughed then, and slowly let his hands drop from his charge's arms. "How about I walk you to your room? I need to earn my paycheck."

He downed the last bit of his drink, and they left the bar together, Matt's arm protectively draped around Jessie's shoulders. When he let her go at her room, Jessie slipped into the washroom and slowly drew her toothbrush back and forth across her teeth, eyeing her reflection with a critical eye. In the end, she sighed, spit, rinsed, and had a pee before padding quietly into the children's room to ensure both were lost in safe worlds of fairy-tales and rainbows. Bawwet-dowwy was on the floor. Picking her up, Jessie tucked the tutu'd doll safely under Emily-Grace's arm next to singer-dowwy.

She kissed her children gently and stole back into the main part of the suite, where she slipped off her boots and jeans, unbuttoned and removed her sweater, and pulled her white lace top and bra over her head. Shivering in the cool air, and being cautious of where she placed her feet in the semi-dark space, Jessie made her way to the big bed where Jacob seemed to be off in his own slumbering fantasy world.

Sliding quietly in behind him, Jessie debated whether or not to try to snuggle up to him. She was feeling just a little too cracked and unsure tonight, about both of her men, to want to be pushed away. Jacob answered for her. He rolled over onto his back. Without speaking, he placed a hand behind her head and urged her closer. His kiss was tender at first, before becoming urgent, as if he were in such desperate need for this connection that he might wither and die without it. He sucked what energy he could out of Jessie this night, rolling on top of her, straddling her, taking her body roughly, his message to whatever God was listening that he loved this woman, body and soul, that he wanted her, and that he could take her now, at will, while Josh could not.

Jessie received his want loud and clear. She responded in kind, quickly allowing Jacob free control over her body and its available pleasures. Always passionate in making love, he was moaning before she was as, with both hands, he forced her wrists above her head and pinned them to the pillow while he opened his mouth over a nipple and sucked and tongued. He moved rapidly to the other breast before finally letting her hands go so she could help guide his mouth lower on her body, and when his tongue flicked against her she, too, cried out. Rolling onto her belly, she let him palm her and lick her, too, then he went inside, as deep as he could go, and they came together that way, Jacob hanging onto the woman he loved for dear life, his lips buried in her upper back as he panted against her, while Jessie's wet tears fell unnoticed.

They took turns going to the bathroom to clean up afterwards. The last words they whispered to each other before settling into sleep that night were three of the smallest and most powerful in the English language—"I love you."

When Jessie awoke in the morning to the feel of a small child burrowing next to her, and golden ringlets on her cheek, the other side of her bed was already empty. She didn't see Jacob again until twenty minutes before their show, when he wandered into their green room tent for a vocal warm-up. He didn't meet her eye and, once again, Jacob and Jessie took the stage, but their magical bubble did not.

Chapter Eleven

$\mathcal{M}$organ was working a few tents down, standing sentinel for the new Canadian band 'Running In Squares.' It was still raining in Montreal, a grey misty pissy rain that leaked in little rivulets down the interiors of some of the white tents, and that served to annoy the organizers of the five-day festival, but did little to quell the excitement of most of the revelers.

Wooden pallets were nailed together under the green room tents, at least, which were all connected via interior canvas walls, so the artists' feet remained dry, but overall the air was damp and cool, and it made Morgan cranky.

He was on edge anyway. Nadia had given him explicit instructions. They had talked through the details of her plan over and over, and she expected a definitive and final outcome. She wanted her film star and his family back. And she intended to pull Josh back into her arms by virtue of killing his spirit entirely.

As he stood guard outside the band's tent while anxiously eyeing the yellow jacketed local security guy currently minding Jessie's tent, the only glitch that really pissed Morgan off now—besides the knowledge that if he wanted his wife back he'd likely have to share her—was the unplanned arrival of the Sawyer children. Even now, they were playing inside Jessie's tent; he could hear them babbling even over the piped in program sound of Jacob's set.

Jessie had done her bit on stage—she'd already played the first part of the set with Jacob, it was his slot in the beginning, anyway, and Matt was doing his usual thing, hanging out backstage keeping an eye on Jacob, trusting the local security to watch over Jessie and the kids. Had he and Ulysses known in advance the children were going to be there, they might have had time to fly Susanne or Dan in. But Ulysses was now with Charles and Dee, and Big Dan and Susanne were off doing whatever they did when they weren't working. So local security it was, outside Jessie's tent—a smallish white guy with a ponytail who was chewing his fingernails and looking bored.

Backstage security itself was pretty tight. But there were tons of people around—band members, managers, assistants, make-up and hair gals, security, volunteers, festival organizers…Morgan knew he would not be noticed wandering over to Jessie's tent and ducking inside. She was in there alone now—well, apart from the kids. Miranda had left a while ago, her job done and Jessie happily waving her off to go do some other artist's hair and make-up. Jacob's set would be ending in less than ten minutes.

Morgan leaned to the right and tried to stop the dry-heaves from accosting his belly.

Damn, the kids, he thought, wishing to hell they wouldn't be witness to their mother's murder. But what choice did he have? Even now, Nadia's sensuous curves and her willingness to share him with Josh was enough candy to make Morgan sweat in delicious anticipation. It wasn't Morgan's first choice, but it was something, at least. And more than that, he and Nadia shared the loss of a child. Sure, she never talked about Darin, ever—his sweet face and playful laughter as he and Morgan moved the Ninja Turtle action figures around—but still, Morgan knew she felt the loss as deeply and profoundly as he did. So they shared a soul thing. She understood his pain, and he totally 'got' hers. He needed her, for the sake of his sanity. He needed her, period.

Jacob started on his last tune. *Fuck,* Morgan thought, thinking of Nadia and willing her to send him strength. *It's now or never.*

Clutching the handle of the knife through his black rain jacket so it wouldn't fall out or draw attention to himself, Morgan shot a backwards glance through the open slit of the tent he was supposed to be guarding. The young twenty-something band hadn't moved in ages—they were entertaining girls at the moment, flirty scantily clad members of a girl band also on the day's festival repertoire. Things seemed to be going well—their female guests had the boys' full attention. The band likely wouldn't even miss their somber guard.

Approaching the pony-tailed guy outside Jessie's tent, Morgan quickly slipped up behind him and applied a hold he knew would render the guy unconscious in an instant. The dude didn't even see him coming, which made Morgan laugh outright. No one else spotted his little trick either, both because the tent hallway was dimly lit, and also because Morgan timed the knockdown perfectly, scanning the space and hooking the guy's neck to pull him backwards instantly, before applying his 'quick drop' method.

One more scan each way, wait 'til two dancers pass, and then...Morgan was inside Jessie and Jacob's green room tent. He had the old black balaclava on in an instant—it was stowed in an outside pocket for easy access. The kids were bent over an oriental carpet on the right, making *putt-putt* sounds as they moved miniature toy cars around. Emily-Grace saw him first. She didn't cry out. Instead, a little three-year-old gasp accompanied her fright and, in remembered terror, she froze. David had his back to Morgan. Oblivious, the toddler continued to *vvrrooomm* a tiny police car around.

Jessie was at the far end, picking up some food from the craft table for the kids, but the tent wasn't large. It was about thirty feet deep. Morgan knew a maybe eight-inch diameter metal tent pole would be in the center of the space—all of the artists' tents were constructed that way.

Raucous applause sounded over the small speaker in the tent. Jacob had finished his final set, and would be back soon, Matt striding confidently along beside him.

Hearing the rustle of the tent flap, and sensing a presence, Jessie turned. When she saw the figure in the black balaclava standing between her and her children, she cried out—didn't scream loudly, for which Morgan was thankful—and bolted for the kids. He caught her instantly, belted her on the side of the head, and flipped her around so he wouldn't have to look in her eyes, and so she couldn't see his. He had duct tape in his hand now, a large strip he'd cut off earlier, and he threw her limp body against the metal pole and yanked her arms up over her head, then wrapped the strip around both wrists. It went around twice, and she hung there, not quite on her knees, but almost.

Yanking the knife out from under his coat, Morgan made a fatal flaw. He hesitated, as a sob started somewhere in the back of his throat. *If I kill this woman I will be a murderer. She was always nice to me. But she fired me.*

If I kill her, those two kids will lose their mother. The world will lose a star every-one adores. If I kill her...I will never hear her music again, or see those pretty pale eyes smile at me again. But...Nadia...

With a final cry, Morgan sliced open the back strap of Jessie's empire style halter top, which fit under her breasts. When the top fell open, he couldn't resist—he reached one hand in and fondled her, just briefly. He gasped with pleasure as he did so, and bent forward, leaning moist lips into the back of her neck. Time was running out. He could hear Jacob saying 'thank you all for coming, have a great night.'

"You won't be having a great night, Jacob, you fucking asshole," Morgan muttered under his breath. He poised the glistening blade over Jessie's back. Three swift cuts on the side of her partially exposed breast and flow-ing onto her side and back, and he was done. That was all he could man-age. Morgan's heart hurt. He cried out when he made the shallow cuts, cradling her body in his arms as he did so, trying not to hear Jessie's semi-conscious cry or see the way she arched her back with the sudden pain. Nor would he allow himself to see her beyond the one-way mirror at the Langley house anymore, in his memory, holding signs up to him telling him she would win, or screaming for help for her sick baby, or—touching herself the way she did that last morning when some dream floated her mind off to a better place.

Her cry was loud enough to startle Emily-Grace into action, to make the child realize what she was seeing was terribly, terribly wrong. Emily-Grace Sawyer stood and started to scream, both small hands over her mouth and her body quaking in fear, both favorite dowwys forgotten, lying in weird, contorted positions at her feet.

Jacob and Matt were laughing on their way down the outdoor hall. A guitar string had snapped in the middle of Jacob's set, just after Jessie left the stage, and so he had a minor emergency in the middle of a song. He was recounting now, to Matt, how the whole set seemed haunted, what with Jessie's distant mood and his uncertainty and the rain and all.

Now, both men instantly stopped moving. With eagle talons, Jacob fiercely gripped Matt's arm. Both well knew Emily-Grace's voice, and both had experienced the three-year-old's occasional tantrum. But this eerie high-pitched screaming was quite obviously not coming from a child throwing a tantrum. This was the terror-stricken cry of a child in mortal fear.

Matt reacted first. He bolted, noticing immediately that the sentry who was supposed to be outside Jessie's tent was not in place. He vaulted into the tent to see a large pair of black work-booted feet exit out the back, under a flap of the tent. Jessie was slumped against the center pole, head hanging limply. She was moaning as blood streamed from her left side. A quick glance at Emily-Grace and David told Matt the kids were fine, not hurt at least, so he ran to Jessie, grabbing a white towel from a neatly stacked pile on the make-up table as he leapt by it.

He could hear Jacob screaming behind him, "Cut her down, Matt, cut her down!" There were children's scissors on the kids' table. Matt grabbed a pair and, although it took a while, he managed to work them through the damp duct tape in the end. Jessie fell to her knees. Jacob had a solid hold around her waist with one arm. He was balancing her head with the other, crying now, falling back on folded knees, sweaty from his show and now covered in Jessie's blood.

"Fuucckkk Matt, fucckk oh Jesus, Jessie, Jessie, please be okay, you have to be okay," he was crying, over and over, as Matt grabbed Jessie's chin with one hand to study her unfocused eyes and the quickly blooming bruise on the left side of her face. At the same time, he yanked his cell out of his pocket and speed-dialed the festival's emergency number.

"Jacob," Matt ordered loudly, firmly, his eyes wide with terror and his breathing coming in short, quick rasps, "the kids. Get a grip. The kids!"

Jacob heard him, and he stopped cursing, but he couldn't stop shaking or crying. *Is this what all this comes down to? All this whining about not having her, about losing her to Josh, is this what it comes down to? She's gonna die in my arms?* He rocked her, still holding Jessie with her back to him, in an eerie weird tableau that mocked the way he made love to her last night, so roughly and passionately.

Soon, security was all over the place, and EMS folks too, urging Jessie from Jacob's arms, trying to talk to her, trying unsuccessfully to get her to say more than her daughter's name. Emily-Grace was still screaming, and not one kindly volunteer could get near her. Even Matt was unsuccessful, but he was swamped anyway, trying to sort out what the hell happened, so in the end Jacob had to let go of Jessie. Ripping off his blood soaked plaid shirt, he went to the child, wildly hoping his blue T-shirt hid the rest of the blood or at least made it less terrifying.

Emily-Grace clung to him the way she clung to her father that long ago day when she and David were found in the Calgary park; her body was tense and molded tightly into his. He turned her away when the EMS team trundled the stretcher with her mother on it outside and into a waiting ambulance. Momentarily, festival security motioned for him to bring the children to an SUV chartered to carry them to the hotel but, before Jacob left the tent, he met Matt's angry, worried eyes.

"Jesus Christ, Matt. What the hell just happened here?" Shivering profusely, Jacob stared hard at Matt, willing him to provide some answer he could live with.

"Jacob, I only know one thing. If the asshole who did this," Matt covered the ears of the trembling child in Jacob's arms, "wanted to kill her, Jessie would be dead. She isn't. She'll get through this, the cuts are shallow. A run through a cat scan will hopefully also reveal no real damage to her head other than a sickening headache Jessie will have for a few days. Take these children to the hotel for now and I'll be in touch in an hour or so. Backstage is locked off. The asshole's not getting away with this."

But he was wrong. Morgan was long gone by the time the backstage area was locked off. He had been careful not to let any of the Jessie/Jacob camp see him at the 'Running In Squares' tent and, with the confusion now, he wasn't missed. He was not on the list of security for the day—he told the guy who hired him over Facebook that he did in fact once work in music festival security, but that it was a long time ago. He had gotten hired under the made-up name Damon Paine.

He figured he was home free.

His simple text to Nadia read *I'm coming home.*

Chapter Twelve

Josh got the call from Matt at 2 a.m. The night manager at the Bowen Island treatment center woke him from a sound sleep in which Josh dreamed he had Jessie in his arms, holding her, protecting her, keeping her safe. So when the harsh rap came at his door in the middle of the night, he intuitively knew it had to do with her.

Suddenly wide awake, he leapt out of bed and whipped open the door. The sleepy guy standing there handed him the rehab center's handset.

"What?" Josh managed, barking into the phone as terror seized his gut. He had been at the center a day. This was his second night, and there were strict rules about outside contact in the first week of residency. Already his stomach was roiling.

"It's Matt, Josh."

"Oh, fuck." Sucking in a breath, Josh leaned back against the wall and bent over, tenting a finger and thumb over his forehead as he did so. "What is it, Matt? Fucking talk."

A heavy sigh prefaced Matt's explanation. It was five in the morning in Montreal. In some way, it was a miracle Josh hadn't heard anything yet, because the Internet was saturated with rumors and grisly tellings. *Thank Heavens for secluded rehab centers,* thought Matt. *With rules about Internet shit, at least in the first week.*

"Jessie was attacked tonight, Josh. She's okay, but she's in the hospital with a bad concussion and some," he gulped, remembering Josh's own agony with a knife a few years earlier, "cuts. But she's fine. Or, she will be."

"Cuts?" Josh had to steel his stomach from emptying its contents all over the floor. "What the hell, Matt?"

Matt explained as best he could. He ended with, "The place was secure, or so we thought. This guy knew how to get on the grounds with a knife."

"Where are the kids? Are my kids okay?"

Another deep exhalation from Matt made Josh's intestines clench. He waited.

"They were there, Josh. In the green room tent."

"Oh Jesus, Matt. They saw this guy attack Jessie with a knife? I don't fucking believe it." *Emily-Grace...my beautiful little girl...she shouldn't have even been there. She should have been with me...but I...*the thought was too horrible to complete. Josh's self-loathing took another solid jump in the wrong direction.

"Jacob has the kids back at the hotel. Jessie's new make-up girl knows them—she's dating Ulysses now, so she's there too. Charles and Dee and Ulysses are on their way." He paused, letting this news sink in. "There's nothing you can do, Josh. Jessie will be fine, Emily-Grace and David are safe and with people they trust, and you're in a place that has the support you need to deal with this latest bullshit. I just didn't want you to wake up in the morning and hear this from someone else."

"My kids, Matt..." It was a whisper.

"Josh, trust me when I tell you they're fine."

"Like I need them bonding with Jacob any more."

"In this case, Josh, I say let them bond. They need him right now." He didn't tell Josh Emily-Grace was still in Jacob's arms, inconsolable, moaning in her sleep. "They won't be forgetting who their father is any time soon."

"I need to be there. I'll get out of here and get a flight first thing."

"No you won't. You won't be any good to anyone if you leave rehab, Josh. Listen, would it help if I put Jessie on the phone? She's drugged up and she has a splitting headache but I'm standing outside her room at the hospital and she's watching me. I think she probably knows I'm talking to you. That whole weird telepathic thing the two of you have going on."

"Yeah, Matt. Yeah. Please. Put her on."

With a sad smile, Matt handed the phone to Jessie. "Here," he said. "Just a few words, Jessie, so he doesn't flee rehab and come to your aid."

She took the phone with her left hand. She was balanced on her right side in a futile attempt to keep the pain of the cuts from slitting her in two. Matt stepped away.

"Josh?" Jessie's voice was drugged, all right.

"You sound like you should be the one in rehab," he said tenderly, sliding down the wall to rest with his back against it.

"Ha ha, Josh Sawyer made a funny," she slurred.

"Jessie…" He lost it then. She could hear him trying to regain control, with big sniffs and a loud inhale at the end.

Jessie spoke slowly, the effort to get the words out making them muffled and vague, so Josh had to hold his breath and focus on what they actually might be. "Babe, I'm okay…in truth, all I remember is…the guy barging in… it was a bigger nightmare…for Matt and Jacob, and…"

"And the kids, I hear."

"Matt says Emily-Grace…is being a bit of a cling-on. Jacob…will bring her in…and she'll be fine when she sees…how silly her momma looks with… these big bandages."

"This is just one big nightmare. And they haven't caught the guy…"

"Matt says…if he wanted to kill me…he would have."

"Somehow I don't find that at all comforting."

"He left a message, Josh…the cuts…they were an X and an O."

Silent, Josh digested that bit of creepy news. "A kiss and a hug."

"Y-yeah."

"Sick bastard."

"Tell me something happy. Tell me…about rehab."

"It's only been a day, kid."

"One day… at a time, right babe?" Shifting her position in the bed, Jessie groaned as the pain of the fresh cuts sliced through her side.

How much more pain can we take? How much more fear can we take?
"Something happy? I know one thing that will make you happy."

"What? I need something…good…Josh…"

"I have a new sponsor. For the whole AA thing, Jess. Someone you know."

"Ohhhh…good. Who?"

"Your old Downtown Eastside friend. Arnie."

"Really? I'm glad, Josh…so glad…Arnie will make you stick to your guns."

"Nice choice of expression there, m'lady. The whole gun thing."

"It was ab-so-lute-lee intentional, dear husband." As the impact of quite naturally referring to him as her husband hit both of them at once, Jessie cleared her throat and added, "Josh, for so long I…I waited for a call…you know…I was so scared…"

"Of what, Jess?" But he knew. Josh knew.

She filled him in anyway. "I know what it's like. To hate yourself so much…to be so lonely. I wanted to die. Not…not in the Langley house, well, not until the end, anyway. No, I mean before, back when…I had to leave you…because of Deuce McCall. And I drank and smoked and tried to hide inside a bottle. I just want you to know…I would never judge you."

Taking that in from his wife who, at the moment, was lying in a hospital bed having pretty much survived an attack on her life, Josh was rendered mute. What could he say to equal that kind of faith and trust in him, that kind of simple unfettered understanding?

Momentarily he spoke, from his place on the floor. He said the only words that seemed to fit. "I love you." They came out cracked and strained. But to Jessie, they were perfection.

"I love you back."

Matt was not surprised to peek back in the room and see Jessie actually smiling. She had that old look on her face, the one revealing Josh's power to take all of her hurts away, no matter how bad. She was almost glowing.

He was startled, though, when he looked down the hall and saw Jacob making his way towards him.

Striding in his direction, Matt cut him off at the pass, hoping Jessie would soon end the call.

"How's Emily-Grace?"

"Charles and Dee got in. She's crying in her grammie's arms." Jacob gestured towards Jessie's room. "She asleep? Hopefully?"

"Not at the moment, no." Matt pursed his lips, unsure. "She keeps waking up. Apparently it's hard to get comfortable when someone slices an X and an O into your side."

"Into your breast, you mean."

"She'll heal."

"I don't personally know how much more she can take, Matt. The psychological fear, for one, if this asshole's gonna wait months before attacking her again, playing some wicked game that might someday…" He couldn't finish.

Matt clamped a hand on the younger guy's shoulder. "We'll find him."

Starting to move towards Jessie's room, Jacob stopped and glanced back at Matt. He narrowed his rapidly darkening eyes and shoved both hands in his pockets. "What, Matt?"

But Matt didn't need to answer. Jacob was close enough now to hear Jessie's low laughter. She was on the phone—the conversation was one-sided. The awareness of who she was talking to sliced Jacob's gut the same way the knife sliced into Jessie's skin. He let his gaze drift away from Matt, and focused on the wall before taking a deep breath and wandering into the room. Once there, Jacob stood with his feet a hip's width apart, and stared at Jessie with glimmering eyes and a 'you-Judased-me' stare.

She didn't drop the phone, but she might have, had Jessie not been able to gather her wits. She hung on, despite the purple haze of drugs and the searing pain and the love in her heart for a man thousands of miles away. Josh was talking, but she missed what he said.

"Sorry, I…I missed that last bit." Her eyes were locked in Jacob's hurt stare. On his end, Josh detected the change in her voice. "Jessie?"

"Uhhh…Jacob's here. He just got here." She tried to make light. "Without Emily-Grace, apparently. There is such a thing as a miracle."

"Apparently there is, Jessie."

Nothing could hide the smile that creased Jessie's face then. Jacob saw it loud and clear. He thought about leaving, but he couldn't. This night was insane, a nightmare, and he needed to know she was okay. Holding that trembling child all night had destroyed much of the resolve and strength Jacob had left. Now, a delayed reaction started in his own toes. A shiver accosted him from the ground up, and by the time Jessie disconnected from Josh, he was downright quaking.

Jessie reached for him. "Please, Jacob," she said at his hesitation. But her expression read *you know I am working my way back to him.* So he turned on his heel and left, bumping into Matt on the way out, almost knocking him over.

Matt stepped into the room and took the phone from Jessie.

"Sleep," he demanded, brushing the backs of his fingers across the bruised, flushed cheeks, where a tiny scar from a burn remained. "I have a feeling you'll need it."

"Oh, Matt," she breathed. "The guy should have…just killed me. This sucks."

"I know you don't mean that," Matt responded gently. "What would the world be without Jessie Wheeler and her music?"

She didn't miss a beat. "Sane," she said, delivering the word in a way that meant two certain people would at least be sane.

"Somehow I doubt that," was Matt's genial response as he pulled a chair forward and collapsed into it, taking her hand as he did so. "Charles and Dee have landed. They're at the hotel and will be at the hospital within a few hours, Mizz Wheeler. Now do as I tell you. Sleep."

He closed his eyes, and within moments was snoring himself. But Jessie fixed her eyes on the door, and fought sleep as she fought life, aching for Jacob to walk back into the room, while through her mind floated images of Josh.

Chapter Thirteen

"Emily-Grace?" Jessie inched forward and touched her daughter's cheek. "Baby, Momma is telling you it's okay to try ballet. The teacher is nice, sweetheart. Do you want to take her hand and show Momma how you can dance?"

The little girl was dressed in a gossamer pink silk ballet skirt over a similar colored bodysuit and tights. Small white leather dance shoes were on her feet, one of which was anxiously bent over on its side as Emily-Grace's fingers played with the loose tassels on her mother's top.

No response was forthcoming. Jessie sighed, and stood up. She held her daughter's hand tightly. "I'm sorry," she said to the kind thirty-something petite ballet teacher. "She's a little on the shy side."

The teacher reached up and absently touched her corn-silk blonde hair-bun. She knew the child's story. Everybody did. Even if they didn't, there was no escaping the haunted, fearful look in Emily-Grace's eyes. It was a look Jessie first started to see in the Langley basement, and which seemed to dissipate somewhat over the last few months with Jacob's bright light in their lives. Now it was back, with a vengeance.

The teacher was understanding. "She's not yet four. Many of the children are nervous at first. Why don't you come sit in the circle with her as we get started? I'm sure she'll come around after a few lessons."

Jessie doubted that, but she smiled sadly and did as was suggested. Later, over dinner at the Madison Avenue condo, she explained the day's trial to Charles and Dee.

Deirdre was too forlorn to comment, but Charles rallied. "You have her until Josh gets out of rehab. That gives you a few more good weeks to help her adjust, Jessie. And the teacher's right. She is young."

"Harrumph," came from Jessie's corner. "In life years she's eighty-five."

They didn't disagree, and picked at their Shish Taouk in silence.

The door to the condo *whooshed* open. Moments later, Jacob wandered around the corner and into the kitchen. Removing his blue wool pea coat, he lazily deposited it over the arm of the adjoining family room couch, then he bent down to give each of the kids a kiss on the cheek. As he sauntered back into the kitchen and dropped to a seat beside Charles at the large modern rectangular table, his eyes lingered on Emily-Grace. She was sitting cross-legged on the family room floor in her ballet outfit, which she refused to take off. Lost in her own little fantasy world, she was making her bawwet-dowwy dance while David floated back and forth between her and his grandmother. The solemn Deirdre was feeding the little guy occasional bites of the succulent spiced chicken.

Jacob avoided Jessie's eyes wholeheartedly.

"How was the gym?" Charles asked him in an attempt to lighten the grey mood of this latest heavy day.

"Fine." Jacob slid off the chair and opened the refrigerator door. Scanning the fridge's contents, he grunted loudly. "Nothing to eat in here," he grumbled.

"Jacob honey, come sit. We have a plate for you. Here." Deirdre patted the seat beside her while Jessie made her way to the microwave and popped in a fourth take-out container.

While the Mediterranean food was heating, she stood with her back to it and tried to cross her arms, but grimaced when she did so. "Fuuuccckkk," inadvertently escaped from between her lips, too quietly for the children to hear, but loud enough for the grown-ups to catch, all of who—including Jacob—looked up in fear.

"Stop looking at me like that," she pleaded. "I'm sorry. It snuck out. It just hurts."

Charles' concerned stare met Deirdre's aggrieved eyes, but Jacob's baby blues stayed on Jessie's. He was standing by the table now, his long face studying her pale lips while she retrieved his food for him. She took the container to the table and set it down before him, letting her fingers graze his elbow as she did so.

"Here, babe," she said tenderly. "Shish taouk. Your fave."

As she moved to go back to her own seat, Jacob let his fingers brush against hers. This day was the first time the two touched, with the exception of nudging small children back and forth, since the night before the Montreal attack, which was two weeks past. They had been back in New York a week now. At the feel of Jacob's skin on hers, Jessie sucked in a breath and let her eyes meet his. Instinct told her to lean forward for a kiss, but she forced herself not to. She told herself she was trying to prepare him, to let him go.

Her heart cried foul and screamed *just love him.*

Jessie knew hanging onto Jacob was the coward's way out. But the thing was…it hurt less to keep him near.

$\sim\!\!\sim\!\!\sim$

"Momma!! Momma!!!"

Propping herself up on an elbow, grimacing from the effort and resulting strain on the still healing stitched-up cuts, Jessie blinked herself awake. Peering at the clock on the nightstand, she groaned. Three a.m. A rustle at her side drew her bleary-eyed gaze. Jacob's shoulders were outlined by the light of the moon. They were hunched, but he was on the move.

"No," Jessie called out to him, tearing up as he headed towards the door of the large bedroom. "I'll go, Jacob."

Another cry chilled her.

Jacob halted, but he remained standing in the doorway. In boxer briefs and a wrinkled T-shirt, he swiped the back of a fist over sleepy eyes.

Fighting the agonizing clench of her belly and an equal urge to vomit from the remembered terror the screams unleashed, Jessie swung her legs quickly over the edge of the mattress and hurried towards her daughter's bedroom.

"Third time this week," she mumbled, anxiety bubbling up from her gut as she rushed passed Jacob's quiet form. Out of habit, she let her fingers rest on his arm as she jogged by. Inadvertently, he extended his hand to linger on her fingers, but the motion was brief, and their touch was over practically before it started.

Emily-Grace was screeching by the time Jessie got to her daughter's bedside.

"Momma's here," Jessie soothed, carefully scooping her baby girl into the curved warmth and safety of her sore body. Settling into the child's candy-floss pink ballerina duvet, she held the trembling child close to her breast, using her good right arm to tightly cradle the little girl. Jessie's left arm, out of habit the last few weeks, savored and protected her left side, but she let that hand float gently onto Emily-Grace's small back.

"Momma's here, darling. It was just another of those silly dreams."

Rocking slowly, she had to fight to keep from breaking down in the child's presence. *These damn nightmares. All because of stupid me. What was I thinking, having children? I destroy everyone around me.*

Buried in her mother's chest, Emily-Grace's whimpers began to ease, but the quaking continued. "I'm so sorry, baby." Jessie's attempt at a calm voice was doing the trick, despite the frenzied armies battling in her belly and the wetness trailing down her cheeks.

A shadow cut the dim yellow light at the doorway in two. Wordlessly, Jacob stood still and watched Jessie cradle her daughter, a million scattered thoughts firing in his brain. The image before him, of an injured mother pacifying her traumatized child, was enough to make him want to stay in New York. He was acutely aware how much it hurt Jessie to even hold her child now—the cuts were still healing. But he also knew Jessie—she wouldn't even feel the complete impact of that pain until later. *Now* was about her daughter, about finding a way to help her get through another night fraught with the terrifying remembrance of a very bad day.

As if she could read his mind, Jessie looked up and met Jacob's tragic stare.

"I don't know how to help her," she wept. "My own baby girl."

Moving slowly into the room, Jacob knelt before the sweet tableau of two of the three people he loved most in the world. "You are helping her," he murmured, extending strong fingers to rub Emily-Grace's damp, quivering back. "Just by being here, Jessie. By holding her."

"It's not enough!" The sobs were coming more furiously now.

"It's enough for now, Jess. It's what she needs—her mother close by, loving her." Bending his lips to the small girl's ear, he whispered, "Right, Emily-Grace? Just having Momma close by is everything, isn't it?"

"Jacob…" Jessie shook her head in warning as she snuggled her daughter closer.

Frowning, he looked up and locked himself in Jessie's eyes. "I just meant that it's good you're here, Jess." He didn't add the word 'alive,' but he may as well have. The moisture in his baby blues divulged that profound deeper gratitude to a universe he prayed would not betray them again.

Despite the fight in Montreal the night before Jessie was attacked, Jacob was staying in New York with his little adopted Sawyer family when he wasn't touring or committed to other engagements. Sometimes Jessie travelled with him when he had no choice but to honor his obligations, but most times she opted out, partly to stay close to her children, and partly on Matt's advice— Matt, who was once again fighting a difficult battle fraught with worry and occasional bouts of despair where Jessie's ongoing safety and security were concerned.

Everyone tiptoed around Jessie and the children, for the most part. Despite their constant mixed worry and relief, they all took turns to stay with her, with complete disregard for their own personal safety. Even Carter and Ashley made the trip from L.A. to keep her company for a weekend. And once again, Jessie's home was a gauntlet of security, which Ulysses and Matt conspired to make happen, and which the singer grudgingly accepted, more for the sake of her children than concern for herself.

She and Dee spent much of their time with Emily-Grace, hoping to once again find the light they missed in the little sing-song voice, but the child's ongoing nightmares—and daylight terrors—mostly locked up the much-cherished smile which, if they saw it at all, didn't reach the little girl's eyes.

Jacob knew he had to go. But he couldn't make the break—he simply couldn't. *I'm just a pawn in this game,* he told himself. *I'm here to facilitate someone else's happiness. I'm suffering, and someone else will win this vicious game.*

But sometimes, and more and more as the weeks passed, he seized happiness. He softened around Jessie, and they did okay by avoiding the truths haunting both of them. Partly this was from fear of what might have happened—twice now, Jessie had survived attempts on her life, although the second try seemed to be just a questionable attempt at best, and more of a message, really.

Jacob fell to his knees more than once to thank God for Jessie's survival—he still had her in his life. He told himself the universe was speaking to him—*take what you can get. She's alive. That should be enough. Anything else is a bonus.*

Sex helped. Sometimes Jessie initiated, but often it was Jacob who pulled her to him, careful not to hurt her healing scars—the blatant X and O that marked her as some sick person's fantasy; the fading burns that marked her as someone's prey.

Their lovemaking was less desperate these days, still passionate, but gentle, as if there was indeed some security in their relationship, and not another man standing in Jacob's shadow, as he himself had ghosted Josh for years. Often, as early morning autumn rain fell outside the graceful arched window in the master bedroom, Jacob traced Jessie's scars while she was still asleep beside him. Beneath his fingers, the rough skin was a harsh reminder of a terror still weighing heavy on them. Wondering if the fear was perhaps why she hadn't demanded he leave, Jacob accepted the role of caretaker, father figure, sanctuary, and lover.

Sometimes his hand strayed to other parts of her body. When Jessie's hips started to move and she ducked her face into the pillow with small gasps, Jacob eased her over onto her back and showed her how much he loved her, how desperate he was for her to love him back, and how much their souls were in sync. She always responded to him, she never turned him away as he heard other women sometimes did when they had a headache, or were tired. Sometimes Jacob thought it was because Jessie, too, was counting their nights together, cherishing them as they came, celebrating their urgency, and loving him in the moment.

There was another reason for avoiding hard truths. Josh was sober. So, with Arnie riding his ass, the actor was busy. He was working again—shooting another film, finally, in Vancouver, an FBI drama. And so he wasn't around. If Jessie talked to him on the phone (and she did, occasionally), she did it away from Jacob. Why was she not gravitating towards him now that he seemed to be doing well? On the good days, Jacob told himself it was because he was winning her over; on the bad days, he was damn well aware it was because she was simply afraid to make the leap.

Emily-Grace's fourth birthday was November 9th. Jessie and Dee wanted to give the little girl a happy day. They wanted—no, *needed*—to see the light back in her eyes. To that end, the birthday party they planned was a celebration the whole clan was invited to attend, Josh and his AA sponsor Arnie included. The day of the party, Jessie took Jacob by the hand and settled him next to her on the foot of their bed.

"This day is for Emily-Grace," she said to him. "No drama. I promise, Josh promises, and I need you to promise."

Shrugging, Jacob agreed. Because he was feeling a tad bit more comfortable in Jessie's company these days, he sincerely believed he could make today work, and he prayed Josh could set aside his tough personal feelings as well. Also, apart from wanting to see Emily-Grace happy, Jacob really *needed* to make this day work—otherwise, the next few weeks would really suck.

The two *Mystic Nights* stars were scheduled to shoot a film starting the following week, in New York. It was the rom com Jessie had told Matt about, featuring two musicians on the prowl in the city. Contracts had long been signed for the eighteen-day shoot, so it would happen regardless of its two stars' attitudes towards each other. But…working together would suck if Jacob and Jessie were on less than amicable terms.

Now, his fingers entwined in hers, Jacob attempted a small smile. Jessie's eyes were bright, shining, happy, not fearful and guarded as they had been since the attack. Loving her this way was easy—Jessie exuded warmth and gave off a raw aura of love.

"Jessie," he started, crossing his heart, "I will try my best today. I swear. This day is for Emily-Grace. You have my word."

"Good," she replied, grinning mischievously. "Because I have a big reward planned for you, Jacob Ryan." Climbing onto his lap, straddling him, she wrapped both arms around his warm body and kissed him heartily.

"Oh, I get my reward first? I am liking this party already." Laughing, Jacob laid back on the bed, taking her with him. Jessie's squeals raised the eyebrows of Charles and Dee, who were hanging balloons and streamers in the wide hallway.

"No, you dork!" she yelped as he tickled her. "This is just the teaser."

"Oh, so that's how it works."

"You're in the film business now, Ryan, you oughtta know what a teaser is."

"If by that you mean I am making a film with my girlfriend next week, then yes, I am in the film business."

"And the other films you made in the past two years? What were they?"

"They didn't count. This is the only one that counts, because I will get to make love with you on camera."

"Not really," she grinned, slipping both hands under his shirt and pressing her palms into his belly, "at least, I don't think so. Geez. Maybe. Some directors are going for that now."

"Realism. It's called realism." Jacob lay back and closed his eyes, relishing the feel of Jessie's tingly warm fingers moving up and down his body.

"I'll give you realism." Shoving his shirt up towards his neck, Jessie leaned down and tongued a nipple. "Mmmm. I like you, Jacob Ryan. I'll do whatever they want on camera, or off camera in the trailer, for that matter. Anytime."

Curving one side of his lips up in a smile, Jacob folded the woman he loved into his arms and savored the moment. Eyes still closed, he, too, let a small *mmmmm* escape. But, despite the fact that tensions were relaxing of late between he and Jessie, he wasn't entirely fooled. Josh was coming to their home today, clean and sober, they all hoped. This little prelude on the bed was Jessie's anxiety showing itself, like exposed nerves on her skin—at the surface, painful, red, raw and sore. She was trying to still the ache, to warn Jacob that today would hurt, despite everyone's promise to behave for the sake of a child who needed safety, security, love and happiness in her life.

After a few snuggles, a quiet knock came at the bedroom door. It was Deirdre. "Jessie honey, I'm sorry to interrupt but I thought you would want to know that Josh and Arnie are here."

She was still in Jacob's arms. He felt her tense; he was not surprised that her breathing stopped for an instant. Jacob thought he heard the words *sweet Jesus, give me strength* escape from between the beloved tender pink lips, but he wasn't entirely sure whether the appeal was actually Jessie's prayer or his.

He sucked in a breath as she slowly raised her head and searched his eyes.

"I do love you, Jacob," she told him, before pressing her lips to his for one final lingering kiss.

And then she was gone, to welcome her estranged husband—the man Jacob knew Jessie would love always and forever—into her home.

He lay on the bed another few minutes before entering the fray. *She said it,* he considered ruefully. *She said, 'I do love you, Jacob,' like she's admitting I'm the booby prize.*

How was this day going to land? Jacob had no clue. All he knew for certain was that it would be tough, despite all their good intentions—perhaps it would even be decisive.

Shoving himself up to a sitting position, he pulled his shirt back down over his stomach where, moments before, Jessie's warm fingertips were sizzling over his skin. Uneasy, he wiped a hand through his curls.

"Into the breach," he breathed.

From the large front room, he could hear the happy revelers already joyously socializing. Voices were raised high in greeting—even Emily-Grace's tinselly words could be heard as she greeted her daddy.

Steeling himself for battle, Jacob eased himself off the bed he shared with Jessie, and made his way forth.

Chapter Fourteen

The first weird glitch in the day occurred when Dee decided she needed a family photo. She wasn't doing it to be thoughtless, Jessie decided. Instead, sometimes the powerful woman was, well, a tad headstrong.

Eyeing Jacob carefully as she took her place beside Josh, who had David in his arms and who, like her, laid a hand on one of Emily-Grace's small bony shoulders, Jessie inhaled to a count of six. She couldn't bring herself to look away from Jacob—he was trying, she knew, but the crossing and uncrossing of his arms and the way he held his shoulders so high, in that taut manner, was giving him away. The eyes...well, the cobalt eyes were shining—not from happiness—and he was doing that 'biting his bottom lip' thing.

An unbidden thought crossed Jessie's mind. *I should have let him go. I should have made him go.* Because now, with her husband beside her—with one of their children in his arms, and the other beneath their hands—Jessie's family felt complete. She told herself the feeling was real, that it was not a charade. Most overpowering? She knew Josh was being seduced by the old magic too. And...Jacob knew it.

Trying not to appear emotional, Jessie avoided meeting anyone else's eyes while photos were snapped. She knew if she did she might lose it, turn her face into Josh's arm, grab him, and hold on for dear life. There was a moment when she actually had to will herself not to. It was the image of Jacob standing there just outside the circle of well wishers, with that hurt puppy dog look on his face, that prevented her from making a public overture towards the man she ached for in her sleep.

It helped to have a big crowd on hand for Emily-Grace's party. Carlotta was there with both her grandson Eric as well as her gardener man, Matt was there with Julie and their daughter Katy (who took Emily-Grace under her wing and did wonders to help the child relax), Steve and Sophie were there with baby Caleb, Charlie and Jane were there with busy Stella; Maggie and John, Carter and Ashley, and even Sue-Lyn and her new partner, whom no one was really surprised to discover was a woman, all came around for the party. Arnie brought his wife, too, but the biggest surprise for Emily-Grace was her Aunt Sara and Uncle Kevin, all the way from Peterborough, Ontario, who towed along their fast sprouting, growing teenagers, Mark and Ren.

Jonathon stayed for the day, visibly annoyed because Giselle was on his back the whole time trying to encourage him to mend fences with Josh who, despite acknowledging that he lost the job on *The Wyatt Boys* because of his inability to deal with the harsh reality of last winter, was still hurt over being fired by his own father. Steve, too, was a little awkward to be around that day. The popular TV series was starting production the following week. Fences were not mended, and conversation between the three remained short and stilted.

Still, it was a busy party so opportunities for Jessie to talk to Josh were limited. By the end of the day she was growing increasingly anxious to get him alone for just a few quick words before he once again exited her presence. As mid-evening approached, the partygoers lingered. The exhausted and over-stimulated little ones were being tucked in for the night—the families with younger children were staying at the Madison Avenue condo. Parents were finally heaving sighs of relief, and were starting to congregate in the spacious front room.

After leaving Emily-Grace's room, Jessie peeked in at the family room. Ren and Mark were hanging out in there, being quite capably entertained by Jacob and his X-Box, judging by the roars of delight and groans of defeat escalating in volume as whatever game the boys were playing was leading them through fantasy villages peopled by computer generated images.

Jacob didn't notice her furtive glimpse into the room. Jessie took advantage of his seemingly complete absorption with the boys and their game and, with a last surreptitious scan over her shoulder towards him, she started tip-toeing towards David's room.

Josh was just making his exit. Closing his son's door, he yawned, then smiled at Jessie's cute grin when she stopped a few feet away, crossed her arms, turned an ankle over, and watched him from behind a curtain of loose curls.

Stepping sideways, Josh met her at the wall to his right—and to her left—of the back hallway. They leaned there, opposite each other, where they could chat in relative peace and solitude.

"I got you something," Josh started, his eyes bright. "I hid it so…" He inhaled slowly and shrugged. "Well, you know."

"Oh," Jessie breathed, delighted. "What'd you get me? And where'd you hide it?"

He beamed at her enthusiasm. "Not telling what it is. You'll see. It's in the coat closet. That thing is big enough to be a bedroom."

When Jessie threw her head back and laughed, the light caught her hair. Josh couldn't help himself. Reaching out a hand, he let his fingers float through the auburn-tinted tresses. He'd been aching to do that all day.

"Ahhh." Watching his face change when he touched her, Jessie almost moaned. There was something about the way Josh's breaths shortened and the way his eyes lit up as his fingers wound through her locks that completely disarmed her. It was like some magical soul light she dearly missed was finally reappearing. "You're killing me, Sawyer."

When the chocolate eyes dropped to meet hers, Josh's smile faded. Now, the lips Jessie longed to extend a finger to touch were a straight line.

For Josh, bringing his hand down from her curls was tough; it was intoxicating to be there, even just to touch a few strands of hair…to be lost in Jessie's essence again.

Eyes wide, he shook his head slowly. "I'm sorry, Jessie, I just…I don't know…"

"It's okay," she said quietly. "I do. I know."

"Can we talk? Not now, I know, it's a madhouse in here today despite how friggin' crazy huge this place is, but I…I really would like to talk. In person."

"You've been doing good, huh Josh?"

"Yeah. Yeah, I have, I'm terrified of Arnie so I don't have much choice, really." Laughing nervously, he leaned forward into her a wee bit more. "The guy's a brick wall."

"He's a good guy. He's been through the same shit, as I'm sure you know. Years ago, but still…"

"Yeah, he told me a bit of his story. Over ginger-ale, mind you. Lost a little in the translation as a result, I'm sure."

This time, Jessie's cheerful laugh was loud enough for Jacob to hear her in the family room. He paused, and cocked his head to listen. *They have a right to chat,* he told himself, recognizing Josh's low voice. Still, he couldn't prevent his legs from walking him out to the doorway, where he could lean against the doorframe and just barely see Josh and Jessie around the corner.

They were standing close, to be sure, and Josh's head was inclined enough towards Jessie that his layered hair was cascading near her face. One of his big hands was resting on her hip, hooked in a belt loop on the long tunic she was wearing over leggings. Jacob couldn't see Josh's other hand.

Watching Jessie's back, Jacob swallowed. He saw her lift a hand and place it over Josh's on her hip. They were laughing about something, but Jacob couldn't make out what was so funny. Then he spotted Josh's other hand, finally—it came up to Jessie's cheek. Not surprisingly, hers followed—she raised her fingers to cover Josh's. She rubbed his hand, too, and by the way Jessie's head was cocked and the way Josh was looking at her now—so lost, so still all of a sudden, as he gazed at her—Jacob knew there was a mist covering the pale sea-pearl eyes he loved.

He didn't need to wonder what it meant—he knew. He'd always known. He was a coward, though. Jacob needed her. He was immobilized by fear.

Moving then, as the world started to spin in some unforgiving orbit around him, Jacob sucked in a breath.

Out of the corner of his eye, Josh caught the flutter somewhere behind Jessie. He looked up, straight into Jacob's piercing stare.

Raising his chin defiantly, Josh let his hands drop from Jessie's hip and face. The nerve on his cheek twitched, and he twisted his lip and sucked on a corner of it as he inhaled.

Jessie stilled, and closed her eyes.

"Fuucckkk," she moaned. "Let me guess."

"Jessie," Josh started as, behind her, Jacob left his post and headed towards the door, "I'm going to go. But I want to see you. Tomorrow, okay? Text me some place in Central Park, maybe."

"Where," she asked, swallowing past the sudden lump in her throat, "by the fountain so everybody can film us and put videos up on YouTube?"

"Someplace private. Come on, you know the area. Just text me."

Jacob was no longer there, watching them. Josh looked up to be sure, and then he bent and kissed Jessie's forehead, letting his lips linger there.

"I love you," he murmured. "Always and forever, remember?"

His warm breath on her skin was too much. Eyes closed, Jessie pulled him close, finally, regardless of where she knew Jacob might or might not still be. "I love you back, Josh," she whispered into his neck. "I'm so, so glad you're doing better."

"I'll see you tomorrow," he breathed hopefully, holding on for a few extended moments before squeezing her hand and brushing by her as he left.

Everybody got a little quiet when Josh made his way to the big front room. He scratched his chin with a thumb and forefinger and nodded at Arnie. "I'm good," he told him. "Stay if you want to. I need a walk."

Matt hesitated. "Josh, let me go with you, at least. Or take Dan, maybe, if you prefer."

"Nah, really," Josh replied, backing away. "I just need a walk. The hotel's not far. I'm not gonna mess up, I swear. I'm too…" He almost said 'close,' but at the last second he knew that wasn't something he could communicate to this crowd at this time.

"None of us are sure you're not a target here too, Josh," Matt said outright, standing. "You need some security on you here in New York."

"No Matt, I don't," was Josh's definitive answer. "I'm outta here. I'll see you all somewhere, sometime, okay? Thanks for a really great day."

The room was silent as the door closed behind him. Slowly, Matt sat back down as Jessie made her way to the front room, eyes misty but ebullient. She scanned the room for Jacob.

"Is Jacob…?"

Steve answered solemnly. "Just your luck, Jess. They're both outside. Only Jacob has a head start so my bet's on him to win this race."

Sophie swatted him. "It's not a competition, Steve."

He watched Jessie flounder as she pondered what to do. "My ass it ain't," was his candid response.

Looking up, she met his eye. Sighing, Jessie glanced at the door, but chose to sit by Sophie instead of bolting to follow Josh. She leaned her head on her friend's shoulder, as Sophie smiled and wrapped an arm around her.

Jacob arrived home at one a.m. There were still a few stragglers sitting around the front room, but he just hung his head and made a beeline for the master bedroom in the back corner. Jessie was in the kitchen showing Steve where the bread was so he could make a snack. When Jacob ghosted by, she glanced at Steve.

"G'nite," she said. "See you in the morning." Steve and Sophie were bunking with them, as were Charlie and Jane—the friends with small children. The rest were staying in nearby hotels.

In the bedroom, Jessie approached Jacob, who was facing the window, waiting.

Leaning into his back, she wrapped both arms around his waist.

"I'm such a fucking coward," he admitted disconsolately to the inky darkness.

"No," she whispered. "No you're not, Jacob. I'm the coward. I can't move forward and I can't move backward. All I can do is stay still."

"What are you afraid of, Jessie? He seems to be doing all right."

"You," she murmured into his neck. "I'm afraid of losing you. Forever."

He turned, then, and faced her. "I'm afraid of you losing me forever too," was his tortured response, as he finally broke down after the hard day. "But I know I have to go."

"I know you have to go too," she breathed, as her body melted into his. "But that doesn't mean I want you to."

That night, they made love with an intensity borne of an impending good-bye. It was heartfelt, it was passionate, and it was a tender ache in a raw, open wound.

After, Jessie waited until Jacob's breathing steadied before she slipped out of bed and padded down the hall towards the large coat closet. She had to root around a bit to find Josh's gift for her; in the end she discovered it hiding behind an old pair of boots at the back of the closet. Wrapped in yellow paper, it was rectangular-shaped, about ten by eighteen inches in size.

Planting her bum on an inner ledge of the coat closet, swiping a few pairs of kids' shoes and sandals out of the way to make room for herself, Jessie turned the package this way and that, like a child, shaking it gently before opening it.

The tape came away easily; she slid her fingers underneath the paper slowly, loving it, cherishing it, caressing it because it came from Josh's fingers, this paper, these bits of cellophane. This gift was born of him; his touch imbued it with a much-missed deep-seated love.

Inside was a simple box, one of those cardboard clothing store boxes given away with purchases at Christmastime. Inside that was a framed picture. Holding it up to the light, Jessie gasped. It was an old crayon drawing of Emily-Grace's, of a lovely arched multi-colored rainbow; next to it, shining brightly out from the faded paper, was a large roundish happy-faced sunshine. Below those were red-crayoned words, scripted in Jessie's own handwriting—*Always and Forever.*

Tearfully humbled at both the simplicity of the gift and its thoughtful presenter, Jessie let her eyes linger over every aspect of it. She traced her daughter's crayon scrawls and the letters she herself so carefully wrote on a very dark day in hers and Josh's history. Then she turned the framed picture over. Taped to the back was a second gift—the locket Josh gave her the night he proposed, which she'd left in her jewelry box at the UBC neighborhood house the day she fled Vancouver in a mess of tears and pain.

That was enough to make her crumble once and for all. Jessie removed the locket with shaking fingers, and held it to her chest while her shoulders shook. She wanted this, she wanted it so bad. This was what she'd been waiting for—an overture from Josh that begged her to understand his past sorrow, that clearly said he wanted her back, that meant it was time to move on, to…let Jacob go.

After a while, she gathered her rattled emotions and stood, then bent to snug the picture back in behind the boots until such time as she got a chance to move it somewhere more permanent. The locket she dangled between her fingers, before hiding it deep inside her make-up bag in the master bedroom's ensuite washroom.

Jessie peeked in at her children before planning to slip back into bed behind Jacob. Matt and Julie's Katy was snuggled up in bed with Emily-Grace. Hopefully the security afforded by a sweet friend's body would, tonight, grant Emily-Grace a respite from the horrific nightmares that haunted her.

Stealing softly into her room to grab her iPhone, Jessie snuck back to the girls and took a picture for Matt and Julie. Smiling, she kissed each of the children in turn. A short walk and a pee, and she was back in bed, perhaps, she thought, for the last time with Jacob. Jessie lay awake for a long time, a victim of adrenalin and longing. As she did with the drawing, she traced her fingers over Jacob, memorizing him, loving him, missing him.

But it was Josh's chest she saw in bed beside her, his white T-shirt coming up over his head, his breath on her neck, on her body, his hair falling onto her cheek as he pulsed inside her, loving her. She envisioned his arms safely tenting her as his breathing slowed.

I'm sorry, Jacob, she whispered. *I do love you.*

Chapter Fifteen

*N*adia was so angry with Morgan for screwing up that she got careless. She knew about Josh attending his daughter's birthday party at Jessie's place in New York, because everyone knew. The caterer's assistant leaked it by sharing pictures of the child's five-layer ballet-figure birthday cake on social media—Twitter was wild with tweets. Most Josh and Jessie followers were so devoted to the couple they searched their names weekly. Some, like Nadia, searched daily.

Well, thought Nadia, shoulders squared as she sat before her computer, *I have a few pictures of my own I can forward. And...I also have a video.*

It didn't take her long, just a few minutes frigging around with a program she downloaded from the net. She used it to place a date stamp on the images to make them look like they were taken a few days before the party. They weren't all that harmful anyway, they were just shots of Nadia and Josh together at a bunch of society functions. Making sure to only choose a few that were generic in nature, so Jessie wouldn't suspect them of being fake or touched up, or not recent, Nadia popped them into a folder on her iMac desktop in preparation for emailing.

The video was a breeze, too. She just ran it through a video editing program Josh liked to play around with back when he was living at the condo. First she resized the video so the date could no longer be seen in the bottom left edge of the frame. Next, she edited in numbers to take the date's place. She chose a day last week.

Nadia emailed the video Sunday morning, early, after wrangling with ornery Morgan for Jessie's personal email address, which was the hardest part of the whole desperate shebang. Jessie didn't get it until their visitors left, after lunch, just as she was about to text Josh about a private place to meet.

Jacob was packing his clothes into a duffel when he heard Jessie cry out. He was a mess, dealing with his own personal shit, when he stepped up behind her and saw her watching a poor quality porn video. It took him a few moments to realize the male star was Josh, and that there were two women in the video as well, one of whom was the exotic, gorgeous Nadia.

Dashing forward, he grabbed the wireless mouse.

"No!" Jessie cried. "Leave it!"

"Like hell," he told her, holding the mouse away from her, blocking the screen. "Who the hell sent you that garbage?"

"I don't know," she answered him truthfully, trembling. "Darin something or other at gmail.com. I opened it because I thought maybe it had something to do with our shoot this week! From an AD or something!"

Incensed, Jacob whipped around and looked at the email address. It wasn't one he recognized. Jessie took the opportunity to grab the mouse from him. She dropped it on the desk and started the video again. This time Jacob watched too, floored.

Finally, he turned back to Jessie. "He's drunk, Jessie, in this video. And when's the last time he was in Toronto with Nadia?"

She was shaking uncontrollably now, trying to speak in words he would understand. "That's not Toronto," she cried. "It's fucking Vancouver. It's the Sheraton. Look!" Jessie pointed out the nightstand, where tourist brochures were clearly visible. "And it's last week, according to the date on the bottom of the video! He's still drinking, Jacob. And he's still with Nadia."

The reality of that hit them both at the same time. Jessie backed away from Jacob, already crumbling, both hands covering her mouth. She made it to the ensuite bathroom before puking. After a bit, Jacob crept in and held her hair, cursing to himself for always having to pick up Josh's crap, and wondering again why this girl insisted on loving such a damaged man.

Vomiting until she had nothing left in her stomach, Jessie pushed Jacob away. "Go," she insisted. "Get the fuck out. I don't want you here. I don't want you here!"

No, you've made it pretty damn clear who you want, Jessie, Jacob thought.

But the kids were playing in the family room, and lo and behold, their mother was once again a royal mess.

Feeling rather nauseated himself, Jacob padded out of the washroom into the master bedroom and lifted a couple pairs of jeans out of his duffel bag. He tucked them neatly back onto a shelf in the wide closet, leaned a hand on the shelf's edge, and exhaled deeply.

~ ~

Jessie climbed onto her big bed and grabbed the edge of the gold duvet. Yanking it up so it covered only her head and shoulders, she sobbed into it until she had nothing left to pour out into the unforgiving world. Sleep took her away, but not before she had time to ponder the heartbreaking end of the video—her husband breaking down after having sex with a young woman who was very likely working in the profession Jessie once spent time making videos for. On one level, because of her history she could let that part go, and not blame the girl, but Nadia was there with them, her perfect body and glistening skin a flawless jewel Jessie's husband obviously craved.

No, what hurt Jessie the most was the realization that Josh likely broke down because he knew he was breaking a promise to himself to remain sober which, of course, curtained a hope Jessie knew he was clinging to—the same hope she ached for until the cruel video landed in her inbox and she opened it.

There were photos too, of Josh and Nadia in Vancouver, at society events, it seemed, her clinging to his arm and him looking affectionately down at her. So he was seeing Nadia again, and apparently exercising his right to explore a shadow side of himself that Jessie hoped was not one he would ever consider acting on further.

When Jacob squeaked the door open later, he stepped quietly inside and gently removed the duvet from over Jessie's head, tucking it around her body instead. Her face was flushed, dried trails of tears telegraphing the level of hurt this latest fiasco had caused. Scratching his chin, Jacob padded back out of the room. At the door was Emily-Grace, wringing her fingers.

"Momma sick?"

He bent down before her. "Yes, sweetheart. She needs a little nap. How about you and me make some chocolate chip cookies for her? For when she wakes up?"

At her nod, Jacob took the little girl by the hand, led her into the kitchen, and propped her up on a low stool by the kitchen island. He opened cupboard doors and pulled out flour, baking powder, chocolate chips and the other ingredients for the recipe his grandmother taught him to whip together on snowy days when he was young. Today felt like a snowstorm—a big old whiteout to once again erase what must have seemed, to Jessie, a clear future ahead.

Glancing over to the family room, where David was puttering happily, Jacob pondered his future. It seemed bleak as far as Jessie and these children were concerned. But as he helped Emily-Grace measure cups of flour, he counted softly to himself.

"Eighty-seven," he said. "And likely, at the very least, eighty-eight."

Wondering if he would see ninety, or maybe a hundred nights with Jessie in total, he reflected that he likely got more time with her than he initially thought possible. Still, that time came at a heavy price. He felt so ingrained in this new life that it was impossible to consider even a day without Jessie and the kids. Relief washed over him that he was not, at this minute, on an airplane to Vancouver, which was where, a few short hours ago, he thought he'd be.

He couldn't help but smile at Jessie's little girl now. She was wiping white flour dust over her pink dress, and it was on her cheek now, too, as she brushed loose hair off her face.

"You are one special little girl, Emily-Grace," he said to her as he used a thumb to wipe the flour on her cheek away. "You know that?"

She looked at him for a moment before a smile of her own appeared. She raised her shoulders, and Jacob thought he saw her blush. The smile reached her eyes, and lit them from within, a rare feat for this traumatized child. He couldn't help himself—Jacob leaned forward for a hug.

"I do love the Sawyer women," he murmured. Brushing his lips against the little girl's cheek, he smiled warmly, glad for another day with this beautiful family.

⌒～～⌒

Jessie tiptoed out to the family room at eight that night, to find Jacob asleep sitting up on the sofa, Emily-Grace snuggled up under his arm on one side, and David snoring in his lap. The large screen television was on, at a low volume, playing Winnie-the-Pooh reruns. Plucking the remote off the square coffee table, Jessie flicked off the TV. Mentally she snapped a picture of Jacob here with her children; Jacob, who by all appearances it seemed did what she was incapable of doing that day, which was feed, entertain, and bathe her and Josh's children.

And love them, she thought, guilt hitting her like a ton of bricks as she thought about what she almost did that day, at how their lives almost changed irrevocably yet again. *I need to be hit over the head with a very large stone,* she thought. *Josh is not worthy. He's not the same guy I fell in love with. He lies, he drinks, he has ménage-a-trois' with the girlfriend he says he cares nothing for. He's not worth losing Jacob over.* Yet a twinge twisted Jessie's heart at those thoughts, which she knew came from some haunted place deep inside her soul. Counterpoint to those were other thoughts...*Josh is hurting. He needs understanding, not judgment. He needs his family back.*

Squeezing her temples to force her mind to quiet, Jessie pushed away the seemingly never-ending angst. Bending forward, she whispered to her daughter, "Emily-Grace, come with Momma. I'll tuck you in your bed, sweetheart."

At the little girl's movement, Jacob's eyes fluttered open. He blinked sleepily around and did a one arm stretch before hoisting himself up with David in his arms.

"Thank you," Jessie murmured to him, leaning forward to brush her lips against his cheek.

He couldn't answer. Jacob couldn't tell Jessie that today was a gift. That it was an extra day, an extra beat on his 'counting them in,' a day that was supposed to be an ending for him—for them. He couldn't tell Jessie he hoped this was the end of their tough times, and that he was praying for the good times to begin, and that their future together could now be long and fruitful.

Ducking his head, he followed her out to the wide hall, and around the corner to David's room. Laying the little boy on his side, tucking him in and leaving him with a light touch and a kiss on his forehead, Jacob sighed. Where might he have ended up tonight? Alone in Vancouver, that's where, in a lonely apartment on Southwest Marine Drive. Likely crawling into a fetal position and crying himself to sleep. It wasn't lost on him that Jessie did the very same thing that day, and not because of hurt over him.

He pulled David's door almost to a close, and met Jessie in the hallway.

"She wants you," she told him quietly. "Emily-Grace needs a kiss and a hug from her beloved Jacob."

"Okay," he said, touching her arm but unable to smile as he moved by Jessie.

Afterwards, he found her in the family room, staring at a blank screen. He settled in next to her, hesitant, thinking she might push him away, but she didn't. Instead, Jessie lay down with her head in his lap, positioned an arm over his legs, and soaked him in.

"I'm sorry, Jessie," he murmured to her, running a hand through her hair. "I know things aren't working out the way you want them to. I'll leave tomorrow, okay?"

"No," she said softly. "No, it's okay, Jacob. We'll figure this out. We have to shoot this movie, anyway. One day at a time, babe, okay?" She flipped around on her back and stared up at him, at the gentle hurt eyes, at the love and concern she saw there, and at the tiny glimmer of hope she saw flicker across his face.

Touching his cheek with the tips of her fingers, she felt a shiver run through his body. He bent and pressed his lips to hers, while Jessie placed her hand around to the back of his neck and ran her fingers through his hair.

They made love that night, and then the next and the next. But Jessie hardly spoke. Instead, she watched Jacob with her children, in her home, playing with them, caring for them, offering a continuity they desperately needed. At night, she cherished him for that, and so she held tight to Jacob's body as his back arched taut while he poured his love into her. But sometimes, in the darkness, she closed her eyes and turned her head away from him, overcome in the knowing that she was lost and hurting over what felt like yet another betrayal from a man she loved more.

⁓ ⌒

Josh waited until the last second for the promised text from Jessie that never came. Arnie rapped on his door at the last minute. It would be a stretch to make their flight back to Vancouver. Before the knock came, Josh was sitting on the end of his bed, the iPhone cradled in his fingers, letting his frazzled mind try to analyze what was likely going through Jessie's head. Certainly all indications over the last bit were that she was willing to talk about reconciliation, and Josh knew by the fear in Jacob's eyes that he knew it as well. So what the hell happened? Why wasn't she texting?

Finally, as he stood and pulled a brown leather bomber jacket on over a black hoodie, he figured despondently she must have decided in the end what Josh knew in his heart but, with the recent positive reinforcement from the treatment center on Bowen Island, was trying to talk himself out of— the knowledge that Jacob was the better man. It sickened him. Would there be another chance? Was this it? Was the perfection he found with Jessie and their small family finally over?

"No," he admonished himself. "No fucking way. I'm not giving up." But in truth, he wondered if she had given up. His final text to Jessie also went unanswered. *Please just call me when you can.*

But no call came that day, or the next or the next.

Josh was taking the kids for the duration of the shoot Jessie was starting with Jacob in New York. On Tuesday evening, he met Matt and the two little ones at the Keating jet after they landed at YVR. After he got Emily-Grace and David buckled into their car seats in the back seat of the King Ranch, Josh leaned against the truck and studied Matt's eyes.

"She okay?"

"Doesn't seem to be," Matt replied honestly, watching Josh's expression flicker into curiosity. "I'm not sure what's changed. She's gone back inside herself. Barely talking."

"Except to Jacob." Josh frowned.

Matt shook his head.

"Not even to Jacob?"

"Especially not to Jacob."

Something tweaked in Josh's heart. Jessie retreating inwards was never a good thing; when it happened, something set the behavior off. *Maybe Jacob found Emily-Grace's framed picture of the sun and the rainbow,* Josh thought. *Or maybe the picture and the locket were too much for Jessie. Or…maybe she's just not ready. Maybe the idea of reconciling is just too terrifying…too big a chance to take. Jacob's been her anchor now since June…*

Driving the kids back to their Vancouver home, he considered that this 'shuttling back and forth thing' every few weeks might indeed end up being their lives for the next many years. It wasn't ideal, and it hurt like hell for all of them, especially since they were separated for so long last fall...around this time, in fact.

Thinking about that horrible day—the shattered window in the SUV, the fear of the unknown—caused palpitations in Josh's heart, and a new pounding in his ears. He peeked in the rearview mirror at his kids. Emily-Grace was sucking her thumb, clutching both of her cherished dowwys, staring out of the window, and David was babbling away, playing with one work-booted foot. A smile creased Josh's face. He and Jessie sure made beautiful children. Would there be more? Not likely, if these last few days were any indication. The smile turned upside down as he concentrated his vision back on the road in front of him.

Jessie, he thought, *give us a chance. Please.*

He hoped she heard him. He begged her to hear him.

One last turn and they were home. Josh steered the truck into his driveway, helped Emily-Grace out of her car seat, and waved to Matt in his sedan as the man checked in with Susanne, who was parked at the end of the driveway waiting for them. Josh waved to her too, before reaching in the back seat of the pickup for David.

Matt watched the small family wander over to the flagstone walk and disappear from sight. He, too, was remembering this time last year, just after Emily-Grace's third birthday, and the call from Jessie that ended in a bone-chilling scream.

Sighing, he leaned both hands on Susanne's car window. He had to review security protocols with her now that Josh was back in Vancouver with his kids. When they were done chatting, Matt wiped his brow and rested his hands on his hips, hesitant to leave the family to whom he had once again grown so attached.

Josh had left the suitcases and assortment of children's things in the back of the pickup for the time being. Nodding at Susanne, Matt wandered forward and grabbed the kids' bags. He figured he'd help Josh out. Some things were just too hard to leave behind.

Chapter Sixteen

After a few gigs with Michael and Kelly, and a much needed week at home with Julie and Katy, Matt arrived on location where Jessie and Jacob's film was shooting in New York. He was switching off with Dan. Susanne remained in Vancouver to keep an eye on Josh and the kids, and Ulysses was travelling with Charles and Dee. The Keating security team was definitely missing Morgan. Ulysses, in consultation with Charles, was loath to hire anyone new at this point in time, at least until they made some headway with the guy who seemed to be on the prowl after Jessie, leaving cryptic messages carved in her breast and back.

Landing in a cast chair beside Jacob, near the built wooden set where Jessie was currently shooting, Matt arranged the short tails of his dove grey wool herringbone coat behind him so he wasn't sitting on them. Following Jacob's example, he propped his leather shoes up on a chair opposite him.

Jacob yawned, stretched, and flipped closed the script he was studying. He pulled ear buds out of his ears and set them, along with his phone, on a nearby chair. "What's new, Matt? Miss us? How're Kelly and Michael getting along?"

"They did a Farm-Aid concert last week in Texas and a weekend tour in Cali, and they're both still talking to each other, so I'd say they're doing all right."

"Humph."

"Thought you were happy for them." Matt gave Jacob a sideways look.

Jacob switched his feet around by reversing his ankles so the left was now over the right. "I am. I'm glad some of us old *Mystic Nights* alumni are talking, I guess."

Raising his eyebrows, Matt waited.

"She's not really talking to anybody, though, so I guess it's not just me on her shit list."

"If Jessie's in that kind of mood, she's the only one on her shit list, Jacob."

"I know. And maybe Josh, I guess." He looked away.

At that, Matt's ears perked up. "Why Josh? I thought they did okay at the party."

"Too okay," mumbled Jacob. He rallied. "It wasn't the party. Something happened the next day. Some asshole, likely Josh's girlfriend, sent Jessie photos and, well, the kind of video your mother wouldn't want you watching. A sex video. Featuring loverboy with her and some other young woman."

Taking a moment to digest that, Matt raised a hand to his gelled hair and absently patted a few spikes down. Dropping the hand back to his side, he chewed on a lip before responding. When he glanced again at Jacob, his eyebrows were burrowed into inquisitiveness and shock.

"Ouch," he finally said, as the reason for Jessie's funk was suddenly illuminated. "Why the hell would Nadia do that at this point in time? I'd think she's figured out by now that Josh is no longer in her camp."

Mumbling, Jacob eyed Matt. "The video was taken shortly before the birthday party. The date was on it. Suffice it to say it wholeheartedly crushed Little Mizz Sorrow."

At Matt's silence, Jacob looked over and furrowed his eyebrows at him. Matt was fingering the tiny hairs on his chin and looking rather pensive.

"What?" Jacob asked him.

"Josh hasn't been with Nadia since before rehab, Jacob. Since a ways before, if I remember correctly."

"According to the video, he has."

"It was dated some time during the week before the party, you said?"

"Yeah, and Matt, he was pissed drunk."

"Did Jessie happen to clarify that with Arnie? I've had a few chats with Arnie. Josh has been going to AA meetings with him every day since rehab. Sometimes twice a day. He hasn't been drinking, Jacob. I don't suppose either of you thought to right click on the video to see when it was created, did you? You can edit those things. Hell, the two of you ought to know that."

Chagrined, Jacob pondered that. "Jessie was in no state to consider anything besides the fact that any chance at reconciliation she had with Josh was toast, Matt. She was devastated. And I wasn't about to go looking at Josh's prowess in the bedroom again, thanks anyway." He settled deeper into his chair.

The studio bell rang to announce that cameras were rolling. An AD yelled *rolling* as well to the assembled cast and crew, and so the guys had to whisper. Jacob cringed when he shifted and his chair creaked. The crew guy recording the sound was set up close by—he treated Jacob to an evil glare.

Waving and mouthing *sorry*, Jacob leaned towards Matt. "What I don't get is how Josh can stand being with a woman whose ex-boyfriend's name is tattooed on her breast."

At Matt's raised eyebrows, he added, "It was on the video." He used a finger to demonstrate where the tattoo was. "Right across her left boob. David or Dennis or Darren...some D name. I'd be asking my girlfriend to get that removed." He clasped his hands together, folded them across his lower belly, and stared at them, waiting for the double-bell and the AD to yell *cut* so he could speak in a regular tone again.

Around sets enough to know to whisper, or preferably not to speak at all, Matt bent in close to Jacob. His eyes were curious, thoughtful. "Were you there the day Jessie talked to the detectives? In Vancouver after she was rescued? I seem to recall you being in the room. I know Josh wasn't."

"Yeah. Why?"

The studio bell finally rang, accompanied by a loud *cut!*

Mat spoke quickly. "Jacob...Jessie said something about a tattoo. On the woman's breast when she went in to the basement to check on Jessie, near the end." Pulling out his iPhone, he selected the Voice Memos App. Scrolling down until he found the audio file he recorded that day as Jessie told her harrowing story, he was not surprised to discover it was 45 minutes long. He glanced at the sound guy and frowned. "I'll listen to it later," he said, stuffing the phone back in his pocket. "Send me the video, Jacob." Matt's heart was suddenly racing; his eyes were on fire.

Staring at him, Jacob was astounded. *No way. Nadia?* Stunned at even the idea that Nadia might have had anything to do with the abduction of

Jessie and the kids, he held Matt's narrowed, concentrated gaze. *Does Morgan know? Her stepbrother...Morgan...No way...*

"Lots of women have tattoos on their breasts, Matt," was what he carefully chose to say.

"But how many have tats that start with D? A guy's name?" Matt asked as his mind suddenly catapulted into overdrive.

Jessie appeared and stopped at the nearby craft table for a handful of gummy bears. She stood watching the guys, pushing the gummies between her lips one at a time. Contemplating Matt, she was glad he was once again among them, but she wondered why he and Jacob seemed to be so deeply lost in thought.

Sensing her scrutiny, Matt shook this shocking new clue aside. He stood, and wandered over. Wrapping both arms around her shoulders, he held tight before letting go.

"Thanks, Matt," she mumbled, pushing a green gummy bear between his lips.

A moment later, the First AD popped her head out of the built set. "Jacob, Jessie. We need you for blocking."

While his charges were blocking the next scene to be shot, Matt caught himself staring at Jacob's discarded phone and ear buds on a nearby chair. His hand floated in the air for a moment before he decided he couldn't wait to hear what Jessie had said in the hospital about the woman's tattoo. He reached for the ear buds and plugged them into his own phone. Listening to Jessie's interview from that long ago day, it took him about ten minutes to find the part about the tattoo. Then, there it was. There was Jessie's tired, injured voice, saying the ink was on the woman's left breast, and that she could only make out the first few letters, a 'D' and a small 'a.' Matt scrolled through more of the interview. He recalled that near the end, the detective had brought up the tattoo again. At that point, the fog in Jessie's mind had been clearing some. Clearly, her voice came through the ear buds saying she thought the tattoo read Darins in full, which she thought was a rather strange name.

"That's too close to be a coincidence," Matt told himself, considering whether he ought to call Charles or Ulysses at this early juncture. He stuffed the phone away again when Jessie and Jacob reappeared, suddenly overwhelmed by nausea as he considered Morgan's close relationship to Nadia. "Not possible. No," he muttered inwardly.

Watching as the two cast were touched up by the girls from the on set make-up and hair departments, he could see a definite distance between them, if not even an actual rift. Jessie was jumpy, twitchy. Jacob was silent. Neither met the other's eye, and both seemed sad. When they were called back to set for shooting, Jessie met Matt's eyes before turning to go. He got the feeling she wanted to talk, but there wasn't time right now.

Around him, crew was socializing in small groups. Only the department keys seemed to be on set. The two cast hadn't said anything, but Matt suddenly understood that the scene they were about to film must be an intimate one. Curious, he peeked in the open doorway to a room set decorated to copy the interior of a sound studio. In the corner was a ubiquitous large black leather couch.

Cocking his head to listen, Matt heard the director speaking to his cast.

"I won't call cut until you ask me to," he was saying. "I want this to play out as naturally as possible. We'll shoot handheld around you, and grab close-ups on sticks from the corner so we don't catch the handheld camera in the shot. If you need to stop, just call *cut* yourselves, okay?"

The director seemed worried. Matt understood why—even now, before this supposed intimate scene, his cast were not able to meet each other's eyes. They were the picture of doom and gloom, not the 'very-much-in-love' characters they were supposed to be playing.

Action was called and the studio bell rang once. Immediately, the set fell silent, apart from the odd creak of someone's boots as they shifted their feet.

"Shit," breathed Matt. *I should have moved before they rolled.* He suddenly realized he was stuck, and so he tried to avert his eyes from Jessie and Jacob, whom he could rather clearly see inside the set, artistically backlit by some clever DP/gaffer team.

The thing was, though…once Matt had the two cast in his vision, he couldn't bring himself to look away. They were captivating.

He watched as Jessie took Jacob's fingers in hers, at the same time closing her eyes and turning her head away from him while she went to some place deep inside to connect with her character in order to make the scene work. Jacob seemed at a loss. He was studying her, waiting for cues to help him get on track for this difficult scene. When Jessie let her gaze float back over to him, he had what he needed. The way his lips moved and the way he angled his head, just slightly, in concert with his gently probing cobalt eyes, said way more than he had apparently spoken to Jessie since Emily-Grace's birthday party. A deep sadness was buried there; it was infused with longing and a silent desperation. Her eyes were similar. They spoke of loss and sorrow; his were slowly transmitting sorrow and desire.

Matt sensed what they were actually saying to each other was *what the hell are we doing?* He knew Jacob loved the children and felt they needed him. He also sensed Jacob needed *them.* The dissolution of the relationship would mean more than just an ending for Jessie and Jacob. Matt could see it all now, all the hurt and fear and pain, playing out in a safe, wordless environment and captured on film for the world to see.

Enthralled, unable to look away, Matt watched as Jacob reached for Jessie and unbuttoned her cotton plaid top from the top button on down. He did it while searching her eyes the entire time, as if he could undo the outer layers protecting her so he could once again connect with her soul. She let him, placing her fingers over his as he moved them over her.

When the top was unbuttoned, Jacob slipped his hands inside and pulled the top away and off her body. She was not wearing a bra—Matt sucked in a breath, not expecting that. His eyes darted down to his feet as he swallowed uncomfortably and wished to hell he could move. Everyone else seemed to be taking this in stride, it was everyday business to them, but to Matt it was another kind of business—he was Jessie and Jacob's security. He was not meant to watch a difficult and painful love story unfold in front of him in a very real and sorrowful way.

Yet he looked back. There was magic at play between the two, that was no surprise, even with the stakes piled high against them in so many ways. The manner in which Jacob was caressing her now, the way she held a hand against the back of his head while he bent to suckle her, the way she tilted her head back and let him sink to his knees, his arms around her waist. It was surreal, but it wasn't sex. It was love Matt was seeing unfold in front of him, and so it hit him with the force of a big gusty wind that the price this couple would pay if they split up would be irreconcilable and final—because it would have to be. There would be no other way to stay in each other's lives this time, should Jessie reconcile with her husband. The price was too high, the pain already too great.

They were saying goodbye here, today, Matt thought, studying Jessie's misty eyes as she let Jacob love her. He could see it there plain as day, in a watchful, almost detached gaze that drifted over Jacob's body as she forced off his shirt to reveal the Celtic cross tattoo she loved inked across his back.

On set, Jacob laid Jessie on her back now, and pulled her jeans down. Thankfully, Matt told himself later, he couldn't see everything as it happened, from his vantage point, but still, what he did see completely disarmed him. Jessie, arching her back and responding to Jacob, fondling her own breasts as her eyes closed, the pleasure of the way he moved his lips up and down her body taking over. She seemed to come, in time, which floored Matt. But then he remembered her history. It both sickened and touched him deeply at the same time.

After, she lay panting as the cameras still rolled. No one seemed to want to call *cut*, especially the two cast whose entwined destinies seemed in jeopardy.

Starting to come down off her high, seemingly aware of where she was again, Jessie let her head roll slightly sideways. She caught Matt's gaze at the door, and held it, biting her bottom lip and watching what seemed to be a confused, remorseful desire slip across his eyes. She blinked back at him as Jacob started to disentangle himself from her, and then she reached for her top and slipped it on, unable to look away from Matt who, as the bell ultimately rang twice and someone finally yelled *cut*, walked away.

⁓ ⁓

Jacob had to stay late to shoot one more scene, so Jessie went back to her trailer, grabbed a few personal items, and quietly accompanied Matt to a rented SUV.

Inside, neither spoke until Matt's discomfort and confusion got the better of him and he managed a small, "I'm sorry." He couldn't look at her, but Matt knew what he would see if he did. Jessie's experience with sex in her lifetime was not the same as most people's...she looked at it differently. But she was wise enough to discern the level of his shame and discomfort, which, to her, made him an honorable man.

"I get it, Matt," she said in a small monotone voice, looking out of the window as busy New York slid by.

"I get it now too," he replied, his voice tremulous as he knifed a shaking hand through his short, spiked hair.

She looked over at him, and waited.

"You and Jacob," he said, still unable to meet her eye. "I'm sorry, Jessie."

Turning her head to gaze back out of the window, Jessie reached for Matt's hand and squeezed it.

"Jesus," he said, shaking, sweaty. "I need a drink."

"Have I scarred you for life, Matt?" She was still quiet, unsure.

"On the contrary," he said, after a moment to think. "Two people in love is a beautiful thing, Jessie." He thought about the video he planned to go home to watch that evening once Jacob got a chance to send it. Doubting very much he would see love in it, he worked to calm his breathing.

Jessie held his hand all the way back to Madison Avenue, and even though he needed to use the blinker a number of times, Matt didn't try to remove his from under hers.

Chapter Seventeen

It was nine by the time Matt opened his email and saw Jacob's name in his inbox. Matt didn't hesitate. He right-clicked on the video link immediately. Clearly, the creation date of the video was much earlier than he knew Jessie believed it to be. Exhaling slowly in relief, Matt closed the 'get info' box that had opened under his right-click, and he double-clicked on the video instead.

What he saw was disturbing—a very drunk out-of-sorts man quite obviously being told the woman on the bed was a gift. Said man looking confused and scared. Unbalanced in every way possible. Woman on bed looking enticing, moving in a way to make said man want her. Third person—Nadia—purring, encouraging.

Uncomfortable with his second exposure in one day to sex by people he knew well, Matt swallowed and forced himself to remain objective. When Nadia's tattoo was visible on her breast, he stopped the film, exported from QuickTime a static jpeg file of the frame, and zoomed in. The video was pixilated at this point, and the tattoo difficult to make out. But clearly the name started with a D, was apparently six letters, and was inked across Nadia's left breast.

"Jesus Christ," he mumbled. "I don't fucking believe this." Again, his mind went to Morgan and his very recent close proximity to Jessie and the children. He didn't like the kid much, but Matt sure as hell couldn't imagine the weird guy having anything to do with the abduction. But then…he groaned. Jessie would lose it if she got wind of this possibility.

Within five minutes, Matt booked a flight back to Vancouver, set up a time to meet Josh, and arranged through Ulysses to call Dan back to duty in New York.

Jessie thought he was upset with her when he didn't appear at her condo the next day. He knew she would think that, so he called her, but Matt didn't tell Jessie where he was going.

That night, she went to bed unhappy, but Jacob eased her pout, starting by biting on her bottom lip as he laid his body on hers. They weren't talking in words. Their bodies were speaking for them.

And for once, Jessie was glad.

～～～

"A video landed in Jessie's inbox a few weeks ago, Josh. The day after Emily-Grace's birthday party."

"Hmmm?" At the kitchen island, Josh was dropping pepperoni slices on a pizza he was making for lunch. An alarm bell went off. He stopped moving and looked up at Matt. That was the day Jessie was supposed to text him. "What kind of video?" Lowering his hand to the counter, he gave the pepperoni a break for the time being.

The kids were nearby—he could see them playing in the adjoining room. Judging by Matt's tone, Josh knew he would have to speak quietly and not overreact should the need arise. The whole 'little pitchers and big ears' thing…

"Do you remember making a video, Josh? With Nadia and, uh, a young blonde? Maybe more than one? In the Nadia days?"

"No," Josh said, sinking on to a high stool at the island, his voice a few tones lower than usual even without the pressing need for subdued words. "I don't remember making a video. Uhhh, filming…anything."

"Well, you were filmed, Josh. At the Sheraton, I think."

Oh, fuucckkk. Josh cleared his throat. "The Sheraton. I was there, uh, with Nadia, once. Yeah. And a…well, uh, a…a blonde she hired. I left for Toronto the next day. I couldn't…look Jessie in the eye. I was fucked up." Stopping, he thought for a second. "Nadia filmed us? That's baked. I didn't see a camera, Matt. Not that I was looking for one, but there was no obvious camera in the room. She must have used a small Go-Pro or something." Clenching the counter tightly with his free hand, Josh's knuckles went white. "Why would she…she sent it to Jessie?"

125

"Ammunition, Josh. Making the video. As far as emailing it, well…she pulled out a gun and fired." Blinking, Matt realized that if Josh was able to isolate the day this video was filmed, then likely hotel room drunken ménage-a-trois with young blondes likely weren't a regular part of his and Nadia's sex-capades. Meaning hopefully no more videos would surface to throw Jessie into a deep funk.

Anxious to get to the heart of the matter, per se, Matt leaned forward and rested both forearms on the island across from a shocked Josh, whose heart, it seemed now, was racing, given the panicked expression flickering across his face. "Josh, two things you need to know. One, Nadia or whoever sent this on her behalf seems to have edited a date into the video. Jessie thinks it was made just before Emily-Grace's party."

"All right." The words came out in a croak. Josh tried to sit straighter and appear focused and calm, but he wasn't wholly successful. "That explains a lot, actually, Matt. Damn." While he pondered what to do about that revelation, Josh emphatically added, "I wasn't myself, Matt. You know that."

"Jessie will understand that too, Josh, once we clue her in to the actual date. But this video has raised another issue. I've been wondering about something." Matt sat back now and thrummed his fingers on the island. He didn't want to raise any unnecessary red flags yet, but…he needed to know about the tattoo. "Nadia's tattoo…over her breast…did it not drive you nuts? An ex-boyfriend's name?"

"The tattoo?" *Jesus, Matt saw the video…me in all my glory…Jessie saw it. Fuuucckkk.* A toe-deep exhalation preceded the next words, which seemed unavoidable at this point as the words *shame on me* settled deeply into Josh's mind. "It's not an ex. At least, if you can believe her, it isn't. It's for her son. Cancer. He died when he was five."

"Her son? He was five?"

"Yeah. God. That's only a year older than Emily-Grace."

"What does the tattoo say exactly, Josh?"

"It's the kid's name and his age. Darin5. Darin with an i, like D, a, r, i, n."

Darin…with a 5…not an s, not Darins. Okay. Matt felt sick and exhilarated at the same time, but he tried not to let the wild emotions ping-ponging across his brain like an old Atari game get the better of him.

Josh noticed anyway. His eyes narrowed. "What? What's the tattoo got to do with anything?"

Grabbing a slice of pepperoni from the cutting board in front of him, Matt shoved it between his lips and rose from the stool. "You doing okay these days, Josh?"

"Yeah. I'm fine. I finished the film, I have the kids, I do AA at least once a day, yeah, I'm great. How's Jessie? Or should I say how are Jessie and Jacob?"

"Struggling. Getting through their film. Then I guess we'll see, huh, Josh?"

"You rooting for me, Matt?"

"Hell, yeah." Matt waved an arm towards the kids. "For this family, Josh. Maybe that's the only thing pushing me in your direction, that they're yours and Jessie's kids. Because I have to tell you—Jacob is a good guy, and he loves the heck out of her. And your kids."

Ignoring that, because he bristled at Jacob's name while at the same time soaked the guy in gratitude for caring for Emily-Grace and David—and Jessie—Josh couldn't help but add, "You think she'll talk to me once you straighten this godforsaken video shit out?"

"There were a few photos too, Josh, clean, just of society events you and Nadia went to. Am I right to assume those as well are from late last spring or early summer?"

"Hell, yeah! Matt, I am not seeing Nadia. I haven't seen her in months." Frustration edged Josh's exclamation. He glanced at the kids, hoping they didn't hear him raise his voice. Emily-Grace was looking up at him, pale eyes wide and apprehensive. "It's okay, sweetheart," he mumbled in her direction. "Daddy and Matt are just having a chat." At that, she sat back on her haunches and seemed to calm, but she watched her father for a few extended seconds before appearing to fully relax.

Matt watched her settle before he continued. "Well, the downside of it all is that she still very much obviously wants to see you." Slapping the counter lightly, he motioned towards the door. "I'm off. The big guy calls. Oh, one more thing. Is there a friend of Nadia's I can talk to in Toronto? So I can find her?"

"She'll likely be at the condo, Matt. Go there."

Hedging, Matt said, "I want to see if I can dig up a friend first. I want to know what kind of mood she might be in before I drop in."

"Why the hell would you want to see her, anyway? She won't respond to threats, Matt. And if there are more videos, they're not threesomes. That was the only, uh…" He colored. "I've got proof in the name of the hulk, Arnie—who Jessie trusts—that I have not been seeing her."

"She still needs to know that sending videos and photos to Jessie are not the way back to your heart. Quite the opposite, I think."

"Fair enough, I guess. I suppose I'd rather it was you than me." Josh thought for a moment. "There's a Samantha. I only met her once. She works at a bar called the Olde Feathered Hen, somewhere on Yonge Street. Try her. Although I feel like there's something you're not telling me, Matt."

"If there's something to tell, I'll tell it, Josh. Right now there isn't. Good enough?"

Josh spoke slowly as he watched Matt back out of his kitchen. He tossed him another slice of pepperoni. "All right. Helluva short visit, Matt. And aren't you supposed to be in New York this week?"

"Needed to see Charles about something. I'll drop in before I leave tomorrow." Matt gave each of the children a little rub on the head as he passed through on his way to the back door.

Mystified, Josh stood immobile for a moment before he resumed making the pizza. A small smile touched the corners of his lips as the realization of why Jessie wasn't responding to his texts or messages sunk into his bones. He decided to give Matt a few days to let her know the truth about the offending video before he tried texting her again.

As he dropped the rest of the pepperoni onto the pizza, Josh planned a relaxing evening with his kids. The movement was accented by a larger hopeful smile, despite an unwelcome, intrusive, equal measure of shame.

On the flight east to Toronto with Matt, Charles nervously fingered his silk tie the whole trip. If Nadia had somehow engineered the kidnapping of Jessie and her children, suddenly Josh's downhill spiral into decadence and booze was soaked with a deeper layer. Her involvement might also answer a lot of questions currently frustrating the investigating detectives, although

Charles couldn't for the life of him see past why Nadia would not ask for ransom money. He decided to wait until they talked to this Samantha gal before making too many speculations.

There was one thing he and Matt agreed on right from the start. They would not involve Josh or Jessie until some truths were unearthed. For one, who was the male involved in the kidnapping? *God forbid, it better not be Nadia's stepbrother, Morgan.* He better have been no more than an innocent pawn in Nadia's game. Or…was Nadia under *his* thumb? And where was she now? If they discovered that one of Jessie's kidnappers was indeed Josh's ex-girlfriend, at least they could likely discern who was still apparently threatening Jessie. If Morgan was involved…no. *No way could the quiet guy have sliced Jessie open, held her against her will…raped her…*

However, regardless of who it was, finding out the identity of Nadia's accomplice would at least eliminate some of the escalated fear they were all living under since the attack in Montreal.

The Olde Feathered Hen was a seedy Irish bar, not noticeable in the cluster of modern office buildings and classier beverage rooms surrounding it except for a faded wooden sign that creaked ominously back and forth underneath the awning of the small, narrow place. Inside, it stank of fried onions on beef and stale beer, both served by mini-skirted servers wearing ruffled blouses a size too small.

Charles and Matt found Samantha easily; she swooped in from the kitchen on tight knee high black leather boots thirty seconds after the men inquired after her.

"Gentlemen?" she asked with an aristocratic English accent Charles immediately felt was put on, but he shoved the notion aside after the brief consideration that there were likely more than a few folks in Nadia's world who were also not legit. "What can I do for you?"

She licked her lips, which had Matt on the defensive immediately. Over the last few days, he was overcompensating for what he considered bad behavior on his part for watching Jessie with Jacob on set. No way was he going down the dark road Josh had apparently succumbed to, at least on one videotaped occasion.

Matt stepped back from the vivacious redhead flagrantly flaunting cleavage in front of him, and let the more austere Charles do the talking.

"We think we have a mutual friend, Samantha."

"Nadia." She didn't hesitate. As far as Samantha was concerned, Nadia was the only person in her circle now wearing Gucci bracelets and designer heels. These two elegantly dressed men would fit right into the gal's new world. "But we no longer socialize. She traded up. I'm guessing you know that."

"We just have a few questions about her. Do you have a minute?"

"Are you police, then?" The way she said it made her intentions quite clear—a quick lowering of the eyelashes and a casual turn of the hip meant 'I'll play your game if you'll play mine.'

Charles glanced behind him at Matt before continuing. He placed his hands in the pockets of his tan overcoat and widened his stance. "We're not police, Samantha. We're just…concerned friends. Look, how well do you know Nadia? Did you go to school together, did you work together…how do you know her? How long have you known her?"

Samantha shifted her own footing then. Pausing, she angled her head towards the floor, holding her gaze long enough at some invisible spot on the scratched hardwood that both Charles and Matt looked down. The fake Brit accent called them back to her.

"We spent a lot of time together at the hospital. Our kids were sick."

"I see. And your child…?" Despite the urgency of the impromptu meeting, Charles did have manners, especially when unwell children were part of the equation.

"He's fine," she answered obediently. "He's on the rugby team in high school now." Raising her chin, she frowned. "Nadia didn't do so well with hers. She lost him."

"That must have been a tough time for both of you."

"Tougher for her. She was never the same. Mothers never are, after, you know."

Matt finally spoke up. "In what way was she never the same?"

Samantha shrugged. "All of the ways. It was like a light bulb switched off when Darin died. She closed up. Her marriage suffered, she stopped going out, she even changed her name. It was like she no longer wanted to be the same person." Lowering her voice, she added, "I went over there, a while after he died? Just to see how she was doing, you know? And the kid's room was still the same. This was six months later. There were still toys on the floor, those action figures the boys like, you know? And his bed was unmade but all the sheets and stuff were still on it. It was kind of creepy."

Digesting this, Matt continued. "You said she changed her name. Her last name?"

"Both names, honey. First and last." Samantha's gaze drifted down Matt's body. He was rather GQ chic in his new grey jacket, the double-breasted her-ringbone wool one he had worn in New York.

He flinched at the obvious intent behind her scrutiny.

"So," Samantha offered, still eyeing him. "Her name's not really Nadia. It's Nadine. And her real last name is Kumar. Her mother was in one of those arranged marriages, she told me. Brought over from India. I suppose that's why she wanted to 'change up.' Nadine, Nadia, take your pick—she never quite felt worthy on North American soil, although she was born here."

"Her mother divorced, or her partner died? She married a white man eventually, right? A man with a son?"

"Hmmm? No, I don't think so. Her parents are dead, I know that, but I'm pretty sure her father was Indian too. He just happened to arrive here a few years earlier than Nadia's mother."

Exchanging glances, Matt and Charles were wondering the same thing. Where did Morgan fit into Nadia's—or Nadine's—life? Charles was the one to ask. "She has a stepbrother, though. Morgan. He's white."

At that, Samantha raised her chin higher and hooted, loud enough for the few patrons in the shabby bar to turn their heads in wonder. Fixing her gaze back on Charles, she told them loudly, as if they were idiots, "Morgan's not her stepbrother. He's her husband! Or was. They split up when she started a new relationship."

A shocked silence overtook both men then. There was suddenly a lot to consider. Thoughts churned in their brains, toppling over one another like socks in the dryer.

Matt found his voice first. "Morgan's her husband?" His handsome face was suddenly an interesting shade of green.

Samantha took pity on him. "Like I said, he was. I don't know their status now." She wrinkled her brow. "Why are you surprised? Because Nadia was seeing that actor, Josh Sawyer, for a while? She kept Morgan on a leash, even then, like a puppy at first, and he followed her around like one too—still does, I hear, although I honestly don't know if they've officially gotten back together now that she and sexy Josh ended things. Doesn't matter anyway—she always knew who she wanted, Nadia did. And if she wanted someone, she slept with him. Or her, apparently. Regardless of Morgan. Not before her son died, mind you, only after. It was like she no longer cared about social filters or graces or whatever you want to call it. She just wanted to suck the marrow out of life, you know? And I think she did a pretty good job. She's got a fancy condo now, she's got expensive jewelry, her shoes are to die for, and those dresses, mm-hmmm. Am I jealous? You bet your ass I am. Do I ever see her anymore? No. Like I said, she—"

"We know. Traded up." Charles sighed deeply and made a mental note to really get to know his staff in future. All this time…and Nadia was Morgan's *wife*, not stepsister. Bewildered, he considered the times Morgan would have been on duty with Josh's kids while Josh was sleeping with Nadia. That must have driven the man insane! Or…more insane. Because how sane can you be if your wife is sleeping with another man under your nose, and you know about it? You don't just tolerate it, you condone it, apparently! The whole strange scenario was appalling to even consider.

So…was the man so angry he was capable of attempted murder? Of someone they all thought he worshipped, who was kind to him? How could he have taken Jessie and the children and hidden them away, after knowing them? After travelling with them? He would have carried the kids even, on occasion. Could he have raped Jessie that last morning and then drained two plastic containers of gasoline on the floors above her head? And lit a *match*?!

It was unthinkable. It didn't seem plausible. None of this seemed plausible. Why? What was the motive?

"Trading up," Matt said later when they were at dinner in their usual upscale Toronto hotel. "She wanted money, but she wanted the film star with it, and the glory, the life, the dinners," he nodded at his own mouth-watering perfect sirloin steak, "the social occasions, the expensive dresses…I suppose hooking up with Josh would get her a certain street cred. Not to mention a more, I suppose you could say 'honorable,' way in. As opposed to frankly asking for money and going on the lam so she's never found out."

"And she had to get Jessie out of the way first to make that happen. But the kids, Matt? Why the children? And why the hell would Morgan participate, if indeed he did? He adores Jessie and the kids."

"But…Charles, if he had it in him to, uh, *hurt* Jessie, he likely isn't too fond of Josh. Not that he ever let that be known. He was always so quiet we just assumed he was fine with everything. He must have had his fantasies." Matt cringed at the thought.

"He always seemed so protective of Jessie. And she was good to him."

"He sliced her breast open with a knife, Charles. He could have killed her."

Grimacing, Charles went white at the memory. "But he didn't. Why?"

"Because he couldn't. He cares about her."

"According to Samantha, he's head over heels in love with his wife. God, Matt, this is twisted. Thank God you and Ulysses let him go." He paused. "Do you think it really was him? Or was Nadia just using him to get her in the door with Josh? Maybe Nadia's got someone else on her payroll. Or she's on someone else's payroll…"

"Wishful thinking, Charles. You and I both know Jessie will go off the deep end if we have to tell her Morgan was the kidnapper. But consider this… there was never an ask for real currency, here. Nadia…Josh was good to her, sure, but Jessie saw their bank statements—she found the Gucci bracelet on there. But she never mentioned Josh handing over large sums of money. So Nadia wasn't likely paying anyone else…"

"So you think it *was* Morgan. Why did we not know who he was married to? Why didn't the investigators check that out?"

"I'm sure one of the detectives did, Charles. They likely got the connection—Morgan's ex dating Josh—but just assumed the two met, as they did, in fact, through Morgan…they fell in love…" He swooped a hand over his steak. "People hook up that way all the time, at parties, whatever, through their partners. I don't think it would have raised any red flags beyond some good office gossip. And people do continue to work together after they've split up, although I can't imagine how."

"And as for us, we didn't care enough to bother checking to see who he was married to."

"Morgan spent his time with Jessie. Nadia was in Toronto. Their paths didn't cross—lots of people don't involve their partners in social events for work. Why would we bother chasing that down if he didn't want to bring his wife around in the old days?"

"He introduced her as his stepsister, Matt. At our post-Christmas party."

"Exactly. And Nadia offered to be Josh's nanny that night. Stepping into Josh's life was clearly orchestrated, Charles. Returning the kids when they did was orchestrated so Josh would need a nanny."

"It had to be Morgan, then. Damn."

"There's something you don't know, Charles." Quietly, Matt told him about Morgan's admission to watching Jacob and Jessie have sex. His face flamed red as he told the story. In a sick way, he kind of understood now how Morgan might have been curious, and not been able to tear his eyes away at the time, especially if the guy harbored some secret fantasy about Jessie. It crossed Matt's mind that the kid likely had all kinds of access to her...six and a half months in a hole in the ground, apparently. But he only took advantage of her on the last morning...

Charles' fork clattered to the table, startling Matt out of that interesting reflection. "We have to call Vancouver, Matt. We need an arrest warrant drawn up for this couple."

"We will," Matt agreed. "But for now, eat your steak. They're not going anywhere."

But he was wrong. Samantha might not see Nadia much anymore, but she still had her on Facebook. Before Matt and Charles had even left the Olde Feathered Hen, she had her phone in hand and was messaging Nadia to tell her *two rich guys were in asking questions about you.* She ended the message with *they thought Morgan was your stepbrother! How weird is that?*

When Nadia got the message, she high-tailed it out of Toronto on the next plane south. Her seatmate was Morgan.

Chapter Eighteen

*J*osh got a call from Nadia that night while she was waiting to change planes in Philadelphia. She was leaning against the wall in a narrow hallway by the women's washroom, watching Morgan in the distance as he stood at a Jugo Juice counter waiting to order.

Josh had both hands in sudsy dishwater when his cell rang. Without scanning the caller ID, he wiped one wet set of fingers on a dishtowel before grabbing the phone and voicing a casual, "H'lo."

Her voice was unsure, low. Hearing the familiar syrupy intonation, though, startled Josh. "I just need to talk," were the words that came over the connection to Vancouver.

After a moment to regain his equilibrium, Josh fought with his emotions before answering. "Nadia, I'm not interested in talking to you." But he didn't hang up.

She reached into her bag of tricks for some fake attempt at an apology. "Josh, I'm sorry about how things went down. I know I got a little shopping happy there for a while."

"Nadia, do you think I care about the money?" he started. "I don't, trust me. I've learned not to care about the money. What I care about is in New York."

"She's not coming back to you, Josh. That train has left the station."

"You don't know that, Nadia, and I'm not really interested in discussing my marriage with you. I'm sorry we got so involved because I know it sucked when I left, but I'm trying to pull my life back together now. And you've been seeing some tennis star, I see, so I'm sure you're doing fine without me."

"If by fine you mean being wined and dined, yes, I'm doing great, Josh. But I want you." The last bit was easy to picture emerging from between the pouty lips, all sad and puffy, accompanied by an insincere shoulder slump.

"I don't think you know what you want, Nadia, unless it's booze, parties and nice clothes. Somehow I think I was just a chess piece for you to move around in some little game. For you to use to claw your way up on your upwardly mobile climb."

Oh, you have no idea, she chuckled inwardly. *But my game is not yet over.*

Out loud, Nadia reverted back to her earlier statement. "I know Jessie is not going back to you, Josh. And do you want to know how I know?"

Josh spit out his response. "If you think your few photographs and X-rated video are going to keep her away, you're wrong, Nadia. Matt figured out that you added your own choice of date to the video. And he knows how to prove to Jessie when the video was created. She's upset now, but once she hears the truth she'll get over it."

"No, honey, that's not why," Nadia purred. "It has nothing to do with the video. That was just, shall we say, something I figured someone with her history would get a kick out of. Oh how the tables can turn, as they say."

"Nadia, I don't know what I ever saw in you. Seriously." Josh was standing with his back to the kitchen sink now, the dishtowel tossed over one shoulder as he held the phone to his ear. "I must have been out of my fucking mind."

"Sex. You needed it. Plus you were in need of a handler, Josh Sawyer. I was only too happy to fulfill that role. Even now, I can taste you. Mmmm." She licked her lips for emphasis. "Where are you getting it from now, big boy?"

The ploy worked. Memories came rushing back, of good sex, and lots of it. A tingle started in Josh's groin, but he fought it. Thinking of the state he was in when the video was made helped fight it. Picturing Jessie watching him in the video…that eradicated the tingle altogether.

"Tell me why you don't think Jessie will come back to me, Nadia. I want to know what great wisdom you have that I don't. And if you say it's got anything to do with Jacob, I'll say you're wrong. They're already not doing so good, according to Matt."

Nadia drove the knife in deep. Her voice was a snarl Josh did not recognize, but for some reason he could picture the blood red nails and vicious darkness in her eyes when she spoke.

"Because she will be dead, that's why."

The resulting sharp intake of Josh's breath gave Nadia a thrill she didn't expect. She savored it as it tickled her toes, legs, the small of her back, the back of her neck.

"Nadia, you're sick. That's a helluva thing to say." But somewhere in Josh's brain was a pounding red light screaming at him to pay attention, that these terrifying words were more than an empty threat from a jilted lover.

"We've tried twice now, Josh. But our wicked game is not over. In fact, as you will see, it is just beginning."

From his post at the kitchen sink, Josh stopped breathing. Pushing himself away from the counter, he counted to ten before he spoke. When he voiced his thoughts, his words were a low, throaty growl. "You've got to be fucking kidding me, Nadia. Tell me you're fucking joking."

"Did I tell you Morgan's not my stepbrother, Josh? He's actually, in fact, my husband. Estranged, to a point, or—well, he was, when you and I—well, he's a ditz sometimes, but he's a good steady beast, so I keep him around. He usually does what I tell him, although he fucked up royally in Montreal. Got a little too close to Jessie over the years, I think. Couldn't drive the knife in quite deep enough. But he told me he got a little fondle in before he sliced open her breast. I'm sure Jacob enjoys running his fingers over the scarred X every night."

Sliding to the floor, his chest heaving with large gasps, Josh bent over and tried not to vomit. *Nadia* and *Morgan* executed the kidnapping of his wife and children? Why?! Out of his mind with grief and anger at his own stupidity in not seeing the truth about her—them—he was wailing before he heard the phone line die.

It was ten full minutes before Josh got his wits together enough to call Matt. When he got through to him, he was not at all surprised to find that Matt already knew the truth. And so did Charles.

None were surprised to find, when the Toronto police raided Josh's Toronto condo, that it was empty.

~ ~

"We are not telling Jessie at this point, Josh." Charles was adamant. "She doesn't need to know someone she trusted with her and the children's lives for the last many years tore her family apart and lit a match above her head."

"And raped her and sliced her and did irreparable damage to our daughter."

"Emily-Grace is coming along well, Josh." Matt was always a calming voice. "She's getting through this."

Charles continued. "We will also not be telling Deirdre, or Jacob, or Charlie, or anyone else at this early juncture. There are warrants out for the arrest of Nadia and Morgan. They will be found. And at least now we know who we are looking for."

"I have to tell Jacob something. He knows I'm looking into the tattoo." Matt was insistent.

"Lie to him."

"I think we should tell Jessie," Josh maintained, his voice rising in pitch as fear of the unknown saturated his every moment. "She needs to know who to stay away from, who to be on the lookout for..."

"Morgan won't get anywhere near her. While the police search for those crazy lunatics, Jessie can finish her film with Jacob and then take a break from work."

"She won't take a break, you know Jessie!" Josh was losing it. "She's likely already got a number of gigs booked, doesn't she, Charles? With Jacob mostly, I'm guessing!" Pacing the floor, his hands were sweaty, his vision cloudy. In short, he was barely hanging on. The reality of Nadia's manipulation and betrayal was too much. Why would she hurt Jessie and his kids this way? Why would Morgan? It didn't make sense. Matt's 'trading up' theory was believable to a point, but there were still holes none of them understood.

Of course, they all knew Nadia had expected Jessie to die in the fire. But what could possibly be gained by partnering with a man as angry—and in such grief—as Josh?

Arnie was at their impromptu meeting, as was Ulysses, which was being held in Charles' Robson Street board room. The elongated room was lined with wood on all four walls, so the men had a private space in which to talk, far from the eyes and ears of Carlotta and Deirdre. Dee was resting at La Casa today after the couple's many hops, skips and jumps around North America of late, travelling to music conferences and checking on the women's shelters Dee and Jessie built.

Now, arms crossed and biceps bulging beneath a charcoal grey hoodie, Arnie spoke up. "Let me work with you, Charles." Twisting around on his torso, he appealed to Ulysses. "I know you're short handed. Short on trust too. I'm with Josh a lot anyways these days. I can help keep an eye out for him and the kids. And if you see fit to send me to New York, you know Jessie trusts me."

"She'll wonder what the hell you're doing working in the Keating camp, Arnie," Charles stated justly. "She knows none of us are thrilled with you procuring a gun for her, swifting her away and keeping that diabolical secret for a year and a half!"

"You need help. I happen to be here. She knows I'm Josh's AA sponsor."

"She will love that you are watching over her children, Arnie." A small smile touched Matt's lips. He felt they were finally making progress, and he couldn't imagine a more trusted man than Arnie to take Morgan's place. Most of the trust was coming from Jessie's opinion of the man, but to Matt, that was the biggest deal of all. He looked at Ulysses and nodded. "Can we get this man some off-the-cuff training in the next few days?"

And so it was that Arnie joined the Keating security team, and showed up in New York with Josh and Jessie's kids after the film she and Jacob were shooting wrapped. Josh, too, was there. No way was he losing an opportunity to talk with Jessie face to face.

At that point, Nadia and Morgan were deep under cover, and no one had a clue when they would surface. Were the men still keeping their eyes open for other threats? Yes. Just in case. But it seemed probable, given Jessie's description of Nadia's tattoo, plus Nadia's call to Josh and Morgan and Nadia's unbelievable lie about their marital status, that Morgan and Nadia were the kidnappers.

In New York, Jessie was supervising the placement of a new baby grand piano when Jacob approached her in the cavernous space and held up his cell. "Matt just called. He's flying in with your ex and the kids tonight. They'll be here around six. Apparently they're bringing someone new who is working security for Josh and the kids. Matt says you'll like him."

"Harumph," was her disinterested answer. Jessie turned back to the new piano, an ebony Steinway & Sons Model S. She managed a smile to the four men who delivered it—legs unattached, to get it in the cargo elevator and upstairs—and one to the man who, now, was running scales in preparation for tuning. None seemed in a hurry to leave.

Studying the new toy, Jacob made his way closer. "It's really something, Jessie. We'll have to write ourselves another mega-ballad."

Scowling, she shrugged his arm away.

"Or not." Jacob pivoted around and slunk off towards the kitchen. About halfway there, he rallied. "Want some lunch?" he tossed over his shoulder. "I'm warming up last night's leftover donair panzerotti."

The thought of food made Jessie's stomach turn. Clutching a hand over her belly, she moped, "No. No food right now."

He stopped moving and, looking back, examined her. "You're a little green there, Jess. Are you okay?"

"Nerves," was her quick one-word answer.

"I bet," thought Jacob as he sucked on one corner of his lip, turned the corner, and dug the panzerotti out of the fridge.

He didn't notice when Jessie snuck by the kitchen's entry, bypassed it, and tucked herself into a position on her knees in front of the toilet. She vomited twice before settling back against the vanity.

"Oh, fuucckk," she moaned, hanging her head. "Just…no, God. No."

Sliding onto the piano's bench seat later, Jessie let her fingers float silently over the keys. Jacob was still in the condo. She wasn't in the mood to play anything he might hear. No, Jessie's inaugural tune on this magnificent new toy would be played some day when he was off to a gig in which she wasn't involved. Then she would play for hours, like she used to do on the baby grand in her Downtown Vancouver condo.

Sighing, Jessie reflected on her life now in New York compared to what felt like the 'good old days' in Vancouver. Sure, New York was exciting, and they were still spending some time with Maggie, which was a mixed joy to Jessie and becoming more of a chore for Jacob, but Vancouver was Charles and Dee, Charlie and Jane, Steve and Sophie, and Josh…and her children full time, not just a few weeks at a time.

Sometimes the sorrow of the past year still got to Jessie. Even now, she often ran her fingers over the scars from the burns, although the small one on her cheek had almost faded. The knife scars on her breast and back were harder to bear; they were someone's signature, a reminder almost of the Deuce McCall days, since they were an X and an O. *Will I always be someone's target,* Jessie wondered? *Will my kids be?* She touched her belly again, and studied the way her hand lay flat against it, remembering the times it stretched and grew to accommodate her growing babies. Another wave of nausea grabbed her, but she fought it, clenching her teeth and willing it to go away.

Voices in the hall distracted her from the weary thoughts. Looking up as Dan, on current security in the foyer, opened the door, Jessie slid off the bench seat of her prized new toy. David's small babble was pure delight. Emily-Grace's silence was deafening. Jessie ran the last few feet and grabbed both of her children at once.

"Oh, you two gorgeous munchkins! You have no idea how much I missed you!" *I can't stand it,* she thought as tears sprang to her eyes. *I cannot stand one minute away from either one of you. I've had enough time away from you.*

Looking up, she caught Josh's eye. As far as she knew, he was seeing Nadia again. And drinking. Hurt flashed over her face before someone she recognized stepped in from the foyer, where Matt had been introducing him to Dan. It took her a minute. Then she jumped on him.

"Arnie! You're the new security? Matt, you made my day!" Then the tears were flowing, but they were happy tears. Cherished parts of Vancouver were now in her home. Suddenly the expansive condo felt fresh and new again, vibrant and sunny.

"I figured we should go over some of the self-protection moves I taught you years ago, Jessie," Arnie was saying, his kind eyes glistening. "Someone's got to get you back in shape after all the ice cream Matt says you eat at Serendipity."

Her upturned lips warmed all of them.

Jessie and Josh helped the kids shrug off their coats and boots while Matt gave Arnie a tour of the space. David was already asking for Jacob. Jessie sent her son off with Emily-Grace's supervision to find him in the family room, where she could hear Jacob chatting with Matt and Arnie. Listening, she watched Josh for his reaction when Jacob and the kids spotted each other. Raucous roars and cheers and much laughter and giggling ensued. She couldn't help but broaden her smile.

Josh tried not to respond in any way, but his gentle smile flipped over and ended up in a frown.

Bastard, thought Jessie. *You deserve that.* Immediately she chided herself with *get a grip on those hormones, Wheeler.*

Noting the little flickers of anger in the eyes he loved, Josh took a steady breath and jumped in. "Jessie, before you keep shooting imaginary bullets at me, can I please just tell you that Nadia's nefarious video is not current?"

"I got that line from Matt already, Josh. And I was almost convinced until I saw references to you and her on Twitter yesterday."

"What? What references?"

"There were tweets. Pictures of the two of you, and they were this week. Jesus, Josh, you have the kids for a few short weeks, could you not stay in? Must you always be running the roads with your gold digging social climber?"

Speechless, Josh held his arms out to his sides. "I am not seeing Nadia, Jessie. Trust me on this one, okay?" Momentarily, he wondered about spilling the beans to her. He wouldn't have to bring Morgan into it...yet...

Josh was saved by Jacob, of all people, who entered the big room carrying Emily-Grace. "Sorry, guys," he said, a little too brightly. "This little girl wants to try Momma's new toy."

"Sure she does," Josh muttered.

Jessie shot him one of the aforementioned bullets. She accented it with a pointed trigger finger, narrowed eyebrows, and a low-toned *ka-pow.*

Josh emitted a slow *ppffffftttt* in response, narrowing his eyebrows right back at her.

For the remainder of the day, Josh did not get a private audience with Jessie, although he got a few minutes with her at the end of the evening while the others stared at his back. Still, it was a pleasant visit overall as everyone played with the children, shared a cozy lasagna and Caesar salad dinner (Arnie was the main chef, with Jacob and Josh as his mostly 'not-speaking-to-each-other' assistants), tucked the kids in bed with stories and songs, and sat around the family room.

There was a ghost in the space, though; Jessie could feel it but she couldn't put her finger on it. It struck her funny that Arnie was now on staff, although she was thrilled. It made sense in the greater scheme of things; in the end she decided with a shiver that everyone was still afraid her Montreal attacker might return, so they needed someone they knew she, at the very least, trusted. Arnie was also Josh's AA sponsor and, in a way, that comforted Jessie too. Angry as she was with Josh, Arnie was an angel to her. Maybe he would, in the end, set her drinking, cheating ex straight.

Jacob enjoyed the guys' company, with the exception of Josh, who cranked his nerves up the wrong way. Jessie's silence and long-term pout over the duration of the film shoot had been hard to take. Today, finally, there was laughter again. Even Josh seemed somewhat relaxed, although Jacob grew increasingly uncomfortable with the way he looked so longingly at Jessie all night, as if he were memorizing her. A few times Jacob saw the two of them connect; their eyes caught, like fireflies captured in opposing thin mesh nets. Glowing and surreal, the two sets of eyes contained a mystique no one in the room understood but that all of them craved, and which Josh and Jessie were powerless to set free.

Eventually one did have to look away from the other, but even Jacob could see it was a hard fought battle to let go, and while they were connected, there seemed to be no real anger, only loss and remorse. It killed Jacob to see them this way, but he still had fight in him. He wasn't giving up yet, hell, he had counted over a hundred days and nights with Jessie now, not including all the times they were separated for work, and he was still counting, despite her reticence to meet him even halfway these days. He hoped having the kids here would help his case some. The little ones loved having him around, and Jacob adored them. Their small faces and rosy cheeks were good little icebreakers.

It was as the fun evening was coming to a close that Josh approached Jessie. They weren't alone, but he wasn't leaving without saying his piece. He spoke quietly, grasping her elbow to prevent her turning away from him.

Looking around first to see if Jacob was watching, Josh inhaled slowly. The guy was indeed watching—he had both hands shoved in his back pockets and a threatening *I bloody dare you* scratched across his stubbly face. Josh sent him a hard look back—*take a fucking hike, Ryan,* but Jacob planted his feet firmly and refused to move.

Jessie spied Jacob watching them too. She swallowed, and blinked confused tears back at Josh.

"Look Jessie, I am telling you the truth, okay?" Josh kept his voice low. "Nadia is long gone. You have to trust me on this. The whole Twitter thing is bullshit. It's someone's idea of fun, of gossip mongering. You know all about that. And I'm not drinking. Ask Arnie."

She yanked her elbow free. "I don't know what to believe anymore, Josh."

Josh's back was to Jacob. He took a chance and whispered, "You mean about Jacob."

"I mean about everything." Forcing her eyes to stay locked on him instead of scooting over to Jacob, who would then instantly know for certain, instead of just speculating, that he was the subject of this conversation, Jessie trembled and willed Josh to understand.

"I get it, Jessie. I do. But some things have changed."

At that, she blinked again. "What do you mean some things have changed? I know something's going on Josh, but—"

"No, no," he backtracked quickly. "I just mean with us. Time has changed things." The nerve on his cheek twitched. Clenching her jaw, Jessie shifted her weight to one foot and crossed her arms.

He tried again. "Emily-Grace's picture. You wrote on it. Always and forever, like we always said."

"I was delirious. I did that the day I moved to New York. When you were fucking Nadia."

"You weren't angry at me at Emily-Grace's party, Jessie. Matt told you the video was manipulated to appear recent. Why are you so mad now?"

Peeking over at Jacob, who was temporarily distracted by a wise Matt— *remind me to thank Matt later*—Jessie jumped in with both feet, sucking in a bottomless Yoga breath first.

"You saw a semi-nude photo of me, taken when I was much younger and stupider. You never saw any of my films, and I'm glad you didn't. But I got to see you, drunk and out of control, fuck some young girl and your girlfriend at the same time, and then collapse in tears afterwards. The memory is fresh, Josh, and although I now understand where it's coming from, where you were coming from, and how long ago it was made, it still sucks." She watched Josh fade and shrink in front of her before she motored on. "Add to this, me making a film over the last three weeks with Jacob—a love story, mind you, with a decent spattering of sex and a very liberal director—and I am feeling a little displaced. A lot displaced. I thought I knew what I wanted. I thought I wanted you, until Nadia resurfaced and reminded me how terrifying and lonely it was when you were with her. And how much you didn't want me."

Shifting her stance again, Jessie spit her last few words out at him, again fighting an attack of nausea that left her slightly hunched over and eyeing the nearest washroom, which was just off the main hall. "Jacob keeps reminding me you're always going to be a flint waiting for a spark, and I'm starting to think he's right. Because, Josh, since you—apparently, so you say—sobered up, he has now become someone I've been missing since before we even got together, and that hurts too." Finishing strong, Jessie melted as she threw out recklessly, "Sometimes I think I just want to go away again, so everybody can be happy without me!"

Angry tears welled up in her eyes, but she valiantly swiped them away. She was spitting out the words in a low tone, so no one else could hear what she was saying, but it was clear to the assembled men in the room—from her body language—that the words were potent. Also abundantly clear was Josh's hunched posture, telegraphing that what she was telling him hurt to hear.

He shook his head. "You believed in me before."

"Call me young and naïve."

"I don't buy that. And I don't buy your shtick about everyone being happy without you. Been there, done that, Wheeler. Bought that truck and decided I hated it. In case you haven't noticed."

"What I've noticed, Josh, if you want the truth, is that I'm scared now. I want my family back, but I'm fucking scared of what I will probably lose if it doesn't play out the way I want it to."

"So it's safer to keep Ryan than risk losing everything, is that it? Never knew you to be one to play the safe stocks on the market, Jess. You've always been a risk taker."

"Well maybe that's my problem, Josh. I am not so bloody damn interested in taking too many more risks. I have scars from burns, I have scars from some sicko knifing me, and my insides are so fucking scarred I can barely breathe. And I'm still scared of the asshole out there who seems to get a charge out of burning and cutting me. Provided that's even the same sick person, may I add! I don't want to think anymore, and I am so bloody damn tired of missing you, and thinking about missing Jacob…that I miss myself." Jessie thumped her chest to accentuate the point, while Josh held his breath.

Nadia's vicious threat was suddenly running through his head.

She'll be dead.

"I don't know what to tell you, Jessie, except there are things at play here you don't understand. Someday you will, but not tonight. And tonight is obviously not a good night for me to plead my case. But I beg you, don't shut me out. Please." He grasped her elbows, both this time, then bent forward and brushed his lips across her forehead. One of Josh's hands rose quickly to erase a lone, trickling tear. He paused and searched the sad eyes before wheeling around, being careful to avoid Jacob's furious stare as he did so.

Josh and Arnie were going to Josh's usual hotel down Madison Avenue for the night. Dan would crash in a room at Jessie and Jacob's condo; Matt was on hall duty until Dan came back on at eight. Everyone was quiet as they waved their goodnights.

Sliding into bed by Jacob later, Jessie didn't hesitate to wrap an arm around his chest as he lay on his back in their big bed.

"Is that a good sign?" he whispered to her. Lately she had been less than forthcoming with any affection for him.

"I was missing you," she murmured. "I just need to feel you, Jacob. Your skin."

"I was missing you too," he said in response, staring at the ceiling and wondering what had changed. Hoping it was something…well…permanent. Relaxing noticeably, he smiled at her. "Sure is good to have the kids back. They bring so much light to this big place."

He felt her small smile even as she yawned. "So do you, babe. So do you. I love you, Jacob. 'Nite."

They didn't make love that night, but it was okay. Both were tired from the late night as well as the emotional angst wrought by Josh's appearance in their home.

As Jacob drifted off to sleep, he dreamed of the very real possibility that he could have Jessie in his arms forever. A wide smile sent him off to dreamland when the additional thrill of maybe having more children to raise with love and joy played across the slideshow in his mind.

As Jessie drifted off to sleep, she thought of Josh, and his rather strange comment about things she had yet to understand.

Her night visions were colored with the harsh *clomping* of her captor's big boots as they rushed overhead in the Langley house. Counterpoint to that distressing memory were the drips and *swoooopps* of carelessly tossed liquid, and the acrid smell of gasoline that accosted her nostrils with fury and fear.

She woke quaking at the lighting of a match; its quick *ssshhffffft* flare suddenly morphing into a knife slicing through her back.

Chapter Nineteen

"*E*ither you end this thing or I will."

Nadia was adamant; her wrathful stance echoed that fact. She was standing with her feet apart, in designer jeans and expensive leather boots. A red cashmere sweater draped itself tightly over her hips and bust, revealing the top of the D in her breast tattoo.

"It's already over, Nadia. May I remind you we're in hiding in godforsaken Timbuktu, if you haven't noticed."

"There are worse places in the world than Houston, Morgan." Resting a finger lightly on a bronze cowboy figure in their luxurious hotel room, Josh came to mind. Nadia well remembered the day he knocked a similar bronze to the floor of the *Wyatt Boys'* set, in a frantic display of anger and sorrow. Josh, in whose body she reveled…whose company she desired, whose heart she craved.

"We can't hide forever, Nadia. They're looking for us now. We're a big blonde white guy and a gorgeous East Indian. They won't be long in finding us."

"We won't go outside together, Morgan. We're fine until we sort this out."

"What's there to sort out? We turn ourselves in, we go to prison for a few years, it's done. We move on."

"A few years? Hmmpph! Consider our lives over if we turn ourselves in, Morgan. Kidnapping, attempted murder…" The sensuous eyes blistered.

"You need to get help, Nadia. You need therapy to get over the loss of our son—"

"Stop!" Covering her ears with her hands, Nadia dropped her body down

148

against a sea of pearl-blue cushions on a wide taupe chaise, and hummed until her husband stopped talking. But as soon as she removed her hands, he started again, which set off the old anxiety in an almost unmanageable belly twist.

"You can't avoid him forever, Nadia! Darin walked this earth at one time. He laughed, he played, he loved, and we loved him back. He was here and now he's gone. It fucking sucks, but that's life. It's our life. We lived it, we're still living it, although parts of us died with him, but we have to go on living. We can't keep pretending he didn't exist!"

"I can do whatever the hell I want, Morgan." From the deep chaise, legs now tucked to the side, Nadia faced her husband. He was pacing the room, trying to find a way out of what seemed an impossible situation. "And right now what I want is to nudge my way back into Josh Sawyer's bed. We agreed— you and I can still see each other, like we did before. You'll get your bit on the side. Josh can provide us the luxuries we deserve."

Incredulous, Morgan stopped moving and waved his arms around. "Like this? This fancy hotel room that's sucking us dry? Josh is not coming back to you, Nadia. He did his stint at rehab, he's staying sober, and he's got hope again. Yeah, you broke him, but he fought his way back and he deserves to live his life again without your fucked up mind fucking with his! He wants his wife back, Nadia. He wants his family back."

"I want his family, Morgan. I lost mine, and I want his. And the only way I am going to get that free and clear is to eliminate Jessie! Think about it, Morgan. If what you say is true, and he still loves her and wants her back, he will break again if she dies."

"He knows what's up now, Nadia, you sick bitch. If Jessie dies, he'll know it's us who killed her! What in God's name makes you think he wouldn't? What part of your brain can't compute that simple fact?!"

"We'll make it look like it wasn't us. We'll frame someone else! That's how!"

"We are not Gods, Nadia. We are not smart enough to execute a crime like that. Even if we were, I don't want to. I don't want any more involvement in your wicked game. I'm done. I want you. I want you because you are the mother of my son. Because I know how much you hurt. But you need to get help. And we need to turn ourselves in. There's nowhere left to run."

"I will not be turning myself in, Morgan. You do what you need to. I'll do what I need to."

Watching her, Morgan understood the level of pain driving his wife to make her appalling choices. He understood because he'd lived it too, the nightmare of watching his child fade until Darin no longer had the strength or desire to lift his own much-loved toys. Morgan knew the heartache of burying a child who was only just beginning to live. He, like Nadia, now watched happy families—at the mall, or on their way to school—while consumed with a debilitating sadness. It drove him nuts that some of the parents didn't seem to appreciate their children, or each other, for that matter. But Morgan knew Jessie and Josh did. They were a couple so deeply in love *before* that their children couldn't help but be cherished and adored. Now what did they have…a traumatized daughter, and a new history of painful addiction to drive them apart. Bi-coastal living where their children were shipped back and forth like merchandise. Sadness, despair, pain. All because of Morgan and Nadia.

Disgusted with his own inability to see a way out of this mess, and whipped by his despicable participation in the breakdown of Josh and Jessie's love story—for a wife he knew was motivated by a debilitating pain that caused a dissociative fracture somewhere in her heart and brain—Morgan slumped down onto a sofa.

"You're on your own, Nadia," he told her heatedly. "I can't do this anymore. I thought I could, for you. But I can't."

He waited for her to come to him, like she would have in the old days, or to call him to her. But she didn't. Instead, the woman with whom Morgan once shared a beautiful soul-love turned her head away. She let him rise from the sofa and stare wordlessly at her before he turned on his heel and stormed away.

When the hotel room door slammed behind him, Morgan didn't look back.

Chapter Twenty

Jessie wasn't feeling any better at the end of the month, when she and Jacob were joining the *Mystic Nights* cast for a reunion concert at 'The Theater at Madison Square Garden.' Josh once again had the kids, only this time it was Charles and Dee who had flown to New York to pick them up and supervise their transport back to Vancouver, which made it easier for Emily-Grace to adapt to the change and leave her tearful mother.

Michael and Kelly flew in for rehearsal the night before, and joined Jacob and Jessie for a catered dinner at the Madison Avenue condo afterwards. Matt was there too, happy to have time with his busy brother, who was thriving under Kelly's devoted affection and their shared love of music.

He asked about their upcoming schedule so he could sort his time between their camp and Jessie's.

"Dragon woman Martinique has us booked for the next two years already," Kelly huffed.

"And that's a problem because…?" Jacob queried with a grin. "Ch-ching, Kelly Kelly."

"It's Kelly Reilly, still," she mouthed off to him. "Or if you prefer, Kelly Reilly Kelly." She winked, and her eyes twinkled. Forking up a bite of spinach and avocado salad, she added, "It's a problem because we would like to get pregnant. My man has finally agreed to trying for a baby. That'll change things."

Frowning, Jessie eyed Kelly, and then let her eyes drift over to Jacob, who was seated across from her at the long modern rectangular table. He noticed her lingering gaze on him, but when Jessie realized he was clueing in, she quickly looked away.

"Huh," he thought, his heart suddenly leaping at the thought that maybe Jessie would be open to the two of them trying for a baby of their own. After all, the whole 'reconciliation-with-Josh' thing didn't seem to be going so great. Lately, Jessie seemed to be coming back to her old cuddly self, although she was still quiet and restrained, most times.

"Jessie seems to manage okay with the kids and work," Michael was saying, laying a hand on his wife's thigh. "We'll sort it out when the day comes."

"And you still don't have a nanny, Jessie?" Kelly asked without thinking.

"Hmmm. Josh did. But when the bitch ended up in his bed, the dynamic kind of changed, Kelly. Somehow I think the kids were no longer her priority. Or his, for that matter," she muttered.

Matt tensed, and the table got quiet. Jacob's eyes dimmed, and he held his beer mid-flight for an extended pause.

With a callous touch, Jessie finished her thought. "I wouldn't suggest you go that route. Or else don't hire a nanny with a voluptuous body and bedroom eyes." Glancing at the shocked faces around her, she shrugged. "When I need to, I hire a sitter for an event. Dee's assistant Pam has a list of gals she trusts."

"Or, like, when we shot the film, Sawyer kept the kids an extra week." Jacob, who hoped he sounded helpful, exaggerated the *we*.

Pointing a fork at Jessie, Michael jumped in. "I remember when you were shooting *Mystic*, Deirdre was around a lot."

"Yeah, and I wasn't there all the time, so it made it easier. Jacob helped then…and now…" Jessie drifted off.

"Mmmm, you guys are adorable together. Any plans to make this a permanent arrangement?" Smiling slyly, Kelly caught Jessie's eye and sent her a *'good-on-ya-girl'* wink.

Her fork halfway to her mouth, Jessie paused. She set it down and telegraphed *'careful'* back to Kelly.

"What?" Kelly asked, as Michael gently squeezed her thigh in warning. Matt had versed him on the ongoing tension and grief that still seemed to be plaguing Jessie where Jacob was concerned.

Annoyed, Jacob piped up. "I have to convince her to get a divorce first, Kelly."

Mizz *'I-have-no-social-filter'* Reilly was all over that one. "So do it, Jessie. What's the holdup?"

Now, Jessie downright glared at Kelly. "Ask Jacob. He knows."

Michael and Matt exchanged glances as Kelly *humphed* and stared at Jacob. "So?" she asked outright, tossing her long blonde mane.

Shoulders slumping, he stared across the table at Jessie and managed, "Do we have to do this every time, Jessie?"

"Do what, Jacob? Have me remind you where I stand on the whole divorce issue?"

"What? You don't want a divorce?" Kelly squished her eyebrows together in confusion. "Why the hell not? You and Jacob have been living out of each other's pockets for years now. Seems as obvious to me now as it did when I first met the two of you."

"What's that old saying?" Jacob started, ignoring Matt's silent warning. "'You can't have your cake and eat it too.' The thing is, 'ole Jessie here does. Little bit of princess syndrome, maybe. Thinks she can have it all." Screeching back his chair, Jacob stood, swiping his plate off the table and heading towards a gray plastic high-sided tray the caterer had left for dirty dishes. Wheeling around, he met Jessie's hurt eyes. "It's true, isn't it Jess? Or should I say, Your Highness?"

Jessie's fork clattered to the table. "A divorce isn't going to change anything, Jacob. It's a piece of paper."

"Sure it would. It would mark an ending, Jessie. And a new beginning. For us. For you and me." He stood at the far counter, ankles crossed and one hand on a hip, leaning a bit sideways, tense.

"New beginnings, huh? After Emily-Grace's birthday party, you were packing up."

"Things changed. You saw the light, courtesy of a porn video starring your husband."

"And why would that bother me?" she lied, as Kelly and Michael froze at the sudden frost crystallizing the air. "I'm well acquainted with the sins of the flesh, Jacob, having made a few such films of my own back in the day. Oh, and pretty much one recently with you, in fact, as Matt here can attest to."

Jacob's eyes flicked curiously to Matt, who buried his head in his hands as his cheeks bloomed an interesting shade of red.

"Well, this is entertaining," Kelly mused lightly, pouring herself a third glass of wine and wondering why Jessie was choosing to abstain. "Would you two like to take this outside? I insist. Your childish quibbling's making my indigestion act up."

Instead, Jacob ignored her and glared at Jessie. He veered a little sideways in the hopes of gaining some support from the men at the table, and maybe from the un-filtered Kelly as well. "He's a walking time bomb, Jessie. He will always be a walking time bomb."

Kelly didn't disappoint. Her candid response, fuelled by mucho wine as she licked her lips, was, "Yes. But I suppose he's Jessie's time bomb, honey. He's her husband. And at this juncture in time, may I remind you that you are not."

"Jesus. Thanks Kelly. Always on my side, aren't you? You're just such a delight to have around." With that, Jacob stormed out of the room, both fists clenched.

A few minutes later they heard him tinkling softly away on the baby grand. Cocking her ears, Jessie's spirits deflated further when she realized he was playing a new ballad she knew he was writing for her.

Forcing a half-smile in Kelly's direction, she watched as her tipsy *Mystic Nights* co-star raised her wine glass.

"Cheers," Kelly toasted. "And may the best man win."

Biting her bottom lip, Jessie slid her eyes over to Matt, beside her, who was slowly recovering from Jessie's earlier rather off-color comment.

Looking up, he searched her face. Like Jacob, Matt knew something had changed in Jessie's mind even after he briefed her on the truth about the dates of Josh's sex video and photographs. But Matt wasn't sure exactly *what* had changed. Josh was doing well, according to Arnie, finally being a good father to his kids again, and slowly earning Emily-Grace's trust. Drinking was not an issue, and he had just been cast in a new Coen Brothers film. Maybe Jessie's heartache was easing as she slipped further and further into Jacob's arms and heart. Maybe Josh was going to lose this battle and, thus, the war.

Or maybe it's the fear, he thought. *Maybe she is living in fear again, after the attack in Montreal. Maybe we should tell her we know who the culprits are, so she can relax and know the search has been narrowed down to two people. Maybe that fear is keeping her isolated and alone, afraid to make a move that will change her future once again.*

Jessie seemed to know what he was thinking. She, like Jacob, screeched back her chair and left the table.

They heard her pad quietly out to the large front room. Jacob's playing grew a little more confident and sure. Soon, a guitar joined in.

Kelly went to the kitchen entry, where she could clearly see the two across the room—Jacob brushing the ivories and singing softly, and Jessie with her back to him on the piano bench, accompanying him on the Gibson he bought her, singing harmonies.

Matt and Michael joined Kelly. They watched the private concert in silence.

"Does Josh have a chance at getting her back, Matt?" Kelly asked, suddenly sounding sober.

"I thought he did…now I'm not so sure," answered Matt, remembering the loving way Jacob had intimately touched Jessie on the film set that day a while ago, and the sensuous manner in which she had responded to him, like they were in their own special world.

Regarding Jacob and Jessie now, Kelly voiced her own opinion on the subject. "I'm not so sure either," she said, sighing against Michael's chest. "At least…I know who I would choose. I would choose the guy whose soul touches me with music."

"That so?" Michael wrapped his arms around his wife's waist.

"Yes. That's so."

Jacob's ballad rose to the high ceilings and beyond, drifting out of the arched windows of the capacious space he shared with the woman he loved. As his voice floated with the music, with Jessie's sweet harmonies anchoring and lifting his lyrics, he prayed the Gods would hear his musical call, and let Jessie be his forever.

Chapter Twenty-one

'The Theater at Madison Square Garden' was a 5500 seat venue. A modern affair, it was a more intimate option for performers than the expansive arena. The show was sold out tonight—excited concertgoers were taking their seats under a dramatic ceiling lined with crisscrossed white lights. As *Mystic Nights* fans buzzed over their programs, one of the stars meant to shortly take the stage was on her knees white knuckling her dressing room's toilet.

Dammit Jacob, she was cursing between spasms, *your baby's sure having a different effect on me than Josh's two. And I'm not sure I like it.*

Jessie was rarely sick with her first two pregnancies. This child, or perhaps the nerves surrounding its conception, was making her very ill.

Not that the pregnancy had been confirmed by a physician, at this point. But it seemed likely she was expecting. Given Jessie's rather recent experiences carrying Emily-Grace and David, the subtle body change memories were fresh.

Groaning when she heard a knock on the dressing room door, which was followed by the unwelcome sound of the handle turning and the door opening, she grabbed a tissue and tried to pull herself together.

But her body wasn't done.

As she heaved unmercifully, Matt called out to her. "Jessie?"

His perfectly appointed gelled hair appeared around the corner. Finally, her belly seemed to settle enough for Jessie to stand. Grabbing her friend's proffered hand, she eased herself up off the floor and faced him, wiping her mouth with a tissue as she did so.

Before Matt had a chance to speak, Jacob popped in, as animated and excited as usual before a big show. One look at Jessie and he settled dramatically, his eyes closing over a little. "Were you sick?" Inside, he said *again?*

"Nerves," she whispered, meeting his eyes for just a fleeting moment.

He hesitated first, and then nodded. "Okay. Nerves, then."

Jessie shifted her body so the doorframe could hold her up. "You need something, Jacob?"

"Yeah. We need to do our vocal warm-up."

"Give me ten, okay babe? I just need to settle my stomach a bit first."

"You gonna be okay, Jess?"

Petulantly dropping both arms to her sides, she slunk lower and guffawed at him. "Do I fucking look okay?"

Matt ducked his head.

Glancing at him, Jacob started to back out of the dressing room. "I'll be back in ten," he announced with false bravado as the old hurt puppy dog look danced over his unhappy eyes.

When he was gone, Matt studied Jessie. "Nerves, huh?"

She shoved a forefinger in the corner of one eye to keep it from leaking, stared at the toes of her boots, and laughed sarcastically. "I'm fucked if I do, and fucked if I don't, Matt."

"Josh or Jacob, I assume you mean."

"You assume correctly. And once again, Matt, you are the first to know. Congratu-fucking-lations."

"Jacob will be happy about this, Jessie."

"Well, that makes one of us, Spike. Out of three, may I add."

Pondering the situation, including the immediate need of how to get a woman rather violently overtaken by nausea through a sold out concert, Matt was silent.

"Say something, Matt. Please." Jessie watched him thoughtfully rub a finger and thumb over his chin.

"Well," he sighed. "I suppose I can at least say some things are making sense to me now. Like why you suddenly did an about-face when considering reconciling with your husband."

Sarcasm edged her voice. "Yeah, well, glad I could clear the fog up for you, Matt." Rotating her nauseous body 90 degrees so she could despondently lean her head against the washroom door, Jessie appealed to a wisdom she knew she could count on. "Matt...how the hell do I take Jacob's baby away from him? Even if Josh did agree to raise the kid. Jacob is...he's so great with Emily-Grace and David. He needs this baby. Raising this kid would be a dream for him. A child of his own?"

"Yours. Your child. With you."

"Yes." Jessie wiped a new tear away. "I think this is the universe's way of telling me to stay with him, Matt."

"I think the universe needs to get its shit together, Jessie. Soon. You're on in twenty minutes. This new quandary will wait. Is there anything I can get you?"

"Yeah. A miracle. Got any of those in your back pocket, hon?" At that useless request, Jessie padded over to her bag, which had been hastily deposited in the middle of a nearby sofa. Rummaging around in it, she eventually found some crackers, which, with a sly grin, she held up to Matt. "Recognize these?"

His laugh was spontaneous and authentic. "Julie still can't stand the sight of them."

"Your old advice worked. They do help." Silently, she nibbled on one rounded edge. As an absent afterthought, she moaned, "Geez, I hope I can get through this show."

As if on cue, a knock came to the door. Matt leaned back against the make-up counter and crossed his arms. Meeting Jessie's eyes, he raised his eyebrows.

"It's open," she called out, not looking away from him, commanding his lips remain silent while their pre-show visitor was in the room.

When Jessie glanced away from Matt and focused on the door, she gasped. Her young daughter was tiptoeing into the room, one set of small fingers clutching at the side of a gauzy pink princess dress. The other hand tightly grasped singer-dowwy and bawwet-dowwy. Emily-Grace's pretty ball gown was topped with a perfectly jeweled tiara; tiny white silk slippers peeked out from underneath the bottom hem of the glitzy pink dress. Behind her, in his father's capable arms, was the little girl's younger brother, David, adorably showing off a toddler's suit—dress pants, white shirt, dress jacket, and mini Charles Keating cranberry silk tie.

Jessie knelt to face her daughter. "You are so beautiful, sweetheart!" she exclaimed. "You're a princess." Touching the tiara lightly, she smiled, eyes misty. "And you have a real crown. Look at that."

"It's a tee-aih-a, Momma. Not a cwown. Daddy hepped me get dwessed. He thought you would think I wook pwetty." Glowing, Emily-Grace waited rapturously for her mother's approval.

Jessie looked up at Josh. He was searching the corners of the room, for Jacob, she knew. When he met her eyes, she sent him utter gratitude on an invisible wire. He smiled, the tops of his cheeks turning a little pink.

"Emily-Grace, your daddy has very good taste. You are a lovely princess." Holding her daughter's small hand in hers, Jessie couldn't help but wonder if Jacob's child was a boy or a girl.

"Gwammie did my heah." Emily-Grace touched the tiara. "She had to use a duckie one to hold it in."

"Ah, I see, she did indeed," Jessie agreed, noting the tiny duck hair elastic. "Smart Grammie. I know those ducks are your favorites, honey. That was nice of Grammie to let you wear one with your tiara."

Still holding her daughter's hand, she stood, and bent forward to give her son a hug and a cuddle, but Jessie didn't take him from his father's arms. "Thank you, Josh," she breathed, "for bringing the kids all this way to see me perform tonight. Are you meeting Dee?"

He gestured towards the hall. "She's just outside. Emily-Grace wanted to wish you a good show."

"Did she."

"She did."

"Mmmmm."

"So did David, actually."

"He can barely talk."

"He can say that. Tell Momma good show, David."

The toddler laughed and clapped his hands over his mouth. But he very clearly said, "Good show," to his mother, in his little boy voice, which delighted Jessie.

"And his father?" she asked, melting in Josh's eyes and already seeing the heartache she knew would appear the second he found out about her pregnancy.

Unable to speak, Josh let his eyes wander over Jessie's wardrobe for the night, which Kelly'd already expressed her disapproval over, it being the usual jeans and, tonight, a casual silk navy bandana-print halter top.

"Stop," Jessie whispered, reaching beyond her son's legs to graze the backs of her fingers over Josh's stomach, in her usual favorite spot just above his belt. "Don't look at me like that."

"I need to," he murmured, eyes glistening. "I need to look at you like this, Jessie. And I need you to talk to me."

"I can't…right now," she replied honestly, wiping one clammy hand on her thigh. "I have a show, Josh. Soon, in fact." Swallowing, she tossed her bouncy show time curls, aware that Matt was still in the room, albeit she figured rightly he was distracting himself with something on the counter. "Are you staying?"

Josh busied himself for a second adjusting his son's tie. He fingered it while saying to Jessie, "I can't. It kills me, watching you on stage. Without Jacob and…with him. It's more than I can handle, Jessie."

"Okay." She nodded, trying to accept defeat, her heart sinking. "I hear you. I get that." Jessie added a plea to the end of her acceptance. "Don't go drinking, okay? I know Arnie's going to be in the theater watching the kids from a side aisle. You'll be on your own."

"No more drinking, Jess. I'm done with that. I'll be okay."

"Will you?"

Both of them paused then. Jessie's fingers were now looped over his belt buckle, one hand on the belt and the other on her son's back. The old intimacies seemed impossible to break. Reaching his free hand down, Josh rubbed her fingers. "Please, can't we talk?" he asked again, unable to meet her eye but relishing the feel of the warm hand under his. When he did peek back up at his wife, he was pleading, the somber gaze flecking from dark to light and back again.

Jessie steeled herself for battle, both in her heart and for the sake of his. "It's not going to happen, Josh," she breathed finally. "Us. You told me a while ago there were things I had yet to understand. Well, I'm in the same boat now. There are things now that you don't understand. That just threw a big ki-bosh over any chance you and I had of trying to work things out."

Josh glanced quickly at Matt, questioning. Matt overheard the comment and met Josh's eyes. From behind Jessie's back, he shook his head. *No. I didn't say anything.*

Josh let his gaze drift back over to the mother of his babies. "Just let him go, Jess. Please. Just let him go. We'll be okay, you and me. I'll be okay. I swear."

"I can't," she lamented, running her hand up and down his stomach without even realizing she was doing so, landing back at the belt. "I can't let him go. I'm sorry."

Josh nodded then, forcing his tender scrutiny of her to move elsewhere. Yielding, eyes clouding over, he made a valiant attempt at enduring a truth he was unprepared to hear.

At that moment, David decided to lean forward and drop into his mother's arms.

She held him tight, removed her hand from where it was looped over her estranged husband's belt, and lightly brushed a finger over her baby's cheek. "He looks so much like you," she said softly. "Like his daddy." She was thinking about Jacob again, and the new baby they would raise together. If he was a boy…well, maybe he would have those beautiful cobalt eyes. Letting her brooding gaze float back up to Josh, Jessie studied his eyes. They were a deep chocolate brown. Jacob's baby, whether it be a boy or a girl, couldn't possibly resemble him. Choking a little on that certainty, she leaned forward and tenderly pressed her lips to Josh's.

"I'm sorry," she said again, and turned away from him.

After a moment he pushed the door open. In a voice that was cracked and worn, Josh called out to Emily-Grace. "C'mere sweetheart. Let's find Grammie so you and David can go with her and watch Momma make beautiful music, okay?"

Jessie bent and kissed her daughter, and then handed David back to his father. "I'll see you later," she said to the children, sending them off with a floating kiss and avoiding Josh's sorrowful gaze altogether. Unable then to keep the tears from coming, she spun around and melted into Matt's welcoming embrace.

Hesitantly, Jacob made his way back inside. Surprised and concerned to find Jessie in Matt's arms this close to show time, mascara running down her cheeks, he touched her back and whispered her name.

"Jessie?"

Turning to him, for strength Jessie let her fingers dangle in Matt's warm hand while she spoke. Drawing up her shoulders, she said, "I'm going to ask Josh for the divorce, Jacob. It's time."

His silence filled the corners of the room with uncertainty. Muffled sounds from the hallway seemed louder than they should be—deafening, even.

Filling in the blanks, Jessie finally stated definitively, "You and me, babe. We can do this, right? We can make it work?"

Blinking, confused, Jacob struggled with what to say. "I thought if you wanted to stay with me you'd be happy, Jess. Not holding another man's hand, melting into a puddle." He started backing away. "Not dissolving in tears over letting Josh go."

"Huh? What'd you think, Jacob? I'd be jumping up and down and ordering fucking champagne? You know how I feel about him. You know."

"Yeah," he admitted darkly. "You never forget to remind me." Pausing at the door, he added, "You might want to call Miranda in." Touching a spot below his eye, he stammered, "You've got a little too much joy running down your cheeks."

Chapter Twenty-Two

Scanning the audience from the side of the stage, Matt spotted Charles and Dee and the kids seated in the wing by stage right—so, in audience terms, the left side facing the stage. By his still posture, it seemed David had drifted off to sleep on Dee's lap. Beside her grammie, Emily-Grace, sporting her glittering princess tiara, was already spellbound. Glancing to the right of the family, Matt was relieved to see Arnie, in an uncharacteristic black blazer and tie, ensconced quietly in a side aisle, standing sentinel by the wall, hands folded in front of him.

Eyeballing him, Matt spoke into a lapel mic. "Test, Arnie. Can you hear me?"

Arnie fumbled a little as he searched for the button to activate the mic. "Yeah, Matt, all's good here. Little guy's snoring up a storm."

"Ulysses, you there?"

"Lobby's clean, Matt. Few stragglers, that's all."

"Susanne?"

"My side of the lobby's fine. A drunk getting escorted out by theater security, no biggie."

"Dan?" Matt asked.

Outside Jessie's dressing room, Dan's deep voice came through the ear buds. "Good to go. Jessie will be on the move any minute."

Shortly, the big Scandinavian accompanied his charge to the stage.

Avoiding Matt's eye, but touching him lightly as she passed, Jessie accepted a standing ovation from the audience before she even made it to her microphone. She waved, trying to make her smile meet her eyes, but it was an impossible task tonight.

Jacob was already on stage, having done a few numbers with other *Mystic Nights* cast. Now, he was seated on a stool with his hollow-body guitar, waiting for Jessie to signal him so he could count her in. Emotionally, he was no longer into the show tonight. His mind was now muddled, confused. Something was at play in Jessie's world that he simply did not understand. Could she be pregnant? Was it possible? Or was it just all the nerves from the past catching up with her, in a PTSD sort of way? For sure her birth control got messed up after the incident in Montreal...and he and Jessie hadn't been communicating much lately. So really, he had no clue.

But tonight Jacob had to pull it together, for both of them AGAIN because she was in her hurt place—*surprise, surprise,* he thought sarcastically—and, heck, someone had to steer the ship. Although he was getting damn tired of it. *One of these days I just want to go along for the ride,* he told himself, then quickly chided himself, because Jacob knew in a lot of ways he'd been doing that all along.

The signal came—a raised hand, only a flicker of eye contact—and he counted her in.

The song Jessie was singing now, on her own, with accompaniment from Jacob and a back-line band that included Christian's gorgeous touch on the keys of a shiny baby grand, was a new song she wrote over the last month. It was a slow song, not exactly a ballad, but more a tale of chaos and confusion, about wanting to float above the clouds to escape, to start again. She did what she always did, and disappeared somewhere deep inside herself, away from Jacob's confused stare, and the audience's hushed rustle, and her own inadequate and muddled feelings. As her voice rose into the song's climax, Jessie's hands floated like the lyrics in the song; when they came down again, they wrapped themselves around the microphone stand, and helped ground her as the lyrics and music faded.

When the magic in that safe place wilted and curled up like a pale pink rose in its slow trek towards a graceful death, she stepped back, unwilling to open her eyes until she had to, choosing instead to hide in the music's power to save her, for the briefest time, from reality and its heartbreak and seemingly ever-present fears.

Jessie put a hand to her belly before she opened her eyes and faced the audience. Jacob straightened when he saw her do it. Twisting a little to look at him then, as the audience rose with another standing ovation to thank her for her ability to mystically transport them to some otherworldly plane, Jessie tried to tell him, through her eyes, that she was committed to him, and to them. She wanted to let him know he shouldn't be afraid, that she would stand tall and be the mother he needed her to be, for their child… for Jacob's child.

But he didn't understand. He didn't have the information he needed in order to understand, yet. He could guess, sure, but…what exactly was she telling him? Her hand was still over her belly. She was divorcing Josh. She was willing to be with him, Jacob. For a baby? Was that why she was letting Josh go, for him? If so…it felt like a trap.

Not for him. For her.

And suddenly Jacob knew exactly why Jessie had collapsed in Matt's arms in the dressing room, and why she was now willing to divorce Josh once and for all. It was because she felt she had no choice. The nausea, the distance… she was pregnant, she had to be, with his child. No way would Josh take her back now. No way would she consider aborting the baby.

So she took the corner she was pushed into. And Jacob was the booby prize.

He had to sing a ballad with her now—their ballad, the number one hit in now more than sixty countries that they wrote together a few days after Jessie left Josh in the first place. Jacob wanted to throw his guitar on the stage and smash it. He swallowed the bitter pill he knew had come his way tonight.

Jessie saw the wild look in his eye, and considered whether he'd finally put two and two together. She wasn't sure, but she knew she had to pull Jacob back to her for the sake of this concert. Turning, she took her guitar from the hands of a technician who dashed on stage with it, and she looked to Jacob to count them in as he always did.

But he sent her a blank look and narrowed his eyebrows. It appeared he was done counting.

She gulped and sent him a confused look before starting. "1, 2, 3, 4…"

Thankfully, he started to play, and she strummed along with him, never losing his gaze despite how much it hurt now to keep it. Their baby was a blessing, no doubt about that. But the child was also now the only thing, in Jessie's opinion, keeping her from her husband. Was she over the sex video? Entirely? Nah. Never. But at least Jessie now understood that it was from a time when Josh was so messed up with grief he couldn't see straight. So she could let that go, at least enough to recognize her husband was hurting and feeling very much alone and unworthy of her love at the time it was made. But this baby...this baby was a wall too big to climb over.

Jacob got through the ballad by losing himself in the music the same way Jessie did. Only this time, neither closed the other off. Instead, they reached inside each other the way they always did, enclosed in their protective bubble, and depended on the lyrics and music and harmonies to sing them home. It worked. Somehow in the chaos and confusion, and the crazed, muddled, complicated feelings, they found each other again, deep in the music's powerful embrace, and in the one word message the song imbued within their souls—hope.

Jacob was angry. Jessie was sad. But the music had the power to heal.

Jessie didn't look away from Jacob until the song was in its dying breaths. When she finally broke away from his gaze, the bubble burst immediately, for her eyes caught a movement along one of the side walls of the theater, near a sconce throwing a dispersed white light. The aisle was not the one where Arnie stood over her children, but the opposite one. The movement was Josh, settling against the wall. Later he would tell her a volunteer—a fan—let him in, with no ticket and no seat. *I wanted to see you play one last time. I needed to say goodbye.*

Raising her head as she strummed towards an ending, Jessie saw Josh standing there alone—hushed, desolate, defeated. He wasn't drinking, but he looked like the same guy who she knew did drink. And it scared her. It was like the light bulb was switching off again. Even from a distance, she knew by his stance that he was empty, that he was done. That his eyes were dark and hurt, just like Jacob's.

And suddenly Jessie wanted to run away again.

Jacob was a victim here, tonight. Josh was a victim. Both were suffering because of her. And she couldn't stand it. Jessie couldn't bear being the cause of their pain.

So when the next song started, and she and Jacob were joined at the front of the stage by Michael and Kelly and a few of the other *Mystic Nights* cast members for an ensemble piece about the sanctity of home and love and family, Jessie only lasted a few bars. Her home and love and family were all messed up. She was a hypocrite, standing up here singing about something she so grandly fucked up, about something she wasn't even sure she was capable of believing in anymore. And now she was bringing a new child into the world to mess up with her crazy version of living.

Backing away from the microphone, she swung her guitar off her shoulders as the others kept playing. Jacob and Michael were on either side of her; they were all standing, sharing mics, singing the popular anthem together. Both saw the panicked look on her face, but they had to continue on. Jessie, however, strode off the stage towards Matt. She practically threw her guitar to a technician, then started running towards her dressing room.

Dan followed her. Matt's job tonight involved eyeballing Jacob on stage, and although Matt wasn't Michael and Kelly's security for this particular concert, he felt responsible for them too. He could also see Jessie's children with Charles and Dee from this vantage point. Likely Jessie was just nauseous again. Tense, he stayed put and waited for Dan to fill him in over the lapel mic.

In her dressing room, Jessie started pacing and trying not to hyperventilate. She was in the throes of an anxiety attack—she recognized the signs, and worked on skills Trudy taught her in order to try to dissipate it. As she counted quickly—panicked, pacing—and slowly regained control of her breathing, her eye caught her cell phone on the nearby counter where she'd left it prior to taking the stage.

A Facebook banner alert caught her attention. Someone wanted her to Friend them. The woman's first name was Nadia.

"No way," she cried to herself. "No fucking way. Fucking awesome timing, Nah-dee-ah."

The FB account was her private page. Rarely did she accept any friend invitations on it, knowing that fans would find her fan page instead. But tonight she grabbed the phone and swiped over the banner. Facebook opened up. Hesitating only for a second, thinking *what are the chances,* in her frazzled state she accepted the invitation.

Seconds later a message came in. *I know you're involved with the Mystic Nights concert but can we talk after? Please?*

"Seriously? Seriously." Staring at the message, Jessie was angry enough at the world and her place in it that she answered with a lie—*I just finished my part in the show. Why?*

I just need to clear the air. So I can move on. Pls.

Fine. Jessie's thumbs flew over the keyboard. *Where? Are you in NYC? I can meet u now.* To herself she breathed, "And I will give you an f-ng piece of my mind." Tears pricked her eyelids as she replayed all the lonely nights picturing Josh with Nadia, and wondering whether she might have had a chance if the woman hadn't butted in on her husband.

The response was swift and decisive. *Central Park, Strawberry Fields Memorial. As soon as you can get there.*

Jessie didn't hesitate. *I can be there in thirty minutes*

C u soon

Fine

Can we talk in private? No entourage

"Huh."

The mood Jessie was in made that answer a clear and concise *Fine*.

Big Dan had already told Matt Jessie was inside her dressing room. But when she rushed past him, throwing her leather aviator coat overtop her halter, he hollered, "Hey, hold up there Jessie," before grabbing her arm and whirling her around to face him. "You're not going anywhere without me with you. What's the rush?"

"Let go of me, Dan. Matt knows sometimes I need my space."

"Not these days, you don't."

"I can't live my life worrying that some sicko is going to knife or kidnap me, Dan! And I've got news for you. If it happens tonight it'll be a goddamned blessing. Let me go."

Staring daggers at him, she tried to shake him off.

As she growled and roughly yanked her arm out of his grasp, Dan reached for the button on his lapel mic.

Eyebrows furrowed in angry flight mode, fists clenched, Jessie was backing up, looking for the right moment to run. The opportunity came when Dan spoke into his mic.

"Jessie's leaving, Matt—she's pissed," sputtered Dan, rather hurriedly. "And she doesn't appear to be open to company."

Whipping around, Jessie bolted.

"The hell she isn't," Matt fumed. "Get down here, Dan, I'll tail her. Arnie, go out the front door, now, see if you can head her off. I'll be right behind you."

"Copy, Matt. Heading her off at the pass." A moment later, Arnie's voice was huffing a little when it came over the mic. "I have eyes. Jessie's running. Give me five, I'll get back to you."

Cursing her for setting such a quick pace, Arnie was grateful for his training as a boxer. Jessie was in great shape, quick on her toes. Despite her adrenaline fueled run, he caught up with her almost immediately.

Slowing, she threw him an angry sideways glance.

"Jessie, if this is the way you normally treat your security, I can't say I'm surprised Matt gets pissed at you. Have a little respect for us old guys, girl!"

"I need some air, Arnie. And some space, which Matt, in fact, has learned to appreciate over the years. And which, if you stick around, you too will learn to give me."

"Tonight's not the night for space, Jessie."

"You know Arnie, for once I am going to say you don't know what the hell you're talking about. This has been a helluva day, and in fact the last year has really kind of sucked. I have never left a show like that in my life. So if you think this is not the night I need space, you've got another think coming."

He was moving backwards now, in front of her, facing her. Storming past him, Jessie quickened her pace again.

Hollering from behind as he, too, stepped up his stride, Arnie's words tried unsuccessfully to hit home. Memories of sending her off on another journey years earlier filtered through his mind. He wondered if Matt was worried that she'd take off like that again. "So things are messed up right now, Jessie, what are you going to do, keep running until you fall off the end of Manhattan?"

"I was thinking of going a little further afield, Arnie. Like I'll maybe head for fucking Ireland this time. I'll fucking swim if I have to."

"Jessie, at some point you've got to stop running. Face your problems like the rest of us!"

Whipping around, she stormed back to him. Poking a finger in his chest, Jessie cried, "You don't know shit about my problems, Arnie! I'll face them any damn way I please!"

"Ah, so this is the spoiled superstar Dan warned me about. At the time I thought he was full of shit. It appears I was wrong!"

Her furious glare would have silenced anyone else, but not Arnie, the angel of Vancouver's Downtown Eastside, who knew from a personal vantage point this woman's shady history and nefarious past.

She was quaking with anger, so he let her speak. "You have a lot of nerve, Arnie. I didn't ask for any of this. I don't want security on my tail tonight, I want to be alone. So in my opinion that actually makes me the exact opposite of a spoiled superstar!"

"I beg to differ, Jessie. I'm out here instead of in there watching your kids! You have threats on your life, so whether you are interested or not, you *need* security, as you damn well know. You know better. Stop running, and either come back inside or let me walk with you. Or behind you, whatever, I can do the 'give the spoiled celebrity her space' thing!"

"I said no! Leave me alone, Arnie! Go! Now! Far the fuck away! And I swear to God, if you call me spoiled one more time—"

Whipping around again, Jessie lit into a full tilt run. Arnie started to speak in his lapel mic but Matt slid to a stop before him.

"Arnie, Dan's at stage right now. He can see the kids. Susanne's in the lobby and Ulysses is alerting the theater's security that the Keating team is suddenly minus two. You and I are following this crazy girl. I hope you're in shape."

"I was missing my usual run today anyway, boss," Arnie replied, somewhat relieved Matt was now beside him, and rather disturbed by Jessie—not by her treatment of him, per se, but by her obvious messed up emotional state.

"Good. Because we can't lose her. Try and keep up."

With that, Matt, who was well accustomed to running with Jessie in the old days, and who had gotten a few runs in with her since starting to work again with the Keating camp, took off ahead of Arnie, although his swanky desert boots proved less than satisfactory for a run on a busy streetscape. Jessie was running in her old brown boots, though, so although she was fast out of the gate, her footwear was slowing her down too. Arnie fared better—he had Nike Trainers on his feet.

Neither man had any inkling of Nadia's surprise appearance in the city. They simply supposed they were following a very upset singer who would, eventually, settle down and wander back to the theater with them.

Jessie didn't look back. She had twenty minutes now to find Nadia, and her curiosity was peaking. What could the woman possibly have to say to her? Not that it mattered. Jessie had a few things to spit right back, one being *enjoyed your video, thanks.*

Growling at the blisters threatening to form on her heels, she dodged a couple of pizza-eating teens wandering down the sidewalk, and moved towards an uncertain future.

Chapter Twenty-three

*J*osh panicked when he saw Jessie back up, swing her guitar over her head, and leave the stage. He saw the fear in Jacob's eyes, too, but Josh had an advantage. He wasn't on stage in the middle of a gig, like Jacob.

He got backstage before Jacob did, but by the time he wormed his way through local security to get there, he was still too late to catch Jessie.

Dan was now pacing near the stage, where he could eyeball Jacob and the children, as per Matt's orders.

After leaving Jessie's empty dressing room, Josh snaked a trail to the stage, thinking that although it was rather unlikely, given her apparent mood, Jessie may have had second thoughts and gone back that way.

Shaking his head, Dan's hasty words fuelled the actor's unease. "You missed her, Josh. She took off like a bat out of hell. Matt and Arnie are both tailing her."

"She'll love that, if she's in the kind of mood I think she's in." Josh bit on a corner of his lip and wondered whether Matt or Arnie would have any luck bringing Jessie back to the theater. He knew she was scheduled for more numbers in the show. Earlier, he'd half thought about going back to his hotel, but he felt like shit and didn't want that distance from his kids, from her, yet.

After listening to a few of the show's opening songs, which gave him time to process what she'd said to him, Josh had decided he wasn't buying Jessie's *it's over, Josh*. He refused to accept that they were done. He needed to see her again, tonight, before he flew back to Vancouver in the morning. Their magic couldn't end. Not after everything...

Glancing towards the stage, Josh noted that the song Jessie walked out on was over now. Raucous applause filled his ears. Not at all surprised, he watched Jacob practically toss his guitar to a tech and stride offstage towards him.

"Where is she?" Jacob growled, knuckles white.

"Slow down, tiger. She's out touring New York City with Matt and Arnie. What, the two of you have a fight before you hit the stage? Some act you got going on there. People watching you sing that ballad might think you're actually in love."

"I'm not in the mood, Josh. She's in the next number."

"You obviously don't know our girl that well, Ryan. Jessie took off. And by the look on her face I can say from experience she's not in a hurry to come back. You and your little Miami sunshine gang might want to improvise the rest of this show."

"Oh, for Christ's sake." Jacob leaned back against the wall in the hallway and glared at Dan. "What's Matt got to say?"

"He's saying he wished to hell he had his Nikes. Josh is right, Jacob. She's after some privacy, and she appears to intend to get it."

"Lovely." Thrusting his chin out and crossing his arms, Jacob looked up at Josh to find him staring. "What."

"You oughtta be dancing, Ryan. Not leaning against the wall looking like you just lost the Olympics."

"And why, pray tell, is that, Sawyer? Because Jessie's finally asking you for a divorce? That's supposed to make me happy?"

As his face fell, Josh's heart hit the floor. He wasn't sure how much more he could take here, tonight. A divorce…well, that was not mentioned earlier, in the dressing room. If it were true, if Jessie intended to go there, well…it would be pretty damn final.

Closing his eyes, Josh migrated away from Jacob. After a moment in which he ordered himself to breathe, to stay cool, he forced himself to look back over his shoulder at the depressed musician holding up the wall.

"One of us ought to be happy," he said to Jacob, confused at the guy's sunken demeanor. "And it sure as hell ain't me."

"She just walked out of our show, Josh. In the middle of a goddamned song! A song about family, and love, and good times, in case you didn't bother listening to the lyrics. On what level do you think she's happy about choosing me?"

Josh swallowed. "She wouldn't stay with you if she didn't want to, Jacob."

"Now who doesn't know Jessie?" Hoisting himself away from the wall, Jacob ran his fingers through his hair. "I'm prepared anyway, Josh. Just so you know. To be with her, I mean, whether I'm still second prize or not. You fucked up too many times and she knows you're a risk. And I want her. I waited a long time to get her back after Scotland, and I fucking want her. But it still sucks that she wants you more, you know? Especially because you're such a loser. It sucks."

Josh was silent, but his heart quickened as he digested Jacob's words. *She wants me more? Still?* He wondered what changed, why she was choosing Jacob. Was it still that damned video? *But I'm sober now. I can be the better man.*

Jacob had more to say. "I was leaving, you know. The day she got that video. I was packing. It was after Emily-Grace's birthday party. I saw you with her, touching her, and the way she looked at you was the way she always looked at you. Looks, I should probably say. And I had a weak moment when I thought *I can't do it. I can't compete with that guy.* I was tired—of trying, of hoping, of wishing and wondering…and then the universe stepped in and said 'Jacob Ryan, Jessie needs you again because her asshole ex fucked up. Again.' So I stayed, mostly because she was such a mess someone had to step up and take care of your kids. But it hasn't been easy, Josh. Something's changed. She's been doing that little disappearing act again, the one where she holes herself up in a little box and refuses to communicate."

"It means she's sad, Jacob. She's feeling alone."

"I fucking know what it means, Josh! Goddamn it! Do you think I'm stupid? But I can't stand it! And now, I come in here tonight and she's crying and telling me she's going to ask you for a divorce. Finally. I should be happy, you're right. But she was crying, Josh. Not throwing her arms around me and celebrating. And now she leaves the show in the middle of that song…but I still don't care. I'll help her, like I always do. She'll warm up to me again and we'll be fine. I'm not about to give up the best thing that's ever happened to me."

"Do you want to know what I think, Ryan?"

"Not really. But I have a feeling you'll tell me anyway."

A few cast were making their way down the hall. Crew were starting to stare as well. Josh eyed them, then led Jacob—and Dan, by association—down the hall, where he shoved open the door to Jessie's dressing room. "In here. This is not something the entire cast and crew of *Mystic Nights* needs to hear."

Dan watched the guys disappear inside the dressing room. He debated letting Matt know their argument seemed to be heating up, but he figured rightly Matt had his hands full. Cocking an ear to the door in case he needed to break up a fight, Dan tried to relax, and stood with his hulking back against the door. Over the mic, he notified Susanne to step into the theater so she could eyeball the kids.

Inside the small room, Josh faced Jacob square on. "This is what you need to know. And Jessie doesn't, for her own sanity at this point, know this, so don't fucking leak it, Ryan." He stared at Jacob as if he wasn't sure the guy was ready to hear what he had to say. Then, inhaling deeply, Josh dove in. "Nadia kidnapped Jessie and the kids. Nadia, who then seduced me and took care of my kids, is the one who abducted the kids in the first place."

It took a moment for the truth to sink in. Then Jacob's mind reeled and the room spun. "What? Matt told me it wasn't her. We were talking about the tattoo…" Rubbing his forehead now, Jacob tried to wrap his mind around this new revelation, the one he and Matt had considered, but which Matt recently told him didn't pan out.

"It was her. Only Jacob…you know she didn't do it alone."

"The guy…wait a minute. Do you know who the guy was? Is? And by the way, as fucked up as this is, what the hell does it have to do with me?"

"The guy was her husband, Jacob. Morgan. Morgan is Nadia's husband. It was some sick attempt to hurt Jessie, I guess."

"Morgan? What? This is too much." Dropping into the high chair by the counter where Jessie had sat earlier to have her hair and make-up done, Jacob stared at Josh, incredulous.

"The police are looking for them. They figure they've long since fled the country, though, so we may be looking over our shoulders for these two our entire lives. But this is what gets me, Jacob, as far as you're concerned."

Josh chewed on a pinkie fingernail for a second, pondering the right choice of words, before illuminating Jacob who, to his credit, given the rather insane news just delivered to him by one of the hapless victims of Nadia and Morgan's crime, listened.

"Nadia put herself in my bed. She fed and changed my son; she cradled and rocked my daughter. She read the kids stories, she made us dinner. She held David when he cried. She was my date, she was my companion, and she was a parent to my children." He paused. "Remind you of anyone?"

Jacob caught on immediately. "How dare you, you goddamned booze-hound. You're forgetting one rather important component of your dramatic telling, Josh. You didn't love Nadia. You never did. I love Jessie. I always have, and I always will."

"Nadia loved me. You see, Jacob? It's no different. Yeah, maybe my feelings for her weren't as love-struck magical as yours for Jessie, but I did care about her. For a while, in my messed-up haze, anyway. You did the same thing she did. You walked into a family that's not yours! They don't belong to you! My family does not belong to you!"

Leaping out of the chair, Jacob stood nose to nose with Josh. His eyes were on fire. "Jessie invited me in! I didn't manipulate my way in. I didn't kidnap your kids and try to set your wife on fire! Jesus, Josh. Get a grip! I love her! I love her, and I love the kids!"

"Now you're sounding just like Nadia!"

"Yeah, well, barring the fact that Nadia apparently caused all the shit, there is in fact one thing she and I do have in common, Josh."

"Oh and what's that? Can't wait to hear this." Eyes blazing too, Josh stormed around the small room.

"She and I took care of your kids. We stepped up when you and Jessie were both so fucked up you couldn't see to feed them, or tell them a story. I know you went through hell but you both gave them to Charles and Dee, willingly, may I add. And what did the children do to deserve being taken away from their parents, huh? And to be shuttled back and forth between the U.S. and Canada every few weeks? Nothing, Josh. Nothing! I stepped up. I did. I love those kids the same way you do. And I will take care of them, and love them, and never let them down the way you did."

"Don't you try to tell me you have a sweet clue what I went through when they were taken, Jacob. I'm glad you were there for them, and for Jessie too, for that matter, when I couldn't be. But I'm doing better now, and I always loved them—that never changed!"

"You need to step back now, Josh. You need to step back now and just do the occasional father shtick, and stay the hell out of my way so I can be the rock those kids need. And if I'm Jessie's number two, fine, I'll be her number two, and one of these days she will see that I've been her number one all along."

"They're my family, Jacob! Not yours! And that will never change."

"Being a husband and a father is not about pieces of paper, Josh, that say you are a husband and a father!"

"Well, that's damn good to know, because a divorce is a piece of paper too. So I guess we finally agree about one thing."

Outside the dressing room, Dan was considering opening the door to see whether he needed to step in, since the guys' voices were rising as their tempers flared. Just as he had his finger on the button, though, Matt's hurried voice came over the lapel mic.

"Dan? You say you have eyes on the guys, Josh and Jacob?"

"I do. Well, more ears than eyes right now, but—"

"Where are they?"

"In Jessie's dressing room, just about to come to blows, by the sounds of things."

"Let 'em. In fact, lock them in, Dan. Guess who's in the city—it would appear we have eyes on Nadia. But we don't have eyes on Morgan. Capiche? Ulysses, Susanne, you copy? Dan?" The words tumbled over each other as Matt's pulse pounded in his ears.

"Yeah, will do, boss. Jesus. Going for a custodian with a key as I speak. Locking the guys in. Watch your back, okay?" He didn't have to tell Matt to watch Jessie's back—that was a given.

Ulysses and Susanne responded in kind, acknowledging that they were to be on the lookout for Morgan.

Matt added, "Ulysses, call for backup. No lights, no sirens. This woman's got her finger on the trigger. I don't want to tell you who her bulls-eye is."

"Damn. You got it, Matt. Where are we sending them?"

"Central Park, John Lennon Strawberry Fields Memorial. Stat. And not a word to Josh or Jacob, Dan. Or to Charles and Dee, anybody."

Trembling a little, Dan signaled a custodian, then he hurried back and pushed open the door to Jessie's dressing room. He met the guys' eyes for a brief moment, trying to hide his own quickly accelerating heartbeat as he did so. He was thinking *I hope to hell you guys have someone to fight about by the end of this hour,* but aloud he just said, "Try not to kill each other, boys. I'm locking you in for the time being."

"What?" Jacob leapt towards the door as it closed before him. "I'm in this show! Dan! What the hell?!"

Josh was quicker to figure out what was going on. He shoved Jacob aside and pounded on the door. "Dan! What's going on? Dan?"

Turning to Jacob, he paused and his eyes darkened. "Jessie," he asserted. Jacob was speechless. The blood ran from his face.

"Something's going down, Jake old buddy. What do you think the chances are that Morgan and Nadia are in town?" Collapsing onto the sofa on the east wall, Josh buried his face in his hands. "My kids," he moaned. "Oh, God. Will this nightmare ever end?"

Watching him suffer, Jacob felt his own heart clench. Jessie and the kids did feel like his family now, hell, they *were* his family as far as he was concerned. A wave of utter powerlessness washed over him.

Quietly, he slid back onto the high stool and closed his eyes. "Please, God. Let them be okay. Please."

Josh pulled out his phone—Jacob's was in his own dressing room. Staring at the small screen, Josh pondered what to say. Where was she? Would she even get a message from him now?

Slowly, he picked out the letters to spell *always and forever,* and he tapped *send.* Josh held the phone between his palms and waited for an answer that never came.

Chapter Twenty-four

"Arnie, swing in closer to Nadia. I'll stay with Jessie."

Matt watched the boxer slip away. There wasn't a lot of cover at the site, mostly just some trees and brush along the perimeter of the space, so neither Matt nor Arnie could get as close as they liked, but they could stay under cover of darkness, at least, so that helped.

Jessie, however, unaware of Nadia's involvement in her diabolical kidnapping, moved towards the light.

"Didn't I teach you anything?" Matt muttered, eyeballing her angrily. But he knew she had no reason to be afraid of Nadia. Not yet...

But Matt was trained RCMP. Both he and Arnie had already discerned that the heavy weight dragging Nadia's pocket down was a pistol.

Nadia, the vixen herself, was leaning against a tall tree in a small landscaped promontory just behind the flat, circular, in-asphalt memorial that, at its center, featured the word *Imagine,* for John Lennon's beloved song. She heaved herself away from the tree now but stood only a foot or two away from it and, hands in the pockets of her brushed suede car coat, she stared at Jessie.

"I'm almost surprised you came," she said, the usual sensuous voice rather flat.

"Why wouldn't I, Nadia? You look better in person, by the way. Although you could use some time in the gym. You've been hitting the booze a little hard, maybe."

"Quite the little bitch, aren't you, Jessie? I don't know why he put up with you as long as he did."

He loves me, that's why. Jessie bit her lip and didn't speak. She was still

179

getting her breath back after her run, and was sweaty but could feel the November chill starting to seep in underneath her aviator jacket. Beneath that was just a thin navy halter designed for stage lights…she shivered.

Nadia noticed. "Not afraid of me, are you, Jessie?"

"Why would I be afraid of a gold digging social climber like yourself, Nadia?"

"Oh! Josh didn't tell you?"

Frowning, Jessie tensed. "Tell me what?"

Huh, Nadia thought, tucking that one away for later. She switched gears.

"I want to explain something to you, Jessie. About your husband and… about mine."

Cocking her head, Jessie smothered a *what?* Aloud she said, "You're married, Nadia?"

"I am." *This is going to be fun.* "But I'm married to someone who is sad all the time. Who lost the light a long time ago."

"Hmm. So you went after someone even sadder."

Nadia shook her head. "No. Not sadder."

"How can you be sadder than not knowing where your children are, Nadia?"

"Knowing they're dead. That's how."

"Oh. Jesus, Nadia. I'm sorry. I didn't know." Truly, Jessie's heart ached at hearing that. Nobody should endure that kind of pain—ever. Even a nasty mistress.

"How kind of you to express condolences, considering…"

"Mmmm. Considering you wanted my guy for a while there, huh?"

Nadia perked up at that. "Wanted? Past tense? Nuh-uh. *Want,* Jessie."

"He's free for the taking, Nadia. Sink your little claws in as deep as you want, sweetheart. I'm asking him for a divorce."

Purring, Nadia half-smiled. "Well, I'd say that's a start, hun, but it's not enough."

"Meaning?" Tilting one ankle over sideways, Jessie waited.

~⌁~

Matt, watching, felt his skin prickle. He knew what Nadia meant, well and clear.

"Arnie," he muttered into the lapel mic, "get the hell closer." He was trying to stay as close to Jessie as he could without attracting attention to himself. It meant practically crawling on his hands and knees underneath the many benches that lined the perimeter of the narrow road leading towards the stones laid in the ground commemorating John Lennon. At that point, the path opened wider, and Y'd off to either side of the grassed and treed area where Nadia was standing.

Jessie had her back to Matt, so she wouldn't detect his presence unless he erred and crunched on a leaf or twig, which he was careful not to do.

Arnie had jumped over a bench further back, and was taking a wide berth through the low shrubs and trees, trying to come at Nadia from behind. But he hit a snag.

His calm, steady voice came over the mic to Matt. "Glitch in plans, sir. We have company."

"What? Who the hell…?" But Matt knew before Arnie told him. Morgan was along for the ride.

"Morgan's watching Nadia. He hasn't seen me. He has a weapon—a gun. Can't tell what it is from here, some sort of small pistol."

"Trained on Jessie, of course. Jesus Christ."

"No, sir. Trained on his wife."

"Uhhhh," Matt breathed, sickened. "This just gets weirder and weirder. Keep him in your peripheral vision, Arnie. Stay on Nadia." Then, to Jessie's back, Matt breathed, "Stay cool, girl."

Inching forward, he digested Arnie's news. He prayed the local cops knew what the hell they were doing. The last thing he and Arnie needed right now was a bunch of rookies triggering Nadia's already jangled nerves.

Back at Jessie's dressing room, Josh was frantic. Hammering on the door, he demanded Dan let he and Jacob out. "Jesus, Dan, what the hell's going on? Let us the fuck out of here! My family's out there!"

Dan fisted the door hard enough to dent it. "Cool it, Josh. We don't need you and Jacob jumping into the middle of the fray. Matt and Arnie are with Jessie, and the cops are on their way."

"What the hell, Dan? Talk to me!"

Dan broke. "It's Nadia, Josh. She must have messaged Jessie and asked her to meet her. They're in Central Park. Which is one reason why you are where you are. The second reason was Morgan, but you don't need to worry about your kids—Arnie spotted him with Nadia."

"Are you fucking kidding me? Dan, let me the fuck out! Jesus, Jessie. Why the hell would you go off to meet psycho Nadia?!" Struggling to remain in control, Josh was quickly losing the battle.

Behind him, Jacob was immobile, recalling the attack in Montreal or, more accurately, visualizing the blood running down his girlfriend's back when he ran into their green room tent.

Jacob hung his head between his knees and gasped for breath.

In the park, Jessie was starting to realize Nadia was unstable. A jilted lover, like Jessie's old friend Deuce, she wasn't functioning on the usual normal scale. And she had an extra component to fuel her irrational thinking. She was the mother of a child who no longer walked the earth.

All right, she said to herself, facing Nadia. *Let's get this over with.*

Nadia stepped forward and stood just behind the row of benches arranged around her in a semi-circle at the end of her little promontory. Her hands were in her pockets too, but that didn't concern Jessie. It was bloody cold, cold enough to see Nadia's breath, which escaped her lips like dragon fire, and disappeared into thin air.

"Meaning," Nadia answered Jessie's earlier question, "despite your wonderful divorce news, apparently your ex doesn't want this." Her hands came out of her pockets then, and Nadia gestured to herself. Jessie froze. At the end of Nadia's hand, dangling from fingers that had touched Josh intimately, was a gun. It caught the light on its upward arc and danced there, while Jessie watched hurt and betrayal rocket across Nadia's coffee skin.

In a nano-second, Nadia had the gun sorted in her hand. She pointed it at Jessie. "Apparently he still wants you."

Swallowing, Jessie thought *this is what I get for telling Arnie to leave me alone. Oops. Nice one, Wheeler.* Her second thought was *hope the boys can learn to get along. They just might be raising Emily-Grace and David together.* She didn't consider Jacob not being involved in her children's lives. It was a given. They adored him.

"I told you, Nadia. I'm asking him for a divorce. I'm staying with Jacob."

"Liar. Jacob was always the booby prize, the consolation prize, the runner up. The loser. What's that they say? If you don't win, you lose. I know you want your husband back."

Tears pricked at Jessie's eyes. "I might want him back, Nadia. But that doesn't mean I can get him back."

"Why wouldn't you? God, he's everything!"

"Like, the answer's somewhere between 'kiss my ass' and 'it's none of your damn business,' Nadia!"

The old Sawyer nanny just stood there, and cocked her head. Waited.

Finally, Jessie heaved a great sigh that consumed her entire body, toes to ears, and she shifted her weight. "Nadia, it's because I'm pregnant. That's why. And it's Jacob's baby. Obviously," she added unnecessarily.

Matt heard Arnie snuff at that. This was news to him.

"Where u at, Arnie?" Matt whispered. He was now about twelve feet from Jessie, on an angle behind her. And Matt was ready to spring. He kept his eyes trained on the gun.

"Fifteen feet from a guy with a gun. He hasn't moved."

In front of them, the stand-off continued, its eerie tableau ghostlike in the night, its diabolical scene playing out atop a stone representing a song that preached world peace.

"You've got to be kidding me." Nadia was incensed. "You've got it all, don't you, Jessie? The perfect family, two healthy children and an adoring husband, a sexy lover who worships you, and now you get to have another child. You make me sick."

"I had a family, Nadia. Now it's broken, or haven't you noticed? It's just a big mess!"

"Oh, honey, I noticed. Believe me, I noticed. In fact, I bloody broke it! My husband and I destroyed your family. I watched you from the other side of that mirror, breast-feeding your baby, coloring with your daughter…crying yourself to sleep. I didn't do a lot of watching, mind you, my husband got to do most of it, and then he did his watching while I was fucking *your* husband…which was cool by me because once we lost our son, Morgan kind of died too, you know?"

Jessie's ears perked up. The pitch of her voice rose dramatically. "What did you say? Nadia?" Not even aware of the movement, she shifted her feet so as to suddenly gain some balance.

"Which part, girlfriend? The part where I admit it was me who abducted you, or...oh...the Morgan part? Yes. Well. Yes, I am talking about the same Morgan who watched over you the last few years. Who all of you thought was my stepbrother. Who carried your children and made sure your premises were always secure, who kept you safe from, well, from crazies like me, I suppose. And yes, honey, he was the guy who knifed your back. And breast, if I recall correctly. Told me he copped a little feel too, by the way. One day when he was mad at me he admitted that little tidbit. Didn't bother me so much as the rape, though, the morning he tried to set you on fire. Only he didn't see it as rape, you see. He thought he was doing you a favor, he said, since you had apparently already started that little party."

"I don't believe this. Morgan wouldn't hurt me. He wouldn't steal my children from their father."

"Apparently he would, Jessie. And he did."

"Why, Nadia? Why? If you wanted Josh, you could have tried to seduce him on your own!" Tears at Morgan's betrayal were playing wickedly under her eyes, threatening to fall. All those days at the gym...his presence on tour...his access to her kids *after*...

Off to the side, Arnie watched Morgan react. He, too, was crying, his face a weird twisted mask of silent pain.

Nadia laughed outright. "Honey, the way that man looks at you, no way was he ever going home with another woman. And anyways, you still don't get it. It wasn't him I wanted, at least not entirely."

"You wanted the money. The fame, to hang with a film star."

"No." Her declaration stunned Jessie. "What I wanted was a family." Nadia choked at the admission. "You have no idea what it's like to have something so perfect and then lose it. Morgan and I, we were in love, I mean really in love, the way you and Josh are. We were blessed with this perfect little boy...and I mean perfect, Jessie. Sweet, and happy and fun..."

Nearby, Morgan was really losing it. Tears were running freely down his cheeks now, as he watched his beautiful wife stand in front of Jessie with a pistol aimed in her direction, finally—finally!—speaking aloud about the child they lost. Finally opening up…telling a stranger, Morgan's old employer, in fact, about their beautiful son.

Close by, Arnie's heart did a double take. Morgan was now succumbing to grief, and the pistol he held was sinking. He was losing focus. *Maybe I can get to him, grab that gun…*

"Then he got sick," Nadia was continuing, her voice constricted with remembered pain. "You can't imagine, Jessie, I mean you just can't. You can't explain to a child that young what's happening, all you can do is watch him fade. You're helpless. Immobile. You try everything, the best doctors, second opinions, psychics, naturopaths, shark cartilage, every hokey remedy known to mankind…nothing works. The child becomes a ghost, in front of you…your child. And then after, when it's over and he's reduced to dust, you realize your husband is dead too! He died with him! Didn't you ever notice that about Morgan? His eyes? There's no light, there, Jessie! Only pain. Sadness, sorrow and pain. He used to talk, he used to chat, he was the life of the party at one time. Now he's a skeleton. He goes to the gym, he goes to work, occasionally he'll have a beer. And all of you, you just walked by him with your *hello Morgans,* and *get me coffee, Morgans,* and *carry this, Morgans,* and *stand over there, Morgans.* And while he guarded your life, and Josh's life, and the lives of your children, he had already lost his own."

"You're wrong, Nadia. I always liked Morgan. We all did. He was quiet, yes, we knew there was something there that was different, but he was good at his job. He was dependable…"

"He was a robot, Jessie. That's what he became after our son died. A goddamned robot."

"And so one day you programmed your robot to destroy a family."

"It started as a game. He saw Josh touch some young woman on the set of *The Wyatt Boys.* Morgan was very devoted to you, you know that about him. He couldn't stand that Josh was acting in what he thought was an inappropriate manner, although he seemed glad he didn't take the woman back to his suite. I told him any woman could get your husband in bed if she really wanted to. But I knew it wouldn't be possible unless, well…I knew we had to break Josh first. No way was he cheating on you with you around. So the surefire way to break him was to destroy what meant the most to him."

"His family."

"You got it. And once I saw how incredible it was to be a part of that… a family…again…"

"You programmed your robot to spread gasoline above my head and light a match."

"Those stupid firemen. They should never have found you. They got there earlier than we thought they would."

"They're pretty efficient, the Langley bunch. We had a few barn and house fires on *Drifters*. Oh, and once we even burned a church. That was quite the dramatic episode, in fact."

Jessie was grasping at straws now, trying to buy time and configure a way out of this new mess. At the same time, she was almost buckling over with cold and nausea; nausea from the pregnancy as well as from the incredible story Nadia was telling her…Morgan's involvement was unbelievable. She was sickened, not just at Morgan's ability to hurt her so deeply and permanently, but also because of this young couple's terrible personal loss.

Arnie moved forward then, and a twig crunched underneath his foot. He cursed, and lay flat on his belly. Morgan looked over, decided it was an animal, and let it go. Nadia didn't notice, nor did Jessie, so lost were they in Nadia's grisly telling.

"The thing about Morgan, though, Jessie, was that he was too devoted to you. He couldn't close the deal, if you know what I mean. So…well…" She waved the gun just slightly.

Afraid to move, Jessie spoke slowly. "Nadia, all you're going to accomplish by killing me is getting yourself a death sentence. For murdering two people, may I remind you. You don't think Josh wants you. But don't you see, that could change…you could walk away from me and have the life you want again. Because now that you know I'm divorcing him, Josh is up for grabs…and I know the two of you had a lot of good times together… he knows it's over between us. That'll change the way he feels about you. I know it will."

The thought of Josh being with Nadia again wholeheartedly disgusted

Jessie, but she was starting to panic. As far as she knew, she was alone with Nadia. The chances of ducking a bullet and outrunning the woman were slim.

Immediately a calm overtook her. *I am tired,* she blinked as she caught herself thinking maybe…just maybe… *I'm tired of sending my children back and forth across the country. I'm tired of the constant push and pull between Josh and Jacob, and most of all I'm tired of loving two men and not being able to have the one I really want. Maybe it won't be so bad…the kids will be fine. Jacob will make sure they're fine. Josh will be a mess…again…*

She felt like a traitor to Jacob for wanting Josh more, but Nadia, in this weird situation was, quite surprisingly, concisely nailing Jessie's thoughts down for her.

Now, filled with sadness and remorse, the woman put a tidy bow on the package. "Why would you divorce him, Jessie? I don't get that. He is a good man; he's the father of your children…why would you let him go? And don't give me the pregnancy story. He loves you. He'd stand by you."

"Because…I have to consider Jacob. And anyways, it's irrelevant. Josh can't stand by me if I'm dead, Nadia."

That simple declaration chilled Matt. He could see Nadia thinking about what to do. She was a woman who felt she lost everything, and now that she knew the police were looking for her, she had nothing left. She needed to end this one way or the other. Taking Jessie down would give her the release she desired.

"Pshaw, Jacob. He's adorable, but he is not your husband. God, you're so stupid, Jessie! You had it! What I wanted so fucking bad! You stubborn, prideful bitch! You could have it again! You piss me off!!"

Shocking everyone, including Nadia, Jessie threw her arms out wide. Matt almost cried out, and Arnie flinched. Morgan sat taller and re-aimed his gun.

"Just shoot me, okay Nadia? Just do it if you're going to! I'm so sick of trying to survive in a world I don't understand. My children are suffering, and I don't have the courage to leave someone who has been so good to me for someone who is a loose cannon. Even though I love that loose cannon beyond all doubt. Even though I cry for him in my sleep! So end this for me, will you? And maybe you will end the boys' torment too. Because none of this has been easy for any of us. And since you started all this bullshit with your wicked game, you need to step up and end it. So do it. Please. Fucking shoot me and stop the goddamned bleeding. Please."

Weeping openly now, Jessie dropped to her knees and hung her head. "Please," she begged. "Just pull the goddamned trigger, would you?"

"Jesus, Mary and Joseph," cried Matt inwardly. He saw the mask on Nadia's face register surprise and then he watched as a certain calm settled there. It was an eerie peace he saw many times in his career with the RCMP.

The gun steadied in her hand.

"All right," she purred. "I will end this for you, Jessie. In a way I am sorry to be ridding you of the demons that haunt you because it's too easy this way, you know? Ending the suffering by dying? But I'll do it because killing you will empty my pain too. And you know something, hun? Most of all I just want Josh to hurt. He doesn't want me. I had two families for a while, mine, and then yours. Morgan is already dead. Josh will die, too, when you are gone. I know, because he was half-dead when I met him, and there was still some hope then."

"Just fucking do it, Nadia! Just do it!" Jessie put her hands over her ears and closed her eyes. Her shoulders shook as silent cries convulsed her. She waited.

"Sing us home, hun? Okay? Sing us home."

She's gonna kill herself too, Jessie thought wildly. Trying not to puke, she focused on her children as she shivered and shook. Her rattled mind drifted to Josh and Jacob and the great love she was blessed to share with both men. She prayed they would find a way to help each other survive. Bent over, retching, her thoughts fluttered back to Emily-Grace and David... *I love you, babies,* she breathed as her body trembled.

Jessie was wondering if Nadia was thinking about her son, when the gun's blast pierced the still, dark night.

Chapter Twenty-five

"What the hell is happening, Dan? Dan, what the hell is going on?"

Still hammering on the door, and now futilely throwing his body against it, Josh was desperate. Weirdly enough, the concert was continuing on stage; program sound being piped through the small speakers in the dressing room was loud enough to freak Josh out. Nothing should be normal now. Nothing felt normal, nothing was normal, and live music should not be being produced on stage at a concert Jessie walked out of, and which now Jacob, too, was conspicuously absent from.

Charles' voice broke the silence outside the dressing room door. "Dan, what the hell is going on? Where're Jessie and Jacob? Dee's losing her mind!"

Sticking his ear against the door, Josh listened while Jacob moaned quietly behind him.

Dan's voice was urgent and panicked. "Charles, shit's going down. Jessie got a message from Nadia, she took off to meet her."

"What? What the hell? Where?"

"In Central Park. Matt and Arnie are with her. Matt's not answering the lapel mic now. Arnie came on for a sec but he's not answering now either. He said the cops are there and two shots were fired. He's not saying anything else."

"Let's go, Dan. Now!"

Dan glanced behind him at Jessie's locked door.

"What, Dan?"

"Matt ordered Josh and Jacob locked in there for the time being."

"Leave them." Charles pulled out his phone to text Dee. *All is well back shortly*

He palm-slapped the dressing room door. "Boys, I'll call when I know what's up. You both know as well as I do you're better off where you are. Suck it up. And say a few goddamned prayers."

Josh groaned and leaned back against the door. Sliding to the floor, he hung his head before whispering a quiet prayer and letting his eyes drift up to meet Jacob's terrified countenance.

"I know they're right," Josh admitted. "But I'm going to fucking kill Matt when I get out of here."

Jacob's words sucked the air out of the room. "Did you hear what Dan said, Josh? Two shots fired. And Matt's not answering. You may not have to."

He rubbed his stubbled chin and sucked in a breath. "And I wonder where the other shot landed."

When the bullet cracked its way out of Nadia's gun, Matt was already vaulting for Jessie. He knew the shot was coming; he had the training to discern the pregnant moment between crazed fear and desperation, and the calm that accompanied a final definitive decision to take action. It came after Nadia said her final words, just as Jessie started to sing, in a tremulous low voice, the first few phrases of 'Josh's Song.'

He saw the woman's finger move to put pressure on the trigger, and he knew Jessie was close enough for Nadia to easily hit with her particular pistol, even without a history of target practice. Without considering the possible outcomes, Matt leveled Jessie in one fell swoop. She landed hard on her right shoulder, hitting her head and scraping her right cheek on the asphalt as she went down. Crashing down on top of her, he felt the red hot sting of the bullet as it sliced through the front of his left shoulder and exited through the back.

Strangely, Matt considered his injury as he fell. *Small diameter bullet, not a hollow point, so it travelled straight through without opening a wider path, I don't think it hit bone or a joint so the most significant issue is going to be blood loss from two wounds, front and back. I'm fine.*

Still, he instantly felt nauseous, but not enough to miss the report of a second bullet, almost immediately. Screaming at Jessie to lie still, he turned his head away from Nadia's general direction, and covered his face with his hands, his body partly between Jessie and Nadia, and partly on top of Jessie, whose violent quaking he could feel through his own body, and who was still singing although now her song was more of a high-pitched scream.

No more bullets flew through the air. After a moment, he heard Arnie hollering as a rush of New York City's best came flying in. Twisting his head around, Matt saw Nadia laying still, her body at a weird angle. Arnie had Morgan on his knees in front of him. The cops were cuffing the old Keating bodyguard.

"Thank God," Matt gasped. "Thank God."

Still lying half on top of Jessie, he bent towards her and brushed wisps of hair back from her face. She was trembling wildly, eyes squeezed tightly shut; shaking fingers were crushed tightly over her pale lips.

"Jessie?" he asked, then a second time, louder, "Jessie, listen to me. It's over. It's over, kid. All of it." Grabbing her left wrist, he pulled that hand away from her face. The tears on her cheeks broke his heart. Would the girl ever again find peace in her lifetime? Happiness? Joy?

Stroking Jessie's cheek, Matt studied her. An officer bent down by the two of them.

"We're fine," Matt told him with a desperate urgency. "We just need a minute." To Jessie, he spoke softly. "Look at me, girl. Please."

She did, finally, and she stopped singing, but the tears kept coming. "I thought that was it, Matt. I thought I was dead."

"You, my girl, appear to have nine lives." Relieved that she was cognizant, and not hiding in some dark 'Emily-Wheeler' abyss, Matt wiped away another tear.

"Thank God you were here, Matt. Thank God you followed my stupid ass. God, I'm such a fucking idiot!"

"Come on. Sit up." He helped her, but she moaned in pain and favored her shoulder. Her cheek was bleeding from road rash, technically, and her head was splitting. Yet she ignored her own pain and gasped when she saw the blood soaking through Matt's grey coat.

They helped each other stand, then, and Jessie used her left hand to move the expensive garment off his shoulder. Around them, police were getting organized, and they were told EMTs were on the way. Now, Matt stood quietly while Jessie pushed his coat off the other shoulder. It fell to the ground. His crisp white shirt was soaking through as blood leaked from his left shoulder.

"It's fine," he said, resisting the urge to sink to his knees, wanting to vomit. "Not fatal, at least. The bullet went in and out."

"Jesus Christ, Matt," Jessie moaned. "You took a fucking bullet…for me!" Sobbing openly now, she started to unbutton his shirt, leveraging her bad arm as well in order to undo the buttons.

To Matt, it was all surreal—standing there under pale strips of white light, opposite Jessie, who he recently watched as Jacob undid her top in the same way. But now she was tearful and stricken with fear, in shock, shaking profusely so that she could barely work the buttons. He was still coming down off the adrenalin too, and was cold and nauseous, and relieved and injured, so he remained quiet and watched her face, thinking about her kneeling there before Nadia, begging to be killed.

The sorrow of that need tore through Matt at a much deeper level than the bullet.

Jessie continued to unbutton him, and then she slipped her cold hands under the shirt and widened it. Her hands on Matt's chest and stomach shocked him, in a strange way. She was his charge, his responsibility. Yet she still had a power over him, as he knew she did over many. This time, though, in his rather altered state after the events of the last forty-five minutes, he saw things differently. He saw a sad, lonely girl who he had helped through some tough times—who had become family to him—now struggle to help him, for a change.

He grabbed her wrist to stop her icy hands from moving over his body, from touching him, from trying to take his shirt off, and he spoke to her.

"Jessie," he said simply.

She looked up from scanning Matt's chest for wounds, and met his eye. There was a calm there, a peace about him she was surprised to see.

"I have to stop the bleeding," she whimpered. "I have to make it stop."

"Yes," he said in response.

He knew she wasn't talking about his wounds.

She half-smiled then, and let her worried eyes drift over his chest and stomach one more time. "Julie sure is a lucky lady," she breathed, letting her good hand remain on Matt's body, and hugging the other tightly to her own. With a few more nudges at his shoulders, Matt's shirt dropped to the cold ground.

"Yes," he said, one corner of his lip turning up. "She tells me that all the time."

"Oh God, Matt," she moaned. "She's gonna hate me."

"Nah. She'll just think I'm sexier. And Katy will think I'm cool."

"You took a bullet for me."

"You said that already."

"It's worth saying twice." The diaphanous eyes pleaded with him. "I wanted to die and still you dove in front of a bullet and saved me. You could have been killed," she choked. "Why, Matt? Why?!"

Frowning then, he posed a question back to her as she bent down and grabbed his shirt, then wadded it up and held it against the wound on the front of his shoulder. "Are you asking me why I wanted you saved, Jessie? Because the answer's obvious."

"Because I'm pregnant?"

"Because you're you." Touching her chin lightly, he searched her eyes. "You make music that makes the world go round. When you aren't out there captivating people, we're all shriveling up, a little every day. We need you. All of us."

"I'm so messed up, Matt. Whatever I do, I end up hurting people. My children…Jacob…Josh…"

"What happened to you and Josh is the direct result of this woman who tried to kill you, Jessie. She was right. What you had is something a lot of people crave. Don't be so quick to give that up. Don't surrender."

"But what about Jacob? I can't hurt him, Matt. I can't. Even if Josh agrees to get back together, considering…"

"Jacob is a big boy. He had his time in the sun, Jessie. He had you longer than he ever dreamed he could."

"I can't imagine living my life without him in it."

"Then don't. Find a way to make it work."

She shook her head. "He won't. He says he can't."

"Then I say it's his loss, kiddo." Glancing around him, Matt reflected on the organized chaos around Nadia's still body. Turning back to Jessie, he said, "It's over, girl. You can rest easy now. You can rebuild the life you cherished. And that you deserve."

Placing her good hand over her mouth, Jessie crumpled. "I didn't go through all that hell to give up on Josh, did I, Matt?"

"No, sweetheart," he said, clutching his reddening shirt to his entry wound. "You didn't."

The EMTs arrived then, and led Jessie and Matt to their vehicles for assessment and on-scene treatment. Jessie rose from the bumper of one of the emergency vehicles when two officers walked Morgan by her.

She raised a hand to stop them.

"Can I?" she asked. "Just a few seconds."

Arnie was walking behind them. He stopped and listened. Matt, too, cocked an ear, despite his pale face and more urgent need to puke.

New tear trails swept down Jessie's cheeks as she faced her old security. Allowing her eyes to deeply search her captor's, she finally saw what Nadia did. Morgan's eyes were tired, sad, distant. Robotic.

"Poor Morgan," was all Jessie said. "You lost your son. And now you've lost your wife."

She touched his cheek with her left hand. He didn't pull away and, instead, leaned a little into her and closed the vacant eyes.

It was not a surprise to Morgan—or to Matt or Arnie—that Jessie reacted the way she did. Even as the realization was sinking in that he was her abductor, her captor, her watcher, her rapist and...her attempted murderer...she still had the capacity to see him for what he was. Which was, in fact, a father in deep, deep mourning. And now he was also a man who just shot and killed a woman he deeply loved.

"He was destroyed by life, Jessie," Matt told her after the police walked Morgan away. "But you are a survivor. Don't ever forget that. You have to choose to survive. No matter how great the pain."

The EMT helping Jessie, a young Asian girl with captivating almond eyes, helped Jessie back to her seat on the back of the ambulance. Arnie wandered closer as the woman adjusted a sling around Jessie's arm in order to stabilize her shoulder.

Matt finally gave in, angled his face away from Jessie, and vomited in a bag the EMT had handed him a few minutes earlier. He felt Jessie's good hand reach around her body and grasp his left forearm to offer solace as he did so.

Arnie's voice radiated towards them. It was accompanied by crossed arms. "This'd be a good time to apologize for yelling at me, Mizz Jessie fancy-pants Wheeler."

"Ahhh," she groaned in response. "I'm not normally like that, Arnie. Ask Matt."

"Occasionally she is," Matt grinned, looking back over at them. He winced as the male EMT treating him put pressure on his wounds. "But mostly she's all right. You just have to let her in one ear and out the other."

Smiling sadly up at Arnie, Jessie apologized. "I am sorry, Arnie. I suck. Really."

Down the road a ways, an angry voice they all recognized demanded access to the now cordoned off crime scene. Charles was on the rampage.

Matt nodded at Arnie and gestured with his head towards the voice. "This is your true test, Arnie. And you thought Jessie was a handful."

"Eek, Arnie. Good luck," Jessie said in a subdued voice, leaning forward past Matt to see if she could spy her producer.

"The way I see it, girl, you're gonna be the one needing luck when Charles finds you. Taking off like that." Arnie tweaked her on the nose with his thumb and forefinger, and wandered off to find his boss.

"Leave it to Arnie to always tell it like it is," Jessie grumbled, tilting her head sideways so the pretty Asian girl could clean and cover the road rash on her cheek.

Arnie was right. Charles was livid, in a relieved kind of way. But he calmed down when he saw that Jessie and Matt were mobile and talking. Standing back to converse with Dan and Arnie while Jessie and Matt were transported to the hospital, he remembered his promise to text Dee as well as Josh and Jacob.

Dee was first. *Had an incident, all is well, when concert over let Josh and Jacob out of dressing room, Custodian has key*

Josh and Jacob's messages were a duplicate text, but Charles had no way of knowing Jacob didn't have his phone.

In the dressing room, where both men were praying profusely, Josh stood when the text came in. He grabbed the door handle for support and read it silently to himself before sharing it with Jacob.

Over now, Matt ok Jessie ok, few minor injuries, all is well

What Charles did not tell Josh was that Nadia was dead. The producer was well aware there were some feelings between Nadia and Josh, despite the terrible truths that eventually came to light. That kind of news was best left told in person.

Jacob slid off the high chair and faced Josh. "There were bullets fired, Josh. But she's alive." He was crumbling.

Nodding, Josh agreed. He tapped his cell against his thigh and tried to find words. There were none.

Eyes settling into a misty cerulean haze, Jacob thrust out a hand. "However this all lands...Jessie, me, you...I want you to know I get it, Sawyer. All of it. How bad it was. How bad it still is. How bad it's going to be."

Taking his hand, Josh shook. "I get it, too," he said in response, the nerve on his cheek finally calming.

That was the closest they got to apologizing to each other for the hell of the last year. But it was something.

Shortly, a key turned in the lock, and the door was opened by a custodian, who stuck his afro'd head in and hollered, "Yo, boys. I been tole ta set ya free."

"If only," Josh muttered.

"How the hell Jessie did it for six and a half months is beyond me," was Jacob's sharp retort.

In the hallway, a very concerned Dee had David in her arms, sound asleep. Emily-Grace was dozing in Susanne's capable grip. Josh reached for her, and Jacob took David.

Her arms finally free, Dee touched Josh's hand. "I'm calling Charles," she said. "What happened?"

As she speed-dialed her husband, Josh sighed. "I have no idea, Dee. We were just told everything's okay."

"Well, sit tight then. I'm about to find out."

The guys were stunned when Charles arrived and filled them in. Jacob routed his cell phone from his dressing room, and found a few texts from Jessie. When he called her, she answered on the first ring.

Josh watched Jacob pace as he talked to her. When Jacob was done, he ended the call and asked to be driven home.

"Jessie wants to stick around and be sure Matt's shoulder is okay. He's having some tests done on it to see about any internal damage, although she says he can move it and all. Just safety stuff. Precautions, I guess, against any further damage." He looked at Charles. "We'll touch base tomorrow, okay?"

A final look at Josh ended a long night of stress and insecurity. "I'll take the kids home so they can be in their own rooms. Jessie will be along in a few hours. I'll get her to call you tomorrow, okay?"

Josh frowned. After the hellish night, he wanted to talk to Jessie now. He considered calling after Jacob was out of sight. To Jacob, though, he said, "All right. Who's driving you, Susanne?"

"I can," the tall blonde replied amicably. "Here, honey, come with me." She accepted a very tired Emily-Grace from Josh, who eyed his daughter anxiously. He glanced at Jacob. "Precious cargo," he managed in a croak.

Staring at his phone after they left, he wondered if he should make that call to Jessie. Instead, he accepted a ride from Ulysses, and made his lonely way to the hotel.

Chapter Twenty-six

At seven a.m., just as a subtle pink light was starting to peek through the lovely graceful arched windows of the Madison Avenue condo, Jessie made her way home. Ulysses had picked her up at the hospital, but now she sent him away.

"I'm fine," she insisted. "I'll lock the door behind me. It's all good." She kissed his cheek, and he went off to his hotel, where Miranda was waiting for news and a snuggle.

Jessie stood just inside the door of the condo for some time before going further in. She thought about the framed picture in the coat closet, still hiding, her precious locket that was taped to its back now buried in her make-up bag, unbeknownst to Jacob.

I am a traitor, she thought. *Jacob deserves better.*

Enchanting notes drifted her way from the grand piano; Jacob was playing with a light touch, presumably because the children were sleeping. When Jessie finally rounded the corner and looked over at him, her heart stilled and her eyes glistened.

He was hunched over the keys, playing a melancholy melody that rose in waves and sank in whispers. Like all of Jacob's music, it was elevated and tranquil, sublime and surreal. He wasn't singing, this time. Instead he was simply lost in the piece, in its rhythms and cadences and in its perfect lilting tone. He moved slightly as he played, feeling the music and letting it carry him to some safe place in his heart and mind. Backlit by the window, Jacob was silhouetted, a ghost…a man lost in time, and stuck in time, who needed to secure his place in time before his spirit disappeared.

With her good arm, Jessie pulled out her iPhone and opened her camera App. Zooming in, she tapped on it and took his photo, preserving this man she loved in a static frame forever. Then she touched the 'record' button and filmed him until he suddenly came outside of the music for a moment and noticed her standing there. With a discordant crunch, Jacob stopped playing.

"Jessie," he exhaled, surprised and relieved.

"Babe," she whispered, moving in his direction and meeting him half-way. Burying her face in his chest, she inhaled deeply. A slight green apple scent filled her nostrils.

Oh God, she ached.

Jacob pulled her onto the couch. She settled on his lap. He studied the sling and lightly touched the bandage on her cheek.

"I'm not going to ask what was going through your mind tonight, Jessie, on stage or off. But I will tell you I am not impressed that you took off after Nadia."

"She's dead now," Jessie whispered. "She's gone. It's over."

"Yeah. I heard. I can't believe it was her."

"And Morgan. I can't believe it was him. They were married, for God's sake. She was his wife, Jacob. Not his stepsister."

Peering at him, she wondered whether to ask the next question on her mind. In the end, she went for it. "Does Josh know? That Nadia's dead?"

"Yeah. Apparently Charles went to his hotel and told him."

"How's…how's he doing?"

"Jessie, please, do we have to talk about Josh right now?"

"Yeah. Yeah, we do, Jacob."

And Jacob's world came crashing down. Again.

He saw it in her eyes, first, in the pale, startling ice-blue eyes that won him over in the first place. Next, he heard it in her voice, in the tired, aching words he would replay again and again for the rest of his life. But most of all, he felt it in her body. She was rigid, and tense. Poised to run. And he knew it.

Knowing what was coming but unable to deal with it or accept it, Jacob turned his head slowly from side to side. "No," he said in disbelief. "Just no."

Jessie swiped at her eyes, which she squeezed shut. When she opened them, she peered intently into his. "We always knew," she said. "You…always knew…"

"Last night you said you were going to ask him for a divorce. You told me, Jessie."

"And you saw how much it hurt, Jacob."

"You can't. You can't end it this way. Not after all this time. Not after this crazy night, Jess. You're not thinking straight. You're probably not thinking at all."

He bowed his head and buried his face in her chest, clinging to her waist with both hands. When Jessie touched a finger to his chin and lifted it, she found only grief in the eyes she loved. It trickled down his cheeks in rivulets that she pressed her thumb into, and tried in vain to erase.

"Don't do this, Jacob," she begged. "Babe, you know things haven't been going so good between us lately. You knew we were on a downhill slope."

"The only slope we've been going down, Jessie, is the one where Josh waltzes back in on his white horse and pretends he's something he's not." His voice was thick with emotion.

"He was a pawn in a wicked game, Jacob. He never had a chance. With Nadia…he never had a fucking chance."

Unable to respond to that, because he knew it to be true, Jacob moved out from under Jessie and heaved his suddenly heavy body off the couch. He turned to look at the woman he loved, who stood also, and faced him.

"If I leave, Jess…I can't see you again. I can't work with you…I can't see you…"

"I know," she whimpered, a current of fear rippling through her body on a cobalt wave of heartbreak and loss. "I understand." Her eyes caved in, then, and her shoulders shook. Sinking her good hand in her back pocket, Jessie's legs almost gave beneath her. Tossing her hair, trying to compose herself, she asked him, "What did we get to, Jacob? On our count?"

"I stopped counting," was his answer. "We were making music, you and me. I thought we were good. I thought we'd made it."

"Okay. All right."

He sat on the sides of the kids' small beds before he left, letting a finger linger over David's cheek, and brushing back a ringlet of Emily-Grace's hair. Jessie waited on the couch, granting the small family's savior the time he needed to say good-bye.

When he emerged from the bedroom, a duffel bag in one hand and a guitar case in the other, Jacob stopped and tried to find the words to let go.

Rising with great effort, Jessie made her way over to him. She placed her good palm on his cheek and kissed him tenderly.

"My darling Jacob," she breathed, "you are everything."

"Apparently not," was his stark answer. "Apparently I'm nothing. Apparently I'm an island, Jess. Something to float on for a little while when you need it. I had it," he added. "I had the most precious family. And now it's gone."

The door closed behind him with a final *shwoop*.

"Not entirely," Jessie wept, placing a hand on her belly as his footsteps faded away. "It's not entirely gone."

Only later did Jacob remember Jessie's nausea. In the end, given their break-up, he decided it was, indeed, just a bad case of nerves.

Chapter Twenty-seven

"You knew," Jessie was saying to Josh, in a quiet non-judgmental voice. "You knew Nadia engineered the kidnapping. For how long did you know?"

She was slouched in a Windsor chair at a long rectangular walnut table, in the chair nearest the end. Kitty corner at the opposite end was Josh, sitting three-quarters on to her, his right elbow resting nervously on the table, the thumb and finger of that hand rubbing two-day chin stubble. At her spoken realization, he dropped his hand to the table and followed it with his gaze.

"Not long," he said, as her heart hurt for him. "A month, maybe."

"You cared about her."

He cleared his throat but continued to stare at a crack in the table, which he absently traced with a finger. "Enough."

Enough for her death to hurt, Jessie thought. *Enough to hurt for why she did all this to you in the first place. Enough to be lost in a haze of confusion by a mess left over by a lover's deep, dark betrayal.*

"I'm sorry, Josh," she murmured. "I really am."

"Me too," he answered after a moment. "About everything."

Sighing, Jessie let her eyes drift up to Matt. He was standing across from her, his right hand holding onto the back of a matching Windsor chair, his left shoulder bandaged and that arm in a sling, the opposite of her. Her right shoulder was bruised and sore, but would heal; his injury was from a clean bullet wound Jessie was chilled to know would have killed him had it been a slightly lower, more accurate shot.

Frowning at her now, watching for signs of breakdown and trauma, Matt's gentle eyes were a comfort on this difficult day.

Matt knew about the breakup with Jacob, Josh did not. No one else in the 80's era New York City Police meeting room knew, not Charles and Dee, not Arnie, not the police themselves. They all attributed Jessie's pale face to the dramatic night before; they felt that her shaking hands were telegraphing her angst at a horrific ending to a terrifying standoff. Josh's sadness they took for the unbelievable treachery by a woman he cared enough about to keep her in his life for months.

The impending Sawyer divorce was also unknown to everyone in the room but Jessie, Matt and Josh. And Josh, to be honest, was pissed at Jacob for not being here to support Jessie today.

This day would not go down as a favorite of the year for either party.

Matt sent Jessie a small nod to say *you can do this. You can get through this day.*

Puffed cheeks accompanied by a deep exhalation was her fatigued response.

Matt filled in holes.

"What we now know, mostly from Morgan's statement, partly from Nadia herself, is that Nadia started this as a game, or as a challenge. Morgan saw Josh as weak, as someone he felt might inevitably go down a bad road that would hurt Jessie. Nadia picked up on that and decided she would give him a little push. They schemed and planned, rented the Langley house under the table, pretty much, installed the fence and one-way mirror, and set up the abduction. They intended to return the children to Josh on Christmas Eve, but instead did it a week earlier because David needed medical attention. Nadia drove the kids to Calgary but she wore a mask and apparently didn't speak, so Emily-Grace wouldn't recognize her when Nadia finally got to know Josh, which was at La Casa the night he admitted to needing a nanny. All of you were introduced to Nadia as Morgan's stepsister. We now know she was his wife."

"Why would Morgan accept his wife dating someone else?" Deirdre couldn't get over that fact.

"Because he was trying to hang onto her. He loved her. He wanted to give her what she craved in the hopes she would come back to him. And, in his words, the 'game' was supposed to end once Nadia proved she could win

Josh. But it backfired on Morgan, whose intention was always to let Jessie go. So in the end he got stuck with a wife in love with someone else, who determined Josh's love for Jessie was in the way."

He looked at Jessie to see how she was doing. She met his eyes and pressed her lips together in a tight line, and slouched further. In the end, she completed the remainder of his thought. "So she decided I had to die."

Breathing in, Matt acquiesced. "And it was up to Morgan to make that happen."

"But he didn't succeed. The first time, he maybe only tried it because he thought I was dying anyway, I think. The second time…maybe he thought I was trying to live again."

"He cared about you, Jessie. He still does. Morgan says you are one of the only people who ever really saw him."

"I saw him," she looked up at Matt, aggrieved. "But I didn't *see* him. I didn't look close enough, Matt."

Charles broke the quiet pause that followed her remark. "Morgan was at the hospital…with the kids…for two weeks…was Nadia at the house in Langley?"

"No." Jessie's voice was small. "There were times no one was there. I thought maybe…" She shrugged sadly. "I thought maybe he wasn't coming back. But he always did, in the end." Shifting in her seat, she stammered, "I still can't believe it was Morgan. When I think of all the times…" The tired voice drifted off.

"Jessie?" Matt encouraged gently, to keep her with them, to draw her out of the Langley prison.

Focusing on the table, she sighed. "He could see in the room. I always knew when he was there, I heard his boots on the stairs, and I heard him moving around. I made signs…basically to tell him he would not win, that none of you would give up on me."

Chancing a glance at Josh, she saw his layered hair fall over his cheek as he sank deeper into his chair. His tan leather jacket rustled when he tried to shove the hair back behind his ear. Swallowing bitterly, she ached to rise, to move towards him, to climb into his lap and move the rogue hair for him, and to follow up with a brush of her lips against his cheek, and tender words whispered in his ear.

As if he could discern her thoughts, Josh looked up and met her searching eyes. He held her gaze. Their sorrow for a past that could not be undone flitted on an unseen wire between them.

Charles spoke, then. "I feel responsible. We should have asked to meet Morgan's wife. We should have looked more closely into who he was when we hired him."

"And why did none of us know Morgan lost a child?" Dee was beside herself.

No one had an answer.

But after an uncomfortable pause, Jessie trained her sight down the table on Josh again. The two children they shared were light; they were everything. If they were gone…

"I can't imagine any deeper pain than losing a child," she decreed quietly, losing herself in her estranged husband's chocolate eyes. As they sat in this institutional place and pondered the last many crazy months, Jessie knew Josh, too, was picturing David's sweet innocent face, and Emily-Grace's loving nature.

By Jessie's simple truth, Josh knew, as did everyone in the room, that despite the turmoil and grief haunting them, hovering over them, she had already forgiven Nadia and Morgan.

Dee had another difficult question to put to the room. "Why did Morgan kill Nadia? If he loved her—"

"To end her pain," Jessie whispered, unable to meet Matt's scrutiny, but feeling his heart twist all the same. "He loved her enough to let her go."

Rising from his chair near the middle of the table, Charles stepped around to Jessie and laid a hand on her good shoulder. "It's over now, Jessie. You were the victim of a couple of jealous, misguided and overwrought people. Now it's time to heal."

"It's interesting to hear you say that, Charles." Jessie reached up and touched his fingers. "Because, unlike the whole Deuce McCall stalking, I was never the victim. I was just an annoying pawn that had to be removed."

She met Josh's aching eyes then, and, in her next sentence, told him she understood it all—the drinking, the pain, the sorrow, the lust for Nadia, even. Mostly, Jessie needed him to know she understood the fear that drove

Josh to become a shadow of his former self, a ghost that walked in her husband's place.

"Nadia wanted Josh. She wanted the strong, devoted husband I had. She wanted children. She wanted a family. Josh was the victim this time."

Again, the room fell silent.

There were more questions to be asked, more details with which to try to come to terms. In the end, Arnie walked Jessie to the door while the others buzzed around, recoiling, struggling, trying to find a way to pick up the pieces and, too, mourning Morgan's pain and how they felt they let him down.

Arnie turned Jessie to face him. "I didn't like watching you last night, Jessie. Asking Nadia to pull the trigger. I can't go back to Vancouver wondering if you're going to be okay. I need to *know* you're going to be okay."

"I will be," she answered, trying to smile but unable to pull it off. "I just see this all differently now. Nadia knew the only way to get Josh—and my family—was to break him. So she did. Only when I got back I didn't know how to put him back together."

Josh was already in the hallway, but he was watching Jessie with Arnie. He saw her start to dissolve, and he tensed. Arnie looked over Jessie's shoulders and met his eyes. Even Arnie, the strong Downtown Eastside angel, was crumbling under the strain inherent in caring for someone he loved in pain.

Training his sight back on Jessie, Arnie sighed. "He's been doing great, Jessie. Really. He's so good with your kids. Josh is not alone, so you don't have to bear the entire weight of putting him back together, as you say. He has me, now, and Trudy and Frank, and some really good friends in Charlie and Steve." He placed a finger under her chin and tilted her face up to his. The wounded eyes killed him. Recovering, he continued. "As you know, it's one day at a time with addictions. But I promise you, there are a lot of people not willing to see him go down. Myself included."

Like a rainbow after a storm, a small smile lit up Jessie's face. "Good thing he's terrified of you, then. Fear alone will be enough motivation not to touch a bottle."

Arnie's hearty laugh surprised them all. Even more so, the tiny twinkle just starting to flicker in Jessie's eyes was a beacon of hope.

"Go talk to him, Jessie. He's looking a little lost today."

She glanced back over her shoulder to spy Josh leaning against the wall in the hallway, hands in his coat pockets, staring at the floor. "Yeah," she whispered to Arnie. "I guess I should." Leaning forward for a gentle hug, she murmured, "Thank you for everything. Having you around lately has been a dream."

"You've come a long way since East Hastings, girl. Keep on keepin' on, as they say."

"As who says?" Her smile widened, and she tilted her head in a teasing way.

"Who knows? Some wise guru, I suppose."

With a squeeze of his fingers, Jessie let go of Arnie's hand and wandered over to Josh. She stopped a few feet in front of him and tried to think of what to say that could help erase a year's worth of anguish and torment. Slowly, as she focused her gaze on the toes of his boots, she moved her foot so she could step on his, lightly, as if a renewed connection had to start in one small place—at the bottom—and work its way up.

Allowing one corner of her lips to curve up slightly, Jessie tossed her hair nervously and met his eyes.

"Hey," she started, her voice like dried sea grass on a hot beach, crisp and crackly.

"Hey yourself," he managed, as she withdrew her toes from on top of his.

"You're flying out in a few hours?" It seemed the safest place to start.

"Yeah. You're all good with the kids for a bit?"

"Yeah, they're, uh, with Susanne and Dan now. And Carlotta. Between all of us, we can handle the little rug rats. We're demanding Matt go home to Julie. Ulysses and Miranda left this morning for Vancouver so he could get back for his father's birthday party tonight. We'll be fine."

"Yeah, Jacob's good with the kids. Charles likes the guy, so, well…"

"No Jacob," she said softly, training her sight on Josh's belt buckle. At his silence, Jessie looked back up to his curious eyes. "He's gone. He left this morning after I got back from the hospital."

A thousand emotions ran through Josh's mind then, accompanied by a gazillion rushed thoughts, which lurched around and over and under each other like tumbleweeds in the sand. "Gone…like to his dad's for a bit, gone?"

"No," she said, pressing a finger to the corner of one eye and trying to smile through the sudden gut-wrenching pain that missing Jacob demanded. "Like gone gone. Like never coming back gone." Burying herself in Josh's eyes she added, "Like forever gone."

Josh shifted his stance, unsure. He said the only thing he could think of that could possibly equal Jessie's suffering on this awful day. "Awww, Jess... I'm sorry. I really am."

He wanted to hold her, but it didn't seem like quite the right time. Snuffling, Jessie looked away and tried to laugh. "You're sorry, Sawyer. Okay. Good. I guess."

Drifting back over to him, she reached out and hooked her fingers over his belt buckle. Her forced smile turned upside down and she inhaled deeply, trying to get a grip. There was nothing left to say, so Josh laid a hand over hers. He rubbed her fingers lightly, then clasped them tightly in his.

She looked up at him one last time before letting go and backing away. "I'll see you, Josh," she said. "I'm coming back to Van for a bit in a few days. I'll make sure you get to see the kids, okay? David needs his daddy. I think he already wants to learn how to shave." She touched her chin and mimicked where chin whiskers would be. "He's outnumbered with just me and Emily-Grace now, so..." She shrugged, knowing she was rambling, then she spun on her heel, went back inside the meeting room, and melted herself under Matt's good arm.

Matt smiled and gave her a one-armed hug before glancing behind him to see Josh watching them. Nodding to Josh, he accepted what he saw transfer itself from Josh's heart to his—*thank you*. Sending him back a big *she's worth it, Josh*, Matt's steady scrutiny lingered. *Fight*, he seemed to be saying. *Don't give up. After all this... just don't give up.*

Quietly, so no one would see him leave, Josh heaved himself away from the wall, removed his hands from his pockets, and headed for the airport.

Chapter Twenty-eight

In Vancouver, Charles and Dee were keeping the kids at La Casa for Jessie. Her downtown condo wasn't set up for children, apart from the occasional visit there. La Casa had bedrooms, a playroom, and of course Carlotta, who went out of her way to make snacks and meals the kids loved, like open faced smiley peanut butter sandwiches with Smarties for eyes and noses, and licorice for mouths.

Wednesday afternoon, Jessie sat cross-legged on the floor of the playroom, as Emily-Grace made play tea for her and Deirdre. David, too, was a guest at the floor-level tea party. Already he adored his sister, and she him, and it was fun to watch the two interact. Even Jessie managed a smile when Emily-Grace tried unsuccessfully to correct the way he was holding his teacup.

"She gets that from you, Dee," Jessie said. "You're training her up to be a real little lady."

"Oh, pshaw." Dee waved her off. "I don't hold my teacup like that." She elbowed Jessie and winked. "It's Charles' doing."

"The big teddy bear." Jessie tried to laugh but couldn't quite muster the energy.

"Honey…let's go get ourselves some real tea, okay? These two are in their own little world right now anyway. I'll ask Carlotta to keep an eye on them for a few minutes. She'll love the break from dusting."

In the kitchen, Dee put the kettle on to boil as Jessie climbed onto one of Dee's high Italian leather chairs.

"I'm sorry about Jacob," Dee told her, watching Jessie carefully.

209

"Me too." Jessie studied her fingernails. "I can't stand not having him in my life."

"Have you tried to contact him, honey?"

Shaking her head, Jessie whispered, "No. I can't." She looked mournfully up at Dee. "We'll never be able to leave each other completely if we stay in touch."

"Why not, honey? He's your musical partner. A soul mate of sorts, isn't he? Why cut him loose entirely?"

At Jessie's lingering look, her mouth twisting as if she wanted to speak but couldn't, Dee said, "Oh. Josh. Hmmm?"

"He's the love of my life, Dee. I mean…Jacob is too, in a lot of ways, and it hurts like hell right now, but…Dee…I want my husband back. I ache to have him back. You know?"

"I do, honey. I know what you and Josh mean to each other. You don't need to convince me." She placed teabags in cups and paused, her hands on the cups as she asked Jessie what she thought might be a difficult question.

"Your body's reacting a little differently with Jacob's baby, hmmm?"

Silence. Then Jessie answered quietly, "I guess it's hard to hide when you're puking your way through each day."

Smiling wisely at her, Dee replied, "On some level I guess I'm glad it's not nerves, as Matt suggested it might be."

"Good 'ole Matt. He keeps secrets well. If Josh doesn't work out, I'm not touching another man until he and Julie divorce."

"Jessie!"

"Kidding! Kidding. He's one in a million though, Dee. He saved my life. With no regard for his own."

"Do you know something, Jessie?" Deirdre was thoughtful. "I bet you would have done the same for him, if the situation were reversed."

"Huh. Yeah, Dee. I would have. No question." Jessie accepted her tea from Dee's outstretched hand. "I'm glad Matt and Charles are friends again. And I'm super glad he and Julie are moving back to Van, especially because Katy is so sweet and kind to Emily-Grace."

"Me too, honey. Me too. Sooo…about this baby…and Josh." Dee lifted the teacup to her lips and took a sip.

Miserably, Jessie sighed. "I don't know. What a mess, huh Dee?"

"Are you forgetting who Josh is, Jessie? Who raised him?"

"Meaning someone not his father who treated him like shit his whole life?"

"Well, maybe so, but also…I think Josh may have another perspective on the matter."

"He's less than fond of Jacob. He won't go for it. It's a helluva lot to ask of a man, Dee, to raise another's man's child." Jacob's sweet nature with Emily-Grace and David flitted across her mind.

"Are you worried about his issues with addictions?"

"No. I mean…" Exhaling slowly, Jessie said, "I don't think so. I think he'll be okay as long as life doesn't throw him another curve ball. And before you say anything, I think this baby might only have been that kind of curve ball if I stayed with Jacob. But I couldn't…I couldn't stay with Jacob after…of all people…Nadia reminded me of what I had. And what I let go."

"You let go at a time when you had no choice, Jessie. Both you and Josh needed some time to recover."

"Yeah, but Dee, look what I did to Jacob. I brought him into my life when everyone warned me against doing so. And he's so hurt he'll never speak to me again. And now…he won't be raising his own baby. I did a terrible thing!" Bending over her cup, Jessie watched her tears land on the counter, like raindrops on a warm spring day.

Reaching for her hand, grasping it, Dee smiled in sympathy. "Sweetheart… a baby is never a terrible thing. You and Jacob are magic together. You made this baby out of your love for each other. I'm glad. I'm glad, and I think in time Jacob will be glad too. Once the big hurts are washed over, he'll be over the moon."

Jessie wiped her tears away with a fist. "Thanks, Dee. Really. Thanks for understanding." She sighed deeply, then straightened. "Dee?"

"Um-humn?"

"Would you mind if I went for a drive? I kinda need some time to just… you know…think. And listen to some music."

"Of course, honey. As long as you don't mind Carlotta and I spoiling your children rotten while you're gone."

"Thanks. You're the best, you know that, right?"

"I know. Charles tells me every day."

Emitting a small laugh, Jessie slid off the chair and responded with, "That's what Matt said about Julie. I guess I'm lucky to have such wonderful long-term married role models in my life to show me how it's supposed to be done."

Popping into the playroom to kiss her children and tell them she'd be back in a bit, Jessie stood and watched them for a minute. She leaned into Dee's shoulder and clasped her hand between hers. "They sure are beautiful, Dee."

Deirdre's reassuring squeeze was her answer.

"I wonder if this new baby is a boy or a girl. And how much the baby will look like his daddy."

Narrowing her eyebrows, Dee later wondered what Jessie meant by that comment. But for now, she walked her to the door. "Are you planning to end up anywhere in particular, Jessie? Or are you just going to drive?"

"I was thinking of heading towards Langley, Dee. Not...no, not to the brown house. Or what's left of it. No, thank you. Um, I was thinking of dropping by the *Drifters* set. I miss the old place."

"Okay. Well drive safe, honey, and we'll see you in a few hours, then?"

Brushing her lips against Deirdre's cheeks, Jessie agreed. "Thanks, Dee. And yes, I will plan to be back for dinner. See you then."

It was a cool Vancouver day, and since Jessie had the kids, she was driving a new SUV that Charles picked out for her, a silver Mercedes. She couldn't bear to drive in the vehicle she and her kids were stolen from, on a bad November day when her life spun out of control. Now, she turned the new vehicle east and hit Highway One for Langley.

She did not play Jacob's tunes in the car. Instead, she put her iPhone on *shuffle*, and floated between the honeyed tones of Sarah McLachlan, Eva Cassidy, Hozier, and even some upbeat Tyler Shaw and Maroon 5, which left her feeling slightly more hopeful than when she first pulled out of La Casa's curved driveway.

The *Drifters* sets, for the most part, had long been dismantled. The cozy old cedar-shingled barn remained, though, as did the split rail fence. The big modern building that housed offices, washrooms, wardrobe and gear storage, as well as lunch space for cast and crew, was still standing as well, albeit it was locked up and, judging by the weeds growing up around it, was abandoned, isolated and lonely. After parking, Jessie wandered down the hill where the nineteenth century village was once situated, but it hurt to see the place empty and barren, so she didn't stay long, although the scent of sawdust and new carpentry still tickled her nostrils in memory.

Walking up the hill, she called to mind the tough times, and the magical times, with Josh, back when they first fell in love. Her heart fluttered at the recall of their initial topsy-turvy love affair. The awful night when Charlie showed up and she had to let Josh go for a while seized her heart in a spasm, so fresh did the memory seem now as she stood in the place where Josh's fingers touched hers as he took the reins of her horse and slouched away towards the barn.

Unable to keep from chuckling aloud as she recalled the now infamous 'horse stunt day,' Jessie's eyes started to sting with new tear-filled memories—now overfull with loss and struggle and survival, and remembrance of a man she didn't know back in the *Drifters* days—sweet, sad Jacob.

She ended up behind the barn, under the cottonwood tree where she and Josh spent hours lingering after lunch or during lighting when they weren't needed on set. Sometimes he let a finger audaciously trace her thigh, in the early days. Sometimes, in season two, they cuddled. And sometimes Jessie just moved that favorite rogue piece of hair behind Josh's ear, loving him with a smile and a touch. Music, too, was a big part of those surreal days. The mellow tone of the now-gone 1985 Gibson J-45, her father's, was deeply imbued in the cottonwood tree, in cherished melodies and lyrics conceived underneath the shelter of its heart-shaped leaves.

Aching, Jessie turned to leave, shivering a little in the cool air, but she stopped short when she saw a familiar figure appear by the front of the barn.

He was wearing the same old tan leather jacket she loved on him—his favorite, she knew, because, well, she knew him. He was grazing a finger along the old cedar shakes of the barn, not looking at her just yet, just reminiscing, likely, as she was.

Jessie caught her breath, and wondered…

Josh stopped before her, nervously jingling the keys of the King Ranch in his fingers.

"Dee, mmmm?" she asked knowingly.

"Yeah," he said. "Dee. She called me."

"Mmmm. I see. And what did the grand lady have to say?"

"She said, 'go see if my girl is okay.' So I did. Uh, I am. Seeing if you're okay." He squinted. "Are you, Jess? Are you okay?"

"I will be. So many things…so much time…lost…"

"Yeah. So much time…" He looked around them, remembering good times and enduring friendships, before settling his liquid gaze back on Jessie's pale eyes.

Josh waited.

She took a deep breath. "I want my family back, Josh. I want my husband back."

He started to smile—he couldn't help himself. But then Josh tilted his head and frowned. "What is it, Jessie? Why do I sense a 'but'?" He planted his feet more firmly, but his intestines clenched. He stopped jingling the keys.

It took a minute for her to find the words, but there was no getting around it. He needed to know. Josh needed to know. *Will he run away? Will he yell, how angry is he going to be?*

"Jesus, this is hard," she gulped as she tried to prepare herself for an unknown outcome. Then she faced him straight on and blurted out the difficult truth. "I'm pregnant, Josh."

It was news. It floored him. Josh sucked in a breath, paused, knifed fingers through his hair, and turned in a circle the way a dog does when it's looking for a place to lie down. But he didn't run.

He turned back to her. "Okay." The chocolate eyes were brimming over, though.

"Okay?" *Seriously? Really?*

She whispered the next line. "We don't have to tell him." She felt sick for saying it, but it was true…it was something Jessie was considering.

"He doesn't…Jacob doesn't know?"

"No. I mean, I…I think he may have suspected, but…I'm not really sure. I didn't tell him. So I don't think he really knows."

"Fuuckk, Jessie…this is a lot right now…"

"I know, but…Josh, please, I'm at a loss here. I need you. I need our family.

I tried with Jacob, I really did, but none of this was ever fair to him. It's you, Josh. It's always been you. It will always be you."

"Always and forever…"

"Yeah. Always. And forever. Please."

Jessie knew the moment Josh made a decision—she watched the emotions play over his face the way a bow graces a fiddle. First shock, then fear, and then doubt. He was seeing it all…going through a pregnancy with her, supporting her through the birth and labor, sleepless nights, and then an entire future raising a child who was not his. Who was a product of a time when he, Josh, was not emotionally or physically available to Jessie. When Jacob stepped in and took Jessie's hand, and held her, and rocked her, and cuddled her and…and loved her.

So much pain. So much loss. It was time to let it go.

"Jessie," he started, as the clouds slowly cleared, drifting away like the tide, "Jacob has always been there for you and…for us. When we needed him. When our kids needed him."

"Yes," she said, as a slow nausea rose in her belly.

"He picked up the pieces. And he did a damn good job of it."

"Yes." *Oh God. He is going to tell me to go back to Jacob. To raise this child with Jacob.*

But Josh surprised her. Instead he said, with compassion and conviction, "We will do the right thing by him. We will tell him about this baby. That it's his."

Unable to breathe, Jessie planted her feet and shoved her hands in the pockets of her aviator jacket. She watched the hard emotions play out on the face and in the eyes of the man she loved. He didn't disappoint.

"And he will be involved in this child's life. The kid will have two dads. Two dads who will be crazy about him. Okay with you?"

She nodded. The words, other than the almost mute "We?" were not available to Jessie at the moment. All that was available was a slowly expanding awareness that she, and Josh, were getting back together. And as tears rolled down Jessie's cheeks, she saw his eyes the way they used to be, before all the badness stole the man she knew away from her. They were clear now, and bright, lit deeply from within, filled with love for her, and they opened up again and let her in; they let her back into his soul.

Now, she choked on the overwhelming welcome *home*, and nodded vehemently as he stood across from her, the realization hitting him at the same time that they, Josh and Jessie, were once again…Josh and Jessie.

He stepped forward first, and laid a palm on her cheek. He thumbed away a tear and then let his hand move further back, so he could cradle her head and pull her towards him. Josh placed his left hand on the small of Jessie's back. When she could finally breathe again, and move, she wriggled forward and buried herself wholly and completely in her husband's arms, wrapping her good arm under his jacket and around his waist, and ducking her face deeply into the hollow of his neck.

She heard him sigh, and even moan a little at the sweet pleasure of holding her again, and she did the same, although her shoulders were shaking as a great relief took hold. Releasing a year of unknowns and the brutal agony of watching Josh suffer was painful, but it was necessary, and as Jessie wept in Josh's arms, he rocked her slowly and whispered *I love you* again and again and again, knowing why she cried, yet smiling with his own relief and banished grief.

When Jessie could finally sigh herself, and lift her head up again, she caught an amused glint in his eye.

"I'm sorry," she sniffled, squishing away the last of her tears with her fingers. "I've been a bit of a mess lately."

"A beautiful mess," he whispered. "A stunning, gorgeous, sweet, loving, beautiful mess. And may I add a very forgiving one. I think."

"It was awful, Josh. Watching you hurt like that."

"Never again," he murmured. "Never again, Jessie. I swear. I promise you that. And I promise you one more thing."

"Mmmm?"

"I promise you from this day forward that I will accept this child as my own. He—or she—will call me Daddy and he or she will be my son or daughter. I will never treat this child differently from our other children. Speaking of which…we'll have a few more of those, too, okay?"

She tilted her head back and laughed. "Okay. Yes. We will. But Josh, let's just get through this pregnancy first, okay?"

"Okay." Josh wiped away a loose wisp of hair, and let the backs of his fingers trace over his wife's cheek. Reaching up her good hand, Jessie wound warm fingers around his.

"I'm glad," she murmured. "So glad you came back to me."

His small smile was enough of a response for her. Josh bent towards her, and lightly pressed his lips to hers.

The movement was small, but the sensation—exhilarating. Tingles ignited in Jessie's body that she loved, and missed. She laid her other hand over his, grimacing a little at the ache in her shoulder, and breathed him in as he kissed her.

"Oh God, I love you," she whispered. "So much, Josh. So much."

"I love you back, little one," was his affirmation back to her. "Always and forever."

He pressed her to him again, and they held each other tight before they started walking back towards the parking lot.

"We had some good times here, huh?" Jessie murmured up to him as she settled under his arm for the walk.

"And some tough times." He grinned stupidly, and reminded her of 'horse stunt day.'

"Ahhhh," she said, throwing a hand over her eyes. "I was an idiot that day."

"You had a reason to be. And I didn't help matters any."

"You were getting back at me for initiating you into the ways of filming love scenes."

"Ah, that day. Yes, also one for the memory banks. Speaking of which, I am not, on principle, going to see yours and Jacob's film. I do have to draw the line there."

"Yeah. I get that, Josh. Not so sure I can handle it, either. I think I will be skipping that premiere."

They were at the parking lot now, and both were loathe to climb into separate vehicles. Josh faced her and spoke softly.

"Jessie, I want you to know that I understand now…what he means to you. I know how hard this is for you, to switch gears again like this. And I know how he must be suffering too—believe me, I know. I will never judge him again, or say a bad word against him."

"You knew I would go to him, though. You knew."

"He was always a step behind me, Jess. He was your best friend, your musical soul mate…it wasn't a surprise, put it that way. And I'm glad it was him. I really am. At least I liked him, and I knew he loved you. Uh…loves you, I guess."

"I don't know where he's going to land in all this now, Josh. It's too hard, you know? To see him or even contact him right now."

"We need to tell him about the baby. Before it gets out in the press."

"Why don't you take a few days to get used to the idea first, okay Josh? Then we'll tell him. Or…I will, I guess. I'll fly down to his dad's or wherever he's hiding and I'll tell him. Then the rest will be up to him."

"He'll want you back." The old fear played in Josh's eyes.

"No. He won't. Not now."

Acceptance marched across his face. "Okay." Josh sighed, and kissed her again. "I don't want to let you go, even to drive home."

"Oh…home. Oh, God." A huge smile widened across Jessie's face. "The kids will be so happy."

"Uh, they're going to be confused as hell, Jessie."

Emily-Grace will be lost without her beloved Jacob, Jessie thought sadly. But aloud she only said, "They'll adapt. Kids are resilient. Look, I told Dee I'd be back to La Casa for dinner. I hope you'll come too, Josh. Then we'll take the kids home, okay?"

"You got it. I'll follow you. Drive safe." Tipping his face in, Josh rested his forehead against hers. "Precious cargo," he whispered, eyes alight.

"Luv you."

"Luv you back."

With that, Jessie led the way out of the old *Drifters* parking lot, glancing in her rearview mirror one last time at the cherished place where, years ago, she played a part in a Canadian TV western, opened her heart, and fell in love, not just with Josh, but with a whole new set of friends. All because of a lonely guy she rescued from a pile of garbage, and a little thing called hope.

Glancing in the rearview mirror, Jessie saw him behind her, in the King Ranch, and she smiled. It felt right to have him there again, as her wing man, as her husband, as the father of, well, two of her children, and now as the honorary father of another.

"I do love you, Josh Sawyer," she breathed, before flipping on her iTunes, and singing her way home.

Chapter Twenty-nine

It was a few weeks before Jessie got the nerve to go see Jacob. But her baby bump would be showing soon, and word was bound to get out once she and Josh started telling their friends. So far, only Charles, Dee, Matt, Arnie and Carlotta knew, although others in their close circle suspected, those being Big Dan, Susanne, Ulysses and Miranda.

Jacob was playing a small gig in Dallas, as a guest on one of his father's more exclusive intimate shows. It seemed apropos to tell him there. Jessie asked Charles to arrange for her to use the jet as well as get tickets set aside for her and Matt. She left Josh home with the children.

He kissed her goodbye and told Matt not to let her out of his sight. Then Josh watched Matt back his new Audi sedan out of the driveway, and swift Jessie away to change Jacob's life—again.

Jessie and Matt watched the show first, unseen by Jacob, who didn't know Jessie was in the audience, or that she was planning to see him afterwards.

Jacob played his own tunes, and a few he wrote with his father, but he avoided playing any of the songs he and Jessie wrote together, including the newest chart-topping ballad. Everybody in the audience was disappointed they didn't get to hear the new tune, and when folks shouted at him to play it, he ignored them by ducking his head and swallowing bitterly.

It killed Jessie to watch him. She chewed her fingernails through half of the show, and twisted her sweater around her fingers during the other half. Jacob's sorrow leached into his music, and into his overall countenance. He hadn't just lost Jessie. He'd lost an entire family.

Jessie gripped Matt's hand during part of the show. She no longer needed to wear a sling over her shoulder, nor did he. Their friendship now was on a deeper level than ever before, and Matt had signed on again as Jessie's family's main security, under the thumb of Charles Keating, of course, with Arnie, Ulysses (who just announced his engagement to the exotic Miranda!), Dan and Susanne rounding out the team.

After the concert, with backstage access also arranged by Charles, Matt, with one arm around Jessie's waist, escorted her to Jacob's dressing room. Raising a fist, she swallowed nervously, and knocked.

"It's open," she heard the much-missed voice call.

Slowly, Jessie laid a hand over the door handle. She depressed it and pushed. The door opened, but before she went in she glanced behind her at Matt, who was watching her while chatting with Jacob's father, Tom. Matt nodded at her. *You can do this, Jessie. It's the right thing to do.*

Jacob had his back to her. He was pulling a blue T-shirt over his head, and turned sharply when Jessie's small intake of breath telegraphed her presence in his dressing room. It was the Celtic cross that caused the involuntary sound. Always, Jessie loved that part of him. To her, it was sexy, a symbol of his heritage and thus, of who he was, and it was also Jacob wearing his pain on the outside. The cross was Jacob.

He froze when he saw Jessie in his space, in Dallas, unexpected and, well, unwanted. Biting his bottom lip, he finished pulling the T-shirt down over the waist of his jeans, not losing her gaze as he did so. Jessie reached behind her to close the door.

"Don't," he demanded. "Leave it open."

Noise from the hallway filtered in—a cacophony of voices, some excited, some low in conversation, and some just drifting by, accented with heels and boots. Jessie paused, but then she pushed the door closed despite his wishes.

"I need to talk to you," she started. "In private."

"Asking me for a divorce, Jessie? You don't need to. We were never married." Grimacing, he reached for a blue plaid shirt she loved on him. She swallowed as she watched him put it on, covering completely now, in two layers, the inked cross she loved, the body she cherished.

"Are you always going to hate me, Jacob?"

Pausing, he stared hard at her. His anger and hurt jumped out at her in spades. "Didn't take you long to go back to him. What, a day? Two?"

"I'm not going to apologize, Jacob. Not anymore. No more regrets. I loved every second with you. I love you. I always will. But always, babe, always…there was that pull towards Josh. I can't help that. He is my husband." She tried to make him understand, to see she was sincere, but he had a wall built against her now, a big tough brick wall Jessie feared may never come down.

"Why are you here, Jessie? Can't see you hopping down to Dallas just to catch my show." Jacob's voice was edged with bitter defeat. He averted her eyes by moving around the small space gathering up belongings and tucking them into a knapsack.

"Please, Jacob, stop moving. Can we just talk for a second, please?"

It hit him then, why she was likely there. He stopped, a hand shoved halfway into the knapsack, and he straightened and looked sideways back at her. He asked anyway, for a second time.

"Why are you here, Jessie? For some reason, I don't think you're asking me back." A hopeful yet hopeless upward tip of his chin accompanied the remark. The cobalt eyes were dim. When there was light in them, it was flashing. Like fire.

Jessie's eyes betrayed her desire to tell him in the most fluid, easiest possible way. Swallowing, she tried to speak but couldn't quite form the words.

"Jesus Christ," he glowered, turning and dropping onto the farthest arm of the couch. "I knew it. You're pregnant."

"Y-yeah," she said. "I actually am, Jacob."

"I thought…I thought you might be." Swiping a hand nervously under his nose, Jacob sniffed, then rested the hand on his knee. "I wasn't sure."

"I want you to be part of this baby's life, Jacob. You are such a great dad."

"Not a dad, Jessie. I was never a 'dad' to your kids." He held up two fingers of each hand to air-quote the significance of the word. "I was a nanny. Apparently."

Shock registered on Jessie's face then. She paled. "That's not fair, Jacob."

"Why, because I didn't stow Josh away in a goddamn basement in Langley first? Not really all that much different, the way I see it. Actually," he raised a pointy finger, "the way your 'husband' pointed it out to me. Nadia and me…yeah, we're a team, Jess. Both after a family that never belonged to us."

"Look, I get that you're angry, Jacob. You have every right to be, but you knew right from the start things might change between you and me because of—"

"Because of your ass-whipped boozehound husband, yes, I know, but I'm tired of you reminding me. So what happens now, then, huh? He gets to raise my kid. That's what happens. Jesus." As the realization of that sunk in, Jacob crumpled under the strain of the last few weeks. Pointing towards the door, he bit his lip again and demanded she leave. "Get the fuck out of here, Jessie. And just for the record, I don't know why you bothered telling me. I would never have known the fucking difference."

"For one, I'm sure you can count, Jacob."

"Yeah, that went well…"

"We got over a hundred…" Jessie was panicking now. "We got a lot of days, and nights too, Jacob."

"We didn't get nearly enough, Jessie. Not even fucking close. I told you after that first night…once it was over…it was *over*. And the next night wasn't enough, either, or the next, or the next. I thought it would be, but it wasn't. It never was."

"Don't do this, Jacob. Shut me out if you want to, but don't shut out your child. You thought I mattered? I didn't matter worth a shit! Your child is who matters. The love you will have for this child will floor you. You will be on your knees for love of this kid. Trust me."

"I was on my knees for love of *your* kids, Jess. And look where that got me."

"I know, babe, I know. They miss you too. Emily-Grace—"

"Don't!" he cried, placing his hands over his ears. "Don't even fucking talk to me about her! About your kids. I don't want to hear their names! I don't want to see their faces! You got everything back! What did I get? I got nothing!"

"You got this!" Jessie laid a hand on her belly, then reached for his. He fought against her, but she placed it against her belly anyway, and held on for dear life should he try to pull away. He did, at first, but then Jessie pleaded further. "Jacob, don't you remember? We used to do this with Emily-Grace, and again with David. During *Mystic Nights*, or when we were recording, we'd laugh about it. Jesus, you felt David move before Josh did! Emily-Grace knew your voice better than her own father's, for God's sake!"

He seemed to be settling somewhat, although Jacob's eyes were still misting over, and there were bright red spots of anger and frustration on his cheeks. Staring at his hand on her belly, though, he listened.

"Jacob, babe, this is your child. Yours. Josh will do right by this baby." At that, he tried to pull away again, and groaned, but Jessie held on. "Because you did right by his. When they needed you. When I needed you. He wants you to have this. Josh and me both, we want you to know your child, but more importantly, Jacob…we want this child to know his dad. Please. You and Josh both understand how important this is, to know what it's like not to know your dads. As a kid? Come on, babe. You want this kid out there wondering why his or her father doesn't come to see him? Her? Or take him, I dunno, fishing or something? Or…play shows with him when he's grown? Please. Think about it, at least."

Finally, Jessie let him pull away. When Jacob looked back up at her, his face was spotted with tears.

"Oh, honey," she sighed, trying unsuccessfully to wipe the tears away, because he blanched and turned his head.

"I'll miss it," he said, backing away. "The pregnancy, the labor, the birth… everything…school, report cards, all of it."

"You can be as involved as you want to be, Jacob. I swear. We both want that. With the other kids too. Like I said, they miss you."

"You make it all sound so easy, Jessie. Like I can just wander in and out of these kids' lives, and pretend it's all good. You wrap it all up with a tidy little bow, but you seem to be forgetting the most difficult part…"

Jessie knew what was coming, but she steeled herself to hear it anyway.

"You." He stood before her, trembling. He knuckled his hands into fists. Then he said it again, this time with an air of dead calm, as if the word was dead to him. "You. Loving you. That's not part of the deal. So on that note, which I find intolerable to discuss, and even more intolerable to discuss while having to stand here and look at you, I will ask you one more time to go before I call security. Please. Just go."

223

"This is new to you. You just need some time, to process this—"

"Jessie! Just go!"

"Don't do this, Jacob. Don't let me walk out that door with your child and exit your life. Don't fucking do it."

He wasn't moving, nor was he still hollering at her, so Jessie took a chance. She moved towards him and grabbed his shirt, startling him. He tried to fight her, to push her away, but Jessie was strong, despite the still sore shoulder. She wrapped both arms around him and buried her face in his neck. "I love you, you stupid dork. Your kid's gonna love you. Don't shut us out of your life. I love you."

With one final squeeze and an aching sigh, Jessie flipped around on her heel and whipped open the door. She paused before walking through it, but she had to be strong. Josh and the kids were waiting at home, and Matt was here now to help her stand tall and deal with the heavy emotions the difficult visit wrought.

The door closed behind her with a loud crunch.

Tom Ryan waited a few minutes before knocking and entering.

He found his son on the couch, head in his hands, struggling to stay there and not melt into a puddle on the floor.

"Son," Tom said in his low throaty voice. "If it helps, she wasn't in any better shape than you when she walked outta here."

"It doesn't. But thanks for trying, pops." Inhaling, Jacob wiped his eyes. "Did Matt tell you why she was here?"

"Yeah. He did, kid."

"I can't do it. I can't be involved with her in any way. This is like the biggest kick in the ass ever."

"Why, Jacob? Why can't you get involved?"

"Because it hurts too goddamned much. That's why."

Tom clamped a hand on his shoulder, causing Jacob to look over at him. "I know, son. I know how much it hurts. And look how much I missed."

A small light came back on in Jacob's eyes then. He patted his dad's hand on his shoulder and nodded his understanding.

Tom had one more piece to say to try to help heal the massive hurt of rejection. "Give it some time, kid. It'll get easier. But don't make the same mistake I did. That Josh guy doesn't know shit about music. The kid's gonna need a dad who does."

"The kid's mom knows music. He or she will be fine."

"Pshaw. Jessie's a pop star over-produced by Charles Keating and his minions. The kid's gonna need some soul."

Surprised at the ease with which it hit him, Jacob laughed. "I'm glad you're around, pops. I don't know. I'll see."

"Hey! This is my grandkid you're talking about. Let's spoil the kid rotten and send him—or her—back to Jessie on a sugar high. Every time. We'll wreak our vengeance! Now, about that over-produced Charles Keating shit, when are you gonna come record with me?"

And so a mostly-absent father eased the pain of a man about to become a father, while Jessie laid her head on Matt's shoulder and pondered her unborn child's future. Placing headphones over her ears, she listened to her and Jacob's music on the flight back to Vancouver, remembering with a melancholic fondness the long studio days, the concerts, the laughs and the silly arguments over the years. *Mystic Nights* came to mind, and the new movie she and Jacob had filmed together. There were so many memories…and, lately, so many hurts.

But this child would link them together. *Heck*, Jessie thought, *if it comes down to it, at least I know Tom will be open to knowing his grandchild. And maybe Jacob will come around. I hope he will. I think he will.*

Closing her eyes, she slept on Matt's shoulder (the good one), and dreamed of golden fields. This time, when she turned her head she spotted Josh, and waved to him. He walked towards her through the bearded barley, a new baby in his arms. It was a boy, and his name was Dylan Jacob.

Chapter Thirty

Dylan was born June 1st. Throughout the long labor, Josh returned Jacob's old favor from the night Emily-Grace was born, and held and kissed Jessie's hand while Jacob's son came into the world. Kicking and screaming, the baby was a healthy eight pounds and seven ounces. Josh groaned in jest when the infant's lungs made his presence known.

"Another singer," he grinned. "Good thing David's into cars and motorbikes!"

"We'll start a family group," Jessie offered. "Me and Emily-Grace and Dylan."

"Dylan. Hmmm. I wonder what Jacob will think of the name?"

Disconcerted, Jessie recovered quickly, smiling as the doctor laid the new baby on her belly. Touching his small head, Jessie's heart ached for the father who chose not to see his son enter the world.

Josh caught the small frown before it upended into a smile. "What was that for?" he asked. "That little sad moment?"

"We talked about having kids," she said softly, knowing Josh would understand. "We actually agreed on Lennon for our first baby, whether it was a boy or a girl. It's kind of a unisex name these days. Trendy, I guess, but…after the whole Central Park fiasco at the Strawberry Fields Memorial, I couldn't go there. Dylan is Jacob's other big musical influence." She looked up at her husband. "I wasn't up for Bob."

Stroking her head, Josh sighed. "For the child of two songwriters, I think Dylan is a good name."

"If we went with Lennon I suppose everyone would always be asking the poor kid if he is a Beatles fan."

"He'd have gotten used to it. Could be worse. Could be, I dunno, Sting, I suppose."

Laughing outright, Jessie counted the baby's fingers and toes. "You're okay with Dylan, Josh? He's your son too."

"Hey, I agreed ages ago, Jessie. It's nice. It's a good name for this little guy."

He bent and kissed Jessie's damp forehead, unable to hide a modicum of jealousy for this bond Jessie would share with Jacob forever. Josh pushed the unwelcome thought away as quickly as it assaulted his senses.

For sure, this was harder on Jessie, who hadn't heard from Jacob at any point in her pregnancy. She sent him texts, though, and long emails with images of her growing belly attached. To her credit, she also created a book for him—a keepsake of doctors' appointments, how she was feeling on certain days, even what she ate and what music she played and sang to the unborn infant in her womb (mostly Jacob's tunes, of course).

Now, an ennui came over her as she disappeared for a moment back into her Jacob days. Josh didn't need to ask where she went—he sometimes saw her rocking alone in the room they decorated for the new baby, the same sad expression coloring her pretty features.

"He'll come around," Josh said, tenderly touching the baby's little fingers. "I mean, look at this baby. He's perfect."

"You're really something, Sawyer. You know that?"

"I do. My wife tells me all the time." Josh chuckled when the baby hiccupped and made an adorable baby sound. "He is precious, Jessie. You did good."

As if that was a cue to rest after the long labor, Jessie yawned. "Go home, Josh. Get some sleep. But please take a picture of our son first."

Obliging, Josh retrieved his iPhone from its resting place on a nearby rolling table tray, and he snapped a few pics. After, he held up the phone. "Should I send them to Jacob? Or are you up for it?"

"You do it, please. Just tell him…tell him Dylan's perfect. And to please come meet him."

"Will do, little one. I'm staying, by the way. The kids are fine with Charles and Dee for a few more hours. Rest."

And so Josh and Jessie's family expanded by one. Dylan's father did not visit his son, although Tom Ryan dropped in to the busy UBC household later in the month when he was in Vancouver for a show at the Orpheum.

And then, to everyone's surprise, one day Jacob agreed to perform at an outdoor music festival in Seattle, where Jessie was also scheduled to play.

The festival was held over the final weekend in September.

Dylan Jacob Sawyer was almost four months old.

Chapter Thirty-one

*J*acob was tuning his guitar when a low buzz around the tents alerted him to Jessie's arrival. In his own dressing room tent, three doors down from Jessie, he tilted an ear and stopped tuning to listen. Outside, he could hear a volunteer welcome Jessie. But it appeared she wasn't alone. It seemed, judging by the oohhs and ahhhs, that her children were with her and so, likely, was Josh.

Setting his guitar down on its padded stand, Jacob sidled to the front flap and peeked out. He was right—the whole family was there, standing outside chatting with one of the festival organizers. Josh was holding the new baby. Jacob sucked in a breath. His heart picked up its pace, and his palms got sweaty.

"Damn," he muttered, turning away from the lovely little family scene playing out in front of him. Wiping his hands on his jeans, he grabbed the guitar again, and picked out a few notes, his back to the flap.

By her tent, Jessie was surreptitiously eyeing the backstage area. It didn't take long to scan the names on the artists' tents—Jacob's was down from hers, at the end of their particular section. She was half tempted to pluck Dylan out of Josh's arms and thrust him into Jacob's, but this wasn't the time. Jacob's set was due to start in twenty minutes.

Emily-Grace tugged on her hand. "Momma, I go see Gwammie?"

Looking up, Jessie spotted Charles and Dee making their way to them. "Sure, sweetheart," she said to her daughter, who took off running and practically leapt into Charles' arms. David was in hot pursuit. The smiles on Charles and Dee's faces were wide and bright. This little family was everything to them. It seemed the days before Jessie entered their lives were grey and dim. Now everything was perfect Technicolor.

Jessie greeted them with a wave as Dee reached for Dylan's fingers and let the baby wrap his little hand around her forefinger.

"How's this little guy doing? Jessie, did you bring hearing protection muffs for the kids?"

"He's great, and I did, but I'm guessing they're going to hang in the tent with Katy when she gets here, and probably draw pictures. 'Cept for this little guy. I'll leave him with you guys when I'm on, I guess."

"Have you seen Matt yet?" asked Charles.

"Yep. He's around. I think he went for concert fries."

"As if!" Dee laughed. Charles rolled his eyes.

"That's an idea," Josh said. "Anyone else here starving?"

"I'm sure there's craft in there, Josh. Can you see if there are veggies for the kids?"

"I need salt. Greasy fries."

"Don't you dare feed greasy fries to my kids." Pretending to pout, Jessie reached for Dylan. "If you want to go out to concessions, at least wait 'til Matt gets back." She spotted Arnie approaching behind Josh. "Or...there's Arnie. Get him to go with you."

Always now, there would be an ever-present fear in public places. Josh's star was high, Jessie's was higher. Still, neither wanted to give in completely to the fear. They weighed the risks and made judgments from there. The children came first, always. The couple never left each other without a hug, a kiss, and an *always and forever*. Nothing was taken for granted, not a moment, not a smile, not even the tears that came with scraped knees.

Now, Jessie let her eyes wander past Josh to Jacob's tent. A PA was making his way over, likely to give Jacob a time warning, Jessie thought. She sucked on her lip and waited.

Charles and Dee disappeared inside the tent with Emily-Grace and David, while Josh studied Jessie. "I was kidding about the fries," he said, taking her right hand and pulling it away from her left under the baby's diapered bum. She was making crescents with her fingernails again, a habit she had mostly broken. "Are you going to watch his set?"

"Mmmm, yeah, I'd like to, Josh. Just from the wing, if security will let me."

"You don't want him to see you."

"Not yet. After." She shrugged. "I don't want to throw him off."

"He knows you're going to be here."

"I know, but…it's just awkward, you know? Can you and Dee keep an eye on the kids so I can watch?"

"Of course, Jess."

"I guess I should take Dylan inside for now. I'll sneak over to the stage after I hear Jacob start his set." Lightly, she swatted Josh's belly. "Go get your fries. And bring me some too, will you? Vinegar and pepper. A little salt. Please."

Shortly, Jacob got his five-minute warning, and he headed across the grass towards the stage. Jessie stood inside her tent and watched him go. He moved quickly, favorite guitar in one hand, head down, trying not to look towards her tent. But when he was almost past, he couldn't help himself. Slowly, his head came up. Jessie backed away when she saw him look up— she wasn't ready for eye contact yet. In a few short moments, he was counting himself in, alone, and then singing for a raucous crowd of 50 000 under a warm blue Seattle sky.

Glancing over at Josh, who was back from getting his fries and was getting the kids' toys organized, Jessie smiled wanly. He looked up and telegraphed his thoughts to her—*it's okay. Go ahead.* Moving the tent flap aside, Jessie stepped outside.

She made her way to the stage accompanied by Arnie, who, being the efficient kind of guy he was, had already cleared access to the stage for Jacob's old musical partner. He found her a place in the wing where she could tuck herself behind a large stand-up banner, but there was nowhere to really hide. She was still in Jacob's sightline, should he choose to look stage left.

After a few moments, Jessie felt warm arms wrap themselves loosely around her neck from behind. Familiar lips brushed against her neck. She smiled sadly, and ran her fingers over Josh's warm hands.

"He's angry," she told him as they watched Jacob play. "His songs are angry. They're beautiful, but listen to the lyrics."

"I guess he has a right to be angry, Jess. He did a lot for us, for what? To get kicked aside like a bag of potatoes."

231

"He has a son, Josh. That's a pretty special reminder of the time we spent together."

"Jacob agreed to play this show, Jessie. That's saying something. He wants to talk, to meet his son."

"I hope so."

"Time's a good healer, little one."

"I guess."

A final chord announced the end of Jacob's current song. Sweating, he wiped a forearm across his brow, and turned slightly towards the wings. He froze when he saw Jessie standing there, with Josh's arms around her neck. It took him a moment to pull himself together.

Straightening, tensing, Jessie raised a palm in greeting to the man who held her hand when she was lost. He didn't wave back, nor did he smile. Instead, Jacob let his gaze drift downwards. Studying a piece of green tape on the black stage, he gathered his wits before starting another song.

This one was clearly a message to Jessie.

It began with a solo guitar melody, joined after a few beats by rolling percussion and bass. The lyrics recounted the bad times of Jacob and Jessie's relationship, accented by a chorus reminiscing and remembering the good times and the overall love the couple shared. Jessie knew he was singing to her, because she recognized the personal tidbits Jacob planted in the song, like references to New York, and a particular food, and jumping on the bed which they did one night after a few glasses of wine and before a particularly memorable lovemaking session. Its ending was sudden and almost incomplete, which Jessie felt must reflect how Jacob felt about their relationship.

As he accepted his applause with a shy wave afterwards, Jacob tried not to look back over at Jessie, but once again the temptation was too much. This time when he glanced that way he caught Josh's eye too. It appeared all three of them understood Jacob's message to her, but no one was angry anymore. They were all just sad.

Jacob had a set to finish to a crowd who would give anything to hear him and Jessie play together again. But he didn't ask her on stage. He finished the set and, as he started an encore, he glanced again to the wing. His personal audience of two was gone.

Jessie wasn't scheduled to play until eight. Jacob's set ended at five. Josh was quiet on the way back to Jessie's tent. He faltered just outside, and Jessie turned to look at him.

"What?"

"You're right. That one song in particular was downright nasty."

"Only to my ears. And to yours apparently. No one else cares."

"Still."

Across the grass from them, Jacob was slinking back to his tent. He could see them in his peripheral vision, but he had no energy left to send to Jessie at this time. It was all used up in the song he sang for her, the one he wrote after they split up, the one he hoped to play for her in person some day. Funny thing, though, he thought somehow playing it for her would be satisfying in some weird way, that it would tell her what he thought of her these days, which was a confused mixture of *glad you're alive* and *glad I had you for a while* versus *I miss you* and *it still hurts*.

It didn't satisfy him at all, though. It just felt conniving and mean. And from her and Josh's eyes, in the wing, he knew it affected them the same way.

Jessie watched him slouch across the field towards his tent. She turned to Josh to say, "I'm going over," but Josh was gone.

"Josh?" Peeking inside the tent, she saw him pluck Dylan from his Grammie Dee's arms.

He stopped in front of Jessie. "Give us five," he said. "No more sadness, for you or for Jacob. That sulky singer's got to meet his kid." Just then, Dylan gurgled lovingly at the man he knew as his dad. Josh laughed. "How can you not love this face? He's beautiful."

Leaning forward to kiss Jessie, who was suddenly panicking, he whispered, "Don't worry, little one. Come over in five. I love you."

Jacob was outside his tent now, leaning against a wooden split rail fence that lined the perimeter of the backstage area. Yanking a cigarette out of a cardboard pack, he was about to light up when he spotted Josh striding towards him, the baby in his arms. He rack focused his vision to Jessie, who stepped outside of her tent to frown at him.

"Oh no," Jacob breathed, straightening. "Not doing this now." He glanced around, trying to figure out where to go or what to do, but Josh was at his side in an instant.

Josh didn't hesitate. "Gimme the smokes, Ryan. So you can hold your kid." Grabbing the unlit cigarette from between Jacob's fingers, and then the pack, Josh held them in one hand and finagled Dylan over to his biological father with the other.

"I can't...this is not a good idea, Josh." But Jacob found the baby in his arms anyway, staring up at him. He froze, and stared back.

"Okay. So, so far you've missed the birth of your son, a lot of sleepless nights, many shitty diapers, tons of laundry and, oh yeah, this kid's got a good set of lungs, which the neighbors are already complaining about. I almost forgot to mention the puke. He spits up a lot."

"Yeah? Lungs? Neighbors are complaining?" Jacob hardly heard Josh. He was too lost in those little eyes, and in the miniature fingers.

"No. But Jessie's already got plans to get him on guitar. Look at those fingers." Reaching for Dylan's hand, Josh used his baby finger to hook the tiny fingers and lift them. He grinned. "He's got long guitar and piano playing fingers, Jessie says."

"Oh." Inhaling deeply, Jacob was trying to remain calm. Studying the baby, he managed, "He's got Jessie's smile." He added quietly, without looking at Josh, "How is she? Jessie?"

"She's okay. She misses you."

"Not enough, though, eh?"

"Ha. Yeah. Enough." Josh frowned. "And yeah, he does have her smile. Dylan's a good baby, Jacob. The kid's not colicky like David was. He sleeps through the night. He's easy to take care of."

"Yeah, well, don't get any ideas, Sawyer."

"He's your son, Jacob. And besides the shitty stuff, literally, let me add you've also missed a gazillion of those Jessie-smiles, lots of sickeningly cute baby gurgling, and at least a few attempts at stringing thoughts together. And the neatest thing? He just discovered his hands. That's still new, so you might catch some of that whole laying on his back thing, going 'what the hell are these.'"

A long exhale was Jacob's way of processing this creature in his arms. Dylan burped and looked innocently up at the cobalt blue eyes.

"Ha. I see you've been teaching him all the good parts about being a guy."

"Nah. He picked the burping up from Jessie."

As if on cue, Jessie cozied up to her boys. Lightly, she touched the baby's head before letting her eyes meet Jacob's. One arm she tucked around Josh's waist, as if she wanted to be sure he wouldn't walk away just yet.

"Dylan," she said softly, "meet your daddy. One of 'em."

Jacob's eyes were lost in hers, then. And struggle as he might, suddenly all of this was too much. The angry set he just played, hell, the angry last many months, caught up to him. Jessie caught the flash of frustration and hurt as it crisscrossed his face, but it hurt her too, to see him this way, knowing what he was missing and the hard truth about how he felt. She couldn't speak.

Josh could though, and so he did. "Jacob, I know you're pissed. You have a right to be, believe me. But the way I see it, you have two choices here. You can remain angry your whole life and turn into a bitter old man, or you can take this child into your life and salvage some kind of friendship with Jessie. And with me, if you'll have me. I know you won't have it all, the regular school days and all the usual shit, but you'll get lots of this kid, Jacob, if you'll make time for him. And believe me…you and I both know this kid needs his own dad around. His real dad."

"Josh," Jessie started, uncomfortable with that.

He cut her off. "No, Jessie, it's okay." Focusing on Jacob again he said, "I know where I stand with this kid. I know he's not mine. But Jacob, I'm doing what I can to make him feel like he's mine. I'm raising him the only way I know how, and that's with love and devotion. The same as my own two, the way you took care of Emily-Grace and David when they needed someone to step up. So the way I see it, this kid's got the best of all worlds. He's got two dads. But still…what I can do for him doesn't replace the fact that he has a biological dad, a guy who can play music with him if he chooses to go that route, or wants to buy him, I dunno, a plaid shirt and baggy jeans or something."

At that, Jacob sniffled and chuckled, not a big chuckle, but a start of one, at least. The baby was adorable, still half-smiling up at his dad, and holding Jacob's finger now, to boot. With expert timing, Dylan sent a few baby gurgles skywards.

"He looks so serious." Jacob let one corner of his lips turn up.

"He is," Jessie said, wiping a strand of hair away from her son's eye. "I think he's trying to tell you to listen up, Jacob. To pay attention. He wants you in his life. He needs you."

They were all quiet then, reflecting on their lives and what got them there, to this moment. Jacob let his gaze bore into Jessie's again. *I miss you*, he was thinking, but the pain wasn't quite as acute.

A pretty blonde was sauntering towards them, two beers in her hands. Smiling, she held one up to Jacob. "I see you have your hands full. How about I leave this here for you, Jacob?" There was a picnic table alongside them— she set the beer on the top.

"Hey, thanks Talia. Ummm, do you know Jessie and Josh? Guys, this is Talia."

"You were singing back-up for Jacob today. Nice job." Jessie held out her hand, fighting a momentary pang of jealousy, which she immediately shoved under the picnic table with the ants.

"Yes, thank you. It's nice to meet you, Jessie. I'm a fan." Talia switched her gaze confidently to Josh. "Fan of yours too. Cool to meet you."

"You too," Josh replied honestly, curious.

Jacob sucked in a breath then, and held up the baby so Talia could see Dylan more clearly. "And this," he said, a small smile starting on his lips, "is the next generation of Ryan singers. My son. Dylan."

"Ah. For Bob Dylan, of course."

"Of course." At that, Jacob's eyes lit up, and the anger faded. He looked at Jessie. "Lennon just didn't seem to work anymore, huh? Not after…" He eyed Josh nervously.

"Nope," was her one-word answer.

"Dylan's a good name."

She smiled. "Hey, Jacob? We're having a picnic tomorrow, at Zach and Hil's place. Why don't you come? Bring Talia, maybe?" Biting her lip, she glanced at the blonde to see if she was maybe overstepping her boundaries by inviting her. Talia was bouncing, so Jessie exhaled. "Steve and Sophie will be there, and so will Charlie and Jane. Kayla's here too, on the grounds somewhere with Paul. It'll be pretty chill…you can hang with this guy."

Unsure, shifting his feet, Jacob eyed Talia. She was alight. "I'd love to,

Jacob, if you're okay with me tagging along." He nodded, a flash of a smile appearing at the same time a red flush washed across his cheeks.

"All right," he agreed verbally, his voice hoarse. "I'll get directions from you later, Jessie." He glanced up at Josh and Jessie in turn. "Is it okay if I keep this little guy for a few minutes? Just here." He nodded at the picnic table. "I have a few stories to tell him about his mom."

"Ahhh, don't damage him too early in life, Jacob," Jessie laughed. "He's not even four months old yet. Give the guy a chance." She softened, as Josh touched her arm lightly and started wandering away. "Can I send Emily-Grace over? She misses you so much, babe."

Talia, too, took the cue to move away at that. She didn't mind. Josh was close by, and he was a pretty famous guy…and she had some questions about one of the stunts in that old Harley film he got the Oscar for.

Alone with Jessie again, with the exception of his son, Jacob rearranged the baby in his arms and said, "Yeah. I miss her too, Jess. By all means send Emily-Grace over."

"You doing okay?"

"Not so much, no. Not really. But working my way back to the land of the living, I guess you could say."

"Talia seems sweet."

"She is. I've been spending a bit of time with her. I like her okay. You'll like her. She gets the whole music thing."

"You mean there are people out there who don't? I'm shocked!"

Once again, Jessie was treated to one of Jacob's sad half-smiles. "So'm I, when it comes to music."

"Hey, Jacob? Could we do it again, one last time?" Immediately, Jessie covered her face. "I don't mean the sex thing. Oops." Uncovering her eyes, she looked wistfully at him. "I mean the music thing. Do you think you could… I mean would you…um, tonight. I get it if you don't want to…ummm…"

"Play with you? I don't mean the sex thing either, although…" His eyes were bright now, almost back to their usual playful cobalt blue, and Jessie laughed.

"Yeah. I mean would you join me for some of my set tonight. I'm on at eight."

"The ballad, huh?" Softening, he buried himself in her eyes.

"One last time?"

"The world will go nuts. Twitter will crash."

"Let it," she grinned, leaning in for a hug and a quick brush of her lips against his, before Jessie planted a soft kiss on their baby's forehead.

The moment wasn't lost on any of them, that Jessie, Jacob and Dylan now were their own little family, of sorts. Josh took note, pulled out his iPhone, and snapped a pic.

Jacob found a certain inimitable peace in the moment, a peace he sorely needed, and it got even better when Emily-Grace wandered over and took her momma's hand. She pulled on it, and Jessie bent down to smile at her.

"Momma, can I see Jacob?" the little girl whispered.

"You sure can, sweetheart. He's right here."

She picked her daughter up so Emily-Grace could more clearly see Jacob, who gestured to the picnic table. He and Jessie sat on the top and chatted with Emily-Grace about the baby for a bit. Eventually, Jessie stood and let him have some time with the kids, and with Talia, who wandered back over and sat next to Emily-Grace so they could tease Jacob about how to properly hold the baby.

Jessie took Josh's hand. They sauntered away, both pondering the strange way the universe now seemed to be connecting their pasts and reconciling them with the present. It seemed Jacob was now willing to be a part of their lives, although only time, in its infinite mystery, would really tell.

Chapter Thirty-two

"You know, Jessie, your fans are nuts. I'm not sure I want to go back out there. I'm not sure I have the *guts* to go back out there."

Steve was lounging on the top of the picnic table vacated by Jacob and Talia earlier when a PA brought them dinner. Charlie and Josh were close by, leaning against the split rail fence having a man chat, while Sophie and Jane lauded over the children in Jessie's tent, which was getting a little crazy and giving Deirdre a headache with all the little ones taking over inside.

"I wouldn't go back out there if I were you, either, Steve," mused Jessie with a grin. "In fact, you wouldn't catch me in the audience at an outdoor concert. The last time I went to one some guy hauled down his fly and let 'er rip right in front of me. That was at a Rolling Stones show, in case you were wondering. Josh and I caught a concert in Georgia one summer. I think I actually got some of the guy's pee on my foot." She grimaced with the not-so-pleasant remembrance.

Chuckling, Steve tapped her on the knee. "Sophie has an issue with the long line-ups at the port-a-potties. Think you can do something about that, oh Mizz Headliner?"

"Yeah. I'll tell her to stop drinking those venti caramel macchiatos she likes. That oughtta help."

"She's breastfeeding. Coffee's a thing of the past."

"Don't I know it," Jessie groaned. She leaned into Steve's side. "Seriously, Steve, this whole atmosphere is nuts. It just reflects the circus my life has become. It amazes me that anyone wants to stand out there and get knocked about in the fray just to watch me sing!"

"I guess there's just something special about Jessie Wheeler," Steve grinned. He followed the comment with a shrug. "Or maybe it's Maroon 5 they're really coming to see."

"Ha!" she laughed, elbowing him. "I suspected that all along!"

He sobered. "I'm just kidding about not going back out there, Jessie. I'd give anything to see you play. You know that. We all would. All 8.7 billion gazillion of us, in fact."

"Don't get serious on me, Steve." Smiling warmly at him, Jessie poked him in the ribs. "Your job is to make funnies."

"And to rope your cowboy in when he needs a friend."

"Apparently." A sad smile creased her lips. "Thank God for you, Steve. Always. I mean that."

"And thank God for Charlie," he grinned. "Between all of us, we'll keep Josh from ever going under again, okay?"

Words were too much then, so Jessie just smiled and let her good friend wrap an arm around her shoulders. Steve added an addendum. "Of course, we'll expect the two of you to return the favor, should it ever be needed."

A gentle nod was Jessie's response. "Of course," she managed. "What are friends for, huh Steve?"

"That's right, kid. What are friends for?"

Both prayed that from now on, the world would only offer sunshine and rainbows to all of their loved ones. But the odds were against them. Life would never only offer a smooth ride. But at least, for Jessie, it was no longer a lonely road.

Charlie glanced over at the picnic table and sent Jessie a happy wave. There was just something about Josh and Jessie when they were together that sent a bright light floating amongst all of the friends. It was as if their happiness gave everyone else permission to exhale. It was as if their love had a divinity to it that was conceived in the heavens and nurtured from above. It had a purity that, once opposing forces were eradicated, lit up the world around them with a golden white light.

Stella and Emily-Grace bounced out of the tent and bounded into their fathers' arms. Giggles and laughter followed the little girls as their dads teased and tickled them.

Pure joy was present in the gathered friends and family today. There was laughter in the souls of the Sawyer women, and, finally, it reached their sea-pearl eyes.

~ ~

Jessie's set was scheduled to begin promptly at eight, so at 7:45 she kissed all three of her children before she left the tent. The two youngest were already sound asleep in travel cribs, after being tucked in by Carlotta and Dee. Josh was off with Arnie at a local AA meeting, planning to be back in time for his wife's set.

Emily-Grace was tired and craving her mother's attention, but she was a child who got quiet and snuggly when she was tired instead of cranky, so she crawled into her momma's lap and soaked up love a few minutes before Jessie was ready to leave. A real little girly-girl, she had also sat on her momma's lap earlier when Jessie was having her hair and make-up done for her set. Miranda loved having her there, and applied a little blush on the small cheeks, and a bit of lip gloss on the tiny pink lips.

"Momma has to go sing now, sweetheart," Jessie told her now, eyeing the time on her iPhone as a PA stood just outside the tent, waiting to escort her to the stage. "Can I tuck you in before I go? When I'm done I'll scoop you up and take you to our hotel so you can have teddy bear pancakes in the morning."

"Momma stay." Emily-Grace took Jessie's hand in hers and held it.

"I can't, darlin.' All those people out there want to hear me sing. They paid money to hear me sing their favorite songs."

"Can I come watch?"

"It's getting late, honey. You need to put your singer-dowwy and your bawwet-dowwy to bed."

"I'll put them to bed and I'll come watch you sing."

The PA ducked anxiously through the flap and called to Jessie, "Five minutes."

"Okay. Thanks."

Looking down at her daughter in her lap, Jessie gave her a big squeeze. "I don't know, honey. Maybe when Daddy gets back he can bring you to the wing to watch a song or two. Would that be okay?"

"Okay, Momma. Can you help me tuck in singer-dowwy and bawwet-dowwy now?"

"I sure can. Let's tuck them in good so they have good dreams, okay?"

Once she got the dolls tucked in, Jessie picked up her daughter and hugged her tight. "I'll wave to you from the stage, okay sweetheart? See you soon." And she relinquished her child to Dee's care, a little sadly, but grateful the kids were at least close by, well guarded by Dan and Susanne, as well as by Carlotta and Dee.

Charles and Matt were waiting for Jessie just outside the tent. She tucked an arm around Matt's shoulder and sauntered along, wishing Josh was back so she could have a hug before her set. Regardless of where he was or with whom, she couldn't relax until he was in her sight again, if not in her arms. Straining her neck to see if he was coming around the bend, she checked her phone for the umpteenth time.

"Has anyone heard from Josh or Arnie?"

"They're on the way," Matt assured her. "Arnie said they're stuck in festival traffic."

"My own husband, stuck in traffic created partly by me as I'm about to go on stage," she pouted. "How long do you think they'll be?"

"He might miss the first two songs, Jessie, but he'll be here. Stop worrying."

Charles piped up, effectively steering Jessie away from the topic of her husband. "So Jacob says he is going to do 'Believe' with you?"

"Says he is. I think it would be nice to play it with him. The crowd will love it."

"He had Dylan for a while today."

"He did. He was great with him. I hope we see more of Jacob in the future, Charles."

"We will. I've got plans for the two of you."

"Not too many plans, Charles. It's still tough, you know?"

"All right, kiddo. Just a tour, that's all. Sixty-five cities or so. Next summer."

Groaning, Jessie rolled her eyes. "I'm tired just thinking about it."

They were at the stairs then, leading up to the outdoor stage. Roadies and technicians had everything in place, and the band was gathered around waiting for the cue to climb the stairs. Jessie reached for Charles and gave him a big hug, then did the same for Matt.

"I love you guys. Thanks for being here for me tonight. I'll see you after. Please make sure Jacob joins me, okay? Don't let him chicken out. We need this. We need to put some old hard feelings to rest."

Then it was time to climb to the stage. Even after all the shows Jessie did over the years, it was still exhilarating to take her place at center stage, wave to the crowd, and launch into the first tune. It was even more exciting for Charles and Matt, who watched her strike up a dialogue with her audience before she started to sing.

"She's come a long way, Matt," Charles said loudly in order to be heard over the music, watching the girl he honed from a lonely waif into an international superstar. "I think she'll be okay now."

"If by okay you mean a three ton weight came off her shoulders today when Jacob spent time with his son, and didn't run away, then I'd say yes. It was nice to see Jessie, Jacob and Josh able to spend time together as friends, of a sort."

"Closer, even. Co-parents, really. For the child's sake, I hope they can make it work."

"They will. We'll help."

"Damn straight we will."

Narrowing his eyes at Charles, Matt said, "What? You've got that conniving look about you."

Raising his eyebrows, Charles looked at Matt and smiled. He leaned in so Matt could hear him better over the music. "I wasn't kidding about that 65 city tour. We'll make sure Jacob's around his kid."

"What's this about Jacob?" Josh and Arnie appeared behind the men.

"Nothing," Matt said, sending Charles a warning look. Josh didn't need to hear that Jessie's producer—and manager, when you consider who he was married to—was planning to put Jessie and Jacob in close proximity to each other again next summer. Tonight was about healing old wounds, not starting niggling new worries over fresh ones. He turned to Josh. "She's only on the opener. She'll be glad you're here."

Sure enough, when Jessie finished the song and stood back to accept her applause, the first thing she did was glance over to the wing. Just seeing her husband there was enough to bring a peaceful calm over her features. The old electricity had no trouble flitting back and forth across the stage between them. She smiled, a tender calm in the sea-pearl eyes Josh loved, and he lit up from within, simply from being the recipient of the great capacity to love that this woman had to offer.

Later, Jessie wrapped up her set with a fiery anthem that everyone in the audience knew. It was surreal to hear fifty thousand people sing the song with her. But she wanted just one voice after that, to share the stage with her and wrap her voice in honey with his harmonies. Waiting for the applause to die down, she raised her hand in a bid for the crowd to settle, at least as much as they could on this surreal warm late summer September night.

"So I have a surprise for you," she started, and a loud cheering took hold. "There's this little ballad everybody likes." The cheering grew. "It's called 'Believe.' It's about hope when things get bad, and about how one special friend can pull you through the darkness. Tonight, I'd like to ask my special friend to come play the song with me because, well, not only did he help me write it, but he also helped me live it."

It was a good few minutes before Jessie got control of the audience again. Even so, she still had to holler.

Glancing toward the wing, a wide smile creased her face. Holding out an arm in welcome, she said simply, "Jacob Ryan, everyone."

He was standing by Josh, which, to Jessie, was also kind of surreal in itself. She watched as her husband clamped a hand on Jacob's shoulder and leaned in to say something in his ear that had Jacob look back at him and which had both men laughing. Reminding herself to ask Josh what he said, later, Jessie shook her head slightly. No way did she see this day going as well as it was, as far as Jacob was concerned. He had taken an interest in his son. Was completely captivated by him, in fact. And now he was walking towards her, on stage, in front of fifty thousand people, to play their ballad.

Stopping at a mic a techie was placing a few feet sideways away from Jessie, Jacob let his gaze capture hers. Suddenly all sound stopped—Jessie could no longer hear the crowd cheering. She couldn't take her eyes off this man—the guy who held her when she needed him, who took her shopping for a new-old Gibson, who loved her and their children, and who, in the end, suffered terribly for the simple act of loving her.

Loving me, Jessie thought. *A homeless runaway from Prince Edward Island. A throwaway girl. A victim of sexual assault, of stalking….and of another woman's aching need to have a family. Like mine.*

Beyond Jacob she could see Josh, a man she loved from the moment she met him in a garbage pile outside her then-fiance's (and now very good friend's) club. Loving Josh had opened a whole new door for Jessie—one with friends to laugh with, to confide in, to cherish. Sure, it wasn't always an easy road, but by God it was something, to love this man and have him love her back.

Charles was there, and Matt…and Arnie…and back at the tent were her three children, with Carlotta and Dee. In the audience were Steve and Sophie, Charlie and Jane, Kayla and Paul, Zach and Hilary and their growing kids, Julie and Katy…in New York was Maggie, who was sticking with her man, John…and in L.A. was Sue-Lyn, with her new partner, and Carter and Ashley. In Peterborough was a sister and her family, and a grandmother, even. In Canmore was an aunt; in P.E.I. was a mother and an aging friend who once knew Jessie's dad.

Life was so full now. It was meant to be savored. And no moment would Jessie savor more than this.

"Ready?" Jacob mouthed from five feet away.

"Ready." She focused on him, raised her chin, and settled. She said into the mic as the crowd shuffled in breathless anticipation, "Let us sing you home."

He counted her in, but not sadly this time. Instead, the beats were strong and steady, and they started anew, at the number one. Neither Jessie nor Jacob could look away from each other through the entire ballad. This was their sacred space, here, on stage, singing a ballad that had helped Jessie through a very bad time, as it appeared it was helping millions in the world now. The song was a gift Jacob had given to Jessie on a very bad day.

Their bubble was in place. And it was magical.

The ballad ended on a sweet note. *I don't want this to end,* Jessie thought, tearing up at the sight of her good friend—in one of his ubiquitous plaid shirts—ducking his head shyly as the crowd went nuts.

The moment was ripe. A few quick steps and Jessie, who had sung the song at the mic without her guitar, was at Jacob's side. She tugged at his sleeve and he smiled at her, still in the bubble too, and then he hoisted his guitar off, handed it to a quick reacting tech, and took her in his arms.

The pleasure of reconnecting again, through music and through their small infant, was an unequalled perfect pearl on a sweet, sweet day. The forgiveness that emanated from Jacob's soul to Jessie's was tangible, a real touchable gem of hope that they could begin again, as good friends, and carry on.

Music did that. Music had the power that day. It took over, it emanated around them and through them and in them, and it eased the pain of some very dark days and opened a whole new rainbow of hope.

They didn't want to let go.

Off stage, Talia had stepped up by Josh. He glanced at her, and noted a serious frown.

"Hate to tell you this, kid, but you'll just have to get used to that."

"Should I be worried?" she asked him.

He paused before answering. "Not as long as I don't fuck up. And I don't intend to, anymore. Never again."

"I'll make sure you won't, if it means I get to keep Jacob."

"He's all yours, Talia. And, may I say, thank you!"

They laughed and trained their eyes back on their two favorite people on stage.

Jacob finally relaxed his grip on Jessie, pawed away his tears and swiped at hers, and said, "That was a sad song. We need to end happy."

"I hear you, Jacob. What do you want to play?"

Looking past him, she signaled the stage manager. "Couple more?"

The stage manager was thrilled. Union, shmunion. "Play away," he called to her.

Jessie whipped around to the band. "Anyone want to do a few more?"

It was unanimous. And that launched another forty-five minutes of rousing pop tunes that had everybody dancing.

Matt couldn't help himself. He leaned into Charles and said, "She's going rogue again."

With a chuckle, Charles agreed. But for once, Jessie's rogue behavior made him happy.

At one point, between songs, Jessie saw Dee arrive in the wing with Emily-Grace in her arms. Josh took their daughter from her, and danced with her in his arms. Jacob invited Talia on stage to sing with them. She joined in with perfect harmony.

The joy inherent in Jessie then was something all of them rarely got to see. She was too troubled, the memories were too tough, the pain too deep. It started when she was twelve, when the man who taught her about the power of music to heal in the first place rolled his car into the Southwest River, and drowned.

"Dad," she said now between verses, as she stepped back from the mic and let her eyes drift over the sheer bliss evident before her, in the singing, dancing fans, in her family, in Jacob, and in Josh. "Thank you."

Her eyes caught Josh's, and ended up locked in his gaze.

"C'mere," she called, gesturing to him to join her at her mic, as Jacob and the band carried the tune, which was the one she walked out on in New York—the one about family and love and home.

He shook his head but Dee gave him a push. So, laughing, cheeks pink, Josh carried Emily-Grace onto the stage, to the crowd's great delight, and Jessie slipped off the guitar she was again playing, and tearfully—joyfully—kissed both of them. She tucked an arm around her husband's waist, and brought the mic to her daughter, who Josh set on her feet on the stage. Emily-Grace knew all the words, and she sang with gusto, her little red cowboy boots moving in time to the music.

"This is unreal," Jessie whispered in Josh's ear. "Or should I say surreal. I love you, Josh Sawyer."

"I love you back, Jessie Wheeler-Sawyer."

Jessie blushed deeply at the sound of that—she would never get tired of hearing Josh call her by her married name.

He had more to say. "Thank you for believing in me. Always."

"Always and forever," was Jessie's response, as she touched a finger to the silver locket she was wearing around her neck.

"Always and forever."

There was a new bubble in place on the outdoor Seattle stage that night. As Jacob sang with Talia, and Emily-Grace kept up her part of the song at Jessie's mic, Jessie leaned her forehead in so it touched her husband's.

Tenderly touching her lips to his, she closed her diaphanous blue eyes, and blissfully let the bubble float her away.

～　～

The End.

～　～

Hello!

Like what you read? I hope you are enjoying the Drifters series as much as I am enjoying writing it. I am hopelessly in love with Josh, Jessie, Jacob, and the rest of the gang. If you have a moment, please go to Amazon or Goodreads and leave a rating and/or review. Us Indie authors depend on those for our survival in the eBook world.

Thank you!
Happy reading!

Susan

www.susanrodgersauthor.com

Facebook: search **Susan Rodgers, Writer**

Twitter: **@srbluemountain**

www.bublish.com

email: **fatcat@pei.sympatico.ca**

About the Author

Susan Rodgers' first novel *A Certain Kind of Freedom* was a Finalist in the Writers' Federation of Nova Scotia Atlantic Writing Awards for unpublished manuscripts. Her short story from the novel of the same name, published in two anthologies, has received rave reviews, as have the Drifters novels, Susan's all-time favourite books to write.

Owner/Operator of Bluemountain Entertainment, Susan is a 'Diploma With Honours' graduate of Vancouver Film School. She produces mostly documentary style client films and short dramas with plans to one day shoot a Feature Drama based on the novel Atlantic Blue.

Formerly a Museum Curator, in winter Susan lives with her partner Steve and her striped cat Oliver (Lucy Maud Montgomery once said the only good cat is a striped cat) in Summerside, Prince Edward Island, Canada. In summer, she hides in a small trailer in Darnley, P.E.I., where she writes novels, paddles kayaks, and crafts sandcastles on the beach. She makes frequent trips to Vancouver to visit her son Christopher, where she enjoys life in the hippie city while listening to great music and sipping on good espresso.

Books by Susan Rodgers

Drifters series:
A Song For Josh
Promises
No Greater Love
Riptide
Whispers of Home
And Then There Was Silence
Let the Music Cry
If I Could Sing You Home

Other:
A Certain Kind of Freedom
Seasmoke
Atlantic Blue

Feature Screenplays:
The Story of Jack & Emma
Atlantic Blue
Beautiful Jane
They Were Dreamers (adapted)

Short Stories:
S12
A Certain Kind of Freedom
A Gentle Peace